# PRAISE F

## THE FIRST BOOK IN THE APOCALYPSE ACADEMY

"With action so potent the words sizzle on every page…"
Shaun – Amazon purchaser

"Can't wait to read the next book! The characters are well fleshed out and I became invested in their background stories and what happens to them." Timothy Walker – Amazon purchaser

"Well written from the perspective of a former military soldier…" Jeff Simmons-Amazon purchaser

"Recommended by a friend, and not usually a genre I would read, but opening the cover I could not put the book down…Purchase this book, you will not regret it." Amazon purchaser

"If you can only read one book this year, this one is it. I can't wait for the next one to come out. More excited to see how they make the movie!!! Look out Harry Potter this guy's great!" Katherine Davoren-Amazon purchaser (5 Stars)

"A great intro into a dark reality." Colby-Amazon purchaser (5 Stars)

"Although fiction, Kallas draws from inner life experiences- fear, trust, loyalty, love, strength and honor – to create an amazing read of survival and synergy…I can't wait to see how the author develops these warriors and their Spartan bloodline (and also the main characters love interest)! Denise (5 Star Review)

"One of the best zombie military books I've read…The mental fortitude and inner battles to maintain a form of humanity tear at your heart strings. I would recommend this book to any fan of the zombie genre." BCove Amazon Customer (5 Star Review)

"Addictive adventure…I loved this book (I mean I loooooove this book). Original and captivating, I fell in love with the characters, celebrated their triumphs and shed tears with them. It's an incredible blend of nerdom, scifi, Greek Legends and military badasses." Amazon Kindle customer

"With action so potent that the sizzle if the words threaten to set every page on fire Anthony Kallas opens his Apocalypse Academy cycle with the appropriately titled Dark Origins. And what a fire-starter it is! Set against the backdrop of a world where just about everything that can go wrong has Kallas weaves a tale stretching from Xerxes to just beyond today; filling this action romp of a tapestry with the supernatural, bioweapons, zombies, biker gangs, humanities remnant and a military component that feels so real that there can be little doubt that Kallas has lived it.

This book is a must read, and I can't wait for the next one!"

— Shaun (5 Star Amazon Review)


"Recommended by a friend, and not usually a genre I would read, but opening the cover I could not put the book down. The author does a great job of combining past and present events and creates a story that leaves the reader wanting to see what's next. This was one of those books, that when you finish it you are a little sad because it is over. So, I am impatiently waiting book #2! I would highly recommend purchasing this book, you will not regret it."

- Amazon Customer (5 Star Review)

Also by Anthony Kallas

*Dark Origins: Book One of the Apocalypse Academy*

# The Apocalypse Academy

## Book Two:

## Dark

## Odyssey

### Anthony Kallas

# Acknowledgments

First and foremost, I have to acknowledge my father in memoriam who passed away earlier this year. Dad, as promised...the story goes on. I love you and miss you.

To Tim Schulte at Variance Author Services... Thank you for the ever-accurate editing, advice and instruction. You are amazing.

Also, ICHD Designs for the fantastic cover art.

To my daughters: Tabitha (Newt), Gwendolynn (Princess – not War Queen) and Patience (Tink): Your personalities and influence helped me understand the complexity of the female teenage mind and emotional roller coaster of highs and lows that are associated with them helped mold every Academy female Cadet in my stories. Dancer, War Queen, Lotus Jane and all the others thank you as do I. Sometimes I wondered if I would survive those trying times and mind wrenching conundrums even with all of my training but we made it through together. I love you all.

To my Brothers and Sisters in the Military and the veterans that have served. So many of you could step into this story and take over a characters role. God bless. I hope the action and training rings true to you all.

Lastly to the men and women of Law Enforcement who have crossed my path over the years and those who still wear that heavy badge: Spartan and the Phalanx may be action stars in these stories but YOU are the true heroes of this great nation. Forever Blue. Always at your six!

# The Apocalypse Academy

## Academy

## Book Two:

## Dark

## Odyssey

# Anthony Kallas

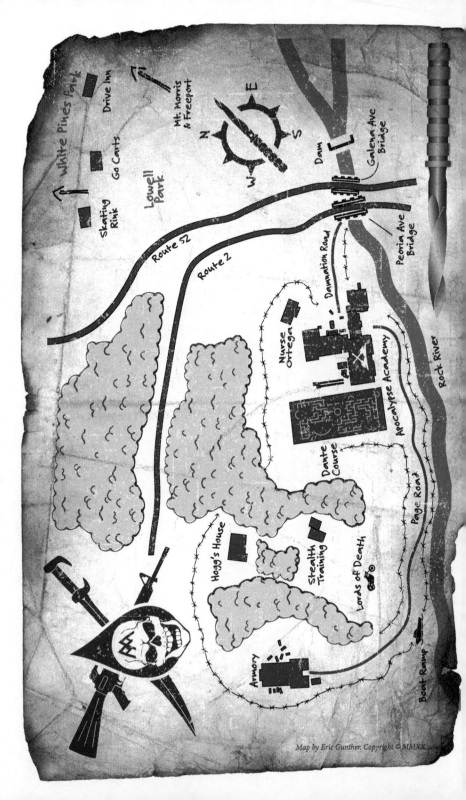

White Pines Park

Drive Inn

Skating Rink

Go Carts

Lowell Park

Mt. Morris & Freeport

Dam

Galena Ave Bridge

Peoria Ave Bridge

Route 52

Route 2

Damnation Road

Nurse Ortega

Apocalypse Academy

Rock River

Dante Course

Page Road

Hogg's House

Stealth Training

Lords of Death

Armory

Boat Ramp

Map by Eric Gunther, Copyright © MMXX

# CHAPTER ONE:
# REST AND RELAXATION

Twelve weeks of learning everything under the sun that there was to learn about "Zs", losing companions and pacifying others made a week of downtime seen invaluable, almost unreal. In addition to the full-length Olympic pool contained in the room adjacent to the gymnasium, there was a bank of hot tubs and whirlpool's that had been previously used for the rehabilitation of sports related injuries obtained on various athletic fields before the rising of the undead. It was in this time of individual mental and physical down time that Spartan, Freak, Cowboy and Gator sat in the whirlpool Jacuzzi allowing the swirling hot waters to relieve the tensions from their minds and soreness from their muscles. Casual conversation floated gently back and forth freely between them.

"So, I gots to ask. You using dis here honor of de Cadet of de cycle. You could have don' gots you whatever it is dat you wan' an you chose de first assignment? Is you cracked? Gator is t'inking that you got less sense dan de bullfrog in the bayou hopping 'cross de busy freeway. Why you don' get a new gun or a motorbike? Hell, even a pros'tute would be better than walking away with de empty hands."

Spartan thought about it for a moment. He really didn't know why he had asked for what he had. He knew that he would never give up the sword of Leonidas. It felt like an extension of his own body and for some reason when he wielded it he felt stronger, more confident. He was more of a leader with less self-doubt; like he could feel the legendary King guiding him. His other weapons and armor were sufficient for his needs and by maintaining them he gave the team consistency. No, Spartan could not really answer why he made his selection, instead he just shrugged. "It seemed like the right thing to do I guess."

Gator chuckled and gave his small whirlpool a splash. "Don' you go frettin' none over that choice Mon Frere. Ol' Gator, he's going to take care of de women of de evening for you hisself when he get back down to da Big Easy. That is of course if they ain' trying to bite his face off on de Bourbon Street."

They all laughed again. Of all the cadets, Gator and maybe Cowboy would've been the easiest to land into serious trouble and laugh about it the entire time with guns blazing. When the team separated, Spartan would truly miss these two specifically. He hoped they stayed safe out in the "Z" infected world.

"Shee-it son! If'n I had won that award, you can bet your boots it would have been a twenty-four-ounce, one hundred percent ribeye from a black Angus Longhorn and tonight I would've been tappin' toes to the sounds of Shania Twain or maybe Carrie Underwood with my favorite (which sounded a lot like fav-o-rite) philly. I would've had a knee slappin' time to carry me through the coming days better than a hog's trough full of corn whiskey and a bowl full of grits-n-gravy to be sure." Cowboy added. "What about you Freak. Your awful quiet. What would you have gone and chose?"

"All my life I wanted to play ball in the big leagues. To walk out into Wrigley field or maybe Fenway Park or even Yankee Stadium and hear the roar of the crowd when I stepped up to the plate and hit one out of the park. Thanks to the assholes in the government that's all gone and it leaves me feeling really empty inside. I guess the only other thing I could want is to learn to play my own blues harp so when the Blues Brothers ain't playing, I could, know what I mean Dawg? Ain't nothing like the blues to soothe the man's soul."

"Amen to dat brother. You've got to come to visit my hometown in de Big Easy. Der's blues on every corner. Harmonicas, saxophones, trumpets and drums. It makes you want to eat de crawfish and drink de beer while you listen to de sweet music."

"Crawfish?" Spartan asked. "I thought they were used for fishing. You actually eat those things?"

"Hell yes homme! Ain't nothin' better than de gumbo pot full of de mud bugs, sausage, mushrooms, corn and garlic. Make them spicy enough to slap yo' mama and drink yo' daddy's beer out from de coola!"

"Aren't they hard to peel? They seem like they have pretty thick shells. I know that it's hard to put a hook through one to be sure when you're going fishing."

Gator smiled. "You don' go and peel them like de shrimp. You gotta pull 'em apart, then you squeeze dem and use your teeth yank out de tail meat. When you finish with de backend, you toss de empty shell on de pile on the table. Then squeeze the heads an' suck out all the juice and brains. Mmmm-mmm, that sure be good!"

"Ain't no way I'm sucking juice out of any bug, Cajun. You're just plain wrong for that. What you really need is some chitlins and red-eye gravy over homemade cornbread. Now we're talking about a meal!"

So it went, back and forth, Cajun, cowboy, athlete and the boy with no past, laughing while they relaxed in each other's company. It would likely be the last time for a very long stretch that they would get to enjoy anything close to normality so they made the most of it.

While the boys caroused together, several female cadets sat and talked of more traditional, feminine dreams. Memories of makeup and salons, manicures and pedicures, jewelry and long gowns shaped their thoughts and words. Eventually the topic turned to men and marriage.

"I want a real wedding" Medusa said. "With flowers and cake, in an old-fashioned church."

"Not me." Dancer replied. "I just want a simple ceremony in a simple white wedding dress. Just me and my Spar… I mean, my man with a preacher." She blushed furiously as she realized that she had almost said Spartan's name out loud. She looked quickly at the other two girls, but neither seemed to have noticed her comment.

"What about you Raven? Do you have a dream wedding?" Dancer asked.

The girl looked at Dancer, emotion showed in her eyes with a wildness that spoke of a love of the outdoors. They shined and seemed to capture the emotion of the moment. "I did when I was a little girl. I wanted a fairytale wedding like in a Disney movie. I wanted a handsome forest guardian to ride up on his horse, sweep me off of my feet and we would ride off together as man and wife to live happily ever after with all of the forest animals as our friends. Like Snow White ya know? But that dream will probably never happen now. Disney is now a land of the dead…" The girl paused, and let out a deep, slow sigh.

6

"But I am not a little girl any longer so I guess I will settle for just finding a nice guy that wants a large family."

"Oh." Was all Dancer could say followed by "Sorry." She silently thought to herself that Raven really needed some sort of professional therapy to cope with the losses that she had obviously experienced during the days and weeks following "Z" night. Perhaps she could talk to Nurse Ortega about the girl's obvious *"survivor syndrome"* and how to best get the girl some help.

The rest of the week of rest and relaxation passed quickly. In fact, it passed far quicker than most of the former cadets would have liked to be sure. The Monday morning PT formation was led by Sergeant Stone and it was grueling. Anyone foolish enough to believe that PT would become easier after graduation was delusional. Ten miles of running up and down hills, while in formation and carrying their weapons made their muscles burn and their boots drag. By the time they returned to the barracks, almost every former cadet, with the exception of Deadeye and Popcorn from Charlie Company, were exhausted. Those two boys barely looked winded.

After showering and chow, the former cadets were all reassembled on the quarter deck. All five of the drill sergeants were also present as was Colonel Slade.

"Well, I guess I can't call you cadets any longer. You have completed your basic training and "Z" survival school here at the Apocalypse Academy. So, the first order of business is to determine what do we call you? Is there anyone that has any suggestions?"

"Soldiers!" Someone shouted.

"Z" police." Came another male voice out of the crowd.

"Z" Mercenaries!" Came a call from someone in the back of the formation, probably from Echo team.

"Z" Knights!" Came War Queen's voice above the shouted voices of the males.

"Z" Warriors!" Said Gator in his thick Cajun accent.

These suggestions were all followed by others such as titans, heroes, and "Z" killers (pronounced Z Killaz), Rangers and the Elite. In the end, Warriors was settled upon by the majority. The name seemed appropriate after all since that was essentially what they had been trained to be and do; create war on the undead. On a personal side, Spartan favored the selection for two reasons. First there was a certain ring to "Spartan's Phalanx of Warriors". Secondly, he had always been a fan of the movie of the same name in which a street gang had been forced to fight its way back to its home turf after being falsely accused of killing another gang's leader. "Z" Night had robbed him of the specifics as to why he got flashes of certain memories from his past.

Nurse Ortega believed that he was suffering from what she called Dissociative Amnesia due to the extreme stress of watching his family be horribly mutilated and eventually turned into the walking dead which subsequently tried to murder him as well. It was a phenomenon well documented in war zones as well as following natural disasters. "Z" night had been both and so much more. She believed that his amnesia was of the generalized type as it held no rhyme of reason to the information that was retained or brought randomly back to mind as opposed to a Localized amnesia type which only applied to the loss of a specific event in a person's mind or the more devastating Fugue amnesia which wiped out cleaned the slate and rebooted the person's mind completely.

In Spartan's case, Nurse Ortega believed that the flashes of memories that he experienced were brought on by his surroundings and that periods of meditation and introspection without outside influence might help him to recover some of the missing parts of his past. Anyway around, it would be a day-by-day process for recovery.

"So now that we have a name for you all, the time has come for a choice. Do you wish to remain a Warrior and part of the team here at the Apocalypse Academy or do you feel a calling to strike out on your own, alone into the unknown lands where you will battle the undead as a Paladin and walk away from the brotherhood of the Apocalypse Academy in favor of a more personal agenda? There is no wrong choice here, let me be perfectly clear. Warriors and Paladins both are valued commodities in this new world. Really they are two sides of the same coin. One just has more personal freedom of choice than the other does."

Spartan was certain that no member of the Phalanx intended to become a Paladin. They had discussed it at length over the last couple of days and had reached an agreement, one and all, to stay together as a team and watch each other's backs. To intentionally isolate yourself seemed to be a quick way to end up dead or worse.

So, when the barracks door behind the Colonel opened up and the girl that had once been the prissy Princess strode out on the quarter deck in full battle ZAP armor with all of her weapons, Spartan was stunned. The girl's golden ponytail swung side to side as the micro servers in the joints of the ZAP armor powered her movements. War Queen had modified the armor by adding plating, possibly from old football shoulder pads to both shoulders, elbows, chest, knees, forearms, thighs and shins. Adorning these black glistening plates were metal spikes of varying lengths. The ones jutting from her shoulders being almost a foot in length while the spikes on her forearms and shins could not have been more than an inch. Draped across her chest and back was a white medieval tabard

11

bearing a Crimson Knights Cross and the AA blood patch of the Apocalypse Academy emblazoned upon her breast. A Mossberg 870 shotgun was strapped to her back and a pistol hung in its black holster at her left hip. Tucked into her belt was a survival knife, perhaps eight inches long. Lastly, she carried the deceased Cadet Knights' longsword at her hip, it's metal scabbard and pommel clearly identifiable even from a distance.

If there was any doubt to any of the assembled warriors that the girl formerly known as Princess had been absorbed by the new persona of War Queen; those doubts dissipated like the fog beneath the morning sun as she stood before them now. Any sense of frailty had been completely erased. In short, the girl looked like a seriously bad-assed Angel of Death.

"I'm ready." She said softly directly to the Colonel. The Colonel nodded once in acknowledgement.

"War Queen has chosen to depart the confines of the Apocalypse Academy and begin a path as a Paladin. She has asked to address all of you before she departs. Please be courteous and listen to what she has to say."

The armored young woman stepped forward; her jaw firmly set. Spartan was sure that he saw a brief rim of tears appear in the edges of the Paladin's thickly black lined eyes, but if it'd been there it was swiftly suppressed. As she began to speak, her voice and words carried with them a mesmerizing power and the assembled warriors stood entranced. The girl looked for all the world like a Goddess of Death incarnate. Her crystal blue eyes penetrated every person that she met. For those who knew her and could see beyond the beauty, there was an unappealing pain hidden deep within those azure orbs; a sadness that would never be healed.

"I love you all," she began "I love you because you are willing to fight. You are all willing to battle the hordes of undead in mortal combat for the fate of our world. Such valor, such gallantry, is the stuff of legends and one day I truly believe that the tales of Spartan, Cowboy, Dancer, Gator, yes even you Cutter will join the pantheon of this world's heroes. People like Odysseus, Perseus, King Arthur, Merlin and Sinbad who have provided inspiration to generations of people through their fabled deeds and miraculous journeys into peril."

"You are armed with weapons of great power. You are also protected with superior defensive suits of armor. You are righteous in your quest to regain dominance of our world from the walking dead. But that is not enough. Be proud of who you are. Be noble of spirit and faithful of heart. Be merciless to the corpses of the undead, be they kings or presidents, movie stars or models in their former lives among the living. Do this without fail and in the end, when your time of eternal judgment comes, whatever God you believe in will surely smile upon you, just as he has cast his final blessing upon my Knight."

War Queen held up her sword arm showing all of the assembled personnel Cadet Knight's plastic identification bracelet that he would've been awarded had he graduated from the Apocalypse Academy. It was fastened tightly about her wrist. Lowering her arm, she passed on a final blessing to the friends she had found in the face of death.

"May whatever God, in whatever religion that you worship cast his guiding light upon you all. Though I walk now into the valley of the shadow of death, I want you all to know that if or when you need me, I will be there. Farewell."

And with that, War Queen turned and began to walk unhesitatingly down Damnation Road towards the gates that would give her access to hell on earth. Dancer hoped that the girl would you have a change of heart before exiting the gates but she knew that that chance was slim. The girl had suffered an emotional breakdown and had assumed a new personality in order to help her cope and to empower her need to kill the undead. The best Dancer could offer was hope and a prayer for the girl's safety. This she did in earnest, although she kept her thoughts to herself.

Spartan heard Cutter's voice from the back of the formation. "That is one crazy, sexy, brave–ass bitch."

For the only time since his arrival at the Apocalypse Academy, Spartan agreed with the Echo team leader. He silently wished the girl well.

None of the other warriors opted to join the ranks of the Paladins. As such, operations meetings were scheduled for after lunch the next day. Alpha team's briefing, the first operations briefing scheduled, was not until 1500 hrs. so Spartan took his team to the sparring gym and requisitioned the nearby aerobics room for an hour from the freckled faced kid at the counter. As soon as all of his team had entered the room, Spartan closed and locked the door behind them.

"Either this is gonna be one hell of a brutal aerobics' event or we're not really here to be Sweatin' to the Oldies." Freak said.

"And they say athletes are supposed to be thickheaded." Spartan replied with a grin and a light tone of sarcasm. "You are right my friend, but the decision that we have to make should be ours alone, with no outside ears."

Together they all sat down on the firm, rubberized blue foam floor matting that covered the entire room. While not fully comfortable, it beat sitting on the ground without any padding at all.

"What's wrong?" Dancer asked, anticipation clearly marking her pretty face.

"There's nothing actually wrong," Spartan replied. "But I have a decision to make. Since that decision involves placing all of us into harm's way with the potential of death or worse, I thought that we should agree upon it as a team."

"Oh, this should be good," Deadeye said poking Freak in the arm. "How many "Zs" do you think we will be lined up against? I say at a minimum, at least a hundred." The boy's cynicism and sarcasm had blossomed since graduation and were as sharp as the tomahawk that he carried.

"Hell Dawg, the Blues Brothers alone can play a concert to a hundred undead folks. It would be like singing *Jailhouse Rock* in the movie. There's got to be at least a thousand if we want the whole band to play."

"I'll do the soundstage." Techno quipped. "And believe it or not… I know how to play the piano too." He added shyly.

17

"I play the clarinet and a little violin too." Dancer put in. "Mum insisted I have a balanced classical education and not just daddy's combat training." She added with a shrug when she saw Spartan looking at her.

"Okay let's get down to business." Spartan said, cutting off the playful conversation. "The colonel pulled me aside after formation to discuss our mission options. I have to make my selection and report to him by 1400 hrs. so that we have time to get our mission briefing."

"This should be good." Freak muttered. "Go ahead and tell us where the Phalanx is going to whup ass."

"We have three choices; each is based on a separate need here at the Academy. The choices for us are as follows: conduct a supply run, intelligence gathering on the Lords of Death who have established a base of operations in a former college town east of here or conduct a search and rescue mission to the north. I have only bare-bones information on each but I'll give you what I've got and we can make our choice together from there."

"The supply run is a ten-mile ruck march west to the nearest town which I believe is either Sterling or Rock Falls. Most of the stores here in town have already been raided and cannibalized down to empty shelves. We get in, find an operational vehicle, load it full of any supplies that we can scavenge and then drive back to the Academy. Simple."

"What's the catch?" Deadeye asked.

"It seems that the target store is a fairly large department store and when "Z" night happened, they locked all of the patrons inside to prevent infection and for their own safety. They also locked in one or more people that were infected unknowingly. Intelligence from the initial reconnaissance says that there are currently no living individuals within the building."

"Do we have an estimate for the number of "Zs" inside?" Techno asked, concern obvious in his voice.

"According to the initial intelligence reports there are somewhere between seventy-five and a hundred "Zs" at this time. The best guess is that they are primarily Romero's but the opportunity for there to be Reapers also depends upon the longevity of the survivors that were inside. At this time there is no intelligence to report the presence of any Husks. So that's a plus."

"OK!" Freak exclaimed. "Dawg, whatever you decide is okay with me but that's a lot of rotten meat. It could get ugly, really quick. Just saying, you know. Besides, that place is going to smell terrible. Besides the "Zs", all that rotten food inside there could make us sick."

Spartan nodded. "The other choices do not get any better. The intelligence gathering mission is forty-five miles of ruck one way to the east, across open country and several small cities."

"What are we scouting?" Deadeye asked. "Person or place? You mentioned the Lords of Death?" Spartan figured that Deadeye would be most intrigued by this mission. As the teams' resident Scout and ninja, the man was nearly invisible no matter where he was, inside the city, or out in the wilderness. With the ZAP armor, there would be no place that he could not get into virtually unseen.

"People actually. Remember during our first couple of weeks here at the Apocalypse Academy, we were on a march and we had to take cover because a bad ass motorcycle gang riding through?"

Techno remembered the incident vividly with a shiver. He specifically remembered the incident because at that time he had been as fat as a tick. When they had run to seek shelter before the motorcycle gang came over the hill, he had clumsily fell and split his head open, knocking himself unconscious. Only Spartan's quick thinking had saved him from being discovered. Subconsciously, he touched the "U" shaped scar on his forehead from where he had struck the rock when he had tripped. The incident embarrassed him to this day.

"You mean Colonel Slade wants us to spy on them?! Is he crazy! They'll kill us!" Near panic filled the boy's voice.

"These are just options Tech. Settle down. It seems that a large group of the Lords of Death have set up a compound of their own inside of a large farmhouse. Rumor has it that they are capturing the living, probably refugees, and feeding them to "Zs" for sport during some sort of motorcycle circus event. There are supposed to be a lot of guns, a lot of bikers and a lot of "Z's". The colonel is concerned that if they continue to grow unchecked, that they may become a much more immediate threat to the Apocalypse Academy. Our mission would only be to scout them out; to gather information, not to engage."

"And the last choice?" Dancer asked.

Spartan exhaled deeply through his nose. This was the mission that he had the most direct feelings about. His own personal choice. However, presenting it to the team would likely result in mixed emotions with Deadeye opting heavily for the scouting mission.

"The mission is a thirty-mile ruck march north through two separate state parks. The Sheltered Cross Home for Children lies in the center of a city that used to house thirty thousand people. Recent radio traffic acknowledged pleas for assistance from the nuns or at least *a* nun, stating that she was barricaded in the church and that she had been using the ductwork for the smaller children to crawl into the cafeteria area and bring back food and water. Every trip into the ductwork places the children at risk for an encounter with "Zs." For now, they are all safe, but they have advised that they are running very low on supplies. The nun stated that they had maybe a week, possibly two more that they could hold out and then they would be out of everything."

"How many kids are we talking about?" Deadeye asked. "It's going to be tough to move a lot of them quietly, especially if they are small. It could get all of us killed."

"Agreed. Plus, there is the inherent danger of infected animals in the state parks. Just for information's sake, there are twenty children." Spartan replied.

"The children will die without our help Spartan. The other issues are not time sensitive. The extra food for the Academy can wait and the bikers will still be there. The kids will not. They will either die of starvation or from the undead." Dancer said a tone of pleading underlying her voice.

"This decision has to be as a team Dance. I understand your feelings, but we all have to buy into this together.

Freak, where do you stand with the Blues Brothers on this?"

"Spartan, you know that you're my boy, and the Blues Brothers and I are Chicago natives. Those "Zs" that is oppressing them po' little children sound like Illinois Nazis to me. *I hate Illinois Nazis.*" He said quoting the one-line pun from John Belushi in the movie and gave Dancer a smile and a wink.

She smiled back appreciatively.

"Techno?"

"Hmmm, let's see… Possible death, certain death, or positively certain death. It seems that our options are limited. I don't suppose that we could pick up an ice cream maker or snow cone machine and stuff to make them with if I said the department store huh?"

Spartan just glared an answer without speaking a word. Techno raised his hands defensively.

"Okay, okay. Go get the kids for God's sake! But I'm telling you now; I refuse to change any diapers. That's so gross!" He said making a face of disgust.

"Deadeye?"

"Each avenue has its own merits, and the colonel is wise to have chosen them. For me, the forests are home. I know the animals and their signs. But where I can move swiftly and surely through the trees and over the rocks and rivers, you may all struggle as we saw during our knife fighting exhibition. Large predators may still roam the parks. Even normally docile animals such as deer and squirrels could become critical encounters. This would be worse if they have become infected. In addition, survivalists and trappers may have sought refuge in the wilds of the parks to avoid the infection. So, the path to the children, while righteous and appropriate, will be fraught with far more danger than the other choices. However, it is better to die for a true cause than to die for stupidity. Let us get the children and the religious mother. It's what my ancestors would have wanted me to do."

Spartan nodded. Somewhere in the back of his mind he remembered his promise to Rooster as well. He would be watching for any signs of the boy's sister.

"Then it's settled. I will go and inform the colonel of our choice. It's going to be a long march. I would recommend bringing our spare power supplies for the ZAP's and Tech I want you to make sure we have at least two solar chargers. Also make sure that we draw field rations for four days. Anything more that we need, we will have to scavenge on the way. Also make sure that we have a complete first aid kit. We don't know what shape these children may be in. I will meet you back at the barracks at 1445 hrs. and then we will head over to briefing."

He stood up and started towards the door, then stopped and looked back at his four teammates. "I'm proud to have you all on my team; as my Phalanx." Then he turned and left the room to go brief the Commandant of their decision.

# Chapter Two

# Briefing and the First

# Operation

The white walls of the briefing room seemed much larger than they had all those weeks ago when Spartan had first in-processed into the Apocalypse Academy. Then there had been twenty-five cadets, five drill sergeants and the colonel, and the room had seemed impossibly small. Now there were only the five teammates of Alpha team sitting together at a single table and the walls felt like they were a mile apart.

While they waited on the colonel to come to the briefing room, Spartan allowed his mind to consider the potential ramifications of the upcoming mission. Five armed and armored teenagers, trained for battle, were going to volunteer to tromp through two separate forests, maneuver through a good-sized city full of the walking dead. Locate and penetrate the walls of an orphanage, rescue a nun and her dozen or so student charges and then march them all back down the same route to the Apocalypse Academy. All of this which had to occur

27

without letting anyone being bitten, scratched or torn apart by "Zs" or infected by wild animals or murdered by crazed post-apocalyptic humans. It was daunting in its scope to be sure, but it had been his initial choice even before he'd gotten his team's opinions.

Spartan looked around the table of Alpha team. They were good people, good friends. Could he put one of them down as he had been forced to do with Rooster if one of them became infected? He honestly couldn't be certain. As team leader that responsibility would fall to him if it needed to be done. That prospect troubled him greatly. A piece of his soul felt like it had been torn away when he had pacified Rooster. He could not imagine what pacifying one of his teammates would do to him. One by one he silently observed them.

Freak was drumming his thumbs on the table and quietly humming a tune. The melody was familiar but Spartan could not place the actual song in his memory. It was probably a Blues Brother's song. The giant was just short of obsessed with the movie. Spartan swore that if Freak could have worn black slacks, a black jacket, the white shirt and a thin black tie with black sunglasses as his duty uniform that he would've opted for that look in a heartbeat. He and Freak had hit off their friendship from the first day when they had stepped in to prevent the eventual Echo team from bullying a fat little Japanese kid who would later also become their teammate.

Techno or Tech looked like the prototypical, nerdy brainiac in any school. He had been a short, fat Japanese American kid who wore out of style glasses, button-down plaid shirts and loafers out in public. A couple of near misses with "Zs" had added an urging towards developing some personal combat skills to the boy as well as the need to be able to run. Twelve weeks of intense physical training at the Apocalypse Academy and a controlled diet had resulted in a loss of forty-four pounds. The new slim-line Techno could run as well as anyone at the Academy as long as he didn't have an asthma attack. Spartan made a mental note to ask Nurse Ortega for a couple of those anti-asthma injections that he had given Tech before the final PT tests. They could be invaluable in keeping the boy alive in the field if they found themselves in a situation where you had to run like hell to escape the "Zs", especially the Reapers. Training every morning with Dancer in martial arts had also helped Techno's endurance as well. Of all his charges,

Tech was probably the most softhearted. He truly cared for people and cared what people thought of him.

Spartan remembered one evening at the barracks when he had found Techno inside the rec room tinkering with what looked like an old-fashioned cassette tape player. When he was asked what he was doing, Techno had quietly shrugged and explained that a female cadet had thrown the yellow and black tape player into the trash because she could not get batteries for it any longer. Techno had taken the player, removed the battery compartment and replaced it with miniature solar energy panels and a lithium battery that he had pirated from somewhere. Now the tape player would be able to charge for eight hours in the sun and then run for two days nonstop. While creative and more than a little efficient, Spartan had not thought anymore about the item until one afternoon, a week or so later, he had seen Lotus Jane walking down the hallway, headphones in her ears and a modified, solar powered cassette tape player in her hands.

Spartan went back to the dorm and had asked Techno if he had given the tape player to Jane, and if so...why? Tech had explained very sincerely that he felt that if he could help any person get a small moment of joy in a "Z" plagued world, then the time that it took to fix something was well worth the extra effort, even if that person was an Echo team member like Jane.

"Besides," He had added sheepishly. "Janie is kinda cute."

*"Janie?"* Spartan thought. *"When the Hell did she go from Lotus Jane to Janie?"* Personally, he could not have disagreed with Techno's taste in women more. Gothic girls and their wannabe vampire attitudes did nothing for him at all but …whatever. To each his own. That choice was Techno's and if he was satisfied with it, then live and let live as long as it didn't affect the team. It did show Spartan that the boy had a very soft heart. If he could go and do something that kind for someone like Jane, who had the moral fiber of a street rat, then he would have probably rebuilt the entire NASA space program from Legos for someone like Princess…err…War Queen or maybe even Raven, both of whom held superior natural beauty.

Spartan's eyes moved over to his scout. Deadeye was point blank focused, blunt and deadly efficient. The boy did not waste energy on unnecessary movement or conversation and was capable of being absolutely immobile for hours on end. It was almost eerie. His native Apache heritage had taught him to hunt and track effectively beginning as a small child and his accuracy with a bow and arrow were as good as or better than most cadets had been with a rifle out to three hundred meters.

Deadeye carried the weight of his father's death heavily, like his own personal crucifix, upon his shoulders. He rarely smiled except when he was with the Phalanx or when he was directly involved in hand-to-hand combat. Spartan remembered the teen's grinning war whoop after he had "scalped" Cutter during the Land Navigation and Survival competition. Deadeye had looked positively possessed with his smile stretching from ear to ear, like a malevolent forest spirit that had just cleansed its lands of the white devil.

The boy was loyal to the Phalanx though. As such, he was an intricate part of their chances of success and survival during the upcoming mission. What he scouted out and reported back to the team would determine the avenues of ingress and egress to and from the orphanage.

Spartan felt that he could not have had a better person for the job. He could trust that Deadeye would report exactly what he found ahead of the team without emotion and without opinion, just cold facts.

Lastly there was Dancer. British born and raised; she had been evacuated to the United States by her military father in a failed attempt to keep her away from the "Z" infection. The girl was a swirl of fiery emotions. No matter which emotion she was feeling at the moment, she carried it to the Nth degree. Happy, sad, angry, scared all were worn on her sleeve in plain view of anyone that was willing to look. Spartan had seen the variances change in the blink of an eye and could tell when the sunny, happy go lucky British girl would transform into the military trained storm cloud of a warrioress. The repeated kicks and knees to Orc and Freak's groin areas were enough to make Spartan wince even in memory.

The girl was capable of such a wide emotional spread from endearing compassion to instant, unforgiving rage that she was something of a wildcard on an operation like the search and rescue of children such as the one that they were about to be briefed on. A meltdown and loss of self-control like the one that she had allowed to overcome her because of the horse in the Dante course could get one or all of the team infected or killed. Perhaps it would be best if he found the girl a high spot where she could provide the team with overwatch and cover from her sniper rifle rather than allowing her to enter the orphanage and find God knows how many disemboweled, eaten or turned children. That could be catastrophic. Regardless of his personal feelings for the girl, he couldn't let that happen to the team. He decided that he needed to talk to the girl before the mission and receive some sort of reassurance that she was steady and understood the need for control.

The side door opened and Colonel Slade and Sergeant Hogg entered the room. Before any of the Phalanx could stand as required by proper military decorum when an officer entered the room, Colonel Slade issued an "as you were" order, keeping the Phalanx seated. The colonel carried a single manila folder with him which he placed upon the front table as he sat down. Sergeant Hogg stayed standing near the room's exit, looking for all the world like Colonel Slade's personal bodyguard.

"Corporal Spartan has advised me that he has selected the search and rescue mission for your team. Rather than waste time explaining that the mission will be dangerous, which should be blatantly obvious to everyone by now, I will instead focus on mission parameters."

Opening the manila folder, the Colonel pulled out several sheets of paper and a couple of photographs.

"Six days ago, we received a low band radio transmission from a midsize town named Freeport. It is located about thirty-five miles from here to the north. On that transmission, a very distraught woman advised that she is was a caregiver at the Sheltered Cross Home for Children. Subsequent research revealed the validity and location of the home to be downtown in Freeport, just east of city center. Communications with the woman, who we have identified as Sister Margaret Elizabeth Tucker; a nun of considerable tenure as I understand it, has advised that she is almost fully out of supplies and is trapped within a barricaded room with apparently approximately twenty children ranging in age from two to ten.

Due to the Chicago nuclear airburst and subsequent EMPs, we will have no available vehicles other than the ones that are to be used on the other secondary missions, so this will mean that you will be humping across two heavily wooded parks on foot. The only other option would be for you to cut your team count by one and take the two horses that we have, riding double. The obvious downside to this of course is that the horses may be of little use and actually a larger hindrance when you get to the city. However, the offer is there to consider.

Spartan sucked a quick breath in between his teeth then responded quickly but smoothly. "Alpha team stays together sir. The horses are not necessary. We can handle the march in and if we do get to the children, they would be more of an issue on the way out if we were trying to ride while they walked. We will improvise for the return trip."

"Very good. On the positive side, there are very few urban areas between your location and Freeport. Apart from the random camper or park visitor that may have been turned, the parks should have been basically empty when "Z" night occurred. This of course, does increase your risk for an encounter with an infected animal of any

36

size. Remember even something as small as a squirrel or even a mouse can be infected. History has shown what a few million infected rats could do in Europe with the Black Death. Do not take any animal lightly regardless of its size. Tree cover will be dense so be certain to assess threats from above, as well as at ground level before moving forward into any area."

"Understood sir."

"Potential encounters that we have calculated range from various "Z's" of all types but probably primarily packs of Romero's and isolated Husks, infected and non-infected wild animals, "Z" infected people and others seeking safe haven. There may be possible survivalists hunting in the woods or holed up in a safe house as well, and the traveling Lords of Death motorcycle group."

"Is there any current intelligence that would lead us to expect an encounter with them sir, or will it just be chance?" Spartan asked.

"The best we can ascertain is that the biker gang actively roams the roadways and cities between LaSalle/

Peru, north up the old I-39 all the way to Rockford, east to DeKalb and west as far as the Mississippi River. They are heavily armed and seem to be extremely sadistic in nature. We are addressing them as a quasi-cult in nature as they treat the "Z's" with a great deal of reverence, believing that they're coming is something out of the Rapture or Revelations in the Bible."

"We also know that they have deviated from a standard biker rank structure in so far as they are all loyal to a single man who has declared himself "the Red Baron." At this time, we have limited intelligence on him other than his nom de guerre and the fact that he was once a soldier." The colonel paused and glanced over at Sergeant Hogg who nodded his affirmation once. "He may be with this gang if you encounter them or in another location entirely."

"So, we're avoiding a fight with these dudes?" Freak asked with a very serious look on his face. "Beggin' the Colonel's pardon but why don't we just take them out once and for all. They're comin' into our turf so we should own them and teach them to respect us. Besides, I saw a show with my granny about those guys. They were all skinny little nerds dancin' around all crazy on the stage. What's the big deal if they learned to ride motorcycles? It shouldn't be no trouble at all to take them out I wouldn't think, now that we are all trained."

Deadeye reached over and lightly slapped Freak squarely on the back of his bald head with an audible crack. "That's *Lord of the Dance* you idiot, not *The Lords of Death*!" The Apache said rolling his eyes.

"Oh." Freak said obviously embarrassed at his confused comment. "My bad Sir. Are they related at all?"

The colonel could not help but to allow faint smile to upturn corners of his mouth. Such bravado was common in combat troops and most often served as an indication that these young men and women were really ready for the assigned mission. Still, he needed them to be focused and to understand the depth of danger that they could be marching into.

"While I appreciate your granny's efforts to educate you in the arts, the Lords of Death prefer to perform their own artistic talents in ways that have nothing to do with metal tap shoes spinning and clapping across the stage. For instance, we have knowledge that the gang routinely captures the living; usually refugees and intentionally infects them through exposure to "Z" bites, thus allowing the living to become prepared for the biblical Rapture that the undead will allegedly bring them. We also have confirmed knowledge that the living are being used for sport in some sort of motorcycle-based gladiatorial setting at the former Northern Illinois University campus where gambling, drinking, drug usage, prostitution and various other more debauched forms of revelry occur almost nightly. Only males are used for the motorcycle arena with females being used for more… traditional entertainments. Human sacrifice, cannibalism and religious devotions and ceremonies dedicated to the walking dead are also rumors that have been gathered by Paladins and Scouts as recently as last week."

"We are definitely avoiding them at all costs." Spartan said aloud as the team nodded his agreement.

Sergeant Hogg's voice came from inside of the room. "If you run into that one-eyed, patch wearing sum' bitch that goes by the name of the Red Baron, you just feel downright free to stomp a mud hole in his ass and walk it dry! You'll know him right off. Red leather on everything. Thinks he's the reincarnation of Germany's World War I flying ace, the Red Baron. Looks more like one 'a the Village People ta me. Just be a crying shame if one of you put a bullet or a blade in his brain. I may even shed a tear in my beer."

"Thank you Sergeant. I appreciate your sentiment but that's enough." The colonel said softly. Obviously, it was loud enough for Sergeant Hogg to hear because he did not say anything further about the Red Baron. The colonel continued.

"Please excuse the sergeant's outburst. We believe that the man who would eventually become the self-styled Red Baron was once part of the Sergeant's Cadre here at the Apocalypse Academy although we have not received one hundred percent confirmation at this time. He created a lot of chaos and murdered several soldiers when he decided to depart what he considered to be the idealistic Apocalypse Academy to join a ruthless gang of death worshiping fanatics in the Lords of Death. He wears that patch on his eye to this day as a reminder from Sergeant Hogg of the cost of betrayal in this new world. Since then, there is an acknowledged blood feud between the Academy and the Lords of Death. If you are captured, you can expect death to be the kindest mercy, and the likelihood of a far worse fate which would definitely include infection being more than likely."

Spartan felt a knot in his throat and swallowed hard to suppress it. The biker gang was definitely to be avoided.

"Favorable situations will definitely be limited during this operation. The next five days weather should be okay for travel. Nothing severe is expected, at least as far as we can tell. As far as we know, there are no Paladins operating in this area; at least not one that is from the Academy or one that has made any type of contact with any of the Academy staff. As we seem to have parallel visions and missions differing in operational parameters, if they were there it seems likely that we would have at least exchanged intelligence and supplies. As of two months ago, there was a farmhouse just north of the village of Mount Morris, owned by the Williamson family. They have survived more or less intact during the Apocalypse and have proven to be receptive to Academy personnel over the last couple of years."

"Jim Williamson Senior is an ex-United States Army Ranger. He served time in Vietnam, Panama and the Middle East. His wife, Jenny, used to be a homebody. She loved to cook and made a fantastic apple pie before the apocalypse. They also have two children, James Junior and Kelly, teenagers of unknown ages, maybe fourteen to sixteen. If you should be wounded, make your way to their home. Identify yourself as warriors from the Apocalypse Academy and they will welcome you with open arms. Jim is a fair to midland combat medic so he may be able to help you in a pinch. I have marked the location of their home on this map."

The Colonel slid the paper across the table to Spartan.

"Please make every effort to conceal your movements from anyone, especially the Lords of Death. The Williamson family has not been forced into an encounter with the bikers as of yet and we do not want to be responsible for bringing them to the gang's attention. Are there any questions?"

No one had any.

"Okay. Two last points. Anyone friendly to the Apocalypse Academy will know the following password and confirmation code. The password is *Whiskey Tango Foxtrot* and the confirmation code is *Alpha Alpha.*"

Spartan heard a small snort and giggle come from Dancer. He looked over her as did everyone else in the briefing, surprised at the uncharacteristic outburst. She quickly tried to hide her smile behind an upraised hand over her mouth and downward look as she apologized.

"Sorry sir."

"Please explain Ms. Dancer. Do you find something amusing about this Op report? Please share your insight with the entire group. I am certain that we can all use a good laugh."

"Yes Sir. As you know, before "Z" night, almost the entire world used cell phones to communicate. Land lines had become a thing of the past and written communications over cell phones known as text messages. Most people avoided actual person to person talking in favor of short, typed messages and that eventually evolved downward even further into the use of three- or four-letter acronyms such as LOL for laugh out loud or LMAO for laughing my ass off."

"Yes, I recall. Please go on." The Colonel said.

"Well sir, to be perfectly honest, the password that you selected; Whiskey Tango Foxtrot; also had its own acronym. WTF used to mean "What the fuck?" in text speak, which in retrospect really seems to describe our current situation appropriately. That's what made me commit the outburst Sir. I sincerely apologize for my unprofessional behavior."

The senior officer said nothing for several seconds, and then burst into laughter, breaking the tension of the moment. He laughed heartily for almost a full minute before regaining his composure. It was the first time the former cadets had ever seen the senior officer laugh.

"Outstanding!" Was all he said, nodding his head and wiping a tear of mirth from the corner of one eye. Recomposing himself, he continued with the briefing.

"One final note that is, after our language and history lesson from Ms. Dancer, a much more sobering one but one that you must all take heed of. If one of you is bitten by a "Z" and infected, you will not be allowed back onto the grounds of the Apocalypse Academy for any reason. You have all been issued pacification spikes as well as your own various weapons. It is incumbent on you all to protect the sanctity and security of the Academy by not allowing any infected including yourselves, onto the grounds. If a new outbreak were to occur, it could potentially destroy what we have built here. You are a team. Live as a team, fight as a team, die as a team and pacify as a team. It sounds cold and I suppose in a way it is. But at the same time that's the way that it must be for us all to continue to survive."

The laughter of the previous moment evaporated like water under the desert sun. The very thought of having to pacify Dancer or one of the guys due to contracting the HUNGER virus was heartbreaking even though it had not yet occurred. Spartan could tell by the downcast looks and nervous fidgeting around the table that his team felt the same way.

"If you have no other questions, then your mission will begin at zero five hundred tomorrow. I am proud of you all. What you are doing, trying to save those children, is the stuff that legends begin with. Follow your quest just as Hercules, Odysseus and Perseus did, and I am certain that you will leave your legacy on history, as well. Good luck."

The colonel stood, turned and walked out of the room without another word. Spartan did not miss the Greek warrior reference. No one from the Phalanx moved or spoke despite military tradition to stand when an officer left the room.

From the side of the room, Sergeant Hogg's gruff voice spoke up loudly. "On your feet troops! Do you need a special invitation to get yer happy asses moving? You all need to draw your MREs from supply. Four days, four meals. Ya can count right? Let's get it done people, assholes and elbows! Move it!"

Alpha team stood up as one and began filing out of the briefing room door.

"Spartan, I need a moment of yer time if you please." Sergeant Hogg said.

Spartan turned and walked back to Hogg. "Yes Drill Sergeant."

"Awww, you can let up on the drill part now Spartan. Sergeant Hogg will do just fine. I told you the other night that you and Band-Aid was like my kids. Hell, I humped you both from the arms o' death so that's gotta mean something. The point is, it wouldn't be right if 'n I didn't send you something to remember your time with ol' Hogg before you go off on your own to court that nasty bitch Death."

Sergeant reached into his pants pocket and pulled out a silver Zippo lighter, then handed it to Spartan. "It's full. Just done filled 'er up for ya. Figured you might need it out there."

"Sergeant Hogg, I can't…"

The burly Sergeant cut him off. "Shut the hell up Spartan. Just take it and don't get dead. I want it back

48

someday and I don' want to have to have to go diggin' through a million "Zs" guts to find it!" Spartan nodded. Sergeant Hogg clapped him firmly on the shoulder once and then walked off. Spartan looked down at the silver lighter in his hand and read the inscription imprinted on the metal side:

> *To Sergeant J. D. Hogg*
>> *For valor and bravery in saving an old war horse's life.*
>> *Thank you.*
>> *General Isaac Spears, 10$^{th}$ mountain division.*

Spartan silently vowed to hear that story when he returned to the Apocalypse Academy in five days. Then he went to find his team.

If a night could've been any more restless, Spartan did not know how. As he cinched the buckles and clips to secure his ZAP armor he wondered how the rest of his team was holding up against the anxiety of first mission anticipation. Careful to ensure that every overlapping segment of armor was fitted snugly to ensure that it allowed no bare skin to show, Spartan buckled on his web belt and thigh holster over the top and fastened the Velcro straps around his thigh. After press checking his Glock 21 to ensure that it was loaded and chambered, he holstered the weapon. His thigh holster carried at level III retention rating. That meant that it contained three separate security features to prevent it from accidently falling out while he was running or from being accidentally taken away by grasping hands as the undead attacked for his flesh. This particular holster required that the weapon be pressed downward, rotated slightly outward and rocked forward to be successfully drawn. It also had a leather flap over the top to help keep his ammunition dry and a spare magazine pouch on the front.

In addition to the holster, his belt carried four more magazines for the Glock, two ammo pouches containing three thirty round magazines for his M4, his combat knife, and a field trauma kit. After the op briefing, Spartan had made it a point to visit Nurse Ortega to obtain some field supplies that potentially the children or his team may need traveling to or from the Sheltered Cross Orphanage. Bandages, antiseptic spray and basic splinting material were placed into the trauma kit along with a separate small box of vials and syringes.

"What are those?" Spartan had asked, referring to the vials.

"The brown ones are morphine. No more than two cc's per four hours. That can be safely doubled but will probably render the patient unconscious so be sure you're holed up somewhere first. The five yellow vials are epinephrine. For them, you use the longest syringe and inject it directly into the heart. These are important if you have someone who is suffered a heart attack or various other heart stopping instances such as a concussion blast etc.... The needles on those syringes are specifically designed to fit between the links of your ZAP armor so that you do not have to waste precious time trying to unsuit a dying teammate. I included enough for one for each of you just in case of emergency."

"And those two?" Spartan asked pointing to the last two vials containing four cc's of a clear liquid in each.

"They're for your asthmatic friend. It's the same juice from the day of the final PT test. But they are not really there so I'm not sure exactly what you're talking about. You must have been mistaken and thought that you saw something."

Catching the clue and the Hispanic nurse's wink, he shut the kit and placed it into the outer belt pouch of his ZAP armor.

"Thank you ma'am. I won't forget this." he said to the woman that was looking out for his team. "May I ask why? Why are you so willing to help us?"

The nurse smiled a pretty, but sad smile. "You are all going out to face death and you're trying to save lives. If bending one of Colonel Slade's precious rules here or there helps to keep you alive longer, then we will all benefit from it." She said and started to turn back to her cabinets, replacing various supplies that had not been needed in the Medkit. "Besides…" She added quietly. "It's what my husband would have wanted me to do."

Spartan remembered the "Z" in the lab coat that the nurse and Sergeant Boomer had pacified to demonstrate the near invulnerability of the undead and the technique needed to place them at final rest to the cadets. He remembered the nurse's pain and emotion as she had run from the tent after allowing her husband to help save lives one last time, through his request to be pacified for the knowledge of the cadets letting them actually *see* the results of the pacification process firsthand for themselves.

"Yes ma'am. I'm sure he would. Thank you." Spartan left the nurse's station and returned to the barracks, not wanting to see the Ortega's tears.

His web gear securely in place, he slipped the scabbard for the sword of the Leonidas over his head and slung the blade across his back. Over this he added his rucksack containing his supplies, extra ammunition and spare power supply for the ZAP. Normally, he wore the scabbard at his waist but the pack would help keep it in place as well and keep it from slapping against his armor if he needed to move silently. Lastly he picked up his M-4 and his helmet. He debated whether or not to turn on his armor's power but decided to conserve the energy and clumped loudly along the hall heading for the quarterdeck to meet up with his team. Walking out of the barrack's doors, Spartan found the rest of his team already waiting for him. He walked up to them, clumping in his armor and weapons.

"Thought you were gonna sleep in boss. We've all been out here 'bout an hour. Glad you're here now though. Any longer and I think the incredible nerdy kid over there would have started to disassemble all of our ZAP armor to see how it works." Freak said, jerking an armored thumb over towards Techno who sat on the low retaining wall around the quarter deck with a micro-flashlight held in his teeth and a screwdriver in one hand. The teenager looked up upon hearing his name and the light from his glasses gave him a faintly owlish appearance as he spoke around the flashlight.

"Wha...?"

Spartan shook his head. "Tech, now really isn't the best time to be modifying anything on the ZAP's. Everybody geared up and ready? Let's do a quick inspection. Any last-minute issues or equipment problems?"

"No." They all responded.

Spartan walked over to each of them in turn. Freak stood like an armored gladiator. As intimidating as the massive teen was naturally; Spartan thought that the hulking armor made the man ten times more fearsome. Like a living monolith. The Blues Brothers formed an "X" behind his bald head.

"Game time brother. I'm ready to play ball!" Spartan nodded. He knew that he could count on Freak to be up tempo. He moved over to the Apache scout.

Deadeye stood quietly, every piece of equipment in place and secured to prevent any excessive noise. The blade of his tomahawk had been blackened to prevent reflection of light as had the blades of the razor bow that was slung across his back. War paint streaked across both cheekbones, peaking at the bridge of his nose.

"Ready?" Spartan asked.

"Yes." Was all the Apache said in response to the question, his tone serious.

Spartan nodded again. The Apache warrior was capable of superior mental focus and was not one to mince unneeded words. He continued on over to Techno.

Tech had replaced the screwdriver into the mini toolkit that Spartan knew that he requisitioned from Sergeant Surfer. He needed to check and see what else the boy had obtained.

"Holding up okay Techno?"

"I guess so." The teen appeared nervous, licking his dry lips and looking around repeatedly, as if a "Z" would just pop out of thin air in front of him and attack. Spartan did his best to calm him down by focusing him on the requisitioned gear.

"How are we for explosives? What did you draw from the Armory?"

The question seemed to snap the way out of his panic. "Four pounds of C4, fifty feet of detonating cord, two Claymore mines with hand actuators, a dozen detonators, two pull tab shock tube initiators, six one minute to thirty-minute timers and one light antitank weapon." The boy stated casually as if reading off the mix of chemicals for a chemistry experiment. "Oh, and two fragmentation grenades apiece, five smoke grenades; enough for one each, five flash bangs; one apiece and one white phosphorus grenade that Sergeant Boomer gave me as a personal gift." He added matter-of-factly. The Benelli combat shotgun hung limply at his side, as if insignificant in comparison to all of the explosives.

"I have a gift for you as well from Nurse Ortega in the Medkit if you should need it." Spartan said nodding towards his rucksack.

Techno didn't need to say anything aloud in response because the smile on his face said it all. Spartan patted the boy's shoulder and moved over to his last teammate.

Dancer sat in the lotus position upon the two-foot-high retaining wall, opposite of where Techno had been.

With her brown eyes closed she seemed so at peace with the back of her hands resting lightly on her Kevlar covered knees, forefingers and thumbs curled forming small "O's". Her hair had been braided and pulled into a tight bun on the back of her head.

"Dance, it's time to go."

"I'm ready." She replied opening her eyes. She stared at him for a long time as if searching to find the right words to say. Then she spoke. "In the field, I need you to promise to be a leader, not my boyfriend. If it comes down to hard choices, then you do what needs to be done based on the team, not just me or us."

"I promise." He said softly. He had been considering how to voice the same issue most of the day.

She smiled, stood up and grabbed her naginata from where it was leaned on the wall beside her. Then she adjusted the sling for her sniper rifle and kissed Spartan lightly on the cheek. A soft "Ooohhh" came from the other members of the Phalanx, teasing the young couple. "Honey, let's go get the kids." She said and walked over to where Freak, Techno and Deadeye stood in a silent huddle watching the entire interaction.

"Don't act like such silly little schoolgirls ya bloody prats!" She said as she flounced up to them, intentionally over exaggerating the sway of her hips. They all laughed.

"All right. Let's get going. Ranger file, ten-meter increments. Deadeye's on point. Dancer, me, and then Techno. Freak you've got our backs. Let's move people, we've got a long way to go. Deadeye; set us a solid but not too brutal pace. Be sharp people."

Spartan initiated the power supply on his ZAP armor and watched his HUD display as the other armors LEDs blinked into life on his view screen. Seeing no anomalies, he silently fell into line behind Dancer as the Phalanx marched towards the gated bridge that would allow them to leave the Apocalypse Academy for the first and possibly for the last time. Each warrior's mind was awhirl with "what if's" and various other doubts. Then as if in response to the need for focus, the brassy sounds of an orchestra began to play the Star-Spangled Banner across all five helmeted comms, just as the sun peaked over the horizon, breaking dawn in its wake. Goose flesh rippled across the teenager's arms and neck.

"Oh yeah boy. Game time. Play ball!" Freak called out as the national anthem ended. Obviously Techno had made a modification to his ZAP armor to incorporate music that can be played outward to the entire team. So together they marched down Damnation Road with no fanfare, no assembly of their peers, no witnesses and only the pounding bass and drums of Ozzy Osbourne's *Crazy Train* to accompany them on the journey into potential hell. Had they looked up, they might have noticed Cutter silently watching them leave from the barracks. In his hands he silently balanced one of his fighting knives, standing on its tip and slowly spinning in circles between his fingers back and forth.

# Chapter three

# The March

After exiting the gates from the Apocalypse Academy and experiencing the near legendary trepidation and anxiety associated with walking Damnation Road; the three mile walk north out of the city limits was a piece of cake. There were only three near encounters with wandering groups of "Zs". All of which were Romero's, which produced hardly any excitement at all. Armored in the ZAP battle suits, the Phalanx chose to simply outrun the shambling bags of decay filled flesh and keep to the original mission parameters without having an unnecessary engagement. Stopping at the northernmost point of the town behind an old Dairy Supreme ice cream shop, the team caught their breath and strategized their approach to the first park.

"Skirting the park altogether may limit our chance for encounters with infected creatures or roving bands of "Zs", however it will also add to our visibility to anyone that may be watching the roadway. I think it's better for us to use the concealment of the park to hide our movements." Deadeye said.

"Dude, what the hell are you going to do if you run into an infected mountain lion or a bear or something?" Freak returned. "That little hatchet on your belt ain't gonna do you much good against something like that."

Deadeye seemed completely nonplussed by the giant teen's comment. "That's very true. However, you seem to be forgetting one important detail my gargantuan friend."

"Oh yeah? What's that Tatanka? You got some ancient spiritual wisdom to share with me or something?"

"Indeed."

"Go for it. Let's hear what you have to say Dawg!"

"Okay... Should we, as you say, encounter an infected bear, a mountain lion, or even a large pack of infected "Zs" that we cannot deal with individually or as a team; then I do not need outrun any of them. I will simply only need to outrun you. At your size you will seem like a mobile buffet table set up for a Thanksgiving feast. With all of those creatures otherwise occupied feasting on your dark meat, my tomahawk will be more than sufficient for handling the one or two stragglers that are left over and that may be interested in me." Deadeye flashed a wicked smile inside of his Helmut as he finished talking.

"Dude" Freak said licking his suddenly dry lips. "That is seriously messed up. I mean, I guess I can't blame any creature for wanting seriously high quality, Grade A prime rib like me but, man, that would so suck."

"Don't worry Freak," Techno added from behind over the intercoms within the zap's helmet. "I heard a new study on "Zs" was released. It seems that they are far more holistic than previously assessed and they prefer only organic food that hasn't been tainted by injected steroids. You should be perfectly safe." He said, chuckling.

"Screw you too Tech. Everyone knows that "Zs" prefer little round oriental donuts like you. You are easier to digest. There are no thick, powerful muscles like mine to bite through." Freak replied.

And so, the banter went back and forth for miles. Even Dancer got into the spirit, claiming to be a "crumpet rather than a cream puff; but still just as sweet." Only Spartan did not participate in the conversation, seeming to be completely focused on the mission at hand.

Topping a small rise, a row of small country homes stood empty off to the left side of the hilly road. The helmet's visor registered no thermal imaging to Spartan indicating that there was no one hidden within the structures; at least not alive. Similarly, his audio boosters registered none of the common Romero moans of torment or the screams of rage that traditionally came from the Reapers. There was only an occasional breeze, catching the leaves and causing them to rustle.

The first house on the left looked to be a solid one-story brick home. In the rear of the home, beyond the chain link fence, Spartan could see the upper third of the aqua blue colored waterslide leading downward into an in-ground pool. Spartan imagined the splashing and laughter of the children that had probably played in that that pool on hot summer days; carefree in a world that had not yet become infected with a man-made extinction event and suddenly he knew without a doubt that he did not want to go into that home under any circumstances short of an emergency. To see the children's rooms; to imagine the joys of a time before the apocalypse, would only bring heartache and pain for the entire team. It was better just to keep moving.

Seeing that his team had quieted, looking over at the houses, Spartan wondered if they were all experiencing the same pained thoughts that he was. He decided to take their mind off of everything by picking up the pace. Sergeant Hogg had called it "Letting the rabbit run." in the Academy meaning that the point man, in this case Deadeye, would take a couple hundred-meter lead to scout the next approach area. For the team, it meant moving from a march to a jog to expedite finding the entrance to Lowell Park and making sure it was safe for them to enter.

"Spartan to Deadeye" he said over the communications link. Everyone knew that an order was forthcoming from the formal call usage rather than open chatter.

"Go Spartan." Came the immediate reply.

"Movement plan: Phalanx Alpha-2. Two hundred meters. Recon only, do not engage. Stop at the park entrance."

"Phalanx Alpha-2. Two hundred meters. Visual only."
And Deadeye took off at a whispered run. The teen's ZAP
armor was totally soundless as he steadily trotted to the top
of the next hill before pausing to evaluate any areas of
concern that could be lurking on the downhill side.
Apparently seeing none, the Apache scout vanished over
the hilltop.

"All right team. Let's shake it loose. Communications by
hand signal only. Radios on silent. Double time to the park
entrance. Deadeye is on recon. We will rally with him there.
Double time march!"

The remainder of Alpha team took off at a run, in
perfect unison. Intervals stayed aligned at ten meters and
booted feet beat the pavement in a consistent, almost
hypnotizing rhythm. Up and down hill they ran past the
rows of summer corn fields now folded and brown with
the coming of fall, homes of all shapes and sizes and
various red, yellow and orange leafed hardwood trees lined
the road on both sides. After about a mile, Spartan's visor
blinked on the direct communications channel. Deadeye
wanted to talk in private.

"Go ahead Deadeye."

"Over the next hill you will see a small bridge crossing a stream. A large blue vehicle, possibly a family SUV, has run off the road and is nose down in the water, maybe three and a half to four feet deep. Gouge marks on the guard rail indicate a pretty high-speed collision. The metal guard rail was bent and crumpled outward for a good eight feet. All in the vehicle are KIA. The driver, a female, appeared to die on impact. The front passenger, a male, and three children in the back appeared to have been shot. The children were still buckled in car seats. No sign of infection but I didn't get in close. Bodies have been there a while, maybe a month or two and are in advanced decomposition. I recommend that you guide left on the roadway. Keep the vehicle out of sight as much as possible."

"Copy Deadeye. Guiding left. Hostiles?"

"Negative at this time. Bullet wounds could have been self-inflicted or from another source. There was no weapon visible but it could have been looted or fallen under the water. There were several sets of tracks in the mud around the vehicle. At least one set was someone under one hundred pounds. Possibly a child or more probably; a small statured female. The stride was too long and consistent to be a "Z". Survivalists or bikers are a higher probability. Could also be nomad refugees I suppose."

"Copy that. Good job. Rally at the park entrance. ETA?"

"ETA in less than twelve minutes. Approximately two point six miles to target according to my ZAP's GPS."

"Copy, rally in twelve."

"Copy. Deadeye out."

Spartan rekeyed his communications to the general communications frequency, and then activated his helmets microphone so that they could all hear him. "There is a pretty bad scene at the bottom of the next hill by the bridge. There are no survivors. Deadeye has a reconned it and confirmed that everyone in the vehicle's KIA. Guide left and keep moving. Nothing to see but heartache there."

The Phalanx crossed the bridge at a fast pace. All of them had seen their share of mayhem and death since the HUNGER plague had begun. None of them had to fight the urge to rubberneck at the crash site. Exactly twelve minutes later they saw the ten foot long, engraved green sign indicating the entrance to Lowell Park. At the same time, Deadeye activated the communications channel keyed into all of their helmets.

"Quiet entrance into the park. The Information and Welcome Center on the left side of the road just before you enter to the park contains two confirmed "Zs". Both look like they were former Park Rangers. Movement patterns and visual confirmation is that both rangers are Romero's however one is really twitchy; maybe only recently devolved. Rally point is thirty meters north of the Welcome Center in the pinetum." Deadeye advised.

"Welcome Center, two Romero's. Rally thirty meters north on the pine tree line. Copy." Spartan replied.

Spartan led his team quietly around the occupied Welcome Center without incident. They found Deadeye perched twenty feet up in the pine tree, exactly 30 meters behind the building. Quietly the boy dropped to the ground, silent as a starlit shadow on a moonless night.

Spartan rallied everyone into a combat circle and called for a quick ZAP armor status check.

"Power supply check: Deadeye?"

"Ninety-four percent."

"Dancer?"

"Ninety-four percent."

"Tech?"

"Ninety-four percent."

"Freak?"

"Eighty-eight percent.

This caused Spartan to frown as he looked down at his own IED readout which also read ninety-four percent.

Freaks armor was eating up more juice than the others. This could be a problem by the time they reached Freeport. If they got into trouble and the big warrior's armor froze up because his power supply died, he could easily become a casualty before he could replace it.

"Freak, next breakout I want the solar charger on your ZAP's power supply. You used up six percent more juice than the rest of us. Keep an eye on it. If you reach fifteen percent lower than the rest of our threshold, we will break and hold while you recharge the battery. I don't need your big ass turning into a statue out here in the middle of nowhere."

Freak just nodded.

Spartan then asked a question to his team. "Do we pacify the rangers? We might need a secure shelter on the way back with the children. This seems like it would be a good sturdy place. It's off the roadway and only has one avenue of entrance because of the surrounding tree line."

"It seems like we should. I mean, they were rangers. You know, keeping us safe when we were alive. It seems like it's the least we could do for them." Techno replied.

"I agree, at least from the noble point of view." Spartan said. "Dancer?"

The girl paused as if in thought, and then spoke aloud. "I agree with pacifying the rangers; just not right now."

"What do you mean Dance?"

"Well, think of the rangers as watchdogs. If we do get back here and need shelter, then pacifying two Romero's will not be overly difficult or burdensome to any of us, right?"

"Agreed." Spartan replied, wondering where she was going with the thought.

"Okay, so if we get back here and the "Zs" have already been put down…"

"… Then we would know that someone else was living inside the welcome center, possibly the park or at least nearby. Good thinking Dance." Spartan said finishing her thought.

"Freak, anything to add?"

"I always felt sorry for Yogi and Booboo. I mean they were just trying to eat, ya know? I'll put the rangers down whenever you're ready boss. No real preference. But I do call dibs on any pic-a-nic baskets we find."

Spartan smiled. Leave it to Freak to associate Saturday morning cartoons, the need to fill his belly and the urge to kill "Zs" all into one thought. You couldn't help but like the guy.

"Deadeye?"

"I agree with Dancer. Contact is unnecessary at this time." Was all he said.

"Okay. We avoid the rangers for now. We need to get down to the river as quickly as possible. There are three established routes from before the Apocalypse. One is an established bike and small vehicle trail known as the Beehive. I am not a fan of this route as the trees will be tight on both sides of the path, making visibility minimal.

The other two were commercial roadways. One is a casual route through the center of the park and ends at the river by the playground and boat launch. The other one is full of blind, hairpin turns from the road that would be daunting by vehicle, especially if we needed any speed. It is also the northernmost road. It winds its way past several stone pavilion picnic shelters and exits further up the river. Neither should present more of an obstacle than the other as we are on foot.

The biggest problem is that the northern side of the road consists of a three-foot-high retaining wall made of stone and cement and then a 40-to-50-foot drop over a sheer cliff face. If we get into trouble, it will be a fight for certain as we will not be able to just cut and run. Personally, I say we go with the shortest route, which is the northern road, but since we are a team, I will listen to any options or objections before I make my final call."

"The playground could be full of "Z" kids. "Z" kids swinging, "Z" kids sliding, "Z" kids on the monkey bars. I really don't want to see that." Techno said. "I say north also."

"Ain't no bears on the road Dawg. North." Freak answered.

"We chose the park route for stealth and concealment. The jogging trail gives us the quickest access to the riverfront." Deadeye replied. "It's a little tighter but virtually no chance of running into the Lords of Death upon such a narrow trail."

"Deadeye's right about the bikers. The trail would probably be safest. But time is mission-critical here. The children and that nun are starving to death and completely surrounded. We do not know how strong their barricade is. I think that operational need overrides the added risk that we take by taking the roadway. North." Dancer said.

"Okay. North Road we go. Tighten the Ranger file down to five meters. Keep in mind defensive positions as we move. No using firearms unless all other options fail.

The noise of a single shot would echo across this entire park letting everyone, alive or undead, that we are here. Move out. Deadeye; set a twenty-meter point."

There was no need for any further discussion. Deadeye was already on his feet and moving by the time the rest of the team stood up. His razor bow had materialized in his hand with an arrow knocked but undrawn, as if by magic. The rest of the Phalanx followed suit, drawing their hand weapons and allowing the rifles and shotguns to fall onto their respective slings.

Dancer nimbly caught up to Deadeye, insuring the five-meter separation between them with a quick glance at the LED readout on her helmet's faceplate. Spartan, Techno and Freak all followed as well. Moving past the Ranger Station and Welcome Center, Spartan felt an intense sadness for the two rangers. Here were two individuals that had committed their lives to keeping people safe and maintaining a place of harmony in the wilderness, yet they were forced to wander eternally within their welcome center as Romero's until someone brought them the peace that came with pacification. Spartan silently vowed to make that peace not too long in coming. It was odd, he thought as he walked ahead keeping pace with Dancer in front of them, that even though he did not know these two men, he still felt a sense of responsibility to them. Perhaps it was a connection to something from his past that he could not remember, or perhaps it was just that their missions were similar; protect the innocent; and he hoped that someone would care enough to pacify him if and when the time came and the situation was similar.

The black and grey asphalt road wound its way through a dozen twists and turns. Tall pine trees and various oak, maple and birch trees towered over the road providing shade and dappling the scene in hundreds of swatches of colorful and occasionally shadowed dark patches from the sunlight filtering between the autumn leaves. The visual effect even with the helmets optical filters was stunning, producing an almost natural camouflage to the area.

Rounding a bend in the road, they saw Deadeye kneeling near the tree line, a closed fist held up indicating that he wanted the team to stop. A second wave of his open hand horizontally above his helmet let them know that he wanted them to find cover. Passing the hand signal back, Spartan moved off the roadway to a nearby tree.

Looking ahead he could see one of the stone camping pavilions on the right side of the roadway, but no "Zs" or people. Spartan trusted Deadeye's sense of danger and if the scout was using hand signals then he had a reason to believe that contact was imminent. Spartan surveyed the surrounding area. If a fight was forthcoming, he needed to be aware of his team's movement availability options and limitations. The area immediately behind the pavilion was heavily wooded with trees on a sloping hill, maybe fifteen degrees upward. It would provide decent cover versus firearms, but difficult terrain if they had to dodge "Zs", especially if they were Reapers. The roadway itself was lined with a two-foot-deep drainage ditch on both sides and more woods on the downward slope on the opposite side of the road. More the same way ahead for as far as Spartan could see.

Deadeye caught Spartan's eye with a new series of hand signals. Pointing to his own eye area with two fingers split into a "V", he then pointed to the pavilion's rooftop. Spartan followed the scout's line of sight, searching for movement. At first he saw nothing because he was looking for "Zs" or people. Then he realized that Deadeye had not been telling him to look at the roof but instead at the building's stone chimney. Refocusing his vision, he registered the soft, lazy white trail of wood smoke drifting out of the stone chimney and he knew that Deadeye had been right to call a halt to the team's movement. They were not alone.

Spartan nodded once to Deadeye to confirm the Apache's observation. This prompted Deadeye to reissue the "V" gesture but this time he focused his secondary point downward towards the shaded rear of the stone structure. There, camouflaged with several cut branches, sat three motorcycles, the bulky chrome machine and white mounted skulls barely visible in the dappled sunlight. The motorcycles belonged to the Lords of Death.

Engagement with the gang was not within the Phalanx's current mission parameters. Their mission was to rescue orphans; not fight a gang war. From what the colonel had said there was already an acknowledged bad blood between the Apocalypse Academy and the undead worshiping biker's. There was no sense stirring up more hostility in an unneeded skirmish. Then they heard the woman scream. High and loud, it held the sound of pure terror as it reverberated off of the trees, the walls and the Phalanx team members' helmets.

The need for silence was instantly gone. Combat instincts overrode propriety as Spartan keyed his helmet microphone to communicate with his entire team. "Freak, Techno... Back door. Dancer... Pick a high point that you can see both ends of the building through your scope. If it's exiting the building and it's not one of us or a woman running like hell; kill it. Deadeye with me at the front. Let's move people."

Combat training kicked in with the surging heat of adrenaline for every member of the Phalanx. They moved as one, each segment of the team assuming their assigned position smoothly and efficiently. Dancer quickly scrambled up the hill and located a cluster of residual boulders jutting out that provided her a perfect platform for her Dragonov. Unslinging the weapon, she extended the bipod and lay down upon the rocks. Since windage was not an issue here, anyone leaving the building would be a clean shot at nearly point-blank range. Pulling back the charging handle, she primed the weapon with a 7.62-

millimeter projectile and settled into her overwatch position.

Freak and Techno circled quietly to the back of the building site, staying low. Upon arriving they found a fourth motorcycle attached to the side car that had been hidden behind the building out of sight. Dangling from the sidecar was a long, leather dog leash.

"Phalanx Two in position. Be advised. There was a fourth motorcycle. Watch for a possible dog." Techno said as he used his Leatherman tool to cut the ignition wires on all of the motorcycles.

"Phalanx Three, are you a go?" Spartan asked.

"Go." Was all that Dancer responded.

"Copy. Phalanx One breaching in five, four, three, two, one, go, go, go!"

Deadeye used his armored boot to kick open the small pavilion's wooden door and immediately peeled right, raising his razor bow and drawing the arrow back to his cheek as he moved. Spartan flowed left off of Deadeye's decision and surveyed the room. A split second later he heard Freak breach the back door. Two bikers sat at a small table at the rear the room, a bottle of whiskey and a pair of shot glasses on the table before them. Also on the table was a long barreled .357 revolver. A third biker had his back to the team, squatting near a small fireplace.

"Nobody moves and nobody dies!" Spartan ordered; his voice amplified across an external speaker in his ZAP armor.

The drunken biker with his back to the team screamed "Fuck you!" and dove to the side as his partner reached across the table, lunging for the revolver. As his hand grasped the handle and began to raise the weapon to a firing position, Deadeye's razor bow flashed downward; its blade cleaving the would-be assailant's arm at the wrist. The revolver clattered back onto the table, hand still gripping it as the biker fell backward over his chair clutching the crimson squirting stump.

The biker at the fireplace used the distraction to grab a flaming log and spin around, attempting to club Spartan with it. Speed and strength augmented by the ZAP armor, Spartan's left-hand shot upward grabbing the man by the wrist and preventing the arm from descending with the flaming brand. His right hand, holding the sword of Leonidas slashed a single stroke side to side. Spartan followed through the swing and pivoted away from the biker, releasing the man's wrist. As shock assailed the leather clad Lord of Death, he still held the torch high, looking like the Statue of Liberty as he watched in horror while gray-white, ropey lengths of his intestines spilled out of an eighteen-inch-long gash in his abdomen and landed in a bloody pool at his feet. His eyes rolled up into his head and his body collapsed seconds later.

At the rear of the house, Freak kicked the outer door so hard that the molding and the entire framework tore free of the wall, flying across the room like a rectangular missile before skidding to a stop at a Romero's feet. Seeing the threat, Freak initially took two steps towards the undead creature before he realized that it was chained to the wall by a heavy length of heavy dog chain. The creature clearly wore a thick spiked black leather dog collar around its neck to which the dog chain was attached by a large padlock. In its rotten hands lay the slim lower leg, calf and foot of what appeared to be a recent victim. The "Z" had taken several bites out of the fresh meat, but the toenail polish and a Minnie Mouse tattoo just above the ankle confirmed the limb belonged to a female.

Spinning around, Freak saw a tall, greasy-haired biker hurriedly pulling his pants up around his waist to conceal his nakedness. Beyond the bare-chested biker, on the bed lay a naked young woman, barely out of her teens, tied by both arms to the bed's headboard. One leg was tied out to the side by the ankle. The other leg was missing below the knee and wrapped in a very crude and blood-soaked rope tourniquet. A blue colored bandana had been tied across her mouth and acted as a gag, muffling her terrified screams. Embedded in the headboard, out of the girl's reach, was a full-sized machete.

Rage filled Freak's mind as he slowly put the pieces of the scene together. Behind him, the crackle of electricity and thump of a falling body indicated that Techno had just dealt with the Romero that had been chained to the wall.

Looking at the man's belt, he saw the sheath of a machete dangling downward. Looking at the limb still clenched in the immobilized "Z's" hand he noted the clean-cut on the end of the leg, above the calf. The leg had not been chewed off. It had been severed by a sharp, heavy blade. A blade conspicuously similar to the machete stuck above the girl's head on the wooden headboard.

"Tech. Check the girl. Tell me if she's alive."

The biker took two involuntary steps backward, clearly unsure of what was happening.

"You better hope she's still alive sucker. If not, you'll be joining her in a minute." He said as the Blues Brothers swung in alternating counterclockwise circles from Freak's powerful wrists. He looked like he was warming up in the on-deck circle for a Saturday afternoon ballgame.

The biker held his hands defensively in front of himself. "Look, I can…"

"Shut your fucking mouth!" Freak yelled advancing three steps closer before the short sentence was completed.

"Tech?"

"She's alive… Barely. Lost a lot of blood. She's also been raped by the looks of it. Probably several times if I had to guess."

"On your knees… *Lord of Death*…" Freak said, sarcasm and an icy cold tone entering his voice as his eyes squinted in anger. "Or jump for your knife. Either way, you don't survive. But how you go out is up to you."

Back at the front of the building, the biker that had dove to the ground scurried sideways, reaching for the inside of his skull adorned leather vest and struggled momentarily to draw a chrome plated snub-nosed revolver that had been concealed there. Following the movements with his eyes, Deadeye leapt over the table that was until recently being used as the bikers' makeshift bar and tipped its top over in front of him just as the first of five rounds slammed into the wood. Activating his ZAP armor's stealth ability, Deadeye blended with the fire lit shadows and flowed in a sidestep, ten feet to the right as the biker struggled to reload.

Raising the revolver, the biker eased around the table searching for Deadeye or his body. Seeing no sign of either, the Lord of Death looked up in confusion and raised his arm toward the back of Spartan's head by the fireplace.

"Gonna get some for Miko!" He said under his breath referring to the eviscerated biker at Spartan's feet. As his finger tightened on the trigger, he felt an impact to his head and the vision in his left eye went black. It was not unlike getting hit with a pool cue in a bar fight. He had that happen a lot. Reaching up with his offhand he felt a thin wooden shaft sticking out from his eye socket. *"The bastard put my eye out with a stick!"* Was the first thing he thought feeling the warm, sticky blood and visceral fluid running down his beefy cheek. *"He's... gonna... pay... for...*Before he could finish the thought, the vision in his other eye also went black from the arrow that had entered his eye was such velocity that it'd speared his alcohol-soaked brain and exited his skull before pinning the biker to the wall like a leather clad butterfly. The biker known as Chucky never knew he was dying and the confusion still showed on his face even after the dying was over and he had become its post life form... Dead.

Walking over to where he had last seen Deadeye, Spartan looked over at the one-handed biker's slumped form lying on the floor, silently convulsing. The Alpha team leader noted the growing puddle of blood around the severed wrist. Unconscious, and slowly bleeding to death, the biker was not going to survive. Spartan elected to let the man die a clean death and swept the sort of Leonidas downward delivering a coup de grace. There was no room on this mission for prisoners.

"Clear!" Deadeye called materializing next to Spartan.

"Clear!" Spartan echoed. "Freak, Techno, sound off!"

"Clear and covering one piece of shit, slimebag, biker gutter trash!" Freak said.

"Clear. One civilian wounded. Probably terminal." Techno added. "We're in the back of the pavilion."

Spartan and Deadeye entered the room through the door and were briefed by Techno while Freak paced like a caged tiger behind the kneeling biker. Each twirl of his bats made a whoosh through the air. Hearing a soft call from the bed, Techno rushed back to the girl's side. Gently he cradled the girl's head in his arms. "I fought him off mama" the girl said so softly it could barely be heard. "I... fought... him off... But...he hurt me mama. He... hurt... He... He..." Then the girl's eyes rolled into her head and with the double hitch of her breath she died.

The kneeling biker began to laugh. A deep bellowing laughter echoed from the man's lips that defied reason and spoke of the madness of his own impending death. Spartan reached down and jerked the man to his feet by his greasy hair. "Get the fuck out of here!" He said and shoved the man towards the door.

"What!" Freak screamed. "You can't let that fuckin' psycho dude go Spartan! You see what that sick fucker did to that poor little girl? She wouldn't give it up so he cut off her fuckin' leg Dawg; then they fed it to a "Z"! If that wasn't enough, then he and his buddies raped her!"

The biker chuckled. "Yeah. Yeah we did. And you know what? She was a sweet little thing that liked to kick me and the boys. When we took that leg off, she was more than willin' to give it up when she couldn't kick no more!" The biker said and turned, running for the door, laughter trailing behind him.

"Spartan! No!" Freak bellowed, pushing his way past Techno and Deadeye, towards the door to follow the biker. "You can't just let that sick fucker walk!"

Spartan took the sword of Leonidas and held it in a backhanded grip, horizontally in front of the big warrior's chest. "Freak stand down. That's an order!" Spartan said with authority that was magnified tenfold by his ZAP armor's communication systems.

The giant froze in his tracks, muscles quivering and straining to hold himself into a single place. Training overrode his emotion though and he stood fast awaiting the next order.

"Wait for it... Wait for it...Wait...for...it!" Was all Spartan said.

Three seconds later, a single shot rang out just as the biker mounted his motorcycle. The bare-chested Lord of death's head vaporized as Dancer's 7.62 caliber round struck home. The impact blew the biker's body five feet off into the tree line.

Spartan shrugged as he walked past Freak, a silent apology spoken between them. "I didn't want you to ruin your bats on scum like that." Was all Spartan said.

As soon as the battle ended, Spartan quickly assessed the Phalanx's injuries and situation. His team had suffered no physical injuries. For some reason the situation with this girl was having an extreme impact on Freak. Obviously, there was no way that he could've known the girl, but still there was something. He made a mental note to ask the big man about it later.

Using the augmented power of the ZAP armor, Spartan and Freak picked up the motorcycles and carried them across the road and up over to the concrete and stone wall where they then lowered them down to Techno and Deadeye. The two warriors that rolled them down the steep incline into an area about fifty yards away and concealed them next to a rock outcropping with branches and leaves. Almost as an afterthought, Techno re-spliced the starter wires that he cut on all of the motorcycles, under the auspices of *"you never know when you might need a ride."*

The bodies of the bikers were similarly disposed of; dumped in a ravine an additional hundred meters away. Freak fumed and his anger was still apparent when he tossed the biker's headless body into the ravine with enough force to make the breaking of bones audible even from where Spartan stood twenty feet away.

There was nothing that could be done for the unnamed girl. They did not want to leave her to the animals in the wilderness, nor just leave her lying bloody and naked upon the bed. Together, Alpha team settled upon a plan to shroud the girl in sheets as best they could and leave her body in the pavilion until they could return. Then they would take her body back to the Apocalypse Academy with them to receive a proper burial.

Using his Native American wilderness lore, Deadeye brushed over their tracks with a large branch and rearranged the leaves and plant foliage to maximize the camouflage of the motorcycles and the biker's bodies. With any luck, the dead bikers would not be found until early spring; if at all. While Deadeye camouflaged the motorcycles, Dancer, Techno and Freak returned to shroud the body of the girl in the blood-stained sheet. It was the best that they could do given the circumstance. Spartan silently contemplated the team's map. A glimmer of metal caught Spartan's eye as he tried to decide the team's best route. Looking down he saw the thirty-eight-caliber pistol lying on the ground. Without a word he picked it up and tucked it into the inside of his boot. There was no sense leaving a functional weapon behind. Next, he picked up the three fifty-seven revolver from where it lay on the floor and pried the fingers open that still grasped the hand grip. Walking to the doorway he slung that severed hand out across the street and over the cliff side. He intended to give that weapon to Freak. Seeing that Deadeye had completed his camouflage task, Spartan asked him about the trail ahead.

"How far to the riverfront?" Spartan asked, holding out the map.

Evaluating the internal schematic of the park on his HUD, Deadeye advised "About a half to a mile if we stay on the road. If we go overland then probably only about a half mile all told, but rougher terrain."

"Are there any specific threats other than the "Zs", bikers and animals if we go overland?"

"There's always a chance of the deadfall or other trap set by a survivalist. Additionally, ambushes will be hard to spot, but then again so will we and we will be traveling by an unsuspected route which would work in our favor. Also, we do not know if the bikers here were just an autonomous pack looking to get their rocks off on that girl or if they were scouting party for a larger group of the Lords of Death that may still lie ahead of the inside of the park."

Just then Freak, Techno and Dancer returned from their grisly duty. Freak carried his helmet under one massive arm. Spartan recognized the residual red rim from where tears had fallen on Freak's face. He truly felt bad for the massive teenager. Walking up to Freak, he handed him the three fifty-seven revolver. "Take it. It's the spoils of war. Maybe you can put it to good use in the future."

Freak nodded. Sliding hid helmet back on, he took the revolver. Looking at Spartan through his visor and said "There's gonna be a lot of pain for the Lords of Death. That little girl didn't deserve that. She was too young."

Spartan nodded as the team prepared to move out. Their plans to avoid encounters with the Lords of Death had already gone to shit and they were barely even out of the city. He advised them all that they were changing routes and that they were moving out overland. Nobody disagreed. Resuming their marching order, Deadeye walked up the roadway about fifty meters past the stone pavilion and silently entered the wood line. Spartan allowed the scout about twenty meters of lead time before the rest of the team followed. The intrinsic sounds of nature flooded the sensors of the ZAP armor's helmet speakers. The difference between walking on an asphalt road and through the underbrush and fallen leaves felt almost as if they had entered another world entirely. The faux sense of security that the roadway had provided became apparent to them as the various creatures of the woods begin to chit and chatter the Phalanx's presence amongst themselves.

Moving fast on a wave of adrenaline from their recent battle and a fear of the unknown woods, it took less than twenty minutes to reach the park's northern gated perimeter. It was a chain-link fence, six foot in height and locked with a single chain and padlock.

"Over or through?" Deadeye asked.

It was an interesting question. If they went through the gate, then it would become unsecured to any wandering "Zs", thus potentially adding more danger upon their return to the park with the children. If they went over the fence, then the gate would remain locked but it would slow them down significantly if they were trying to outrun an enemy like say, an entire city of zombies, that were looking to snack on bite-size portions of orphans and nuns for dinner and a large portion of Phalanx for dessert. In the end, Spartan called Freak to the front of the line and gave him the order to "break the chain or lock but leave the gate intact if possible."

Freak did not say a word. He merely walked up to the three-inch padlock, grasped it in one gigantic hand and twisted. The ZAP armor's strength enhancer did the rest, snapping the lock in half without making Freak so much as grunt in exertion. Allowing the rest of the Phalanx to pass through the open portal, Freak then re-closed the door and wrapped the chain through the supporting frame of the gate and fence line. Although this would not keep out a human, it would or at least should, keep out any wandering "Z's" that might happen by.

Alpha team then returned to their Ranger file maintaining twenty meters apart and set out at a jog.

# Chapter Four

## Intelligence update

"Sergeant Hogg? You requested to see me?" Asked Colonel Slade from where he sat behind the large mahogany desk. The desk was the one luxury that he allowed himself during his tenure at the Apocalypse Academy. It was an antique from the early 1800s that allegedly had been sat at by numerous congressmen, governors and even President Lincoln himself before his assassination. Just prior to when the "Z" pandemic had struck, he had purchased the desk for more than seven thousand dollars at an auction in Chicago.

"Sir, yes Sir!"

"You may dispense with the formalities sergeant. It's just the two of us talking. What's on your mind?"

"Sir, two separate Paladin reports have come in from the field. One from the east and one from the north. The Paladin, Ryker's, came from the east and has been periodically monitoring I – 88 into DeKalb. As you know, the Lords of Death have been recruiting or slaughtering any survivors on the former campus of Northern Illinois University."

"Go on."

"Paladin Ryker has reported that a heavily armed group of riders has departed their base in the DeKalb area and are currently heading west on I-88. Their final destination is unknown at this time however the Paladin stated that it is reasonable to believe that they may be heading this way."

"What leads him to that conclusion sergeant? Has he captured and questioned any of the Lords of Death?"

"No sir, but he said that the Baron was leading them." Sergeant Hogg replied. "He said he could see that bastard's red leathers from a mile away."

"And is this Paladin reliable?" The colonel asked, a deepening scowl creasing his brow.

"Sir, Ryker is a former Army Ranger. He's usually right on the money in his assessments."

Slade knew that the sergeant was correct. The Paladin known as Ryker was clinical and efficient at destroying both the undead and the Lords of Death. He'd become renowned for his use of an ancient medieval mace that he called "Hell Bringer" in his assaults. His reports to the Academy had never been wrong yet.

The colonel nodded. "And the second report?"

"Something has happened in Madison, Wisconsin. We are unsure exactly what, but a flood of "Zs", mostly Romero's with a few Reapers mixed in, have begun to move southward. The Paladin that provided the estimation stated that the pack was roughly eighteen to twenty thousand in number."

"Eighteen to twenty thousand? Is that number confirmed? If so, there hasn't been anything that large since the weeks immediately after "Z" night. That many undead would crush everything in its path. Any human life is doomed. Where's the pack heading at this time?"

"The pack is on a beeline for Freeport, Sir. Freeport is also the destination of Alpha team if you recall. They were issued orders to perform a search and rescue mission on the orphanage at that location."

"Have we tried to recall the team?"

"Yes Sir we have. Negative contact. EMP residual interference is scrambling the signals. I believe it was probably from the Chicago ground bursts but I can't rightly rule out local jamming as well."

"You're telling me that I have a five-man team of freshly graduated warriors, going on their first mission to rescue small children and they are walking headfirst into a literal meatgrinder of as many as twenty thousand undead and we do not have a way to warn them, is that correct sergeant? Who was the reporting Paladin?"

"The report came in from Paladin King, Sir."

The Paladin known as King was eccentric to say the least. Before the HUNGER virus had wiped out humanity, King had been involved in show business as an Elvis

Presley impersonator. Now he wore the persona at all times, all the way up to the rhinestones and glitz that he had applied to his ZAP armor in the exact pattern of Elvis Presley's famous 1978 white jumpsuit, his pompadour hair style and the rhinestone rimmed sunglasses that he wore wherever he went without his armor. But as strange as the man seemed, he was usually spot on and accurate with his reports.

"I see."

"I do have a suggestion, Sir."

"I'm listening Sergeant."

"Allow me to take my ZAP armor, draw weapons and head out to try to catch up with Alpha team from behind. If I take two spare batteries and push hard, I should be able to intercept them before they enter Freeport. They're moving cross-country and through the parks. If I stay to the roadways for ease of movement, travel light and fast I should really get there ahead of both the team and the "Z" horde."

"Let me recap to make sure that I understand you sergeant. I have a band of bikers, quite possibly led by the Red Baron himself theoretically heading this way and your suggestion is to allow you to leave? You're one of my best warriors. Can we not send King or another Paladin after them instead?"

"Sir, with all due respect, King is in A1 nut ball, whack job. I wouldn't trust him to wash my socks much less bring a warning to my team. He'd end up trying to set the message to crappy lyrics for that guitar he totes on his back. We do not need a singing telegram for this Sir. We need a warning. Besides, as you said the Baron *might* be coming this way. We *know* that Alpha team is in trouble. We owe it to those kids to bring a warning if we can. We sent them out there."

"Very well sergeant, but no heroics and no John Wayne shit. You hustle after them, warn them and get your ass back here pronto. And Hogg…"

"Yes Sir."

"If you manage to pull this off, there's a real bottle of Kentucky bourbon waiting for you back here at the Academy. Not hooch but good old-fashioned black labeled Jack Daniels. Good luck."

"Thank you Sir!" Sergeant Hogg said and spun on his heal heading for the door then he stopped short. "Sir, if that sum' bitch Baron shows up. You just find a way to keep him busy until I get back. He and I aren't finished with the little do-si-do that we started. I got something really special to give him personally."

"I will sergeant."

# CHAPTER FIVE

# THE LONG RUN

Spartan allowed his mind to analyze what he and his team had just fought. Though his legs kept churning, eating out mile after mile, his mind was making careful notation of the location of the battle, the weapons that the Lords of Death had possessed and the people that they had dealt with. Specifically, the young female victim and the Romero on the dog chain. This last bit of information was troubling Spartan the most. *Why hadn't the Romero attacked the bikers? It seemed clear that the creature had been almost domesticated, but the question was how?*

*Or had it been?* As Spartan thought about it, he never actually saw a Lord of Death near the undead. In fact, Techno had already immobilized the creature before Spartan had come into the room. Perhaps it was not tamed at all, only leashed and fed as a way to placate it. Either way, he planned on reporting all of the information to Colonel Slade, if and when they returned to the Apocalypse Academy.

Next he took the time to analyze his team. Deadeye had been mercilessly efficient as expected. Techno had done well in immobilizing the "Z" but had not gone on to address the threat before stopping to render aid to any victims as he had been taught. Mistakes like that could get him or another member of the Phalanx killed. Out in the shit, emotions like sympathy were a weakness. There was no place for it. If they were going to pull off this rescue mission, it could not be by blind luck. They needed to be clinical and precise in their actions. The same went for Freak. Spartan needed to find out why the warrior had flown into such a hulking rage with the biker. Certainly, the raping and murder of the girl was an atrocity, but Freak had been incensed as if he actually knew the young girl personally. If there was a trigger to his actions, then it could be exploited by an enemy. They needed to identify it and ensure that there was a plan in place to defend against the vulnerability for all of their sakes.

"Hey boss." Came a call over to Spartan's internal helmet communications channel. "We might want to take a break from our pace for a bit. Tech's stumbling a little. Truth be told we broke the ten-mile marker a ways back. Me and Tech could both use ten to catch our breath."

106

"Copy Freak. Look for somewhere covered where we can be out of sight." Spartan changed the internal channel to speak privately with Techno.

"Tech, are you holding up okay? Do we need to take ten?"

"10 – 4." Came the gasped reply. "Tens good."

Spartan could hear the wheeze of asthma in Techno's voice. He did not want to have to use one of the special cocktail syringes from Nurse Ortega until it was absolutely necessary. Clicking the all communications icon on the HUD of his helmet's visor, Spartan told the team to begin looking for sheltered area in which to take a break. Five minutes later they noted a small copse of trees that had been left as a wind break in the cornfields where they were currently marching. The creation of the small grove resulted in an aesthetic break in the autumn time sea of bent brown cornstalks and looked pleasing upon approach. Now that the summer greenery had faded into shades of autumn orange, yellow and red, the stand of trees looked far more representative of an enchanted forest hollow than of a farmer's field.

The decision was made to cross the remainder of the field at a full run due to a farmhouse that stood three hundred meters away to the east. The dark windowed two-story structure would provide a fine vantage point for a sniper, especially to a slow-moving team traipsing across uneven rows of dead corn. Fortunately, no such event occurred and the Phalanx arrived in the tree line without incident. Easing quietly into the center of the trees, Spartan directed Deadeye to do a quick survey of the remaining tree area to ensure that they were alone within it. Upon receiving the thumbs-up from the scout, Spartan allowed the team to fall out for break time but reminded them to stay vigilant.

Techno and Freak looked like gigantic black dominoes falling to the ground; Freak crashed down against a log that had fallen during some long-ago storm and Techno just fell flat on his back. Contrary to his other two teammates, Deadeye scaled one of the taller trees to allow himself a heightened vantage point from which to survey the area ahead and around them. Dancer caught Spartan's attention, nodded her head off to one side indicating that she wanted to speak to him privately, away from the rest of the team.

Walking off to the side of the grove, Spartan and Dancer knelt down next to a large oak tree, removed their helmets and surveyed the farmhouse off in the distance.

"What's bothering you? You've been silent ever since we left the Academy except issue a few orders here and there. Talk to me." Dancer said quietly.

Spartan gazed for a long time at the farmhouse in the distance. "It looks quiet enough. But I can't shake the feeling..."

"What feeling?" Dancer asked.

"I don't know. It's hard to explain. It's like ever since we left the Academy, I've had the sense that we were all in imminent danger. Like we were walking into a trap. It's like my muscles want to draw my sword and get ready for combat."

"Is that why you're pushing us so hard?" She asked. "Because if we are in trouble or if we are being set up, then at the rate we're going we will be too exhausted to fight if something does happen."

Spartan considered her words and knew she was right. Techno had not moved from where he had fallen, gasping for breath in his ZAP armor. Freak was not fairing much better. His head was leaned back against the falling log and his chest could be seen rising and falling rhythmically inside the chain mail and plastic plated armor. Glancing up he noted Deadeye forty feet up in one of the larger trees, apparently using the optical enhancements of the ZAP helmet to magnify the view in the distance. Even in the armor Deadeye easily scaled the tree and Spartan marveled at how the boy seemed so comfortable in the treetops. Sliding his helmet beck on, he switched the communications to Deadeye's individual frequency and spoke to the scout.

"Anything in the distance?"

"One cow. Unknown on its status but it seems uninfected. I've never noted a "Z" to graze on grass before."

"Affirmative. What about the farmhouse?"

"Clear. No activity this far. I've magnified to full power and I haven't seen any activity in the house windows or near the barn."

"Okay, I'm going to stretch the break to thirty minutes. Really let everybody catch their wind."

Deadeye chuckled into his helmet's microphone. "That's probably a good call. Freak had been talking to me about the ins and outs of wildlife tracking when we stopped. His helmet communications channel is still keyed open. Currently he is snoring."

"Nothing like a power nap to rejuvenate you." Spartan said with a laugh. "Are you okay up there?"

"Yeah, I'm good."

"Okay." He switched the frequency back to Dancer's individual communications channel.

"Freaks asleep. Deadeye says it's quiet all around us, so we're going to make it a thirty-minute break instead of ten and catch our breath."

"Good call." She said. "We should set up the solar chargers while we rest. Restock the suit power supplies."

"Agreed. I'll get Freak's if you'll help Tech."

Five minutes later they reconvened as they set up their own solar chargers.

"Freaks charger was in his pack. It was like rolling over a sleeping grizzly bear to get it out." Spartan laughed. "Did you find Techno's charger?"

"He already had it set up." She replied. "He was working on a schematic plan to incorporate an inhaler unit into his helmet system to treat his asthma. For five minutes work, he had a heckuva diagram started. He even had the system voice-activated from what I could see."

"I don't know if he even knows how smart he really is."
Spartan said. "That is so impressive that it's almost
ridiculous."

"Mm-hmm. Spartan, I need to ask you a serious
question."

"Go ahead."

"Back at the park, the biker that ran outside... You let
him go?"

"Yes." He replied calmly.

"To be free or to be assassinated?" Dancer asked with
an edge in her voice.

"To be executed." Spartan again replied calmly.

"Do you think that was fair?" Dancer asked.

"He was guilty of God knows how many crimes
including the rape and murder of that little girl. He got

what he deserved. I chose the most efficient and humane way possible. He might have survived two or maybe even three hits from the Blues Brothers before he died depending on how cleanly Freak struck. Deadeye could've taken him with an arrow but since he has a finite supply it was better to conserve them. Techno was trying to treat the girl's wounds and my sword ran the same risk as Freak's bats. No... From the standpoint of fairness, efficiency and mercy; you're single bullet was the best option. It was clean, efficient and painless. In truth it was probably *more* than that scumbag deserved."

"I wasn't talking about being fair to him. He deserved to die. I have no problem with that. I was referring to me. If I am to become just a cold-blooded assassin, then I may as well go to join Cutter's crew of malcontents and thugs now."

Spartan considered her words and the accusation they inherently carried. He had taken an innocence from her by forcing her to kill an unarmed man. No matter the circumstances, he could have at least warned her.

"Your right Dance. I should have at least taken the time to issue the order. Truth be told, I wanted him dead as much for revenge as from the standpoint of justice. Please forgive me. It won't happen again."

"Nothing to forgive Spartan. I just wanted you to know how it made me feel. Either way, order or no order, the end result would've been the same." Dancer replied. "But for the record, the dirt bag deserved to know that his death was ordained on my bullet before I shot his face off."

"Yeah. I agree. Nice shot by the way. Very clean." Before she could answer, he held up a single hand as if to save weight. "I promise to give you advance warning if we ever have another opportunity to allow any fleeing bikers, rapists, or murderous types to run into your fire lane without us killing him first for his crimes. That is completely logical and fair. However, in the full interests of the team, should there be another opportunity during the rescue mission for you to shoot said raping, murdering, fleeing biker types, please do not stand on the formality of orders from me. Just cap his ass and we will sort out who owes who in apology later."

"Okay." She said silently smiling behind her helmet's visor because she knew that Spartan had just basically told her to "shut up and color" because the command decisions were his to make and then apologies were for after the mission over a drink. It was something her father would've said and whether she agreed or not, that paternal comparison made it an order she could live with.

"Good. I'm glad that's settled. How's your ZAP's power supply?"

"Eighty-six percent and charging."

"Okay. I'm at eighty-four percent. Let's just juice up and go get those kids from the orphanage. You go check on Tech and Freak, will you? I'm gonna check on Deadeye."

"Roger. Wilco." Was all she said and walked away without another word.

Spartan just watched her go. She had just gone from a complaining girl to a consummate soldier in less than three sentences. He just shook his head. He was not even going to try to figure out the transition. He was sure that some

116

pre-Z apocalypse head-doc would have correlated hormones, childhood upbringing and being forced to eat red meat into a mishmash of bullshit that sounded socially like psychological wisdom. Spartan felt that it was much better to just let it be and concentrate on how she looked in the polymer plate and chain mail ZAP armor. He wasn't sure that sexy was the appropriate word but he was certain that no one else could make the linked steel plates swing like that. Damn...

He slapped the side of his own helmet and mentally scrambled the image in his brain. They could all die if he wasn't focused. It was time to get back on his game. He quickly turned and headed for Deadeye; a task that he knew would get him back on point. Crossing into the outer ring of trees, he keyed his helmet's microphone on Deadeye's frequency.

"Deadeye, where are you at?" He asked quietly.

"Ten feet forward, and thirty feet up." Came the reply from the Apache.

"10 – 4" Spartan replied and began to walk towards the location that the Apache had indicated. Upon arrival, the scout was still nowhere to be seen. Spartan slowly scanned the trees above him. Red, gold and orange leaves blended together in a fire simulating image amongst the treetops. He still did not register Deadeye's location. Switched his optics, he scrolled from thermal to black and white and even to radiological but nothing outlined Deadeye's armor or ambient heat signature. The technology was that good.

"Where...?" He said again, keying microphone.

The gentle sound of leaves being displaced as if by a breeze and an accompanying soft thump that physically moved maybe six total leaves announced that the teen had jumped from the tree thirty feet up and was now standing directly before Spartan. Deactivating his ZAP armor's stealth capability, Deadeye shimmered into view.

"Report."

"The fields ahead look basically clear. Three pastures up have cows and maybe a bull. It was hard to say even with the enhanced optics of my ZAP armor. There was no sign of any bikers. My audio enhancement did pick up a few undead moans on the wind but they were distant and just of very small number. We should be able to handle them without any difficulty if the need arises."

"Do you have a route in mind?" Spartan asked.

"Yeah. By bearing to the east by five degrees we will cross nothing but farmland all the way to the White Pines Forest State Park. There will be only two business-class structures between us and the next section of open country all the way to the park entrance. An old abandoned drive-in movie theater and a roller-skating rink. I figure both to be abandoned so I have given them both a low risk assessment. From a residential standpoint, the map shows six housing units, also pretty well spread out. The one with the cows in the pasture was also registered to raise various farm life including horses, chickens, goats, hogs and the cows. We can pretty much count on a dog or two there as well. All the other houses were corn and soybean farms with one farm further to the east being licensed to raise pigs. All roadways will be dirt lanes, which decreases the likelihood of motorcycling encounters although it would still be feasible for them to attack if they so desired."

"That sounds great. Well done. How's your power supply?"

"Ninety-two percent. There was really good sun at the top of the trees."

"Copy. Be ready to move out in ten minutes. Dancer and I will wake up the other two. Let me know if anything changes immediately." Spartan ordered and turned to walk back to the remainder of the Phalanx.

Following the thirty-minute rest, Freak and Techno's spirits were greatly raised. So, when Deadeye led the team of warriors out of the grove at a quick trot there was little complaint. The pace, while significantly slower than their original, grueling run, was still brisk. To pass the time, Freak began to sing a low cadence across the ZAP armors' internal communications frequency.

*"Momma, momma can't you see?*
  *What the "Zs" have done to me.*
  *Momma, momma can't you see?*
  *What the "Zs" have done to me.*

*Took away my base on balls'*
*Now I'm splitting undead skulls.*
*Took away my base on balls'*
*Now I'm splitting undead skulls.*

*Whoa oh owa oh!*
*Whoa oh owa oh!*

*Momma, momma can't you see?*
*What the "Zs" have done to me.*
*Momma, momma can't you see?*
*What the "Zs" have done to me*

*Took away the hometown team,*
*Made me a monster killing machine!*
*Took away the hometown team,*
*Made me a monster killing machine!*

*Whoa oh owa oh!*
*Whoa oh owa oh!*

*Momma, momma can't you see?*
*What the "Zs" have done to me.*

*Momma, momma can't you see?*

*What the "Zs" have done to me*

*Learned to fight at the Academy,*

*Killin' corpses, set them free.*

*Learned to fight at the Academy,*

*Killin' corpses, set them free*

*Whoa oh owa oh!*

*Whoa oh owa oh!*

*Ain't no way that I can lose'*

*Long as I'm singin' the A'pocalypse blues.*

*Ain't no way that I can lose'*

*Long as I'm singin' the A'pocalypse blues.*

*Whoa oh owa oh!*

*Whoa oh owa oh!*

*Whoa oh owa oh!*

*Whoa oh owa oh!"*

Despite the seriousness of the mission, Freak's freelance singing brought a smile to all of the Phalanx member's faces. Mile after mile, under the influence of Freak's

cadence, were eaten up. Together the Phalanx ran across
fields, crawled under fences, sprinted through yards and
leapt over ditches; all while being guided by the baritone
voice of Freak and the thoughts of their final objective in
Freeport. In each warrior's mind ran a gambit of scenarios.
Each one varied in its outcome and was molded by
personal emotions of the moment. The potential joy of
successfully rescuing the children, the terrible fear of failure
and of death or worse at the clamping jaws of a "Z" and
the terror of children threatened with harm coupled with
the tranquility of the sun in the fields and blue sky as they
ran. All of these emotions and the various shades of gray
that connected them together ran through their thoughts
and minds, subconsciously driving the muscles of their legs.

Four hours later, Deadeye pulled the team up, slowing
them back down to a march. Carefully they walked,
mindful of their spacing. Under the sheltering boughs of an
enormous pine tree, Deadeye called a halt and requested a
combat circle to discuss options for passing the next
obstacle in their path. A small square building, perhaps the
size of a middle school gymnasium, lay before them. To the
right, a set of tires sat ensconced in an overgrown weed
surrounded dirt track of a go-kart graveyard. Further to the

right, towering high above the pine trees stood the pale white massive drive-in movie theater screen, perhaps a hundred feet tall.

Deadeye keyed the "all communications" frequency in his ZAP helmet on its surface.et, turning his mirrored visor to face Spartan, the anti-reflective layers of metal oxide muting the images to a distorted semblance of colors.

"We need to be cautious. The potential for a wandering "Z" is higher here. Although I do not hear the moan or wail of the undead, I also do not hear the normal sounds of the forest. Something has the animals and birds spooked around here. We need to be on our guard."

"Could it be us in all of this armor?" Dancer asked.

"I do not believe so. The crows cawed at us out in the cornfields, and the cows didn't even flinch when we ran by. This is something else. Something close by."

"What is that square building?" Spartan asked. "Could whatever is there be what is causing the disruption with the animals?"

"It could be. According to the colonel, the building is or more accurately was the roller-skating rink. It has been located out here for approximately forty years. It was popular in phases especially the disco era of the nineteen seventies, but it could've been busy or slow when the outbreak of H1N1GR occurred. The biggest problem is that the building lies upon a main road so it could be occupied by who knows who and potentially have unexpected traffic that we cannot predict."

Just then the sounds of music and laughter began in the roller-skating rink. From the sounds of it, at least a dozen people were gathered and singing "Thriller" by Michael Jackson. Curiosity was piquing Spartan's interest, but the need for expedience for the orphan children of Freeport's sake was paramount. Still, they would be returning back on the same path, so two minutes of scouting to assess future dangers could save all of their asses.

"Diamond formation; Deadeye on point. Freak you're on my six. Dancer and Techno off to each side of me. Five-meter interval. We do not engage. I repeat; do not engage. This is just a quick look-see to know what is here for our return trip. Any contact with hostile's, you are to take off and head up the road to the entrance to Lake LaDonna. Should be about two miles. If you absolutely cannot avoid battle, take 'em down as quiet as possible."

Freak keyed in. "Dude, they got go-karts, roller skates, disco balls and Michael freaking Jackson playing. How bad can it be Dawg? Someone sees us, hell, we will just moonwalk right by."

"Maybe I should just run home and grab my old Bedazzler for you so I can put some shiny sparkles on your ZAP's glove for you too!" Dancer quipped.

"Oh yeah! But then I would have to trade out the Blues Brothers for two new bats. I'd call one Billy Jean and the other S.C."

"S. C.? South Carolina or Southern California?" She asked.

"Neither. It would be short for "Smooth Criminal."

126

"Maybe we could just all start singing "We are the World" and the "Zs" would stop eating people, join hands and become one big, happy family. It was a song to fight hunger after all." Techno chimed in. Everyone laughed.

Spartan hated to stop the nervous banter but he knew that the longer they remained in one place, the greater the risk they ran of being spotted. They needed to move and move quickly.

"If you're all done talking about your favorite music, we need to focus."

As if to emphasize Spartan's point, an undead moan rose over the iconic sounds of Vincent Price's laughter that signify the end of the once popular cultural hit. The sound had only one possible source and it immediately told the team that the living dead were also inside the building. The walking corpses did not laugh. So, the living were present also.

A new song began, carried on the autumn air. The buildup of piano keys and a woman's voice in solo begin to sing of a song that Spartan vaguely remembered as belonging to the disco era of the 1970s. As the chorus hit and the music became much livelier, the revolving lights of a color disco ball began to twirl on the interior the building's artistically frosted windows. Although the living could not be seen, it was clear that they were enjoying themselves inside.

"Deadeye. Take a quick look. Let's see what's here if we have to come back this way. No contact. Look and listen only."

The Apache nodded once and faded from view as he activated his armor's stealth capabilities. There was no sound as he moved off into the night.

"Spartan." Techno called.

"Go ahead Tech."

"I just wanted to let you know, it seems that my armor is equipped with technology interfaces and sensors. I can tell you if we are near electricity, heat, nuclear and even bio electric currents. The identifiers are so clear that I can tell you, for instance, that the skating rink is running off of a five thousand horsepower generator that is diesel fueled. The sound system is a late 1970s model Audiovox arena sound, and it draws minimal electricity, whereas the disco ball draws twice as much power and it was made by the Takagami group in Japan in 1985. There is also a GE refrigerator, full-sized in the back running and a secondary unit that is used to cool beer kegs in the bar area. It even has a lighted Budweiser pull-tab sign."

Spartan considered this information for a full minute. The ability to analyze a target containing living persons was invaluable. Then he had a second thought. "Tech, you said you could analyze the information. Can you alter it? Control things like lighting or music or whatever?"

"I'm not sure Spartan, but it seems possible. Let me see what I can do." A couple of minutes passed as Techno hummed out loud and reviewed the armor's internal schematics. "Watch the exterior light, left rear of the building. If this works, the light will begin the blinking rhythm with music. In three, two, one…"

Sure enough, the light began to blink on and off with the bass from the song.

"That's outstanding Tech. Keep researching. We all need to see what our ZAPs are really capable of."

Deadeye returned a moment later and blurred into view. He keyed all communications frequencies so the entire team could hear his report. "It seems to be a group of survivalists. Everyone is wearing something green and yellow that says John Deere on it, so I'm guessing that they were initially farmers. I counted six men, and four women. Several children were also present. Weapons present included hunting rifles, various pistols and at least one shotgun."

"What about the "Zs" that we heard?" Spartan asked.

"Well, that's the damnedest thing. The undead have been dressed to resemble various rock stars and have roller skates tied to their feet. The undead have everything from leather jackets and rhinestone gloves and wigs to make them look the part. When the songs begin, the "Zs" are shoved out onto the roller-skating rink where they roll around chasing the living for the duration of their song.

Then they are pushed into a bullpen of sorts. I saw at least twenty costumed "Zs" in the pen."

Spartan shook his head. He really didn't know what to say.

"It looked like all of the living were drinking tap beer, even the children. Some looked like they had consumed significantly more alcohol than the others as their moments of bravery during the entertainment increased as I watched and they kept getting closer and closer to the skating "Zs".

"How do they keep the "Z's" from falling on the skates? Techno asked.

"There were two ways that I saw. The first was training wheels bolted through the lower legs. One training wheel per leg on the outside with the bolt running horizontally through the calf and bone and fastened on the interior of the leg. The second method was a length of thin pipe or maybe rebar that has a small wheel welded on the floor end. The opposite end is then jammed into the creatures back somehow. In essence, they turn the walking dead into undead tricycles."

131

"That's just bloody cruel." Dancer said disgustedly.

"Agreed, but it is not our responsibility right now. We can report to Colonel Slade when we get back to the Apocalypse Academy. For now, we need to get past here unseen. Deadeye did you see a route?"

The scout nodded. "It would be better by total darkness but we don't have that kind of time to knock out all of the exterior lights around the building. There's a path between the go-kart stand and the skating rink that looks to lead across the main road. It is exposed but if we move fast and low we shouldn't be seen unless one of the John Deere fan club decides to come outside and take a leak."

"Any guards?"

"There were none posted that I saw. That doesn't mean that there can't be a singular man wandering around alone in the woods. They don't look too sharp for survivalists. If the Lords of Death find this place, these guys are meat."

"Okay. Let's get to it. We're burning daylight. Spread out and assume ten-meter intervals. Low and fast. Cross the road and hit the woods beyond. Deadeye, keep us moving in the direction we need to go."

Without another word, the Phalanx took off; five silent warriors at a run. Behind them, the sounds of ZZ Top's "La Grange" began to beat in the skating rink, and they all entered the national forest beyond with imagined visions of three heavily bearded "Zs" in horn rimmed glasses and blazers, skating in circles while wearing training wheels and chasing the drunken living.

Spartan paused at the edge of the wood line, to look back and ensure that no one was following them. Yes, the world had become a very, very fucked up place. Seeing no one, he disappeared into the woods behind his team.

# CHAPTER SIX:

# HOGG'S CHASE

Hogg pushed his ZAP armor to his physical limit, urging every ounce of speed from the muscle enhancing shell that he could muster. Use of his years of military training allowed him to keep running far beyond the endurance capabilities of an average man. His Special Forces training allowing his mind to override the pain that the physical exertions were causing; keeping clear and focused as he desperately strove to catch up to Alpha team. Twin forty-five caliber semi-automatic pistols hung from each thigh holster and a fully locked and loaded M-4 assault rifle swung freely across his lower back, swaying within easy grasping reach if needed. Two round M67 fragmentation grenades swung in time with his stride from his combat harness: one on either side of his upper chest. Other than two additional water canteens and eight extra magazines each for the assault rifle and pistols, Hogg carried nothing extra to weigh himself down. If he needed to forage for food, he was capable of doing that on the run.

He had exited north out of the city, racing along at better than twelve miles per hour. The ice cream stand that marked the outermost city limits had passed by in a blur, seemingly seconds after he had exited Damnation Road. Less than thirty minutes later he was entering the first park. Hogg did not know which of the three lanes of traffic that Alpha team had taken to reach the edge of the Rock River before they would turn further northward. He opted for the most direct and therefore most expedient route, and charged recklessly ahead, directly down the main roadway. Stealth was great, but it was also slow. There was no time for such finery. With the Baron supposedly closing in on the Academy, Hogg needed to find the Phalanx, warn them of the "Z" migration southward, and get back to defend the base. If he was lucky he might even get a chance to pop a round through his old teammate's eye socket and watch his brain explode out of the back of his shattered skull. Then he might take the time to stand in the middle of the battle, open a cold beer and drink a final toast to his friend who had become his foe.

Multihued trees blurred by in streaks of gold, orange and red. The crunching pieces of fallen leaves under the man's heavy combat boots rattled and swirled away, broken eddies of leaves carried on the autumn breeze. Reaching the end of the roadway, Hogg pulled up momentarily, assessing where he needed to go. The riverside playground equipment stood abandoned. Metallic slides, monkey bars and swing sets stood empty next to the sun glistening river. Hogg silently thought that the playground resembled the bones of some prehistoric creature that had died, and time had picked the flesh from. Far out in the center of the river, a single small rowboat drifted with the current. Seated low in the boat, a solitary man in a weathered and worn boonie hat gazed unflinchingly at Sergeant Hogg in his ZAP armor, apparently nonplussed by the protective gear. The man's low profile in the boat made him a difficult target to distinguish but Sergeant Hogg's enhanced armor could clearly make out the .308 rifle leaned against the man's digitally camouflaged fatigues. The man was obviously a survivalist, and as long as he didn't raise the hunting rifle; he was no threat nor concern to the Academy instructor.

Sergeant Hogg raised a single hand in a waving gesture as a sign of respect for the survivalist. Any man willing to roam the world alone with all of its inherent dangers nowadays was either crazy as a shit house rat, had an intimate death wish or was a brave son of a bitch. Since the survivalist was staying to the deepest water, where "Zs" and other livelier human scum could not easily reach him; Hogg was willing to bet the latter. The man returned the show of respect and quickly drifted from Sergeant Hogg's view. The brief interlude watching the unknown man in the rowboat had allowed Hogg to catch his breath. Now he needed to get back to the mission at hand. Using the internal compass on his ZAP's HUD, he turned due north and again set out at a run.

# CHAPTER SEVEN
## WHITE PINES FOREST STATE PARK

Spartan and his team continued moving through the park up until about an hour after sunset. Deadeye selected a secluded site under a small stone bridge to keep his team out of the general view of any passerby's; living or undead. Breaking the seals on their helmets, the team was immediately awash in the sounds of nature that had been previously filtered out by the helmets audio systems. Crickets chirped, night birds flapped by and the stream over which the stone bridge crossed burbled happily. Spartan addressed Deadeye for the first time in hours without the metallic, hissing ring of the communication system in his ears.

"Think it's safe to build a small fire under here or do we endure and sleep in the ZAP armor for warmth?" The team leader asked, trusting the scout's opinion and expertise in the wilds.

"As long as one of us remains armored and on watch, we should be fine. I will gather up some old limbs for the fire and some rocks to help hide any excess light. Then I will keep first watch."

Spartan agreed and was silently thankful for his teammate's wilderness skills. Slowly he began to unlatch the various fasteners, seals and buckles that held his ZAP armor together and saw that the remainder of his team had done the same, silently peeling away the protective gear. The chill of the autumn air was much more prevalent without the insulation of the armor and the team was grateful for the small fire. After a second search of the immediate area, Deadeye returned with several long pieces of pine bough to cover the entrance, blocking much of the cool night breeze and camouflaging their position. Spartan contemplated bathing in the river, but a whistle of cold air across the back of his neck and the subsequent chill bumps convinced him that it was better to be sweaty than to be cold. He would take care of basic cleanup and personal hygiene in the morning. Besides, the stream was probably as cold as ice itself.

Quick heating their MREs with the included fuel bag, the team sat in silence, enjoying a rare moment of tranquility in the wilderness. Dancer, her meal of Chicken à la King half finished, declared that she was ready to go to sleep and crash out for the evening and that Deadeye should wake her for the second watch. Not wanting the food packet to go to waste, she offered the remaining contents to Freak who immediately accepted. The dark-haired girl pillowed her head on her arm and fell asleep almost instantly in a fetal position. Looking down at her, Freak spoke to Spartan.

"Dude, that's not normal."

Spartan did not understand. It had been a rough day and they were all tired. "What do you mean Freak?"

"Well, back in Chi-town, ain't no girl gonna just lie down in the dirt and rack out without worrying about bugs or their nails and shit Dawg. She drops down like she's been doing this her whole life and without even a blanket. Ain't no way Gran' would come out here."

"Man, my mom would've spazzed out." Techno added. "I remember one year we all went camping and she got mad at my dad because the primitive campground in Yosemite National Park did not have available outlets for her hairdryer and television. She was pissed off all weekend because she couldn't watch Wheel of Fortune." Techno chuckled at the memory. "My dad and I just left and went fishing."

"You don't realize just how tough that girl is. This is nothing for her. Her father was British Intelligence, Special Air Service I think. He pushed her to learn how to survive. She's probably done this a hundred times in the past."

All of a sudden a brutal, gurgling noise emerged from Freak's giant-sized midsection, shattering the silence of the night.

"Uh oh." He said getting up quickly. "MREs are callin' on." As he strode off at a rapid pace into the bushes a short distance from the campsite. Shortly thereafter, there was a grunt that broke the silence followed by an explosion of bodily gases. Spartan and Techno doubled over laughing. For all of their training and threats of constant death, they were still teenagers and flatulence was hilarious to them. Atop the stone bridge, even Deadeye cracked a smile within the confines of his helmet although no one would ever know that he did so.

Ten minutes later, the boys could hear Freak's less than subtle return to the makeshift camp, as he crackled and crunched through the sticks and dry leaves. "Man, who picked this damn campsite?"

"Deadeye, why?" Spartan responded.

"Dude, lemme tell you he picked a real winner. Probably the only haunted trail for a hundred miles in any direction."

"What are you talking about Freak? Make sense."

That was when Spartan noticed that Freak had drawn one of his Blues Brothers baseball bats and was currently handling it with both hands as if approaching the batter's box. The boy was obviously spooked by something.

"When I was a boy, Gran used to tell me stories from the old days back before there was TV or even much radio.

She said back then everything was passed on by word-of-mouth. Kind of like now around the big cities since the nukes and the EMP's fried all of the electronics."

Spartan nodded and noticed that Freak's eyes were wide and there was a real tinge of fear in the teen's voice as he spoke.

"She used to tell me lots of stories. Detective stories, cowboy stories, jungle stories, heck even love stories. They were all cool to hear because Gran had a way of keeping your attention when she talked. Then one night, not long before Halloween, she sat in a rocking chair with her shawl over her lap and had the wood stove burnin' to keep the chill out. Through the little open door, firelight blinked and made shadows dance along on the walls and ceiling. The air outside was cool, like tonight, an' old man winter was just around the corner. Can't remember exactly but we might have even had frost on the ground once or twice already."

Spartan waited patiently. It was obvious that something beyond the MRE gut bomb had upset his teammate. He needed to see what that something was and determine if it was tangible or just the forest night playing tricks on the teenager. Freak's eyes darted towards the shadows of the forest as an animal crunched a leaf under its hoof or paw somewhere in the distance.

"She told me a story one night about the ol' days when she was a little girl. The story chilled me to my bones. I'll never forget it, no sir, not 'til my dyin' day. There had been a period of time when she lived out in the farm country and this big old Scandinavian dude, you know blonde hair, blue eyes, big bushy matted yellow beard, had come into town on his black horse. They said he had the sunken eyes of a man who has seen too much death and his soul had shriveled up like a raisin. On his back he carried a huge sword like they had in the olden times; curved and wicked looking. When he got to the center of town he just stopped and sat on his horse in the middle of the road. Eventually the Sheriff came out and went to talk to the man to see if he needed help. When he did, the dude spoke in some weird language that nobody understood. From his tone and body language the Sheriff knew that something was wrong."

"The Sheriff motioned for this dude to get down off of his horse and when the man started to dismount, that's

144

when the Sheriff noted the fresh blood still dripping from the sword's blade. Of course, he arrested the man and sent out a ten-man search party to the surrounding farms. Upon coming to a settler's cabin north of town, he opened the door and found the bodies of a woman and her four children that had all been slaughtered. Blood was everywhere, on the walls, on the ceiling, and on the floor. Worst of all the corpses had all been decapitated and the individual heads had been lined up in a row on the dining room table largest to smallest. Huge bloody footprints tracked inside the cabin and out of the door. When the report got back to the Sheriff of what the search party had found, the Sheriff who also acted as judge for the town, accused the Norwegian man of five counts of murder and sentenced him to be executed at midnight of the same night by his own sword. There was no trial, no lawyers, and no clemency. The man could not understand English so no one knows if he even understood the accusations against him."

"Gran said the moon was full on the night that fourteen deputies brought the man outside of town to an old oak tree stump. While the men held him down, the sheriff accused him of his crimes and then swung the

145

man's own sword down so hard that he cleaved through the man's neck and embedded into the tree stump. The posse then tied the body to the horse's saddle and slapped it hard on its flanks so that the horse would run off into the night carrying the dead body away, separating it forever from the evil mind contained within the skull. The men then took the accused murderer's decapitated head and threw it down into an old abandoned well. No burial, no prayers, no nothing."

A cool breeze blew and rustled the leaves around the camp. Freak looked to be on the edge of absolute panic. His grip tightened and untightened unconsciously on the handle of his baseball bat. Spartan had never seen the big man so unnerved, even during the Dante Course when he had to cross the river when he couldn't swim. Whatever had him scared was real to his mind.

"The dude's massive black horse trotted off into the dark. Upon reaching the top of the hill, the black stallion reared up on its hind legs as if in defiance of the Sheriff and his posse. As he did so the headless corpse threw its arms upward in pantomimed anger as the moon framed the horse against the night sky. It whinnied and rode off into the darkness. Guided by the jack-o-lanterns that the children had carved to ward off evil spirits, the posse returned to town. They thought the nightmare was over. They were so wrong Dawg. Thirty days later, during the moonless night, the man's vengeance began. Headless corpses began to turn up around the town. Each corpse belonged to one of the ten initial posse members. The town began to talk as rumors circulated that the men had all been decapitated by a vicious, sharp blade and that the heads were never found."

The sheriff, being an educated man, did not believe in ghosts. Taking the surviving four men that had escorted the Norwegian man to be executed with him; the Sheriff went back to the tree stump. When they arrived, they found the sword missing from the bloody tree stump where they had left it lodged a month prior. They returned to the town with tales of vengeful spirits and ghosts. One by one the Sheriff's men continued to vanish at night, only to be found decapitated, with their heads missing the next day.

Due to the religious fall festival tradition and in observance of ancient legend, pumpkins were used to keep out evil spirits. The children carved them into jack-o'-

lanterns and lined every road and every shop front. On Halloween night the Sheriff returned one more time to the site of the Norwegians' execution, intending to have a final showdown with the evil creature. The headless demon arrived atop a black stallion that snorted demonic flames from its nostrils. In his hand, it wielded the same wickedly curved sword that the Sheriff had used to perform the execution. Standing behind the horseman were the spectral figures of all fourteen of his deputies. The Sheriff paralyzed with fear, begged for mercy but never drew a weapon. Gran' said that they heard his scream all the way back in town. In the morning, the townsfolk found his decapitated torso leaning against the same stump that he had executed the prisoner upon. Seated upon the bloody tree stump was a jack-o'-lantern, its candles still burning inside, just above the headless corpse.

The townsfolk have never forgotten those legends and believe, according to Gran, that the creature still seeks heads to add to its collection to this very day."

Techno snorted in derision at the giant's tale. "You big goof. That's the story of the Headless Horseman. The original story was written by a guy named Washington

Irving in the 1800s. It's fiction. I read it in school. Everybody tells the tale to scare people when they go camping."

Freak nodded and then motioned for Techno and Spartan to walk over to the edge of the firelight and pointed with his bat at a sign posted to the bridge upon which Deadeye stood watch. It read "Sleepy Hollow" and on the ground below it sat a dozen decapitated "Z" heads in the tall grass and cattails arranged from smallest to largest.

"Is it?" Freak asked, then walked over and began putting his ZAP armor back on. Techno and Spartan followed suit; an uneasy chill swirling up their spines. "Gran never lies."

# Chapter Eight
# Hogg's hard run

While Alpha team lived their true to life ghost story, Hogg continued to push his body and his ZAP armor to the absolute limits. During his many days as a soldier, he had marched twenty to thirty miles on several occasions during a single day. This included common troop movements and once after his Humvee took an IED through the steering rod and flipped him upside down right in the middle of an Iraqi desert. Truth be told, it was probably more anger than endurance that had made him hump all the way back to base camp in one night. In fact, it was *definitely* anger in the motor pool when the Duty Sergeant refused to issue him another vehicle in the middle of the night so that he could "go shoot the Rag Head bastard that had goat-fucked his Hummer."

That same boiling emotion led to Sergeant Hogg commandeering the Base Commander's personal jeep and driving it back off of the base to get some payback. Of course, he had been courteous and left the General a note along the lines of "Sir, I needed your vehicle because the prick in the motor pool wouldn't let me have one. I will be back for the morning formation and will buy you a beer for the inconvenience."

Despite Sergeant Hogg's best efforts, that definitely did not happen as exactly as planned.

During his return drive to the northern grid, where his Humvee had been blown up previously, Sergeant Hogg came across a column of ol' Saddam's Imperial Guard. After a carefully considered attack plan, revised twice within seven seconds, Sergeant Hogg drove the General's Jeep directly into the column of enemy soldiers, scattering them in all directions. Then, in a moment that even the fictional movie icon Rambo would have been proud of, the sergeant had calmly stood up in the Jeep and utilized the M-60 machine gun mounted on the rear of the vehicle to kill a confirmed twenty Imperial troops. The remaining twenty soldiers surrendered before being chopped up by the 7.62 rounds. Unfortunately, the General's Jeep also suffered as a combat casualty; having burst the radiator and flattened both front tires during Hogg's insane charge.

In the end, Sergeant Hogg ended up leaving his second vehicle behind in the desert and repeating the thirty mile walk back to base camp while keeping the twenty Iraqi prisoners under guard. He became a camp legend overnight.

After a psych evaluation was ordered by the Base Commander, the question asked became was Hogg a hero with brass balls or was he a bona fide grade A nut job? By the end of the evaluation, the consensus was that Sergeant Hogg was a hero who just basically did not give a shit about authority. When the Base Commander had heard the final outcome of the evaluation, he had immediately pinned a medal onto Sergeant Hogg's chest for "gallantry and bravery beyond the call of duty," labeled him a war hero and ordered him shipped outta the war zone to become a Drill Sergeant. In the General's own words *"he needed more men like Sergeant Hogg to teach the warriors of tomorrow how to be real soldiers."* Hogg had then told him just how full of shit he thought the Commander really was but he did not fight the reassignment.

But now it was not anger or endurance that pushed him onward; it was fear. Fear that the team of young warriors he had trained were about to be overrun by the living dead. Fear that he would lose Spartan just as he had lost Band-Aid to the claws and teeth of the "Z" plagued walking dead. Fear that he would lose another adopted son.

So onward he ran, subverting the pain in his limbs, knowing that he had no time to lose. He considered trying to find a vehicle, but it would be dicey at best and time-consuming at worst. Besides a lone vehicle was extremely noticeable on the road; everything from survivalists to bikers to the living dead would be able to see him. It was better just to run. Reaching the north gate of the park, Hogg used the power of his ZAP armor to vault the fencing without ever slowing down. He had to find the Phalanx before it was too late. He had to.

# Chapter Nine
# Cutter's Treachery

Cutter walked across the department store parking lot, with his team fanned out behind him, black armor glistening in the sun and weapons at the ready. Echo team had been sent to secure the store and gather supplies. Although there were reportedly many "Zs" inside, all were Romero's so as long as he prevented his team from being cornered by a large group of the pus bags and the ammunition held out, then there was little to fear. The creatures could not strategize nor conduct tactics. All they could do was form a mob of teeth and claws. His teams were expert killers and had made short work of the walking dead. Even Lotus Jane had gotten into the act. In her ZAP armor, it was nice to see that she had gotten over her unfortunate crush on the little Jap kid in Alpha team. He had known about it of course. Nothing happened on his team that he wasn't aware of but he really hadn't given a shit about the girl's hookups as long as she jumped when he said jump. But picking a slant eyed kid from *Alpha* team of all people was something of a surprise to him.

She had spent a week crying in her barracks room after team assignments had been handed out before she'd suddenly snapped out of it. Cutter suspected that the change of attitude was partially due to the mission to which they had been assigned, liberating a department store. Coincidentally, the store had contained a pharmacy. When Cutter had told her this, along with his intent to leave her behind if she could not get her shit straight the girl wiped away her tears and returned to battle-ready status almost instantly.

Now as his team walked across the cracked and desolate pavement, he had been glad that she had come along with the team regardless of her personal motivations, because the next ten minutes would determine if they would live or die and he might need her gun and knives.

Walking past the abandoned cars and shopping carts stalls, Cutter brought his team to a halt twenty yards beyond the last vehicle. Directly ahead of him stood a single man wearing a black eye patch and a full set of crimson riding leathers. A long barreled German Luger sat in a holster on his hip and the silver skull handle of a Nazi SS dagger jutted from his belt. A black leather belt also ran diagonally across his chest, attached to the shiny black belt around his waist. From the low belt hung numerous grenades, ammunition and his canteen. Knee-high, polished black boots and a World War I spiked German helmet completed the ensemble. In his hand, held by its pommel as the tip rested lightly on the ground, was a heavy, thick bladed sword. The pommel of the sword consisted of a silver skull and two red Ruby eyes that winked evilly in the sunlight.

"Do you know who I am boy?" The man said in a gravelly, harsh tone of voice, his contempt clearly evident.

For some reason the Cutter could not explain, he was compelled to show respect to this man. Normally brash in the face of authority, Cutter was cowed by this man's aura that exuded evil.

"Yes Sir, I do."

"Then you know that killing you or any of the other brats of the so-called "Apocalypse Academy" would not cause me a moment's hesitation or grief?" Although the words were formed as a question, Cutter knew that they required no answer so he only nodded in response.

"Then why do you stand here before me? Why do you raid my store for supplies? And why do you insult me by wearing that ridiculous, superhero wannabe armor in my presence? Do you know what the "AA" insignia on your uniform means to me boy?"

Cutter's head was whirling, struggling to line up answers to all of the questions he had been asked, not willing to forget anything while standing before what was perhaps the world's most dangerous man. Glancing around, Cutter could see furtive movements darting from the shadows along the building and he instantly knew that his team had been surrounded.

"Sir, we were ordered to come to the store by the Commandant of the Apocalypse Academy. The armor was designed to defeat "Z" attacks, both claw and bite. And the "AA" is the logo of the post-pandemic "Z" plague school for orphans known as the Apocalypse Academy." Cutter could feel the sweat on his palms and brow within the armor despite the atmospheric controls. He really wished that he had a blade in his hand; it always seemed to comfort him.

"A rote answer at best and why are you here boy? Why, pray tell, did you send a messenger to meet me and request this meeting and what exactly is stopping me from gutting your teenaged ass and leaving you to the crows?"

"Sir, I am here to offer an exchange of information, sir."

"What could you possibly have to tell me that I would consider of even minimal interest?" The Red Baron brought the blade of his sword up resting it on his one shoulder but with implied malice of action. "And what will keep me and my disciples from feeding you to the chosen ones for entertainment?"

Cutter knew that this was his chance. "Sir, I am requesting an exchange of information for supplies. We are only looking to gain what we have in the trucks currently. Then we will leave without conflict with you or your disciples."

"You've got balls boy. I like that. All right. If your information is good enough, then I let you walk away. If not…" He lowered the point of his sword until it touched the Kevlar beneath Cutter's chin. "You die here today. Let's hear it."

Cutter took a deep breath and focused his thoughts. When he was sure that he had clarity, he spoke to the Baron. "Something has driven more than ten thousand "Zs" in a single band out of Madison, Wisconsin. Intelligence from a Paladin stated that they are marching en masse towards the town of Freeport, just a couple of hours north of here."

"That's it?" The Baron asked his tone incredulous. "That's your all – valuable information that you believe will keep your little skinny ass alive? Of course, there is an army of undead marching southward! They are being led by men under my direct command!"

"Oh." Cutter said swallowing hard. Well, no sir. Actually, that's not all."

"Well then, continue. I would hate to cause you interruption in your all-important information delivery and make you lose your train of thought." The Baron chuckled, swinging the heavy sword side to side like a golfer warming up to tee time. The red blade swished through the air, a low whistling sound emanating from the long blood groove etched into the upper edge of the sword.

"Another team of Academy warriors is currently in route to Freeport on a mission to rescue a group of orphans and a nun."

"Oh – kay… Is *that* it?" He asked. "Knowledge that there are two teams of useless brats instead of just this one? Why should I give a rat's ass about any of the Academy students? The undead will get them all I am sure."

"Actually sir, there are five teams. But I believe the team heading north will be of particular interest to you."

"Really? Why is that? All you academy brats are the same. Chosen ones to fulfill a destiny, my ass! What absolute bullshit! All of you are nothing but meat for the undead that are inheriting the earth."

"No sir. What I mean to say, Sir, is that your information is incorrect or at least partially incorrect if you'll pardon my saying so. Each team was specifically designated and by whom we were trained. For instance, Echo team, which is the team that you see before you, were trained by Drill Sergeant Havoc."

"I see. Havoc is a good man. He understands the need for efficiency and discipline by cutting away the dead weight. Sometimes it takes a real man to make sacrifices and hard choices. He would actually make a good disciple." The Baron replied.

"The team that is traveling to the orphanage is Alpha team."

"And that means…?"

"I was told by Sergeant Havoc to tell you that they were trained personally by Sergeant Hogg. Sergeant Havoc also stated that Hogg even considers the team leader, a boy known by the codename "Spartan" to be his adopted son."

At the sound of his former partner's name, the Baron unconsciously reached a black glove hand up to touch the scar and eye patch that covered the empty socket behind it. A twitch curled his upper lip into a sneer. Crimson rage flushed across his face and he stabbed the blade of his sword deep into the dirt. "And is that… that pig Hogg with them?"

"No sir. The intelligence about the "Z" horde just arrived this morning. Alpha team had no knowledge of the approaching horde from the north. According to Sergeant Havoc, Sergeant Hogg left around noon today on foot to try to warn them. He is traveling light and alone."

*The Baron paused to consider the information. If it was accurate, he could exact revenge on the Apocalypse Academy by wiping out one of their teams of chosen warriors and rain hell on Hogg personally by capturing him and feeding him slowly to a "Z". He would enjoy watching the big soldier being torn limb from limb, bite by bite. Perhaps he would even take one of Hogg's eyes in payment for his own before he allowed the man to die by inches. There would be no mercy. No pacification. Oh, how he hated that man. Perhaps he would kill the adopted son in front of him first to watch Hogg suffer in anguish. The wave of "Zs" that were being herded by his own Lords of Death would*

162

*then arrive at the site of the Apocalypse Academy and Slade and all of the rest of the hypocrites would die as well. Yes, his revenge on the Apocalypse Academy would start soon enough. He would let this boy live…for now. He needed to find that bastard Hogg.*

"Today you are in luck boy. I will let you walk away from here with all of your body parts. But make no mistake, if I ever catch you on my turf again, and you are not asking to become one of my disciples, you and your pathetic group of wannabe soldiers will be food for my Chosen Ones no matter what messages you bring. We are not friends. We are not comrades. You live by my…good graces." He said with a slight chuckle as if the very concept of good was entertaining to him. "Are we clear?"

"Yes Sir."

"Then go. Be grateful that I have found your information at least moderately useful. To me the "AA" on your armor stands for "Always Assassinated" which is what I fully intend to do to you and your teams… one by one as I find you alone. Remember that the dead have risen again in fulfillment of the scriptures and that I am their lord and master. I alone have the power to command them just as I command my disciples, the Lords of Death."

"Yes sir. Thank you for understanding why I felt that you would be interested in this information." Cutter said, and spun on his heel, walking briskly towards the truck containing the supplies he had been delegated to obtain. Behind him, they all heard the Baron's motorcycle as it roared to life, followed by the sounds of more than a hundred disciples immediately following suit. The collective noise sounded like mechanical thunder and was sure to draw every "Z" for miles around to their location.

"Let's get the hell out of here." Cutter said to his team, moving forward to the truck at a run. From around the corner ahead of them, the first of the undead that had been drawn by all the noise, staggered into view.

Jumping into the cab of the truck, Cutter started it up and floored it without looking to see if the rest of the team was on board. Beside him, Lotus Jane silently fumed. She could not believe that Cutter had so arbitrarily betrayed the Academy, especially just out of spite and not even to save his own selfish ass. She had always known that he was something of a self-righteous, preppy, arrogant prick but that described a lot of people that she knew or had known before the outbreak. That particular personality trait was especially common to the silver spoon community; the kids that grew up with money and thus believe that the world owed them a living.

To betray the living for any reason to the undead or their masters required a very special type of egomaniacal mental imbalance. From what she just saw, Cutter was just about as "special" in that category as they came. She had to find a way to warn Techno. The boy was sweet and deserved a heads up to the bullshit that Cutter had pulled. Jane chuckled to herself. Yes, the boy was definitely naïve but he was also nonjudgmental of her past or of her habits. He didn't deserve to be "Z" food. She had to do something…

Then again, doing something always seemed to get her into trouble. Perhaps she should just do what she had always done at home when she knew that a beating was coming. Pop a few pills, drink a little gin and then she could hide within the chemical haze of her own brain and wait out whatever storm was brewing. Feeling the half quart sized bottle of painkillers that she had of stolen from the pharmacy of the department store safely tucked beneath her jacket, she opted for plan B. Quietly she opened the lid and popped four of the narcotics into her mouth. Then she settled back into the truck seat and waited for the warmth of the medication to fill her body as it always did. The truck bounced hypnotically along the road and lulled her into a mellow feeling of euphoria. Her last thought as the world began to stretch and skew and the heated numbness of the medicine began to ease her into sleep was a whispered apology to Techno because she really was a bitch.

# Chapter Ten

## Freeport

The city of Freeport stood directly before Alpha team. Empty buildings stood like the bones of some long dead prehistoric creature jutting up from the ground. The remainder of the forced march had gone by pretty much uneventfully, primarily due to Deadeye's skill at tracking and the team wisely skirting the small village of Mount Morris just north of the national park. It was late afternoon when they arrived in the outskirts of the city. The first red – orange rays of the sun dropping low in the sky made the distant hardwood trees appear to be draped in vacillating flames, the multicolored leaves swaying in the autumn breeze. Seeing the city spread out beneath him, Spartan began to issue orders to his team.

"Techno see if you can raise the orphanage on the shortwave radio." Spartan said, and then turned to Deadeye. "Find a high point. We need an avenue into town, a high ground position for Dancer to snipe from and an idea of how many "Zs" we are potentially going to be facing while we are toting a dozen or so children in our arms."

As usual, Deadeye turned and trotted off without a word. Spartan turned back to the radio.

"Penguin Mother this is the Odyssey over…" No response. "Repeat… Penguin Mother, this is the Odyssey. Do you copy?" Again, there was no response. Techno tried a third time, boosting the radios' gain to maximum. "Penguin Mother this is the Odyssey. If you can copy but cannot transmit, we are coming to get you. Hang in there." No response. "Odyssey out."

Spartan considered the possibility that the orphanage had been overrun. To the best of his knowledge there had been no new emergency message or plea for help. There should have been enough food for at least two more days according to the nun's previous transmissions. So why the hell were they not answering? Perhaps the communications were down or maybe they had lost the power to the building. One thing was certain, sitting still wasn't going to answer any questions. They needed to get moving. Nightfall was only a couple hours away at best. Just then

Deadeye came trotting back up and reported to his team leader over the private communications channel.

"Do you want the bad news, the really bad news or the really, really bad news?" He asked.

"Bring it all. We need to get moving." Spartan replied.

"Okay, by order of importance. One: the road into this city is hazardous at best. The roadways are clogged with vehicles and almost guaranteed to contain "Zs" of all shapes, sizes and even species. The city has a small bridge near what looks to be midtown. From what I could tell at least half of the bridge was collapsed, probably on purpose to slow advancing "Zs". I couldn't tell if the bridge was an overpass or actually overwater. Both present challenges of their own. Overland we will be forced to go around which will eat time. Overwater we will have to swim. Both options leave us vulnerable."

"Item number two: the west side of the city is burning. It looks like the fire is uncontrolled and very hot. If it is a fast-spreading fire, it could present complications, especially if we have to fight to get into the orphanage and then back out again. It would be bad to be caught inside a burning building surrounded by "Zs"."

"Item number three. I saw the orphanage. At least I am fairly certain it is the right building. To put it into perspective for you; do you remember Custer's last stand? The building is ringed by no less than a couple hundred "Zs". They looked like they were mostly Romero's but I couldn't be a hundred percent sure. In a bunch, they all look and move alike. If we have to fight all the way up to the doors of the orphanage, it could get ugly in a hurry, especially since the doors, in all likelihood will be barricaded."

"One small bright spot is that there is a water tower about a half a mile away to the west. It's closer to the fire, but high enough that "Zs" won't be able to climb up effectively and probably won't be able to see a sniper from the ground. It should be a great shooting point for Dancer. Getting there and any problems that she may run into may be another story since she will be alone."

Spartan ran the issues quickly through his mind, contemplating his options. The road hazards were not really unexpected. The city had housed better than seventy thousand people in the days before the HUNGER virus escaped. Many people were likely trapped in traffic, maybe with family or friends that were already bitten or infected. The resulting carnage would have been terrible to watch. The bridge was definitely an issue. Circling around made the most tactical sense but from what Deadeye described the children in the orphanage didn't have much time.

If the city was burning as well, then at least one avenue of egress had been cut off for his team. Running with a bunch of children was going to be tough enough. Doing it with no options was infinitely worse. On a more personal note, he was not overjoyed at the concept of his girlfriend hiking off on her own through a "Z" plagued city to take a sniping position, isolated on a water tower. If the fire spread too rapidly or if the "Zs" shifted to that section of town for some reason, Dancer would be hopelessly trapped and for all intents and purposes, doomed.

Turning to the team, he opened the all comm frequency and quickly briefed them on Deadeye's observations. They all agreed that the "Z" foot traffic was an issue with no real recourse other than being observant and cautious. The bridge was a way more difficult circumstance that resulted in a brief argument between Freak and Techno.

"Dude, have you got a short circuit in that geek wiring in your brain or what? Ain't no way we can jump that. It's gotta be thirty to forty yards across. Ain't you got no sense?"

"Freak, it's merely a matter of associating the proper ratios of speed, angle of incline, distance and weight to accurately assess the ZAP armor's ability to magnify our bodies natural strength to a level sufficient to clear the chasm. Had you paid attention in science class you would understand these ratio values and applications. Instead, you chose the infinitely popular "hit ball with stick class". Now, I see that it may not have been a choice at all, based upon your inability to calculate complex problems. Baseball and its inseparably low need to count beyond three strikes, four balls or three outs is definitely more your speed."

"Did you just call me stupid?"

"No, no, my large friend. Stupid would be calling you ignorant. Ignorant, by its very nature would be implying that you had the capacity for mental growth but it was latent and just underdeveloped. That is not the case in you my friend. You are in fact a magnificent specimen for the Neolithic time period."

"Oh. Well, I guess magnificent is okay; but if I catch you calling me stupid, I'm gonna shove this bat up your ass and turn you into a Jap– sickle." Freak said pointing to where Elwood was holstered over his shoulder.

"If you two have quite finished your male bonding, we need to get down to business." Spartan said with a tenseness to his voice. Seeing he had the team's full attention, he continued. "Dancer, the water tower is just over a third of a mile to the northwest. The "Zs" seem to be focused more on the center of the city than in the suburbs. Can you make it to the tower on your own or do we need to drop you into place and then roll onto our objective?"

Dancer lightly patted the wooden shaft of her naginata. "I will be fine. Give me a ten-minute window as a head start and to make the climb. Then I will be in place and ready to provide fire support."

"Okay. Ten minutes. Copy." Spartan frowned inside of his helmet's face shield. He had not expected Dancer to so readily accept the solo assignment. Although it was the nature of her job as a sniper, it still felt wrong to just let her run off alone into a city filled with the walking dead. "Be conscious of the fire burning through the western section of the city. If it gets too hot, get out of there and we will rally back up outside of the city."

"Deadeye, we need something to draw the "Zs" away from the orphanage."

"Actually," Techno interrupted. "I believe I am better suited for that task. I've been reviewing a layout of the city's buildings. There's a gas station just north of the orphanage at the end of the block. If there is still power on in there I should be able to drop a charge into the fuel well to make a hell of a lot of noise. No "Z" will be able to resist coming to see me."

The plan made sense. Spartan had forgotten about Techno's newly learned explosive skills. He needed to stay focused or they all could die or worse; be turned. Worrying

174

about Dancer was definitely distracting him. He needed to get his shit together.

"Freak, the nun and the children were last holed up towards the rear of the church. Schematics show an access hall that runs from the rectory directly to the kitchen and dining area. Once we breach the doors, the building inside should contain minimal contacts based on the church staff. That's our entrance."

"Dancer, you're our eyes outside. Once we have the children and the nun, we will be looking for the smoothest way out. There are entrances on all four sides of the building, and a second entry point at the rectory where we will be entering on the south side. I will let you know where we are coming out by radio."

"Any contacts and we take them down as quiet as possible unless we get a "Zulu" call from Dancer or Techno. On a Zulu, the mission is compromised and we vacate regardless of where we're at in the mission. Established rally point Alpha will be right here. Rally point Bravo will be back in Sleepy Hollow in the park. Rally point Charlie if needed, will be back at the stone pavilion where we fought the bikers. If we get a Zulu call, take off. Wait one hour at the first rally point, and then eight hours at Bravo and Charlie points. Stay alert. "Zs" are not the only problems out there. The Lords of Death and the skating rink Future Farmers of America "Z" karaoke crowd are also out there. At the rally point the challenge word is *"Three hundred"*. Confirmation code is *"Phalanx."* This is what we've trained to do people. Let's go get those kids and their pet penguin.

"Fuckin' A! Hooah!" Freak yelled.

"Watch your asses' people and we will laugh about this together later at dinner; whether it'll be back at the Academy or dining at the Devil's dinner table in Hell!"

Dancer laid a small hand on Spartan's shoulder. Despite the layers of armor, he could swear that he could feel the heat of her touch. He reached up and placed a hand over hers, while simultaneously keying the private communication channel to her helmet.

"Watch yourself out there Dance. If you get into trouble, run. Don't worry about us, we will catch up."

176

The girl nodded, choking back unexpected tears of concern. "I love you." She said softly.

"I love you too." Spartan replied and gently squeezed her hand. "Let's go save some children."

Dancer stepped back and unstrapped the naginata from where it was carried over her shoulder, unsheathing the deadly blade from its traditional wooden scabbard. The metal glinted in the fire-hued autumn sunlight, reflecting shades of flame around her. Giving a formal martial arts bow, the girl turned and raced off towards the setting sun and her assigned post on the water tower. There was no sense in mentioning that she was scared to death. It would not do any good for her situation and could put the rest of the team in danger if they were busy worrying about her and not be paying attention to the dangers around themselves, especially Spartan.

Surprisingly, her run thus far had been uneventful. She had crossed better than half the distance to the water tower before she saw the first of the undead. It was a shabbily dressed male Romero. In life he was probably a derelict, and now he emerged from his alleyway home with the typical lurching gait of a Romero. A wispy gray beard scraggled his chin and wear lines creased his brow and cheeks. He had probably been close to the end of his normal life before he had become infected. The gaping hole just above his left temple had changed that as a "Z" had bitten an orange sized divot out of its skin, skull killing him instantly and passing on the HUNGER virus, dooming the already cursed man to an eternity of misery.

Despite the urgency of her mission, Dancer could not help but feel pity for the pathetic man. Spinning her blade downward at a forty-five-degree angle, she swept the blade right to left. Steel that had been tempered and folded a thousand times cleaved through the clothing, flesh and bone like a hot knife through butter. In one fluid motion, she amputated the "Z" at the thigh on his right leg and continued downward severing the left leg just at the knee. The homeless old "Z" toppled to the ground as the body no longer had support to remain upright. Face down the creature struggled to turn over and bite at the warrioress. Dancer placed her booted foot in the center of the "Zs" back, pinning it to the ground. Lining up her blade with the undead's spinal column; she smoothly pushed her blade downward between the vertebrae and the skull, severing the spinal cord at the base of the creature's neck and driving the blade into the derelict's brain. Like a light that had been unplugged, the creature stopped trying to struggle and lay still. Later Dancer would swear that she had heard the "Z" sigh, almost in relief as she ended its torment.

"Be at peace old man." She said aloud and after wiping her blade off on the "Zs" clothing, she resumed her run for the water tower. Her team needed her. She would have more time for pity later.

She raced along dodging more than a dozen "Zs" that stood like undead traffic cones in the middle of the roadway, forcing her to weave in and out of the asphalt lanes. At last, she reached the water tower and looked up at the twenty-story climb. "No time like the present." She thought. Reaching back, she strapped the polearm to her back, she began to climb. Halfway up the ladder, she paused and glanced back down. It seemed that she had acquired a something of a following. A dozen or more "Zs" now milled around the base of the ladder. Getting back down from the tower just became much more difficult.

# CHAPTER ELEVEN

## TECHNO'S PREPARATION

Techno eased between the dumpster and the gas station's outer wall, as he tried to swallow back the burning bile that his terror was forcing up into his throat. For all of his bravado to Freak, being alone in a city full of the living dead was so horrifying to the teenager that he was afraid he would be paralyzed by his fear. This in turn would cause him to be eaten despite his ZAP armor and not provide the team with the distraction that they so desperately needed to rescue the children. So, thanks to his stupid ego driven bravado, he was now essentially a dead man walking.

In the back of his mind, he heard Sergeant Surfer chastising him as he had when he had first begun explosives training. *"Distraction equals detonation."* Panicking would lead to a loss of focus towards the mission parameter of creating a distraction for the rest of the team. During the majority of his young life, Techno had been the chubby Asian kid who had also been known as the *"four eyed eggroll"* by his school mates and *"my little dumpling"* by his own mother. As such he had believed in the self-fulfilling prophecy of being a geek and a fat little loser. That is of course, right up until the day that he had been snatched up by the military troops and brought to the Apocalypse Academy to begin his training. From that day on, his life began to change, slowly and inexorably for the better despite living in a world filled with the walking dead and egomaniacal pricks like Cutter and Orc. In fact, it could be rationalized in a purely cold and calculating way that the HUNGER virus had given his otherwise pathetic and hopeless life structure and the promise of a future not filled with Twinkies and pocket protectors.

Techno thought about the unsolicited acts of kindness that had been perpetuated on his behalf. From the fight on the first day at the Academy by Freak and Spartan, to the daily training each morning before dawn with Dancer, learning martial arts and trimming away the fat from his body. Even Deadeye, the teenaged enigma, had acknowledged Techno as a person to be depended upon for advice, support and friendship in his own "*special way.*" No, he would remain focused for the sake of his friends, and his teammates. He would not let them down.

Dodging from late evening shadow to late evening shadow, Techno evaded dozens of "Zs". His instructions had been simple. *"Get to the gas station, unlock the security valves on the fuel cut offs, rig the charge to ignite the fuel supply, and then run like hell."*

The "getting there" part had actually progressed fairly smoothly. The only "Z" he encountered was a long past his prime wino that lurched towards him as he traversed through an alleyway. A quick reach out with the stun baton immobilized the creature and left it lying in much the same position it'd spent most of its active human years; dazed and confused against the wall amidst the trash and refuse.

At the rear the gas station, Techno found the door locked by both deadbolt and padlock. The only windows to the building were large, plate glass types that would definitely shatter but probably activate an audible alarm when they were broken. Besides, the breaking glass alone would draw dozens of "Zs" to his location. Slowly, using every bit of body control that he had learned to silence his footfalls and mimicking the movements he had watched Deadeye perform so smoothly, Techno eased to the side of the building and peered around the corner. A tall, slim

Romero, dressed in the greasy gray overalls of a gas station mechanic wandered aimlessly between the gas pumps appearing to wait patiently for the cars that would never come. Clutched in one hand, perhaps due to years of muscle memory, was a large socket wrench. No other undead wandered nearby that he could see from his vantage point.

Gently he eased the rucksack from his back, trying hard to minimize any ambient noise. His eyes never left the gas station attendant, and Techno slowly began to assemble an improvised explosive device strictly by touch. Opening the bag, he felt the plastic container that held the blocks of C–4. Tech open the lid and tore off a four-inch-long section of the block. Using his hands, he began to knead the sticky, doughy substance until it became soft and pliable. Creating a roughly round white shape, he then removed a two-inch electronic aluminum detonator and inserted it into the clay of the explosive charge. Lastly, he removed a small electronic timer, similar to a kitchen timer, and connected the wiring on the detonator to it. Glancing down he set the time on the digital alarm for thirty minutes. All he had to do now was to get the bomb over to the gas pump, which meant he needed to remove the windshield washer.

Glancing back around the corner, he noticed something that he had not picked up on previously. The maintenance garage door stood open and a sedan, possibly a Corolla sat raised high in the air upon the lift skids to allow a mechanic to work underneath.

A plan began to formulate in his mind and grabbing his bomb and his rucksack, Techno slipped quietly into the building when he was certain the attendant was not looking. A quick visual scan on his helmet's HUD showed no further undead lurking inside. He silently moved over to the safety valves for the fuel pumps and disengaged all of the locking mechanisms. Working quickly, he stripped off the faceplate on the control panel and re-spliced the lines so that even if the circuit breaker blew, the fuel would not stop pumping once it was activated as long as the handle on the nozzle remain depressed. Leaving the counter area, he began to walk back to the maintenance bay. Having a second thought he stopped, turned around and grabbed a half-dozen bags of multicolored hard candy from one of the shelves. Then, moving back through the swinging door, he walked over to the dangling control panel for the lift and pried open its faceplate. Interfacing the ZAP armor's electronic override system with the control box, Techno quickly converted the panel from manual to verbal command. He spoke quietly into his helmet.

"Lower." The lift lowered the vehicle.

"Raise." The lift raised the vehicle back to its full height.

Satisfied, he went about implementing the next phase of his plan. Removing one of the bags of hard candy from the pile, he quickly opened it. Dumping a handful of the rock-hard candy into his gloved hand, he set the others aside and walked to the open entrance of the maintenance bay. Looking outward he saw the "Z" dutifully wandering back and forth between the gas pumps.

Selecting a single piece of striped candy, he cocked his arm back and threw it towards the "Z" as hard as he could. He wished he had played baseball as the round candy flew wide right. A second throw yielded no better results as it flew over the "Zs" head all the way to the street beyond. Sighing inwardly, Techno took the remaining six hard candies and heaved them en masse at the "Z". Four of the six pieces pelted the undead, immediately drawing its attention. Looking up, it spotted the half Japanese warrior and uttered a moan of hunger, immediately abandoning its post between the gas pumps to pursue him.

Tech slowly retreated into the garage, walking past the lift to the far side of the room, then turned and waited patiently. While the Romero slowly staggered towards him, he opened the faceplate on his helmet, unwrapped a green hard candy and popped it into his mouth. The explosion of sweet lime flavor surprised him. But after months of eating salads, it was delicious. Slowly he reached up and resecured the faceplate. The "Z" continued to shamble forward; grease-stained hands outstretched towards the warrior that stood calmly sucking on the piece of candy. When the mechanic was close enough, Techno read the name tag aloud.

"Murphy."

At the sound of Techno's voice, the Romero lurched violently forward, its moan sounding more frantic, almost desperate. As it reached the center of the area between the lift and the Toyota that it upheld, Techno spoke again, but this time it was to the control panel being run by his ZAP armor's interface capabilities.

"Lift power… Engage." Automatic hydraulic safeties disengage." A quick hum followed as the computer complied with the instructions. He suddenly felt a moment of pity as the "Z", as if sensing its impending doom, looked upward at the two-ton vehicle supported in the skids above it. Techno wondered just how many times Mister Murphy, the gas station attendant, had performed the same view servicing vehicles in his day-to-day life before becoming undead.

"Sorry Murph…Lift lower." Techno said aloud. Without the hydraulic safeties to lower the vehicle, the two tons of Toyota plummeted downward and crushed the undead mechanic flat with the crash. Grabbing his pack and the IED, Techno ran for the gas pumps. Setting his pack atop the first pump that he came to; he removed a package of zip ties and fastened all eight pump handles into the on position and laid them upon the ground. Fuel sloshed out, saturating the asphalt and flowing into and around the gas station. Working quickly, Techno placed the IED that he had built against the gas pump and activated the thirty-minute digital timer. He watched for a few seconds to ensure the timer was active, double checked his wiring, then turned and ran like hell back the way he had come. In less than thirty minutes there was going to be a helluva boom and "Zs" were going to flock to the area hoping for a meal. Techno intended to be far away by that time, possibly contemplating the philosophy of Murphy and why the Murph – Z had stopped to look up at the car instead of attacking him. *Were their memories deep inside of the "Zs" or only actions that were repetitive based upon life experiences? What was "Murphy's Law" as applied to "Z's"?*

Either way, Sergeant Surfer would be proud of both his ability to build the bomb so quickly and accurately as well as Techno's philosophical curiosity. On top of that, the team would have the distraction that they needed to draw the "Zs" away and rescue the children.

Everything was going as planned...

# Chapter Twelve
# Approaching the objective

The entrance to the rectory was a single lock, frosted glass door. Deadeye steadily worked on the lock, his picks deftly maneuvering until the latch finally turned with a small click. In stealth mode, he was nearly invisible, the zap armors chameleon-like abilities blending him seamlessly into the environment. As long as he was still, he vanished completely. When moving, he seemed more like the heat waves that rise in the summer from hot asphalt.

"Z's" wandered to and fro, some passing within mere feet of where the Apache knelt working on the lock. The only indicator that the job was completed was the quick opening and closing of the frosted glass door and a double flash of a red lens light that indicated the scout was inside and holding the portal. Spartan knew that when Techno's distraction came, Deadeye would have the door open for them. Spartan used the quiet moment of pre-combat to ensure the isolated placement of the other two members of the Phalanx while Freak stood guard.

"Dancer, this is Spartan. Do you copy?" He said into his helmet's communications microphone.

"Go ahead Spartan." Came the reply. A feeling of relief swept through him, knowing that Dancer had traversed the third of a mile safely and was now elevated high above the reach of any "Z".

"Status check." He called.

"In place. I have a zero on the south side rectory doors and the westside church entrance. Be advised, the church entrance has been breached by "Zs". Unknown if the extraction target is still viable."

"Copy. Church has been breached by "Zs". Any issues on your approach?"

"Negative. One minor contact pacified. For the record, it's a bloody long climb up to the top of this tower and..."

Spartan heard the hesitation in his teammate's voice. Something else was wrong. Something she wasn't reporting.

"Continue Dancer, is something wrong?"

"Not at the moment, no. I am secure. However, when the time comes to leave, I seem to have gathered a larger following than the Spice Girls in mid-America during the 1990s. Egress out may be something of an issue. Hopefully Techno's distraction will pull some or all of the "Zs" away. If not…" She left the sentence unfinished but he knew that she was implying that she would not be returning.

"Do not worry Dance. We will get these kids out, and then we will come and evacuate you as well."

"Negative Spartan. The mission parameters are very clear. The children must be evacuated out safely and returned to the Academy. Am I clear soldier? If you violate those orders, I will charge you with dereliction of duty and relieve you of command placing Deadeye in charge. I am collateral damage if I cannot get out of here. I knew the risk. I have trained for this my entire life. If you value how

I feel, if you value my trust in you as my team leader and as my love, do not put me in a position of always having to wonder if a child or a teammate could have been saved by leaving me behind. Do not dishonor me." The military training that her father had instilled from an early age in Dancer was evident now. There was no hint of worry for herself, only the overriding point of the mission and the safe retrieval of the children as their orders had instructed.

"Copy." Was all he could say return.

"Spartan, one more thing." She chimed over the frequency as the wind blew hard against her armor.

"What is it Dancer?" Spartan asked. He thought he detected a hint of laughter in the girl's voice.

"Well love, this may not be the best time to mention it, but I really need to go to the loo."

Despite the seriousness of the situation and his own dour perspective on his teammate's plight, Spartan chuckled. The loo was British for bathroom. He knew that alone upon the water tower, she could not possibly get out of her ZAP armor, even as flexible as she was.

"Well, I guess you'll have to drip dry then girl because there's no toilet paper four stories up. Just think of it as being in the old West or maybe even medieval England."

"You bloody American savage. I'll do no such thing." She replied. "A proper Englishwoman learns self-control. I love you." With that she clicked off her communications link.

"I love you too Dance. Hang in there." Spartan replied to the empty frequency, looking at the red status light that indicated the girl was no longer transmitting on the personal channel. Orders be damned. He wasn't going to abandon her. He wasn't going to lose her to the "Zs".

# Chapter Thirteen
## Hogg's supply run

Hogg ran harder than he had ever run in his life. Concern drove his legs as he pounded ahead on the pavement. He had long since left caution to the wind and just turned the hunt for his team into a headlong dash.

Reaching the skating rink that bordered the White Pines Forest State Park; he ducked low into the pine tree line and skirted the establishment, avoiding the revelers that he observed there. Guiding east, he passed the go-kart track and raced towards the privacy fence that separated the drive-in theater from the skating rink property. Putting his back up against the wooden fence, Hogg ducked low and knelt to catch his breath. He still had miles to go before he would be in person-to-person communications range. There was no way he would cover that distance tonight. He needed to find a secure place to hole up and take a breather. It was just then that he realized how badly he wanted a beer. No, scratch that. More like a dozen beers. And a microsecond later he realized that he had not brought along any supplies at all, in the interest of weight and speed. He needed to find someplace fast that he could forage and shelter up for the night.

Carefully he peeked between the slats of the wooden fence looking for guards. Ensuring that the 80's skate party were all still within the building and jamming out to "Mickey", which they had synced to a colored lighting system, Hogg turned and boosted himself up over the top of the privacy fence and peered around his surroundings. The gravel parking lot was empty except for row after row of window speakers, resting on their poles. A skeletal set of playground equipment stood in the shadowed grassy area towards the front of the drive-in's massive parking lot.

Alone, mid-center in the gravel stood a boarded-up building that housed both the projection unit and the concession stand. "Perfect." Hogg thought as he began to scale the barrier. "I bet there's no beer but Juju-fruit's, Reese's pieces and a Coke should hold me over for tonight."

Dropping nearly silently over the fence, Hogg had taken about three striding steps towards the concession stand when he heard a familiar hiss – pop of the canned drink being opened on the opposite side of the fence where he had just come from. Need overriding common sense, Hogg raised up onto his toes and peered back over the fence. A lone male figure stood urinating on the base of the pine tree, his back facing Hogg's position. A solitary open can of beer was held precariously in one hand as he stood relieving himself out in the dark. Sitting alone on the ground behind the man, five additional brother beers rested, still ringed in their plastic holding strap. Hogg's mouth salivated inside of his helmet. The man must be really drunk to have not noticed him as he had climbed over the fence.

*"Fate favors the foolish!"* He muttered to himself and carefully rested his assault rifle against the fence, ensuring that it would not fall over. Then, reaching up his armored hands, he grasped the top of the fence and waited for the opportune moment to make his assault. His auditory sensors registered the stream of liquid as it transitioned from constant to intermittent and finally to a drip. The telltale sigh and zipping sound indicated that the man had finished with his personal business.

Using the muscle enhancing quality of his ZAP armor, Hogg squatted as deep as he could and thrust upward with his legs while simultaneously catapulting himself forward with his hands and shoulders. Vaulting the fence in a single motion, he landed in a combat crouched directly behind the man.

Used to the rigors of combat, the drunken man spun around expecting an attack by a "Z" or two. Hands clenched; the man frantically searched for his assailant. He was not prepared for the muscle enhanced, armored uppercut the connected squarely with the underside of his chin. The man flipped backwards, arms and legs splayed, unconscious before he hit the ground. Combat reflexes taking over, Hogg's hand shot out and caught the open can of beer as it spun through the air. Less than a swallow of the rare golden liquid had spilled before he righted the can.

Setting the can carefully in the grass so that it did not spill, Hogg quickly patted the man down. A nice boot knife he left in its sheath on the man's ankle. He did not want to leave any human being unarmed in the "Z" wilderness; even an apparent moron like this. Patting down the man's flannel shirt, he found a long hard leather pouch in the left side, breast pocket.

"No flippin' way I can get that lucky." He mumbled as he opened the case. Inside were five whole cigars, fresh and from the smell, imported. Suddenly he felt bad for the man. Apart from the tacky green and yellow John Deere attire, they seemed to have similar tastes in the important things left in this world. He could not just leave the man on the ground as potential "Z" chow. Looking up to the pine tree the man had just been urinating on, he spied a large branch about ten feet off the ground. Hoisting the man over his armored shoulder, he began to climb. Reaching the fork, he unfastened the man's belt and slid it free from the belt loops. Wrapping the belt around the tree, he resecured it around the man's chest, snuggly holding the man in place. Then, certain that the farmer was out of harm's way, he climbed back down the tree.

After a brief moment's thought, he opened the visor on his ZAP helmet and slugged down the entire open can of beer. Then he discarded the can directly below the man near the drying urine. With luck, no one would believe his story about being assaulted in the dark, and his friends would think that he got drunk, climbed a tree and passed out. Hogg then picked up the cigars and remaining cans of cold beer and climbed carefully back over the fence.

Picking up his assault rifle from where it was propped against the fence, Hogg moved low and fast towards the concession stand entrance. Arriving in the dark with no further encounters, Hogg used the night vision granted by his helmet's enhancements to gauge the door security. A single padlock on a hasp and a turnable door lock seemed to be the only deterrence. Reaching up his armored hand, he grasped the padlock and in one swift motion, tore it from the wooden door frame. Then turning his attention to the door handle, he turned it gradually, using the ZAP's enhanced strength, until the locking mechanism inside bent and then broke with a soft metallic ping.

Opening the door, he raised his assault rifle and scanned the room. Glass counters full of old junk food and dried up soda fountains greeted him. A moldy popcorn machine stood behind the counter, its contents long since picked clean by scavengers. The stale snacks beckoned as his stomach rumbled. Caution overriding his hunger, Hogg cleared the nearby manager's office of any potential threats to ensure that no undead would be surprising him in the night, then took a folding chair wedged it under the doorknob, securing the office closed. Removing his helmet, he opened a beer and selected two pink pickled eggs from a jar on the counter and a box of old Juju fruits for dessert. Taking a bite of the vinegar laden egg, he moved off to the corner of the room to enjoy his fortuitous meal and some much-needed sleep. His last thought as he dozed off was how amazing it was that snack foods lasted indefinitely after the apocalypse.

# Chapter Fourteen

## The Orphanage

The explosion engulfed Murphy's remains, the gas station and the pharmacy across the street. Glass storefronts shattered in a three hundred sixty-degree radius of the rupturing fuel tanks for a mile in every direction. The resulting fireball and mushrooming cloud of smoke, dust and debris filled the sky with the visual notice of death.

Drawn by the vast noise of the explosion, the "Zs" obediently turned and began to stagger towards the sound; their virus rotting brains equivocating sound with food. Seeing the undead's attention drawn away from the church, Spartan and Freak quickly and quietly crossed the street and entered the rectory door where Deadeye stood waiting. As Freak passed through the open doorway, the Apache reached up and twisted the deadbolt secure.

"That was one helluva noise. I hope Techno is okay." Freak said quietly.

"He did his job." Spartan said trying not to think about the young Japanese American's status. "It's our turn to do the same."

"Are we going in quiet or balls to the wall boss?" Freak asked indicating both his assault rifle and the twin bats strapped across his back.

"Quiet." Spartan replied. "We may need the firepower to fight our way back out of here. Deadeye, are we clear?"

The Apache scout replied without turning around. "The first floor is secure. Negative contacts in any area. The door across from us leads upstairs to I assume, the church housing authority. I can clear it or secure it as you choose but I have not done so yet."

"Secure it. If we have to go back and clear later we will. For now, it's not part of our mission parameters and thus not on target."

Deadeye nodded. "Freak, that desk over there oughta do it. Grab one end and I'll grab the other." He said referring to a large oak desk that apparently belonged to the church's secretary. A picture of Jesus handing a little blond girl a flower sat in a glass frame upon the corner. A bloody, red handprint smeared across the glass as if the owner was trying to reach out to his or her Lord for salvation in their final moments as a human being. Together the two warriors muscled the heavy wooden desk into place in front of the upstairs door. When finished, Deadeye picked up his razor bow from where it stood against the wall and laid an arrow across the string. Holding the weapon in his left hand, he indicated the corridor door to the left as the correct path to take.

At a nod from Spartan, the Apache warrior moved forward, silent as a cat. Spartan and Freak followed. Passing an open entrance to a library and then an empty lounge, the team paused at the entrance to the closed male and female restrooms. Pushing the men's door open slightly, Deadeye listened for the telltale footfalls or signature undead groan of the walking dead. Hearing nothing, Deadeye and Spartan flowed quietly into the room while Freak maintained overwatch in the hall. Seeing no one in the stall or the main part of the room, they quickly exited the room and repeated the process of the women's restroom.

Pressing open the door, the team was met by the torn and tooth shredded remains of what appeared to have been the secretary. Her flowered dress was bloody and torn open at the abdomen and long gray ropes of intestine had been unraveled from her midsection. The linked segments of intestine showed signs of tooth marks and had gaps in several spaces. In addition, the woman's stomach had been torn open, exposing the moist, chewed remains of her partially digested potato chips for the world to see as she lay in rigor. An additional wound to her skull had insured that the secretary was past the point of reanimation. Spartan and Deadeye stepped over her remains and cleared the otherwise empty restroom, ensuring that no other threats lay hidden in the stalls. Together, Spartan and Deadeye reentered the hall where Freak continued overwatch in the gloom.

"The secretary's not taking any calls." Deadeye said dryly as he passed the big man and resumed his point position moving down the hallway. An open archway led into what appeared to be the community dining room with an attached kitchen area. Peeling left, Deadeye used the night vision of his helmet to look for threats. Spartan, reacting to his teammate's movement, split right, flowing down the wall with the Sword of Leonidas clenched in his right hand. The rooms were large, perhaps thirty-foot square, with the kitchen divided from the dining area by a large countertop that ran horizontally across the length of the room.

Due to the openness of the room, Freak lumbered into the center aisle between the rows of folding tables. The twin baseball bats that he had dubbed the Blues Brothers alternately twirled clockwise in his hands as he prepared for impending battle.

Although the room appeared empty, the warriors of the Phalanx were taking no chances, cautiously moving forward and peering between chairs and under tables. Ambient light filtered into the room through a dozen tall, slender stained-glass windows, casting the room into a gray – green set of shadows that was occasionally tinged with red, orange or blue. Spartan wondered for the briefest of moments if the designer of the glass works of art had any idea that the color schemes they utilized in making the religious symbology on the windows would also one day become symbolic of the new world of the undead.

Refocusing on the mission at hand, Spartan cleared the right side of the room. A flashed hand signal from Deadeye indicated that he had made visual contact with something ahead in the kitchen area, but from the angle, Spartan could not see past the countertops. Enhancing the audio on his ZAP's exterior communications array, Spartan listened. He was rewarded with the unmistakable sound of flesh tearing and the smacking of a wide-open, chewing mouth. Then the unmistakable sound of several "Z" undead moans rose up from behind the countertop and Spartan knew that undeath lingered in the church's kitchen; feasting on the flesh of the living; savage, brutal and merciless.

Deadeye had drawn his razor bow back to its full extension. The diamond sharp arrow tip glistened green in the stained light of the windows as it sat unwaveringly upon the bow, waiting to be dispatched as an agent of death. Spartan flashed a return hand signal to Deadeye and Freak. He was going to look over the countertop to see what horror waited for them beyond the barrier. Silently he moved forward, each footstep slow and deliberate. Enhancing the optical capabilities of his helmet to starlight vision as he leaned forward, he searched for the sounds of the feast in progress.

Upon the kitchen floor, arms and legs akimbo, lay the bodies of three separate teenagers: two boys and a girl. Tied to the dead girl's wrist was a thin white plastic shopping bag that looked like it contains several canned goods. The bags plastic rattled as a "Z" dressed in a priest's garb gnashed at the flesh on her inner thigh with its teeth. No sound came from the girl as she was savaged. She was, fortunately already dead, having bled out from the previous bite wounds to her femoral artery. Two other adult "Z's" in civilian clothes feasted on the dead boys. From their movements, Spartan could clearly see that they were Romero's. He was about to flash the hand signal to Deadeye as to what he saw when the faintest hint of movement came from the kitchen cabinet behind the undead caught his attention.

Although the cabinet door was closed, Spartan was certain that he had seen it move just a fraction of an inch. It could've been the result of the feeding frenzy below him or even a possibly of rats, but he needed to be sure. Changing the visual acuity on his helmet from night vision to infrared, he quickly scanned the cupboard. The resulting heat signature confirmed what he had feared. A child; a very small child, was curled up inside of the cabinet.

The shifting scrape of movement on his auditory sensors caused Spartan to immediately shift back to night vision. Apparently the "Z" priest had seen the cabinet door move as well and had now raised its bloody mouth from the girl's torn thigh and peered at the exact spot where the child was hidden. As the undead's moan became a wail of rage, Spartan knew that he had been mistaken. The priest was not a Romero. He was a Reaper and it had just figured out that more food lay hidden in the cabinet. Reaching out its clawed hand, it tore the cabinet door from its hinges in a single violent motion.

The child's scream of horror galvanized Spartan into action. Relying on the ZAP's ability to enhance his muscles, he backed up two steps and propelled himself headfirst over the countertop. The headlong vault ended with him crashing into the "Z's" side as it hunched over to grab the once hidden child. Cabinets and rotting bones smashed and various appliances rained down upon the living and the undead as they careened into the wall on the far side of the room.

The other two Romero's looked up at the disturbance and the first began to stand and shamble towards where Spartan fought with the Reaper; still holding the dangling orb of an eyeball from its nerve root. A whistling sound followed by a deep, hollow thunk of an arrow meeting flesh indicated that Deadeye had eliminated one threat, although Spartan could not see the end result as the Reaper was trying to gnaw its way through his faceplate while he restrained its arm to keep it from tearing through his armor. Seeing Freak around the corner, he yelled over the melee.

"The kid Freak, get the kid!"

The giant bull-rushed the "Z" that had begun to rise from its kneeling feast of teenager. Three hundred pounds of Zombie Apocalypse Protection armor, backed by servo enhanced muscle smashed into the undead creature like an out-of-control eighteen-wheeler hitting an insect on the highway. The end result was the same. Pulped "Z" flesh splattered across the armor and helmet as the impact drove the undead across the kitchen where it bent unnaturally backward as its spine struck the metal stove and shattered without a sound of pain. Ignoring the reverse bent and paralyzed creature that now clawed mindlessly at the air around it, the giant reached down and plucked up the child; a blond-haired boy of about six and in one smooth motion spun and slid the kid butt first across the linoleum floor to where Deadeye stood.

"Get behind me." Deadeye said in an amplified voice that to the boy sounded for all the world like a robot. As the child scrambled to follow the instruction, Deadeye loosed an arrow into the Reaper's right kidney, spurting rotten blue-black blood out of the wound. In a human being that shot would be crippling at least and potentially fatal. In the Reaper priest it was less than an annoyance.

Spartan's armored hand was locked under the undead creature's jaw, forcing the head and neck upward, stretching the dead flesh and preventing it from succeeding at biting him. The creature's nails clawed at his ZAP armor's shoulders and arms, gouging and furrowing the plastic shoulder guard with four identical claw marks but not penetrating the armor's levels of protection. Rotten black blood sluiced down the Deadeye's protruding arrow making it difficult for Spartan to maintain a solid handhold or to bring the ZAP armor's strength enhancements to bear on the creature.

Looking to the side quickly, Spartan saw that the Sword of Leonidas was striped on rotten gore and had skidded out of reach during his headlong dive into the "Z". With the Reaper on top of him, he could not let loose of its neck and claws to try to reach his combat knife without risking opening himself up to further attack. They were at an impasse.

The clatter of metal to his left drew his attention. One of the Blues Brothers; Jake; Spartan thought; landed on the ground beside him. Looking up, Spartan had a microsecond to see Freak bring Elwood around in a roaring two-handed, full force swing. The result was comic book spectacular as the "Zs" face just above Spartan's hand disintegrated in a slow-motion explosion of teeth, bones and brain that redecorated the nearby kitchen wall. A single spasm shook the remaining lower jaw causing the exposed tongue to waggle side to side like a rattlesnake's tail, and then the priest's corpse fell over and lay still.

Freak helped his team leader back to his feet. Picking up the Sword of Leonidas and Jake, Spartan handed the bat back to his teammate. The enormous teen took the weapon and keyed his person-to-person helmet frequency, opening a channel directly to Spartan.

"You okay Dawg?"

"Yeah, I'm good. Thanks for the save brother. That was close."

"What was up with that superhero, fly through the air shit? You ain't even got a cape!"

"Did it look cool though?" Spartan responded. He knew Freak was right. The move had been born out of desperation but in reality it was careless and stupid for himself and could've put the team at risk. He had just reacted when he saw the "Z" go for the kid. Dancer was going to come unglued if and when she found out.

"Is the kid okay, did he get bitten?"

"He's okay. He's with the Apache on the other side of the countertops. He's a little shaken up from seeing his friends and the older teens get eaten, but you saved his life."

Spartan nodded. "Thanks again for the save. I owe you one." Then he looked up and spied the boy standing next to Deadeye. Walking over, he knelt on the ground next to the boy.

"What's your name kid?"

"Billy, Mister Power Ranger Sir." The boy replied timidly.

The boys comment took Spartan little bit off guard until he realized that his helmet's face shield was still down. He initiated keying in the internal release mechanism and the tinted shield of his faceplate slid upward, revealing his face to young Billy.

"Wow!" The boys lit up. "That's so cool."

Ignoring the child's gush of hero worship, Spartan asked him a question.

"Billy, how did you get in here with the monsters? Can you show me how you got in here?"

The boys head nodded enthusiastically. The boy tried to grab Spartan's hand but Spartan pulled back. He was covered in rotten muck and he didn't want the boy to get accidentally infected. Instead the boy trotted over to the opposite side of the room where a small eighteen by eighteen-inch-wide metal grill lay on the floor next to the refrigerator, exposing the ductwork beyond.

"Is this where Sister Margaret is? Through here?"

The boy shook his head up and down. His narrow face looked like a pigeon as his head bobbed and the smile that split the boy's face indicated that he was truly fond of the Sister. Reaching down without any obvious display of emotion, the child unwrapped the plastic bag's handles from the dead girl's hand. As the thin plastic loops slid free, Spartan saw the faintest twitches move the dead girl's fingers. She was beginning to reanimate.

215

Quickly he shepherded the boy away from the dead girl, back towards the hole in the wall. Halfway there the boy stopped dead in his tracks and looked up at Spartan. Holding the little bag of canned goods upward with significant effort and strain, the boy asked Spartan a question.

"I'm a big helper huh?" He asked, his eyes full of innocence.

Even in the face of an undead plague, a childlike Billy looked for approval for acts well done. A memory flash surged through Spartan's mind of another little boy with dark brown hair asking him the exact same question when he had gone and gotten Spartan a soda from the refrigerator because he had been too lazy to get up and get it himself. It was a lost memory of a little boy that had looked a lot like himself. A little brother?

"Yes Billy. I'm sure that Sister Margaret thinks that you are a big helper." He tussled the boys already wild hair. "Can you be my big helper too?" He asked the boy.

The boy smiled so widely that Spartan thought his face would surely split in half. He nodded yes enthusiastically.

"Could you go and tell Sister Margaret that we are here for her?"

Again, the enthusiastic head shake and the boy turned around without a word and entered the small air duct on all fours, quickly vanishing from sight. Movement behind him caused Spartan to turn around. The dead girl had completed her transformation into infected Reaper. Sitting up, she scanned the room through red infected eyes. Seeing Freak, she snarled and started to stand up, preparing herself to launch into an attack. Spartan decapitated her from behind. As the head rolled away, Spartan heard Billy calling to the nun from the air vent.

"Sister Margaret! I got the food you wanted and guess what? The Power Rangers are here!" Spartan could not help but to laugh despite all of the carnage around him.

# Chapter Fifteen
## Dancer on High

From her sniping perch high up on the water tower's platform, Dancer considered her position for effective support shooting in order to cover the team's egress from the orphanage. She did not bother to look down to consider her own personal situation. Based upon the number of moans that her audio sensors were registering and the basic fact that she could feel the metal base and ladder supporting the water tower vibrating repeatedly under the impacts of the cadaverous undead that were mindlessly clawing at the metal, she knew that there must be quite a few undead down there waiting to eat her liver and that the entire situation was bollocks. There was no sense dwelling on what you can't change as her father always used to say.

Settling into a prone position after extending the Dragonov's bipod support, she looked through the high-powered scope at the front of the orphanage. Techno's distraction seemed to have worked. Only a few "Zs" remained mobile around the building and the team should, if they moved quickly enough, be able to evacuate the children safely. Looking towards mid-city she could see the fire burning brightly from Techno's powerful explosive device. A huge mushroom cloud of oily black smoke marked the spot like an ink stain on an otherwise gray-blue sky. Scanning the nearby roadways, she looked for any sign of the young Japanese boy but saw no sign of movement on any of the streets surrounding the explosion. She contemplated calling him on the personal frequency but dismissed the idea, knowing that she needed to keep communications open for the assault team. She was disciplined enough to understand the primary mission. Techno would have to fend for himself, if he was even still alive at all after that blast.

Looking back at the orphanage, she saw no change to the "Z" population and decided to chance turning her rifle scope towards the creatures that were flocking towards Techno to get a better sense of a specific undead type and a more accurate number of Reapers and Romero's for when it was time to extract her teammates.

Blinking her eyes to allow them to change her focus from the near target to long-range, she slowly adjusted the rangefinder on her scope. At first she thought she must be off target. She saw no pack formations of undead at all, only a few wandering "Zs". Perhaps they had all been vaporized in the explosion. Craning her neck upward, she looked over the top of the scope, making sure that she was looking at the right spot. No, she seemed to be on target, at least where the target used to be, so where was the pack of "Zs"? Settling back into her shooter stance, she re-sought the range and the pack. Again, she found nothing but a few wandering undead. As her confusion mounted a blur of movement zipped past her scope's lens, like a fast-moving bird passing a window. Glancing up a second time and looking around the water tower's edge she saw no birds in flight and thought maybe it was just a piece of debris that had blown past from the fire. Then a thought occurred to Dancer. Reaching to the top of her sniper rifle, she adjusted the appropriate knobs on the electronic magnification of her scope, decreasing its power. Like a television coming into focus, the image of the pack came into full view. Only it wasn't her pack. It was more like a herd of undead being led straight towards her team by a number of the Lords of Death riding their motorcycles.

"Oh blimey!" She said aloud to no one at all. The view through the high-powered assassin scope was straight out of a nightmare. A horde of "Zs" were literally being wrangled by motorcycle driven Lords of Death. The motorcycles wove in and out of the horde, zipping to and fro, leading them onward, baiting them with their living proximity. Behind several of the more powerful motorcycles, bound living human beings were being drug along by ropes and chains, tied at the hand or foot. These people were being used like worms on a hook, trolling for the undead. Bloodied and battered the tormented faces silently screamed in pain and fear as the motorcycles lured the "Zs" forward. The distant, silent screams of the living seemed to be driving the "Zs" into a massive feeding frenzy in Dancer's scope. Conversely, the living human beings upon the motorcycles seemed to be having the time of their lives, laughing amongst themselves as they wove to and fro just beyond the closest undead's reach.

As Dancer watched, an elderly, bound black man was grabbed by a group of "Zs" that the gang member upon his motorcycle had gotten too close to. Biting and clawing, the undead tore into the man. As the helpless victim screamed in silent agony, the Lord of Death calmly pulled out a large knife and cut the rope that tethered the bloody human to the motorcycle, allowing the powerful machine to zip away. The man was quickly lost beneath the mob of undead.

Rage filled her soul and she wanted with every fiber of her being to put a 7.62 caliber bullet through the gang member's forehead. But doing so would not only reveal her position but also that of her team as well. Easing her finger off of the half-pulled trigger, she activated the emergency all comm feature of her helmet's radio. She needed discipline not emotion right now.

*"Spartan this is Dancer; do you read me? Over."*

No response.

*"Spartan This Is Dancer. I Have A Three Hundred Priority Message Do You Copy!"* Urgency tinged her voice. A three hundred priority message meant that the entire Phalanx could be wiped out by overwhelming numbers like they had been at the battle of Thermopylae in Greece hundreds of years ago.

Static hissed across the open communication line then suddenly a response. *"Spartan to Dancer. Go ahead with the three hundred priority message."*

*"Spartan, there is a horde of an estimated one thousand to as many as ten thousand, I repeat...potentially ten thousand "Zs" being driven like cattle into the city by the Lords of Death. ETA less than an hour. They're using living human beings as bait to lure the horde forward. Repeat...Living human beings used as bait. You need to get your arse out of there asap. Over."* The mental anguish and horror of what she was seeing was evident in her voice.

*"Acknowledged Dancer. We are expediting contact with the Penguin at this time. Fall back to the rendezvous point. Any word on Tech?"*

*"Negative Spartan, on both accounts. I haven't heard from Techno since before the big boom. I also have too many dance partners waiting below me to fall back to the rendezvous point. It seems that they like my perfume."*

A hiss – crackle – pop came across the radiofrequency. It seems that someone was trying to break into the conversation.

*"...rtan..."*

*"Techno is that you?"*

*"10-4...* Crackle... *Pinned...*hiss... *Broken... Sorry...*Pop."

"Hang on Tech. Dancer, see if you can see him from up top. I'm not leaving either of you two behind. Techno, activate your emergency beacon."

"Copy." Came Dancer's immediate reply.

*"Neg...Spart...hurt too ba...burden...leave m..."* The signal trailed off leaving only static behind.

"That wasn't a request warrior!" Spartan yelled into his helmet's microphone. *"Tighten your shit up, shut your mouth and be ready! Do you copy me?!"*

*"Copy."* Came the week reply, and a green blip began to ping on Spartan's helmet GPS. Techno had activated the emergency beacon as instructed.

*"Dancer, sit tight. We will swing by to get Techno after we rescue the children and then pivot back around south to extract you. We will handle the "Zs" when we get there. Try to pick off any that you can while you're waiting around but keep an eye on that horde."*

*"Spartan…"*

*"This is neither a negotiation nor a democracy, Dancer. Follow orders. Let me know how much time we have before we're overrun."*

Her father's ingrained discipline kicked in and she shut off the helmet communicator after a very quiet *"copy."* To herself she said *"hurry"*, as she looked down at the undead below. There had to be twenty or more "Zs" staring upward at her, slavering to eat her warm living flesh.

Turning back to Freak and Deadeye, Spartan spoke rapidly to them. "You all heard that conversation? Dancer's trapped and Techno's hurt… maybe dying. There is no more time for subtlety. If something gets in our path that

225

ain't a nun, a kid or one of us; put it down fast and hard. One-shot kills. Once we have the nun and the children, Deadeye you're going to lead them south to the forest. That's your turf. Keep them safe in the woods until we can meet back up. Freak, you and I will be going for our teammates. We may have to carry Tech, so I need your power. Any questions? No? Good. Freak; take point and move the doors and obstacles out of our way fast. Deadeye you're on our six.

The team transition from hand weapons to firearms smoothly and silently as they moved across the kitchen. Crawling sounds could be heard coming from the venting. One by one, the bedraggled heads of the children began to pop out of the ductwork. Wild hair and terrified eyes reminded Spartan of the gophers and groundhogs that used to make him laugh in his youth. He could find nothing funny about this situation. It was only another useless memory that he would analyze if and when he survived this mission. The last boy to come through was little Billy. Extricating himself from the air vent, the boy stood up and poked the boy of similar age next to him.

"See!" He beamed as he spoke. "I told you there were Power Rangers here to rescue us!" The boy said excitedly.

Spartan did a quick headcount. There were nine children in total. There were supposed to be a dozen. And then he remembered the three teenagers that had been slaughtered on the floor by the "Z's". He looked down at Billy.

"Are there any more children with Sister Margaret?" He asked, nodding at the air vent.

"Only the baby." The boy replied. "Sister Margaret was changing his diaper when we left."

An infant? He didn't remember that from the ops briefing. That could change things enormously because infants tended to squall without self-control. Uncontrolled noise like that could give away their position and location to the "Zs" or the Lords of Death in a moment's notice.

"Is Sister Margaret going to bring the baby through here?" Spartan asked, indicating the air vent.

The two boys immediately giggled as if Spartan had just told the funniest joke of all time. Peals of laughter spewed from the boys until they had to gasp for breath holding their sides. Wiping away the tears of mirth from their eyes, they responded to Spartan's inquiry.

"No Sir, Mister Ranger Sir. She ain't gonna fit in there. She's got too big of a butt." The boys said and giggled in unison again.

Just then, a girl of about nine years of age walked up and stood next to Spartan. Without invitation she spoke up. "What the boys are so delicately attempting to state is that the rotund girth of Sister Margaret will not be able to even enter the ductwork. It would be physically impossible, even if you greased her like a pig and had one person pulling from the front and one person pushing from behind." She said matter-of-factly.

Spartan silently studied the girl's features. Tall, slender with light sandy colored hair and knowing green eyes peered back at him. A smattering of freckles dotted her nose and cheeks and her posture spoke of a girl with a classical education which had included grace, manners and etiquette. She was probably rich before the world went to hell on "Z" night.

"I see." Was all he said in response.

Looking over at the air vent, there was no way in hell that he was going to fit through this small aperture, even without his armor. Freak would've been better suited to go through the entire wall rather than try to wriggle into a space like that. They would have to go around to the front of the building which meant a lot more potential hostile engagement. Well, if there was no choice, then there was also no time like the present. Turning, he headed for the door. He stopped short when Deadeye placed in armored hand upon his shoulder.

"I can make it." The Apache said. There was no drama in his voice, no pretense, nothing more than just simple fact. Spartan loved that about the boy. No mincing of words, just deadly efficiency. Turning back around, Spartan looked over at the eighteen-inch square opening just above the ground. "Are you sure? That's awfully tight. If you get stuck you could be in a bad way if there are any "Zs" in the area."

Deadeye nodded without a word, simultaneously handing Spartan the deadly razor bow. If it came to fight, it would be up close and personal. Smoothly the boy drew his tactical Tomahawk from where it hung on his belt. Black as night, only the razor-sharp edge caught the light. Without another word, the scout dropped to all fours and then down to his elbows. Extending the hand holding the Tomahawk in front of him, he wormed his way into the air shaft.

Spartan keyed his helmet communications system on the all comm frequency. *"Three minutes Dancer; Deadeye is in the air vent going after the penguin. She's too large for the vent so they will be coming out the front doors. Also, they will have a baby with them. Repeat… they will have a baby with them. Thin the herd when you see them as much as you can. Any Reapers or "Zs" in the immediate vicinity; put 'em down."*

*"Freak; you and I will take the children out the side door where we came in, back at the rectory. Then you, I and Deadeye will rally up and hand over the children at the McDonald's up the road four blocks from here. You and I will then get the rest of the Phalanx while Deadeye and Sister Margaret get the children out of town. We will all*

*rally back up at Sleepy Hollow. Repeat… We will rally at Sleepy Hollow. Be ready."* He ordered.

Long seconds ticked by until a single whispered call came across the communicator in hushed tones. *"Spartan this is Deadeye. I'm in and I have the penguin and the child. Waiting for your go on the front door. I have removed the barricades so don't be too long."*

Spartan looked inside himself as rage and anger threatened to overwhelm his leadership and conscious tactical thoughts. It was like trying to hold back a Rottweiler with a skein of yarn. *"Copy."* Was all he responded. Grabbing his gigantic friend by the upper arm just above the elbow, Spartan keyed the microphone on Freak's private channel. "Get them out Freak! I will get Deadeye and the nun!" He growled; his tone brooked neither debate nor argument. His voice sounded gruff on his ears, almost forced, like he had been screaming. Then, receiving the nod from his six man, Spartan strode out the door, ZAP enhanced muscles flexing, drawing the razor-edged sword and swinging it side to side. There was no running now. No tactics, no mercy. Just brutal violence, which was a side of him that had been dormant for far too long since he had last embraced it.

Bloodlust was upon him and all he wanted to do was destroy the undead that had brought so much harm to his world and to save these children and his teammates. His grip felt like hot, hardened steel on the pommel of the legendary king's sword, almost as if it had become an extension of his own arm rather than a weapon for annihilation. Adrenaline surged and a war cry burst from his lips as he saw the first "Z" turn from the front of the church to fully face him and begin to approach. The creature began its mournful moan that called the surrounding undead to a meal of fresh meat. In two quick strides, Spartan was upon the creature, the hawk faced pommel lashing out to smash the creature's teeth into jagged, broken stumps. As the undead's head snapped backwards, Spartan allowed the forward momentum of the weighted pommel to guide the blade outward and upward. Upon reaching the apex of his swing, he reversed the direction of force and drove the razor-sharp blade downward on top of this "Zs skull. Driven by rage, momentum and powered armor, the sword bisected the "Zs" skull into two symmetrical halves all the way down to the creature's chest. The only movement from the creature was an involuntary muscle reaction as its separated eyes rolled up white and it dropped soundlessly to the ground.

Three more "Zs" had answered the voracious dinner call of the first and shambled toward Spartan. Rather than await their approach in a defensive posture, Spartan sprang to the attack. Time was of the essence and despite his inner voice that called for him to dismember the abominable creatures, Spartan knew that he had a very small window of opportunity to rescue the nun, the infant and Deadeye before the undead that were drawn away by Techno's explosion returned.

Sweeping his blade horizontally right to left in front of him, the Spartan sword severed the outstretched fingers of the closest of the three undead. Triple moans of undying hunger echoed in his ears as the audio sensors of his helmet filtered in all sounds, ensuring that he heard everything. To the inexperienced warrior, the sound would have been unnerving, perhaps even terrifying. To Spartan the noise acted almost like a mechanical form of echolocation, making it easier for him to target's undead foes with precision and efficiency.

Reversing the momentum of the heavy blade, Spartan pivoted and brought the swords cutting edge back across the undead's kneecaps. Blue jeans and white bones slashed open as the tendons supporting the legs collapsed, dumping the "Z" face first onto the sidewalk. Without pause for thought; the young warrior stomped his armor-plated boot downward, mashing the diseased skull beneath his heel and ramming shattered bone fragments through the undead's porous brain. Its moan of hunger was silenced instantly.

Looking up, Spartan gauged the other two "Zs" approaching immediately in front of him. The tallest; a middle-aged male perhaps 6' 4, seemed to have been a businessman in life. The creature wore a white button-down shirt and a blue paisley tie that were both stained dark red, evidence from its previous grizzly meals. The second "Z" was a female, perhaps in her mid-20s. A long blonde ponytail hung straight back from her head and above her purple jogging outfit. She might've been almost pretty, were it not for the missing ear and cheek that had been taken by a random "Z" as lunch at some point in the not-so-distant past. The woman could not have been much more than a week or two beyond the Reaper stage of "Z" evolution.

The male "Z", although larger by far, was the more ponderous of the two. Spartan opted to eliminate the female first. The "Z" had obviously not been dead too long, a month at the most. With the exception of the missing quarter of its face, the creature had not yet begun to decay while exposed to the various elements; lavender eye shadow even still clung above the milky red eyes.

Swinging the hawk billed pommel of his heavy steel sword backhanded, Spartan drove the blunt steel into the woman's temple repeatedly. Two, three, four times hammering the woman's temple with ancient steel. The multiple impacts cratered the "Zs" skull, buckling her legs beneath her body and driving bone fragments into the rotten gray matter. The undead was reduced to a quivering pile of dead flesh, effectively inanimate except for the involuntary muscular twitches that spasmed across the creature's body.

As he viciously stomped the female "Z" into the ground, a clawed hand closed across his shoulder armor from behind. Dropping down and to the side, he torqued his armored body away from the slower moving Romero. Taking his sword in both hands, he prepared to lop off the undead's head, ending its unnatural existence. An explosion of flesh, bone and rotten eye fluid leapt outward from the "Zs" face as a 7.62 caliber round disintegrated bone and tissue from the rear forward. The body pitched ten feet to the side of Spartan; driven by the Dragonov's vicious round.

"Perfect timing Dance." Spartan said as he ran forward to the front of the church.

"Save that Spartan. You've got fifty "Zs" less than a hundred meters out and another several thousand or more a quarter mile beyond that. You might want to move your arse mate." The sniper replied.

"Copy. Moving."

As Spartan rounded the corner of the building, the interior doors of the church opened and he could see Deadeye approaching, accompanied by a wall of a woman carrying a baby. Garbed in the traditional black and white habit of the nun, the woman carried the swaddled baby safely tucked between a gigantic fleshy arm and her holy bosom. In the nun's other hand dangled what appeared to be a three-foot-long metal crucifix. The lateral edges of the metallic cross had been ground or hammered flat and sharpened, effectively creating a crude yet efficient battle axe for the nun. The edges bore the slick red – black sheen of rotten "Z" blood upon them. This holy woman had come to set her children free and was not afraid of the risen dead at all.

Pulling the Scout's razor bow off of his shoulder, Spartan quickly handed it to Deadeye and verbally checked their physical status. "Is everyone okay?"

"We had a minor issue with the church's organ player. It was resolved by Sister Margaret, but we will be needing a new…"

Deadeye's quip was cut short as an orange bearded "Z" dressed in the sacramental robes of a priest burst from the shadows within the church and wrapped the Scout in its arms from behind; its jaws open wide to try to bite through both armor and flesh. Reacting immediately, Deadeye drove his body backward, smashing the "Z" between himself and the church's wall. Grasping both of the creature's wrists, the Native American fought a stalemate battle with the Reaper grappling him from behind. The angle of their bodies made it impossible for Spartan or Dancer to react, to prevent the Scout from being potentially infected.

Fortunately, they did not have to. In one smooth motion, Sister Margaret tossed the baby underhand to Spartan like an option quarterback, pivoted and brought her holy axe down upon the priest's skull, lodging the crucifix axe all the way into the "Zs" throat area. It crumbled to the ground in a pile of black and white robes. Putting one foot on the dead "Zs" chest, the nun pulled the crucifix free. Arcing the weapon upward, she brought it horizontally back down, this time severing her former boss's head.

"Child molesting prick!" Was all the Sister said, then she hocked up a wad of phlegm and spit upon the priest's corpse.

"I guess they will need an organist *and* a priest for Sunday services." Deadeye said completely deadpan.

The only response was the nun's grunt as she lifted the axe and brought it down a third... fourth... fifth time releasing years of pent-up rage for the pedophile priest. Each time the axe made a suctioning sound as the weapon came free of the "Z" priest's chest cavity. "I hope you burn in hell, you bastard!" She screamed.

"We have to go... now!" Spartan said, handing the wrapped child back to the blood splattered nun. Not taking time to question the basis for the holy woman's rage or the cleanliness of her religious garb while she held the child, Spartan nodded once and then began scanning the immediate area ahead of them for incoming threats. Turning, he and Deadeye began to trot towards the rendezvous point at the golden arches where he knew his gigantic friend and the gaggle of children would be waiting. Behind him, the nun huffed like an old railway engine. She did not complain to her credit, nor ask him to slow down. She merely trudged forward, red-faced but determined. From far above, Dancer repeatedly picked off any "Zs" that got too close to the team as they moved.

*"If she survives this run, without having a heart attack or a stroke, she will be one helluva an asset to the Academy!"* Spartan thought of the nun. *"That's one tough ol' bird!"*

And through it all, the baby slept, oblivious to the bloody chaos and gunfire in the undead world around it; content in the nun's warm and loving embrace as the team ran for home.

# Chapter Sixteen
# Hogg's Choice

The deep bass and throaty roar of a multitude of motorcycle engines awoke Hogg from his fatigue induced sleep. Years of combat training had taught him how to become instantly alert when sleeping in the field and despite his physical exhaustion, this was no exception.

Grabbing the M-4 assault rifle from where it rested against the wall, the burly sergeant crept over to the front plate window and peered outside between the boards that covered it. Leather clad Lords of Death sat astride hundreds of motorcycles or milled throughout the parking lot of the drive-in theater. The variety of skulls emblazoned on their vests and jackets identified who they were with certainty as much as the emblems and patches that adorned much of their clothing and human skulls that had been painted red and rode upon their steel horses.

Throughout the throng of bikers, Hogg could clearly see many familiar faces. Several of them were former military personnel who had chosen to follow the Red Baron when he left the Apocalypse Academy to pursue his own agendas. There was Herc; the biker Sergeant at Arms who stood flexing his bulging biceps for a group of females who gawked and goggled at his physique. There was Xander, the alchemist. He was the Red Baron's chief procurer when it came to illegal booze, weapons of mass destruction and narcotics. Rumor had it that when his wife refused to join with the Lords of Death at the same time he did, he put her to sleep with a permanent dose of sleeping pills mixed into her martini. There was Hook; a long-haired Gulf War veteran that had lost his left hand attempting to defuse a roadside improvised explosive device, then had been turned away at the Veterans Administration for compensation before "Z" night.

Magik was the only female that Hogg knew of to be named within the group other than being tagged as *"my old lady, woman or my bitch"*. Rumor had it that Magik was a former New Orleans stripper who had also served as her Lord's personal concubine and voodoo priestess. It was said that she preferred to seduce her victims and then free them from the burden of life during the highest moment of ecstasy by slashing their throats and riding them while they bled out beneath her. She was truly a sadistic bitch.

Lastly, Hogg recognized the black and silver spiked hockey mask covered face of the bodyguard known only as Rampage. He was a pure killing machine that allegedly could feel no physical pain due to a genetic disorder that numbed the nerve endings of his body. Worse was the knowledge that the man was a mute. Not because of the genetic deformity, but because he had cut his own tongue out just to see if it would hurt. The man had a machete hung from his side and a cruel looking medieval battle axe that showed over the top of the shoulder. When a killing was needed or when the Baron was threatened, it was Rampage that defended his master. Tales told of the bodyguard not only dismembering his victims to please the Baron but feasting upon their hearts to gain the warrior spirit contained within. Hogg thought this made the man a certified A–1 nut job. Crazy and savage made for a deadly combination. Of all the bikers, he was perhaps the most physically dangerous. At six foot eight inches tall, he was a towering mass of death and destruction.

The massive, masked man stood protectively behind the red leather clad figure of the person that could only be the Red Baron. Hogg would've recognized his old partner anywhere. Not only from his clothing, but from the black eye patch that covered the eye that Hogg had personally removed in their last encounter. His forearm muscles ached to pull the trigger and put a 5.56 round through the man's forehead, but considering the odds he wouldn't live long enough to enjoy it.

So instead, Hogg knew that he couldn't let the ZAP armor fall into Biker's hands. So he did the only reasonable thing he could think to do given the circumstance. He walked over to the floor in front of the concession stand and carefully looked at the boards there. Finding several loose ones, he gently pried upward with his combat knife, minimizing the noise that he made. Once he had enough room with the boards pulled out from the floor, Hogg took off his ZAP armor carefully, gathered up his M-4 and slid them into the hidden space. Carefully, he pressed the boards back into place ensuring that it couldn't be found by the casual observer. As a last-minute thought, the sergeant took a box of chocolate candies and scuffed them into the floor. Then re-buckling his gun belt around his waist, he lit a cigar and walked straight out of the concession stand door. Smoking cigar in one hand, combat knife in the other, Hogg exhaled a plume of smoke and called out to his former partner in the most bluster filled voice that he could muster. "Hiya Red. It's been too long. What you say we finish this dance once and for all?" He asked in his deep baritone voice.

The Baron's response was short but poignant. "Ahhh, the infamous Sergeant Hogg, my old nemesis. How wonderful of you to join our little gathering. I trust that you have not come to beg forgiveness or to petition to become one of my Lords of Death."

Seeing the sergeant place his lit cigar firmly between his teeth and his body shift to a combat stance, the Baron had his answer.

"Hurt him badly, but do not kill him. I intend to do so slowly." So, the party began amidst a flurry of slashing knives, hammering rifle butts and pummeling fists. Hogg's last thought as a particularly vicious blow struck him in the temple was that he could not remember the last time that he had had this much fun. Then the world went black.

# CHAPTER SEVENTEEN
## ONE SHALL FALL

Dancer watched through her scope as Spartan, Deadeye and the nun moved at a full run towards the designated meeting place. Shifting her body slightly, she scanned the roadway back into the center of town. Logic had indeed set in, categorizing the threats for the young lady as she sat high upon the water tower. Bikers were the highest priority (and coincidentally her personal favorite target.) Zipping by on the motorcycles, the Lords of Death could easily catch up to the rest of the team. Any shot she had at one of them she took. So far she had killed three and another took a wounding hit to the thigh before losing control and crashing his motorcycle through the plate glass window of a furniture store. She had seen no further movement from within the building and given that the sniper rifle fired 7.62-millimeter rounds there was a very real possibility that he had fully lost the leg or bled out. The rest of the bikers seemed to have fallen back as she had not seen one for several minutes.

Her second choice was the Reapers. Although they were unable to catch one of the team in the powered ZAP armor, they were more than capable of moving quickly enough to catch a fat nun. Worse, the Reapers seemed to be able to form a crude pack mentality and displayed the disconcerting ability to surround their prey and then an attack en masse. Several of the living that had been towed behind the Lords of Death on their motorcycles had been torn loose of the tethering ropes and literally ripped to shreds by packs of these creatures.

Seeing one such undead run hunched across the crosshairs of her scope, loping almost like an ape, she slowly centered the red dot on the side of its skull. Controlling her exhale, she pulled the trigger. The recoil of the weapon and the subsequent vaporization of the creatures head from the neck up verified that she had again done her job.

Currently she was tracking no less than seven packs of Reapers as the horde surged forward through the town. As an interesting scientific point each pack seemed to be made up of ten or less Reapers. There were no large packs at all, whereas Romero's could gather literally in the hundreds. In addition, there seem to be one "Alpha" male in each pack that guided the groups' hunt and travel. The truly interesting part was if the Alpha was killed, as she had done several times, the next "Z" in line stepped up to lead the pack. No vote, no infighting and no debate. The next "Z", male or female to reach the fallen leader's position of permanent death became the boss. It was actually quite efficient. Dancer mentally made a few observations and verbally outlined them into the ZAP's helmet log. It would be a very interesting conversation with Nurse Ortega and the Drill Sergeants whenever she returned to the Apocalypse Academy.

"Or when they recover my bloody armor after I've fallen to my death and been eaten." She said aloud to no one in particular. She took a moment to gaze downward at the "Z's" that were gathering below her. There were literally dozens now looking up at her hungrily. Sighing, she did the only thing that she could do, she returned to protecting her team from afar.

Of least importance were the Romero's and the Husks. The Romero's, while they could be dangerous if they surrounded you, were generally slow and stupid. One-on-

one they were pretty much cannon fodder; either easily outran or neutralized with a quick strike. Husks were so desiccated that they barely moved at all. As long as you didn't run into them or hit them with a vehicle and rupture their skin, they were of minimal operational impact. She believed that the fast-moving fire would wipe most of the Husks from the field long before they became of any importance to the team.

Dancer let her line-of-sight drift slowly, scanning the roadways between the Phalanx and the rendezvous point. An occasional Romero could be seen wandering aimlessly in search of prey on one of the side streets, but no Lords of Death and no Reapers were observed nearby. Her helmet communicator beeped with the announcement of an incoming message. Seeing it was Spartan on the person-to-person line, she quickly answered.

*"Dance, are you still there?"*

*"Bloody right I'm still here mate. All of the dance clubs were closed for a holiday. I suppose it saved me a few quid. Are you still planning on stopping by for a visit and a pint?"*

*"You're damn right I am. We're at the rally point now. Freak and I are getting ready to depart. Deadeye and Sister Margaret are taking the children and moving out to our secondary rally point. Freak and I will be coming to chat. Have you heard anything else from Techno?"*

*"Nothing. The communications channels have been quiet. He is either laying low or pretty badly hurt. Normally he can't shut up."*

*"Agreed. What's your status up there for fire observation and "Zs" down below?"*

*"Well… The fire has moved at least a half a kilometer in towards the center of town. Another half an hour and I will be able to bake a pie up here. The ambient air temperature according to the AI in my ZAP armor is currently around ninety-six degrees. Winds are gusting at 5 to 10 miles per hour so the fire is being fanned pretty well. As for my guests down below, I must be quite popular. I now truly know how a cat treed by a pack of dogs must feel. There must be better than fifty of the buggers down there now. All Romero as far as I can see but so far none of them have figured out how to climb the ladder."* She responded.

*"Are you secure enough for us to retrieve Techno first or do we need to get you out ASAP?"* Spartan asked.

*"Yes…"* She hesitated before answering. *"To be honest, there is very little that you can do here. The reality is that I may very well not be leaving at all. Be safe love. Find Tech and get him out of here. I wish we had had more time together."* She clicked off the helmet communicator before Spartan could scream his response over the open airways. Readjusting her elbows upon the mesh grating beneath her, she tracked the scope back to the north. After clicking off a quick shot that obliterated a Reaper's upper torso, she shifted her point of focus to search the debris for Techno. If she could at least find him and lead the team to him then her sacrifice would be worth it in her eyes.

A quarter mile away, Techno wavered in and out of consciousness. The few moments that he had been awake, he sincerely wished to be back in the quasi – mystical world of dreams. Dreams that had now been displaced by wakeful agony. Consciousness equaled reality. Reality equaled physical pain beyond his ability to comprehend or control. The immense levels of pain dropped him screaming back into the unconscious world of dreams. It was a vicious cycle.

In a moment of clarity, Techno thought that he had heard a band of "Z's" nearing his location. Buried as he was beneath the rubble and debris, he doubted they would see him; however, prudence said that he should remain still to prevent himself from being noticed. On a separate level he found himself thinking that the ZAP armor needed several upgrades including impact resistance, internal medical systems for injecting various medicines such as painkillers or antibiotics and voice activation for control of the same systems. This last thought came as he crossed the threshold of the doorway back into the world of unconsciousness without being able to reactivate his communication system.

Then, in a cascading sparkle of color that rained down before his field of vision (which was actually his neurons acknowledging the pain receptors in his nerves), he walked back into the mythical world of unicorns, elves and dragons that enjoyed eating ice cream on the ocean shore and he knew no more.

# Chapter Eighteen
## On the move

Spartan and Freak ran as fast as their ZAP armor would carry them back towards the smoldering wreckage that had been Techno's designated target for distraction purposes. The handoff of the children had gone smoothly with Deadeye and Sister Margaret combining to form an efficient yet odd team, hurriedly herding the children south out of town. No radio reports from Deadeye or Dancer announced any imminent issues so now it was merely a matter of reassembling the Phalanx before the thousands of "Zs" flooded the city.

Due to wearing the enhanced armor, Spartan and Freak were pretty well able to avoid confrontation with the wandering undead as long as they kept moving. The occasional swish of Spartan's sword and the thud of Freak's twin bats communicated the end of several "Zs" tortured existences without a word ever being uttered between the two warriors. So smoothly did they play off each other's attack and defensive prowess that they seemed to be coordinated or scripted; like a complex dance.

The ping from Techno's emergency beacon was strong and getting stronger. Rounding the corner of the street nearest a hardware store at a run, Spartan and Freak pulled up short as they viewed the debris field for the first time. They knew that the explosion had been large. They were not expecting the complete carnage that they were looking at now.

The explosion had mangled mortar and brick, as well as sinew and bone. Chunks of debris had shredded the fragile bodies of the undead, tearing them into fleshy chunks of tissue ranging from the size of a dime up to the size of a baseball. The resulting red rain painted the storefronts and exposed interior walls crimson with the rotted black-red blood of an unknown number of "Z's". Torn electrical wiring hung downward from holes that had been rent into the various building's infrastructures. For anyone with a reasonable imagination, the town of Freeport could have been compared to a human being's body; personified by bones built from buildings and nerves of conductive electricity. A body that had suffered a shotgun blast to the chest and now lay in its own blood, as the flesh burnt around it.

Ignoring the destruction, both members of the Phalanx focused on trying to locate their missing partner. From within both of their helmets, Techno's emergency beacon pinged rapidly and continuously. So frequent was the blip that it almost seemed as though they must be standing on top of their teammate.

*"Do you see any sign of him Freak?"* Spartan asked.

*"Dude, there's so much rubble and shit 'round here he could be about anywhere. He's going to be harder to find than a crow on a starless night like my grandpa used to say. That's just if he's laying somewhere in plain view. If he's buried in all of this rubble; we may not be able to find him at all."*

Spartan knew Freak was right. The force of the blast had thrown debris in all directions, building a circle of rubble five foot deep and collapsing many structures entirely. This coupled with the dozens of body parts that had been violently removed from their owners by the force of the blast, added to the macabre setting around them. They didn't even know if Techno was still alive.

A crow winged downward, settling onto the street as it selected a "Z" eyeball from a fallen Romero for its afternoon meal. Gobbling up the still juicy delicacy, the bird cawed its annoyance at the two team members of the Phalanx. Receiving no response, the bird moved to obtain the other eye. With the spear of its beak, it pecked out the former undead's last remaining orb and with a rush of black wings, flapped rapidly to a higher vantage point upon a roof of an unrecognizable store. There it ate its meal in solitude.

Spartan followed its flight, fighting an urge to shoot the ghoulish bird out of the sky. The noise would only attract too many "Zs" anyway. Turning back to the rubble, he keyed his helmet's communication system. *"Techno, we're here. You have to give me a sign so that we can get you out of here. C'mon buddy, talk to me."*

Only a static hiss met Spartan's inquiry. No other response was forthcoming.

*"Damn man, you don't think he..."*

"Shhhh!" Spartan said stopping the big cadet's questioning in midsentence. *"Listen!"*

*Tink, tink, tink.*

There it was again. Metal on metal. The team leader strained his hearing, mentally filtering out any noise that his communication system did not screen out for him automatically.

*Tink, tink, tink.*

Again, the faint sound of three sharp taps of metal on metal. They were weak but they were definitely intentional. Spartan scanned the area, switching from thermal imaging to grayscale to full color. He compared rubble, looking for metal in all of the cement. He saw a stop sign lying in the debris, its metal support pole twisted and snapped off in the wreckage of a doughnut shop. Without a word, he grabbed the sign and threw it off to one side, careless of where it landed or the noise it created.

Under the sign lay a single black gloved hand clutching a stun baton. It was Techno's hand. He was buried entirely beneath a ton of rubble and piles and piles of candy bars.

Grasping the hand gently, Spartan spoke into the microphone, his mouth dry.

*"Hang in their Tech. We're here. Freak and I will have you out soon. Just hold on."*

A faint moan, almost reminiscent of the mournful groan of the walking dead, was the only reply the team leader received.

Freak and Spartan began flinging rubble aside, sacrificing stealth for speed. Thousands of pounds of concrete and mortar as well as several dozen stale donuts had fully buried their teammate in the blast. White and red sticky filling coated the boy's crushed ZAP armor, making whatever wounds there were beneath it seem almost cartoonish in appearance. From the cant of Techno's lower torso, it was pretty clear to Spartan that the boy had suffered a serious back injury. Possibly even broken it.

*"Dude, how the fuck are we supposed to move him like this? He's all fucked up."* Freak said. *"I saw somebody that looked like this after a car wreck back before "Z" night. He died. Then one of the corner boys stole his sneakers before five-oh could get there."*

A long, soul-torn moan came from behind the duo. They're less than silent digging out of their teammate had drawn the attention of a dozen "Zs". Fortunately, no Reapers were in sight. Only Romero's.

*"We've got to immobilize him."* Spartan said. *"And we've got a window of about two minutes before we have undead guests for dinner."*

Looking around, Spartan ran over to the stop sign that he had so carelessly tossed aside. It would serve as an interim backboard until they could find something better. Reaching down, he grabbed hold of the signpost just below the bolts that held it to the sign. Twisting sharply, he snapped the bolts off using the power of his ZAP armor. Running back to Freak, they carefully slid the sign under Techno's spine. Freak then used the enhanced musculature of his ZAP armor to bend the sides of the sign upward, creating a metal cradle for their injured teammate. They then worked quickly together, winding parachute cord from their packs around the boy's torso, securing him firmly to the sign.

Looking up, Spartan saw that the "Zs" were only thirty feet away and closing steadily. There was no time for stealth. The creatures had already begun to emit the telltale low moan that attracted so many other of their kind. Unslinging his M-4 and leveling it at the creature's heads, Spartan began to spit 5.56 ammunition into the undead. From such a short range, the rounds ripped through multiple bodies, tearing away heads, arms and faces. In seconds all twelve undead were down and neutralized. Slapping in a fresh magazine Spartan called Freak.

"We gotta go. There will be more of those things here any second. You get Tech. I've got your back." He hollered.

"Negative. I've got Tech. You get out of here and go get Dancer. Don't worry. They can't catch me, even carrying the fortune cookie here."

"If you run into a Reaper, you could be in real trouble carrying him Bro."

"Yeah, it would be just my luck wouldn't it, if it was my ex-girlfriend that I ran into out there. She always was a

261

clingy bitch. Go get our girl. Don't worry, I got this. I'll meet you either at Sleepy Hollow or the park where we danced with the bikers."

Spartan was torn. Leaving his partner without a six man went against everything they had been taught at the Academy. You didn't abandon a partner. Still, Freak could handle himself. He couldn't leave Dancer to die without at least trying to rescue her. Looking up to Freak, Spartan nodded once, then turned and raced for the water tower. "Watch your ass brother!"

"You too bro." Freak called back as he lifted Techno gently in his massive arms.

Spartan silently prayed as he ran to whatever God that was listening, that he would be in time. That he would be able to save his teammates. And that he would be reunited with the Phalanx ahead of the "Z" horde at the park. It was a lot to hope for.

# CHAPTER NINETEEN
# DANCER'S DILEMMA

The heat from the flames was almost searing as Dancer continued to lay in her shooting position high on the water tower. The fire had burned into the neighborhood directly adjacent to her location, the flames shooting 30 to 40 feet high in some places as rooftops erupted like ancient volcanoes. Occasionally, there was the *whump* of a long-forgotten vehicle's gas tank or an old butane tank attached to a rusty barbecue grill as they erupted from the pent-up fuel that ignited within them but otherwise the scene was silent beyond the crackle of flame.

Looking downward quickly, Dancer could see the "Z" mob still staring upward at her location, oblivious to the approaching fire. They had the patience of Job. The undead reminded her of the analogy she should have used earlier when talking to Spartan; about the pack of dogs, she had once seen that had treed a cat. The pack had wandered aimlessly around the tree until the cat eventually had become so desperate that it had to make a break for its freedom. The pack had then torn it into pieces as it leapt from the tree. At the time she considered it the natural course of the world; survival of the fittest and all that. Now she discovered that she had a newfound empathy for the cat. It seriously sucked to have no options. Worse yet, she sat next to fifty thousand gallons of water and was still at risk of being burned alive by a fire the size of the city.

Her radio crackled to life on her personal frequency. *"Dancer this is Spartan, do you copy?"*

*"Go ahead Spartan. I copy."* She replied.

*"We've got Techno, but he's in bad shape. Freak's carrying him to the rendezvous point at this time. I'm on my way to get you."*

That was cryptic. Either the boy was seriously wounded or maybe infected or even both. Anyway, now wasn't the time for answers. Dancer paused before keying the communication system, once again looking at the pack of undead, and then over her shoulder at the raging inferno behind her. Short of an Abrams tank or maybe a helicopter she wasn't getting off the water tower.

*"Spartan... Break off. Do not... I repeat... Do not come for me. I'm surrounded by dozens of "Zs" below and the fire is less than twenty meters away from my current location. I have maybe ten minutes left before the entire tower is engulfed in flame. If I'm lucky my armor will hold out long enough for the wanker's below to burn, then I will make a run for it. Coming here will only sacrifice yourself. over."*

*"Dance... Set up a repel line to fast rope on my signal. That's an order."*

*"Spartan... Please don't..."*

*"Save it Dancer. I'm already here."*

Dancer scrambled to the edge of the tower's railing and looked down into the shadowed buildings below. There she saw her team leader striding confidently out from between two of the largest buildings. His black armor reflected the flames making the armored warrior appear almost demonic in nature as he strode forward, the Sword of Leonidas drawn, and his pistol in his offhand. Time slowed down as the Phalanx team leader confidently strode into the pack of undead. With a roar of battle fury and sword strikes along with a series of pistol shots, the battle was joined.

# Chapter Twenty
## Running with Children

Meeting back up at the outskirts of the burning town, Freak and Deadeye partner-carried their broken teammate on the stop sign as the burly Sister Margaret shepherded the children forward, urging them to be quiet, bribing them with peppermints that mystically seem to appear out of the voluminous pockets of her robes. Every jolt and jostle elicited an unconscious moan from Techno but speed was more important to the success of their mission than was Techno's comfort. Fortunately, the ZAP armor's protective helmet muffled the sound to an almost inaudible level except to the other members of the Phalanx who clearly heard every little hitch of breath over the communication system.

Sister Margaret continued to huff and chuff like a steam engine, clearly exhausted and red-faced, carrying the infant without complaint in one arm and her priest slaying crucifix/axe in the other. The infant, for its part, could not have been better behaved. Other than the occasional soft cry when her diaper was dirty or when she was hungry, the child cooed and gurgled merrily as the rotund nun bounced along, hence earning her the nickname "Giggles" or "GIGI" for short. The nun was regularly assisted by the proper little nine-year-old girl that the team had met in the church. They had nicknamed her "Sandy" because of her blonde hair and freckles, and the girl was a whirlwind of help. Feeding the baby, chasing stray children and just making sure quiet was maintained. Freak silently vowed to give the child a large bar of chocolate, if they survived this run back to the Apocalypse Academy. The girl was a product of the times and definitely wise beyond her years.

Deadeye led the group into the state forest, guided by his Native American sense of direction. Fortunately, only a couple of Romero's had been seen thus far and they had been easily dispatched by Deadeye with a single, silent arrow to the skull while Freak took over holding Techno's prone form for a moment. As night began to fall, Deadeye gauged that they still had more than twelve miles of travel to reach the pre-designated rendezvous inside the park. They would greatly increase the risk of losing a child if they continued to march forward into the dark. They needed to camp. Searching as he walked, he talked to Freak on the private communications line, helmet to helmet.

*"We've gotta get these kids into shelter for the night."*

*"Copy that, but I'm not seeing a Holiday Inn nowhere Dawg. Got a plan?"*

*"There's a large rock outcropping up ahead on the left. Decent cover if we can get to it and then we can provide overwatch for the children and the nun from above during the night."*

*"What about chow? These kids are starving. I don't think the two MREs that we have in our packs are gonna do it. Can you forage for berries or a deer or something? Use your wilderness skills to find us some food?"*

*"I've got it covered. I have been using my Apache inheritance to scavenge as we move. You just get Techno under those overhanging rocks. I'll do the rest for the children."*

Freak agreed. Taking a firm hold of the stop sign with both hands, he carried his injured teammate alone as Deadeye ran ahead to scout the campsite for the children and the nun. By the time Freak and the nun arrived with the children, Deadeye had tomahawked a dozen pine boughs and had leaned them across the opening of the rocks creating a lean-to with his poncho which provided light dispersal and wind blockage beneath it. A small campfire burned within the cave providing both warmth and heating for what appeared to be several cans containing a red liquid. On the ground lay two loaves of squashed bread and a jar of peanut butter.

Freak laid Techno softly under the overhang, and then spread out his own poncho for the children to sit on. Looking at the food, he keyed his helmet microphone on the channel directly to Deadeye. *"Dude, where'd all the shit come from? You gotta spirit guide that provides food now?"*

*"The land provides for its warriors if you know where to hunt."*

*"Uh-huh... Seriously dude?"* The gigantic warrior asked.

*"Okay, okay. I really got it at the church pantry. I figured the kids would need the food. I shoved all of that into my pack after I aced the secretary."*

*"Oh. That was smart. And the cans are?..."* Freak asked inquiringly.

270

*"A true staple food of camping. They are an invaluable part of Americana and a childhood favorite sure to bring happy dreams to all these young children when they have full bellies."*

*"Which is?"*

*"Chef Boyardee Ravioli's!"* The Apache said with a laugh.

*"You are one really smart freakin' injun."* Freak said and really meant it. Ravioli's just happened to be the one food in the world that his grandmamma had given him whenever he was down or upset. Some people had chocolate; others had ice cream. He had meat and cheese filled pasta covered with thick red spaghetti sauce.

A low agony filled groan behind him meant that Techno was stirring.

*"I'd better check on our wounded warrior. I'm sure he's probably getting hungry too."* The big warrior turned and started to walk over to their injured partner, then stopped and turned back around. *"You think he got her out? I mean, if anyone could be a hero, it would be Spartan, right?"*

271

Deadeye nodded, idly brushing an unseen object from the top of his helmet where it sat next to him on the ground. *"I never thought I could feel sorry for the undead."* He said in a quiet voice. *"Spartan is a great leader. When full battle fury is upon him he is an unstoppable force. His sword moves as if it becomes a magical extension of his will. Each cut precise, each slash devastating. He will be a whirlwind of death. The undead won't stand a chance."*

*"My people had a name for this type of warrior. He was said to be possessed by the great predator spirit of the wolf and called a Nantan Lupan. These warriors were fierce and fearless beyond compare. Often the animal spirits control the fighting frenzy, giving the warrior greater endurance and animal senses. It is believed that this was also the beginning of the werewolf mythos in America. Well, that and the Skin Walkers which were kind of an evil antithesis to the Nantan Lupan."*

*"And did they always win? Throwing down against the undead with a bunch of animal powers sounds pretty bad assed to me."*

Idly the scout poked the fire with a broken branch. *"No."* The boy said softly. *"They usually died in a horrific*

*manner often at the end of some tragedy. Usually, they had suffered*
*more than fifty wounds before they succumbed to their injuries."*

Freak felt his jaw dangling open and silently closed it. Without another word, he turned and walked away.

"Let us hope that our brother in arms has better fortunes than my ancestors." Deadeye said softly to no one in particular as he continued to poke at the fire, casting embers into the night sky and watching as they floated away on the breeze before winking out into the darkness.

# Chapter Twenty-One

## Hogg-tied

*Forty or fifty against one.* It seemed almost unfair considering the overall odds. You would think in a world filled with the living dead, those remaining beings that were still capable of drawing breath would be interested in the older concepts of fair play, honor and personal integrity. Even most punk guided street gangs had a code or rule to guide behavior before "Z" day.

"I guess those sons of bitches don't follow a code." Hogg murmured through his thrice busted lip. He tried to can't his head to one side and look at his surroundings. Strained neck muscles ached imperiously as he lifted his head and looked up through swollen eyes. He was sitting inside of a small room that was completely empty except for a metal drain in the center of the floor. The pervasive scent of cleaning fluids filled his sense of smell. His best guess was that he was in a storage or janitorial closet of some kind. The door was solid, preventing any look at further surroundings and there were no windows in the room at all. A small seam of light came from beneath the door offering the only illumination in the room.

Seeing no electronic monitoring devices like a security camera, Hogg tried to flex his arms. Thick rope bit into his wrists and ankles simultaneously while the metal chair he was seated in wobbled in place. The pain of the rope burns paled next to the needle-sharp agony of circulation being forced into his dangling hands. The room overall was small enough that tipping the chair over in an attempt to break it would probably only result in getting wedged against a wall and more than likely causing himself more pain. He was just going to have to sit tight and see what was going to happen next.

As he mulled over his situation, a variety of emotions swept through his mind. Anguish over being unable to warn the phalanx of the "Z" horde approaching their position; happiness as he reminisced about the crunch of breaking bones when he fought the Lords of Death; frustration at being captured. The most intense emotion of all had been the anger of seeing the smile on his former partner's face as he stood before the fallen drill instructor.

"Don't worry" he had said with a wide wolf-like grin. "It will only hurt… a lot."

The red leather clad man had laughed maniacally as he walked away and the fists and rifle butts began to play a rhythm of pain upon the fallen soldier. The last thing Hogg had seen as he lost consciousness was his former partner, the Red Baron, pick up his still burning cigar and place it into his mouth. Drawing a full mouth full of the pungent smoke, he exhaled and casually tossed the burning tobacco at Hogg's feet. One of the punching monkeys had then subsequently stepped on it in his eagerness to get in another blow, crushing the cigar.

Nothing pissed Hogg off more than waste in the new world that was owned by the undead. Especially good cigars and whiskey. He sincerely hoped that when and if he got loose, he could remember which of the biker idiots had stepped on his cigar. He intended to punch out the man's teeth, one by one, solely based on the principle of the senseless waste of such a rare luxury.

Footsteps approached the outside of the closed door. From the multiple footfalls Hogg could hear, he was certain that there were at least three people; maybe more, coming to visit him.

The lock on the door clicked and bright light flooded the small closet. Blinking rapidly, Hogg fought to focus his vision. Standing before him was the Red Baron, resplendent in his crimson leather biker's outfit. He had added a riding crop that was neatly tucked under one arm and a monocle that fit into his right eye, galvanizing the Nazi image that he was trying to portray. Finally, he had cleanly shaven his head, causing his pate to gleam in the light. All that was missing were the SS bars on his collar and the image would have been complete.

Behind the Baron, his bodyguard Rampage stood like an immobile slab of beef. His black and silver studded hockey mask was secured over his face to conceal all but his dark eyes. The monstrous man's bare chest and shoulders rippled with muscle as he stood with his arms crossed. If it was possible for any man to exude hatred, it was this man. Not just of Hogg, but of life in general.

Next to Rampage stood Hook. Stringy black hair hung down to his shoulders and spilt across the top of his vest in a wave of greasy black locks. His sunken face spoke of emaciation, but whether it was from drug usage, disease or a lack of sustenance, Hogg did not know. Light reflected from the man's hook which gleamed as if it was polished continually.

"So, you are awake. That is good." The Baron said. "For a while I was not certain you would survive. My minions can be overzealous sometimes."

"Like you really give a rat's ass if I live or die, you piece of shit." Hogg snorted in derision and then immediately regretted it as the pain of his obviously broken nose sent bolts of lightning throughout his nasal cavity and involuntarily watered his eyes.

"On the contrary my old friend. I want to offer you a chance to join me. Your death would be the last thing that I want. We have too much history together, you and me. To exult in the command of the undead that remains in the world around us and those the last living elements of humanity that mankind so fears to lose. That's what I want for you. To have you once again at my side fighting against those who would oppose me. In fact, you may have any title you wish as long as you serve me."

"Hmmm, let me think about it a moment." Hogg paused as if deep in thought. "Ok, I'm done." Drawing back a mass of bloody mucus into the back of his throat, he calmly spit the red-black wad onto the Baron's shined leather boots. "Go fuck yourself!"

The mute giant, Rampage moved to pummel Hogg who could only close his one good eye and brace for the impact that he knew was coming. Instead, the masked biker was stopped in his tracks by a single raised hand from the Baron.

"Come, come my friend. There is no need for this pointless show of bravado. There is no one here for you to impress. It is senseless to defy the reality of the situation. We are old warriors you and me. We have stood shoulder to shoulder as comrades in arms in innumerable battles, across the face of this weary world. We have fought the living and the dead as we drank our way across all seven continents and survived to tell the tales. Surely you must see that I hold a superior tactical advantage over the limited forces of the Apocalypse Academy. There is no government anymore. There is no United States of America or Canada or China. England has fallen as has Australia, Africa and South America. The dead walk everywhere and each day another death strengthens their numbers. Another corpse rises to walk the earth, infecting the living in an endless cycle that can only end in the extinction of mankind. Let us reconcile our differences and conquer this land together."

Hogg burst out laughing; a sound that sounded almost like an animal's hack bursting from his parched throat and battered face.

The Baron ignored the outburst, continuing his speech to his enemy, once comrade.

"My army continues to grow. Every day new riders voluntarily join me, swearing allegiance to the Lords of Death and acknowledging me as their sovereign lord. We number more than ten thousand warriors strong. A force larger than any current military unit left in the world. How do I know this for certain you ask? I have driven onto the abandoned military bases of the past. I have walked into the skeletal nerve centers of places reserved for launching missiles and making war. They all stand empty. Pathetic memorabilia of an age past. Useless that is, unless you happen to hold a key or the launch codes. I happen to have both. The nuclear arsenal of a mega power resides in my hands. I could just obliterate the Academy altogether. I could turn the entire Rock River basin into a glowing patch of earth unable to sustain life for the next million years. I could play God."

The Red Baron got a faraway look in his eye, as if he was seeing an alternate reality available only to his mind.

"Instead, I have chosen to be benevolent, not unlike Jesus. I do not destroy. I nurture. I foster the living even into death and then I command the dead as they rise again. Disciples and enthusiasts flock to me and beg for my blessing as I lead them into the promised lands. Lands free of war. Lands under the watchful eye of a living God...my Lord's hands. This is why you must join me. It is in your best interests. Perhaps I shall even spare those remaining at the Apocalypse Academy from my wrath. There is no reason to be stubborn. Join me."

Hogg let his head loll downward, his breath raggedly stirring the hairs on his upper chest. Breathing deeply, the Special Forces soldier carefully formulated his response. His eyes burned with rage as the hatred for the self-proclaimed God of the Living and the Dead that stood before him. Anger boiled off of Hogg in palpable waves and malice shown in his eyes as he looked up slowly at the Red Baron.

"You want a reason you sick sack of egotistical monkey shit?" He said through clenched teeth, his voice barely above a primitive growl. The ropes binding his hands and feet to the chair creaked in protest as he flexed his brawny arms against the hemp. Blood began to trickle from his chaffed wrists as his rage carried him beyond the threshold of pain.

"I'll give you a fucking reason. In fact, I'll give you eighteen reasons. Do you know that number Baron? Eighteen? I will help you out in case your memory is faulty. Eighteen is the number of "Z" day survivors, military and civilian, that you personally murdered as you departed the Apocalypse Academy. Eighteen people that you gunned down and either killed outright or left wounded to die at the hands of the infected dead that entered the compound when you departed, leaving the gates wide open as you fired blindly into the crowd, fleeing the very people that were responsible for your survival. By the way, I bet you didn't know that one of the people that was bitten and infected was your own daughter Kitten?"

Hogg relished the look of shock that registered on his enemy's face. The narcissistic fool had obviously thought his daughter safely inside of the Academies' barracks when he staged his revolt.

"You lie!"

"Now why would I go and do something like that? The truth hurts a shitload more and I just love seein' a dirtbag like you suffer."

The Baron's eyebrows knitted together in consternation and anger. He had given his daughter explicit instructions to remain in her dorm room with the door barred until he came to get her. He had intended to gather her up en route to the gate with his followers as they fled the Academy, but the fight with Hogg had taken too long. He had been forced to leave her behind with the intent to return and free her with his new army. Had she panicked? Had she run crying from the barracks, blinded by her emotional pain and into the undead calling his name as he rode away? Had she suffered because of him?

"How...?" The Baron fought to keep the quiver from his voice, refusing to show weakness before Hook and Rampage.

"Ran right past all of us. Sprinted into the Z's like she was possessed by the devil his self; screaming for "*Daddy!*" the whole time. She fought like a wildcat too. Clawin' and punchin' and kickin' anything in her path as she tried to get to you. I imagine you couldn't hear her over the engines of the motorcycles. When you drove away without so much as lookin' back, she just stopped fightin'. By the time we got to her, she had been bitten several times. None really severe, but you and I both know it ain't gotta be. We knew she was infected for certain." Hogg said calmly, bracing for the emotional storm that he had seen come from his former partner hundreds of times.

"How long before she turned?" The Baron asked, his red gloved fist clenching and unclenching at his side. The muscles in the man's jaw danced as he ground his teeth silently together.

"Three days in the infirmary. On the fourth day, I knew it was close to the end so I took her outside and sat with her next to Lincoln's statue in the park. It's where she wanted to go. That's where it ended."

"Did you pacify her?" The Baron asked, turning his back to his former partner, rage boiling beneath the facial mask that he maintained before his disciples.

Hogg did not answer immediately. Instead, he studied the man standing before him, watching as the man's body language changed. Watching as the man's breathing became more rapid, shorter. Almost hyper-intensive. The man's forearm muscles danced beneath the red leather sleeves as the gloved hands opened and closed into fists. It was clear that the man was struggling to maintain the humanity of a parent that had lost a child. It was almost like watching the animalistic transformation of a man into a lycanthrope…half man, half primitive beast. After a long moment Hogg answered.

"No…I was going too. With God as my witness, I had the pacification spike up to the base of her skull as she took her last breath. It would have been quick; painless. All I had to do was give one quick shove and it would have been over. Kitten would have been at peace. I watched as she quietly faded from life, her eyes on the river."

"And…?!" The Baron half screamed.

"We were partners. Kitten was like a daughter to me too. I was at the park when she was rescued. I watched her grow up remember. I loved her too. The Colonel, he recognized you for the threat that you were. I knew your views on the dead. How they were the chosen of God and I told that to Slade. The meek that would inherit the earth was how I believe you characterized them. I knew that one day you would want her back. So, against my better judgment and without considerin' my personal feelings for her peace, I carried her body back to the Academy at the Commandant's order and locked her in an empty room. Only I have the key. She came back the next day. At least part of her did, but I believe her soul is gone. What's left is nothin' but a shell. To the best of my knowledge, that's where she still is to this day; sitting chained to a chair. Waiting for the time when "Daddy" will come for her. Waiting in her own personal Hell for "Daddy" to come home and rescue her. But that day will never come. You will never see her again you sadistic, sick sum' bitch…and do you know why? I'll tell ya. It's pretty straight forward. I'm gonna kill ya. I'm gonna kill ya for the eighteen people that you didn't give a shit about when you left us behind. I'm gonna kill you for Kitten."

The Baron spun around so fast that Hogg barely had time to clench his jaw closed before the man's red leather clad fist smashed into his nose and mouth. The impact knocked Hogg over backwards in the chair and ricocheted his skull off of the wall and the floor on the way down. Jagged purple lightning exploded behind the sergeant's eyes. Looking up from where he lay on his side, the Baron stood before him panting savagely. The man's silhouette outlined by the doorway glowed red, outlining his features in crimson. Enraged he looked like a demon straight from the depths of Hell.

"Oh, I am going *home* Hogg!" The Baron sneered; his face contorted with rage. "And I will have my daughter, even if it means tearing your pathetic Academy apart brick by brick to find her. But rest assured, you will not be there for the final battle. In fact...you will never leave this place."

The Baron spun on his heel, the rubber sole of his boots emitting a small squeak as he turned and issued instructions to Hook and Rampage.

"Take him to the front of the drive-in. Crucify him high upon the wall with a sign painted below him identifying him as an enemy of the Lords of Death. Do not kill him outright. I want him to die slowly. To die thinking of futility as my Kitten did."

Hogg snickered between his bloody lips, drawing the Baron's attention once more. He felt a sarcastic comment bubbling within him, even though he knew it would probably cause him more pain in the form of a fist in the mouth.

"So, is it too late to get you to fetch me a beer for ol' time's sake?" He called to the Baron, his smile stretched over his crimson and ivory teeth. "I don't think your flunkies are that bright to be able to read the labels properly and bring me back a good brand anyways. Bunch'a retards!"

He was right. The fist slammed into his jaw with a crash that clacked his teeth together and caused him to bite his tongue. Blood poured into his mouth from the injury.

"Guess not." He forced himself to say with a weak chuckle.

Then many more fists rained down upon him and he knew no more as darkness blanketed his vision and he slipped once again into battered unconsciousness.

# Chapter Twenty-two

## Long drop and a sudden stop

Spartan's first three swings with the Sword of Leonidas cast two "Z" heads in one direction and a third opposite of the first two as it met his backhanded slash. Rotten brain, blackened blood and diseased teeth littered the air as he savagely tore at the undead with the ancient weapon. Every slash contained enough force to cleave a side of beef in two, yet he did not pull back on the force he exerted. He needed the creatures to fall with a single blow. Time was an enemy and he was quickly losing ground fighting a face-to-face battle against the undead. For every single undead that he smashed, slashed or shot, two more rose in their place, clawing and tearing at his battle armor. Although the ZAP armor was tough, it was not indestructible. Reflections of flames licked at his faceplate, reminding him how very close the deadly fire was to him and Dancer. Snap kicking the closest "Z" in the kneecap, Spartan dodged to the side as the creatures' shattered leg inverted backwards, dumping it into the legs of its undead brethren and creating a small pocket of space for him to maneuver.

Using the fallen creature as a distraction, Spartan took three quick steps and vaulted onto the hood of an old Ford Ranger pickup truck. The truck's hood stood a full five feet above the ground and offered Spartan a tactical advantage against the undead horde that continually sought to surround him. A "Z" stretched itself far over the front of the truck's white hood, it's clawed hand grasping for Spartan's ankle. Swinging the weighted sword downward in a powerful slash parallel to his leg, he lopped the hand off at the wrist, leaving the appendage dangling from his armored boot. Shaking his leg briefly, Spartan kicked the claw away into the crowd.

A hail of bullets rained down from above as Dancer sniped the undead attacking her team leader to the utmost of her ability. It was a difficult shot as the girl had to hang her upper torso off of the side of the water tower, holding the rifles' full weight in her arms while simultaneously controlling her breathing and trigger pull. Still, the Alpha team sniper was performing spectacularly, as a half a dozen undead lay with splattered skulls from her shooting.

Wiping the gore on his faceplate into a bloody streak, Spartan paused long enough to key his helmet mike as he stepped out of reach from the nearest "Z" that clawed the air near him.

*"What does it look like Dance? Are we making a dent at all?"*

The girl's response was very professional even though her undertone bespoke of a deeper terror that she was not willing to give voice too.

*"The bloody fire is less than a stones' throw away. I can feel the heat from here, even through my armor. Closer to us we have about forty or so undead in our immediate AOR and another ten thousand of the rotten bastards will be crawling up our arses soon enough. I have not seen any more Lords of Death since I was picking them off earlier like sparrows on a wire. Still, I doubt they've left completely, probably just avoiding the fire. And yes…I still have to go to the Lou. All in all, everything seems quite peachy, like a day in the park…Arrrgh!!!*

A single shot echoed in the distance, slowed in its report and magnified by Dancer's scream as it reverberated throughout Spartan's helmet. Spinning in place, Spartan crouched upon the hood of the truck, minimizing his own body profile and frantically searched for the sniper. A single figure dressed in crimson biker leathers stood brazenly upon a building's rooftop three blocks away, staring down at where Spartan now stood. Raised over one shoulder, the man held what appeared to be a bolt action rifle. A tiny coiling river of smoke drifted from the weapons' upraised barrel.

Completely unmindful of the undead that were steadily encroaching upon his tenuous perch, Spartan transitioned the Sword of Leonidas to his left hand while simultaneously grasping the handgrip of his M-4 from where it hung upon a three-point sling at his side. Reflexively flipping the thumb selector to fully automatic, he began to strafe the weapon's barrel upward toward where the assassin stood upon the rooftop. Bullets ate into the concrete, pock marking the brick and mortar as the weapon's natural tendency to raise its barrel when fired on fully automatic walked rounds all around the man. A red and grey cloud of mortar dust billowed into the air, obscuring Spartan's view of the crimson clad man. Switching his helmet's optics to infrared only succeeded in further blinding him due to the nearness of the citywide fire and the waves of heat that it was emitting less than a block away.

Dropping the empty magazine from the weapon's seat, Spartan slammed home a fresh magazine and released the bolt making the weapon ready for further engagement. He desperately scanned the rooftops for the shooter. Had he hit him with his wild burst of fire? Spartan highly doubted it. The man was too confident in his actions to be taken down by a lucky wild round.

A clawed hand reached over the hood of the truck and pawed savagely at the edge of his combat boot, seeking a grip to pull Spartan down from his perch. In his haste to deal with the sniper, Spartan had almost forgotten that he was surrounded by dozens of the walking dead on the ground. His emotions were roiling through his head and his heart jack hammered in his chest. Fear, anger and concern for Dancer and himself all fought to drive his muscles into action. Seeing a second undead attempting to climb the trucks' brush guard to gain access to the hood, Spartan knew that he could not stand still any longer. The failure to act in any situation was most often a death sentence. Even a wrong choice was better than none at all. Kicking his booted foot free of the animated corpses' grasping hand, Spartan swung the Sword of Leonidas downward in an offhanded stroke that parted the undead's head in half just above the bridge of its decayed nose and continued onward to slice through the second grasping corpses' skull at a forty-five-degree angle. Before the second severed skull began to slide away with a wet suction sound, Spartan was moving. Jumping down from the big truck's hood, he evaded the outstretched hands of a half dozen Romeros and raced towards the water tower, keying his helmet's microphone to Dancer's personal frequency as he ran.

*"Dance, are you ok? Dance? Dancer, answer me goddamnit!"* He screamed into the microphone as he ran.

No response. Only dead air came across his helmets' speakers. Either his teammate was incapacitated or she was dead. There was no more time for planning. He had to get to the girl in the fastest means possible. He would have to take extreme measures or they would both be very dead, very soon. Casting a quick glance over his shoulder, he looked for the sniper in red. The man was nowhere to be seen. Thank God for small blessings he thought as he reached the closest tower leg. This action was desperate enough with a high probability of death all on its own without someone shooting at them to make it worse. It didn't matter. Either way he had to take extreme measures or he and Dancer would die from the undead or the approaching fire.

Dropping the M-4 loosely back onto its sling, he frantically dug into his belt pouch. Feeling the rectangles of clay in his palm, he quickly pulled them from his pouch, stripped off the covering of clear plastic and slapped two off white, sticky explosives onto the water tower's closest support leg. Using his offhand to slash at the approaching undead with his sword, keeping them at bay with a series of cuts that amputated fingers, hands and heads, Spartan drew out two digital detonators from his pouch and plunged one into each block of explosive. Jamming his thumb against the start buttons in rapid succession to initiate the thirty second countdown, he began to shove, hack and slash the undead out of his path as he ran back towards the pickup truck. Scaling the hood in a single leap, he ran to the top of the truck's cab and mentally began to count the timer down. At ten seconds he keyed his helmet's microphone and called to Dancer.

*"It's gonna get loud down here! Get ready to take a ride Dance! Hold on!"*

Five...

Four...

Three...

Two...

One...

Spartan dove into the bed of the pickup truck as the dual shaped charges exploded in twin horizontal bursts of flame, cutting through the water tower's leg like a hot knife through butter. He could only hope that Dancer's armor would protect her from the majority of the fall, absorbing most of the impact into the Kevlar padding.

Thirty-five thousand gallons of water encased in a rusted metal shell groaned as the remaining two legs of the water tower buckled inward and steadily collapsed under the increased weight bearing load. Steel and water, Kevlar and flesh fell like an apocalyptic waterfall upon the undead, crushing the Zs under the tons of liquid force propelled by mere gravity. Water flew in every direction as the impact split steel and jettisoned Dancer's armored body through the air; pin-wheeling loosely. There was nothing graceful about the flight nor the resulting impact with the hard ground fifty feet away. There were no movie special effects to show the nimble young woman arcing gracefully over the crushed bodies of the undead only to land gracefully upon a knee, looking around for the next creature to fight. Instead, this fall by his teammate left Spartan thinking of a wounded duck that he had shot while hunting with his father at the age of thirteen. Shot in the chest, the bird had weakly flapped it's wings a couple of times and then plummeted into the water's surface. Dancer's body flew outward, end over end, propelled by momentum as the water tower fell, then began to cartwheel through the air upon descent before ultimately smashing to a stop when mother gravity decided that she had flown quite far enough.

Spartan was on his feet and racing for his teammate before the vibration from the torn water tower and the slosh of the falling water had stopped. Heedless of the smashed and torn body parts that lay mangled upon the ground, Spartan ran straight for the girl that he loved. More than a dozen truncated Zs continued to move toward him; their clawed fingers pulling their bodies along.

Well ahead of the crawling horrors behind him, Spartan slid to a stop on his knees beside the girl and ripped the safeties off of his helmet, Pulling it off. His heart wrenched painfully as he observed the jagged bullet hole in the side of her helmets' protective plating and the slow but steady stream of blood that was trickling out of it to pool on the ground beneath. Carefully he released the helmet's securing latches and chin strap and removed it from Dancer's head. Gently he lifted her head and supported it on his thigh while he brushed away the bloody brown hair that clung to her face and then he inspected the wound to her skull. The helmet's protective Kevlar had absorbed the majority of the bullet's momentum. Despite being a clean shot, the bullet had penetrated only the protective covering before being deflected off target at an angle. The resulting wound had creased Dancers' scalp and knocked he unconscious. It was quite possible that she may even have a concussion. At least she was still breathing.

Glancing over his shoulder at the half dozen crawling Zs that were still advancing upon him and Dancer, he noted that they were still more than thirty feet away. Muttering a small thanks to whatever deity was listening, he grabbed a combat compression bandage from his harness, tore it open the plastic housing with his teeth, and applied pressure to the wound. The resulting groan of pain from

Dancer's lips reminded him of the approaching undead and he quickly wrapped the olive drab green gauze around her head to hold the bandage in place and tied it off onto itself. It was not a permanent solution to the problem but it would have to suffice until he could get them both to a more secure place. Then he called to her softly, gently tapping her cheek with his fingertips in an effort to rouse her back to consciousness.

"Dance? Dancer, can you hear me? It's Spartan."

Dancer's eyes weakly fluttered open, pain evident in her face as she looked up at her Team Leader.

"Crikey…" she said in a voice that barely could be heard over the moans of the approaching dead. Spartan looked hurriedly over his shoulder. The crawling corpses were only fifteen feet or so away now, dragging torn limbs, and shattered organs behind them. The smell of cordite, rotten flesh and shit filled the air making him wretch.

"Can you move?" He asked, grave concern clearly etched upon his face.

"...I think so..." Dancer groaned, her voice expressing the pain that she was feeling as her breath hissed between clenched teeth and her eyes started to roll up into her head.

Spartan shook her gently. He was worried that he would cause her more harm by shaking her, but he was far more afraid of the two of them becoming an undead buffet snack pack. She had to get up and move or they were dead, plain and simple. Any other concern had to be secondary.

"Dance...we gotta move. We are running out of time. I can help support your weight but we have to get you to your feet first. Can you move your arms and legs?"

A second or two passed as the prone girl gingerly flexed various body parts to determine their effective status. A deep cry of pain shot from her lips as she tried to move her left arm.

"Wrist ...broken. Damn that... hurts." She had broken her shin while playing football as a child back in England before the collapse of society. While she remembered that it hurt and she had cried for her daddy, she did not remember the mind-numbing pain that she had just felt when she had tried to flex her hand. The pain threatened to overwhelm her senses and cast her back into the darkness of unconsciousness.

Spartan thought about dropping the girl and going for the M-4 that still swung on its sling from his back. He knew that he was close to being out of ammunition. Even if he could get the weapon up and on target fast enough, there was no guarantee that he would have enough ammunition to eliminate the threat before they got to him and Dancer. They're only hope was to evacuate to a safer location and either meet up with the rest of the Phalanx or find another way back to the Apocalypse Academy.

"Dance...this is it. We don't go now then we are dead meat. We've gotta move! Get on your feet girl!" Spartan screamed, as the first crawling corpse clawed at his boot. The girl nodded slightly. Throwing the girl's non-injured arm over his shoulder, Spartan lurched to his feet just as the undead bit down on the steel toe of his combat boot. Lurching to the side, he drew the armored foot out of the creatures' rotten maw and kicked it forcefully in the temple. Rotten sinew and bone collapsed causing Spartan to lurch to the side to keep his balance; the movement causing

Dancer to cry out in agony. Planting his feet firmly beneath him, Spartan scooped up his helmet and began to half carry, half drag Dancer away from the wreckage of the collapsed water tower and the city that was burning behind it.

Looking back at the undead, Spartan could see their crawling forms, shadowed against the blazing fury of the city behind them: a parody of a scene from Hades. Many sported bright spots of yellow and red flames as the heat from the inferno began to ignite their clothing and hair. He wondered briefly if they would feel the pain as the fire consumed their limbless bodies. Then he realized that he really didn't care. Let them burn for eternity. The damned things had been the cause of Dancer's pain. Both them and the man in red. Somehow he planned to send them all to Hell as payback for her pain. These few were just the beginning of his list for balancing the score.

Turning back around, he helped steady the girl as she wobbled each step away from the city; away from the undead. Amazingly Dancer's Naginata had remained strapped to her back during the fall off of the water tower. More amazingly, it hadn't sliced her in half when she landed on the ground. The Dragunov sniper rifle however was nowhere to be found and they had no time to search for it. She would have to get another rifle later if they survived the trip home. Readjusting Dancer's arm over his shoulder, he let her put as much weight upon him as he could possibly carry. Then he began to half walk, half drag her away from the city, step by wobbling step, as the buildings burned to ash around them. The scores of flame ensconced undead could be heard screeching and ululating in anger behind them.

# Chapter Twenty-three
# Separating the team

The cans of Chef Boyardee ravioli turned out to be a truly lifesaving meal. Bellies full of warm, meat laden pasta, thick red tomato sauce and cheese; the children had fallen asleep almost immediately. The vigor of the previous days' run coupled with the horror of fleeing the orphanage containing the corpses of both the undead clergy and the remains of their fellow orphans had traumatized the children badly. When they had first sat beneath the improvised poncho tent, many had spontaneously burst into tears, crying for lost friends or perhaps for the loss of the only form of security that many of them had ever known. After eating the full meal that Deadeye had so wisely procured for them prior to the flight from the city, the children's sobs had quieted into rhythmical deep breathing and light snoring as they lay in a huddled pack upon the ground for warmth. The sight reminded Deadeye of how newborn wolf cubs massed together when the mother wolf was not present in the den, security provided by body warmth.

So deeply did the children sleep that not a single child awoke to the chuffing and soulless moaning that carried on the wind to where they were encamped. A strong pack of more than fifteen Romeros had wandered by on the road above them during the night. The sorrow filled moans of the living dead had torn through the crisp autumn night silencing the night birds and other small forest creatures instantly. Deadeye noted that the animals of the forest seemed to sense that something unnatural was amongst them and that they needed to be quiet to survive. The hungered and guttural moans of the undead called out endlessly, perhaps hoping innately to spook an animal from its hidey-hole for fresh meat to fill their soulless bellies to rend and tear with tooth and claw.

Had even one of the children awoken and screamed at the sight of the walking corpses on the road above them, the pack would have surely discovered the presence of easy prey beneath the stone ledge and poncho camouflaging. As valiant and skilled as both Freak and Deadeye were at close quarter's battle, fifteen to two were pretty steep odds; especially in the dark of the night and while attempting to protect a nun, multiple children and an infant as well as their own asses.

To her credit, the portly Sister Elizabeth showed no sign of fear at the approaching undead and had nestled the infant gently yet firmly against her ample breast; slowly rocking the child back and forth to ensure that it would not awaken as the walking dead passed the group by. Close to where she sat, her crucifix axe lay propped against the rock face of the wall within easy reach, if hiding became futile and battle between the living and the dead had to be joined. Deadeye and Freak had discussed the woman amongst themselves earlier in the day across the private communications channels within their ZAP helmets. They had found it extremely interesting to note that the holy woman, despite her religious commitments and dedication of her life to God, held absolutely no compunction against hacking up the dead that had risen to unlife in the most graphic manner possible when she needed to protect her little charges. Her ferocity had been clearly displayed in the execution of the undead priest although both of the boys had been of a like mind that there had been something deeper to her anger. There was almost a hatred of the once holy man that had become vividly evident as she had chopped him into pieces. Whatever he had done in life, death had brought vengeance in the form of a crucifix wielding nun who struck out for all the children that the priest had wronged. Deadeye thought that it proved that karma was a bitch. Freak had swiftly agreed with him.

Hearing the pack shuffle further downhill and stepping away from where the children had been secreted, Deadeye leaned over and whispered to Freak.

"I'm gonna take a look. You know, to make sure that those rotting pus bags keep moving away from us and the kids." He said, slipping his helmet back over his head and securing it in place. "I want to make certain that they do not accidentally ramble back this way and stumble across us. The kids will not sleep forever and we can't count on dumb luck to keep them moving in a straight line northward. One of the fuckers could start chasing a squirrel or a fox or something and get turned fully around, sending it right back into our laps. Besides…sooner or later one of the kids will need to pee or want a drink of water. I am gonna try and make sure that there are no "Zs" around when they do."

"You got a plan there Sitting Bull or are you just gonna wing it?" Freak asked with a tone of concern evident in his voice. Though he would never admit it to Deadeye or any of his teammates, being left with all the responsibility of so many children made him extremely nervous.

"Yeah" Deadeye said, the small microphone inside of his helmet detecting a faint chuckle as he laughed to himself. "I figure that the little party at the skating rink that we passed earlier could use some livening up. A special guest appearance…that type of thing. It looked like they would have enough firepower to put down these few "Zs" without too much trouble but it should also be loud and chaotic enough to draw any other Romeros or Reapers in the area to their location and away from us."

Freak nodded in understanding.

"Watch your ass Tatanka!" He said, as he slid his own headgear back into place. Dances with Wolves was one of his Gran's favorite movies. "And don't go getting into any cool ass fights without me. I can't have you one-upping me fo' braggin'rights when we get back to the Academy Dawg!"

Deadeye just slowly shook his head, understanding that Freak meant the name as an endearment. "Tatanka was a buffalo you moron. If either of us was to be characterized as a big furry cow it would be you. I am an entirely different animal." The scout said with a chuckle, but not identifying what his totem animal was. "If I am not back by dawn, then you get your big ass up and get moving with the kids. Put the morning sun on your left shoulder so that you do not get turned around until you get to the state park fencing. Go through the gate and keep following the creek until you get to Sleepy Hollow where we camped the other night by the bridge. That's where Spartan instructed us to meet up with him. I will try to meet you there. If I do not show by the end of that day or if Spartan doesn't show, then you need to consider us casualties and head back straight south to Dixon. Get the kids to the safety of the Academy and turn them over to Slade or Ortega or even Hogg for safekeeping. You're gonna have to be moving pretty fast because we are not just talking about a couple "Zs" chasing you down brother. We are talking about an entire hoard. Ok?"

"I got this Dawg. No worries."

They briefly clasped hands and individually wondered if they would see each other again or was this moment the final end of the Phalanx. Overhead a crow cawed into the trees, drawing their attention. Seeing it as an omen,

Deadeye let go of his friends' hand, picked up his razor bow and stalked silently into the forest.

# Chapter Twenty-four

# Too wounded to travel

The struggling silence of half carrying Dancer brought
Spartan to memories of distant play by play calls and
hollow echoes of sportscasters from his past. Flashes of
memories strobed across his mind as he recalled his father
and brother watching games on the television every
Saturday or Sunday afternoon on crisp autumn days.

Competitive by nature, the games became an extension of
the family psyche. Win at any cost. Never quit. Play the
game all the way to the end!

Just like then, he couldn't quit now. He was nearing
exhaustion. He had been half carrying, half dragging
Dancer's semi-conscious body for hours. His shoulder,
back and neck muscles burned fiercely with every step.
They had been fortunate to outdistance the Z's within
about thirty minutes after evacuating the burning town of
Freeport. The roaring fire and billowing smoke from the
fire engulfed city providing them both cover and

concealment as they moved southward. They had been fortunate not to encounter any undead or Lords of Death thus far. Spartan knew that their luck would only hold out so long. Sooner or later, someone or something would cross their path and force him to decide how to best protect himself and Dancer. All that he could do was continue to plant one foot in front of the other and try to race against the odds to get the girl safely back to the Academy.

Spartan stumbled, his armored boot catching on the asphalt of the roadway as he drug himself along. Fatigue was really starting to wear on him. Initially, he had opted to move with Dancer through the tan and brown cornfields that stood on either side of the roadway believing that they could use the stalks as camouflage if an undesirable, living or undead, had ventured by. An hour's worth of being constantly snagged by the desiccated cornstalks had changed that decision for him. Moving back to the road, he could only hope for the best. He was too tired for anything else at this point. Even with his advanced levels of physical fitness, a massive initial adrenaline boost and the power of the ZAP armor, he still felt bone weary. Although Dancer was a petite girl, with her armor on she still weighed more than two hundred pounds.

Pausing, he glanced up at the sky on the western horizon. Shades of pink, red and lavender streaked the sky like an artists' portrait. Open fields could be seen far out into the distance. An enormous black crow winged silently above the dead fields searching for a last morsel of food that it could snatch. Spartan empathized with the creature. He was starving himself.

Pausing and readjusting his grip on Dancer's hand and waist, Spartan glanced back the way that he had just come. The northern horizon was filled with a massive cloud of black and grey smoke. He wondered how many still living people had escaped from the inferno. How many men, women and children had survived the initial infestation of Z's only to be roasted alive within their barricaded homes? What type of horrible mental anguish had they felt knowing that they would die if they fled their homes to get away from the approaching fire only to find the ripping claws and chewing jaws of the undead, or they would literally be cooked alive if they stayed, praying for the arrival of a fire department that would never come. The thought carried with it a blackness of despair for humanity's future. Shaking

314

his head, Spartan turned back around to face the south. By his estimate, there was still more than twenty miles to travel before they reached the Apocalypse Academy. A few miles less than that to rendezvous with the rest of the Phalanx at the park. They would be there waiting for him until dawn and then they would move on assuming that he and Dancer had both been killed in action. He had to keep pressing forward. Somewhere behind them, the Lords of Death were marching an undead horde towards the Apocalypse Academy. He had to warn Colonel Slade and Sergeant Hogg as well as everyone else that they were in imminent danger of being overrun. Dancer moaned once as he stumbled just a bit and jostled her from side to side. He desperately needed to get her medical treatment as well. Again, a fierce gurgling noise emanated from his belly, this time accompanied by a cramp that threatened to tie his stomach into a knot. He needed to stop and rehydrate himself and Dancer, as well as take on a few calories to boost his energy levels. He would do neither of them any good if he passed out from exhaustion.

He looked around quickly for a secure place in which they could rest. Unfortunately, he saw none. Just as it had before, the horizon stood devoid of any buildings. That was one thing about living in the Midwestern portion of the United States, there was often vast distances owned by farmers that contained nothing more than corn or soybean fields. It was not unreasonable to go for ten or fifteen miles in some stretches and never see so much as a house. In the summertime, the deep greens of the planted crops and the repetitive row after row nature of the planting created a mesmerizing vision, drawing a persons' eyes continually between the rows of stalks and the deep brown lines of the earth between them. Coupled with the never-ending expanses of rising and lowering power lines and power poles, traveling along the roadways had an almost hypnotic nature to it as it produced a sense of calm and passiveness. Spartan remembered a blip of riding on the school buses to neighboring towns for a football game. Half the team had been asleep by the time they arrived to play the game. A chuckle broke through Spartan's gritted teeth. What a strange moment in time to recall a random, lost memory.

Seeing a small outcropping of rock and a medium sized pine tree with low hanging branches to the right of the roadway, Spartan quickly selected the spot as his waypoint and limped with Dancer off of the cracked pavement towards it. Gently he laid Dancer back against the stone, careful to elevate the girl's broken wrist across her chest. They had stopped briefly after fleeing the Z's and the fire, only long enough for him to fashion an impromptu sling out of one of the compress bandages to hold her arm safely across her chest. He was pretty sure that the break was severe. Not quite compound, but he had felt what he thought was bone sticking out of place when he had splinted her hand. She needed more expertise than he could offer her. Basic combat medical training was one thing, setting bones and treating skull fractures was quite another. He could only hope that Nurse Ortega could help her. If not, Dancer may not survive her injuries. Infections, especially the type of gangrene that set in from untreated broken bones could kill a person as surely as a horde of Z's. Spartan cast the dejected thought from his head. Defeatism would only lead to their deaths. He had to think clearly.

Taking a last glance around the impromptu perimeter of their pine tree, he carefully removed both of their helmets and sat them on the ground. He had replaced Dancers' helmet after they had fled Freeport just in case the red leather sniper had decided to take another pot shot at them. Fortunately, that had not happened. Then he unslung his

M-4 and propped it against the base of the pine tree, keeping it within easy reach. Looking down he noticed the blood encrusted hole in the side of the girl's helmet. Given the size of the wound and the post impact damage, she had been damn lucky. The marksman had definitely been an expert shot. His single bullet fired from a few hundred yards away had struck Dancer with precision, dropping her instantly. Spartan knew that he needed to find out who the man was for the safety of his entire team. Was he just a survivalist? One of the Lords of Death? A criminal? A military man? Special Forces? He just wasn't sure. Whoever he was, he had payback coming to him in spades when the Phalanx caught up to him for what he did to Dancer.

Dancer's head lolled forward against her chest, eliciting a groan of agony from the girl's unconscious lips. She had been drifting in and out of consciousness for hours and her inability to stay awake had Spartan worried. Gently he lifted her head and brushed her brown hair to the side away from the matted blood. Dried flakes of blood fell away like crimson snow as Spartan used his fingertips to probe the wound on the girl's scalp. The jagged cut opened at his touch causing fresh blood to trickle out. Cautiously he touched the edges looking for any sign of entry deeper than a surface wound. Not seeing any, Spartan redressed the injury with a fresh compress bandage from his medical kit to Dancers' head and eased her back against the rock. She definitely had a concussion and a skull fracture was still a very real possibility. Next, he checked the girl's injured hand by clasping her fingertips. They felt warm and soft in his hand. That was a good sign. If the break were severe enough, Dancer could have lost circulation to the hand, leaving her fingers cold and dead. Adjusting the sling, He eased the wounded girl's arm back across her chest.

Leaning his back against the bole of the pine tree, Spartan opened a MRE and ate the cold contents as fast as his stomach would allow. Chicken Ala King looked and smelled like old fashioned cat food on its best day. Cold it was a nasty concoction of yellowish fatty gelatin, gooey noodles and chunks of processed chicken. Spartan choked the slimy mess down, knowing that the carbohydrates were imperative to his continued energy and survival. Then he ate the greasy packet of peanut butter by mixing it with his sugar, creamer and hot cocoa packets. Sergeant Surfer had taught them that this was called Ranger pudding and that it was something of a delicacy in the field. To Spartan it tasted sweet and gritty; like eating a mouthful of chocolate flavored sand. At least it hadn't left a slime layer over his teeth the way that the entrée had. Finishing the meal by gnawing on a brick hard cracker, Spartan used the chemical heater contained in a second MRE to heat up the spaghetti packet for Dancer. Maybe some warm food in her belly would help to bring her around to consciousness.

"Dance – Can you hear me?" He asked as he raised a brown plastic spoonful of pasta and red sauce up to his teammate's lips. "You have to eat to keep your strength up. We still have a long way to go."

There was no response from the girl beyond the gentle rasp of her breathing through half parted lips.

Gently Spartan placed an armored hand upon the girl's thigh and shook her firmly, hoping to shake her into being awake. The movement rocked the girl's head side to side and caused her sling to shift downward to her side. A sharp cry sounded as the Alpha team sniper screamed in agony. Lightning-fast Spartan surged forward and covered the warrior's mouth with his hand, talking softly to her. He hoped that her cry had not given away their position to any nearby bikers or Z's.

Studying the girl's delicate face beneath his armored glove, Spartan quietly shushed her cries and eased a spoonful of spaghetti into her mouth. Although her eyes were open, they were focused very far away. Her pupils were dilated and her head seemed to wobble on her neck. She chewed and swallowed reflexively as the Alpha team leader fed her spoon after spoon of the military meal. Rich red tomato sauce drooled from the corner of Dancer's mouth which Spartan gently wiped away without a word. Finally, the girl's eyes fluttered shut; her breathing deepened and she fell back into a disturbed sleep.

So, Spartan did the only logical thing that he could think of to do. Standing up, he insured that all of his and Dancer's weapons were secured to their bodies, and then he lifted the unconscious girl over his shoulder into a fireman's carry. Lifting his M-4 from the ground he quickly scanned all four horizons for any sign of the undead or the Lords of Death. Seeing none he muttered a quiet prayer that the undead not catch up to them before he reached the remainder of the Phalanx. Then, exiting the low hanging pine boughs he began to move southward as fast as he could towards where he knew his teammates would be.

# Chapter Twenty-Five

## Deadeye's Hunt

Deadeye moved like a predatory cat through the tree branches and fallen logs of the woods. Although each footstep pressed down upon the dry autumn leaves and dead tree limbs of varying sizes that littered the ground, not a single sound could be heard to mark his passage through the forest.

Razor bow in hand with a knocked arrow clenched between two fingers, the Apache scout focused on the sights, sounds and smells of the living earth around him. His father had taught him from the time that he was a small child that the spirit of the Earth could guide him during his hunts if only he would take the time to learn its language. A brief image of his father leading him along numerous dirt paths and game trails rose within his mind, learning as the man had identified the innumerable plants and animals of the wilderness around them. His father had been the most knowledgeable Forester in the tribe. By looking at a single paw or hoof print and gauging its depth and shape, the man could almost supernaturally determine the overall size, shape and weight of an animal. Often he could determine if an animal was injured, grazing or hunting just by the creatures' gait; making the animals speed easier to approximate. The great man had been lost on a similar day of instruction when the undead she-bear has sunk it's undead claws into his father and torn him into ragged strips of flesh because of Deadeye's own immature foolishness.

A soul scarred pain of longing gripped the scout's heart. Muttering an Apache swear word under his breath, he pushed the bloody images out of his mind. Concentrating on the past would only get him killed in the present. He needed to focus on the task at hand. Failure to do so would result in not only his death, but the death of all of the orphans, Sister Margaret and likely his Phalanx teammates as well. He had failed his father. He would not repeat the mistake with his comrades in arms.

The irony of the situation did not escape his notice. When he himself had made the lapse in judgment, he had been but a young and naïve boy. Now, although only a handful of years had passed, his mission had dictated that he and his teammates grow into the role of surrogate parents charged with protecting the young ones from the horrors of both the living and the dead.

The sounds of eighties club music echoed its thumping bass through the quiet forest night, riding on the night breezes far away to the north. Moving with preternatural stealth and speed, he had caught up to the Romeros within the first half of a mile after leaving Freak, Sister Margaret and the children at the campsite. He was confident that the children had not seen him leave, their warmed bellies full of pasta had aided in their sleep; so, there should be no outcries of concern for his missing. Circling silently but quickly through the woods until he was in front of the shambling monsters, he periodically gave them a glimpse of himself. He did not get close enough for the "Zs" to attack but stayed close enough for them to continually moan in anguished frustration and march forward to find him. As the undead moans of eternal hunger began to reach a fever pitch of desperation, Deadeye would lead them along the path like the proverbial Pied Piper, guiding their steps toward him as surely as if he had hung a raw pork chop around his neck. Sparing his ZAP armors' batteries, he loped along, staying twenty meters in front of the lead undead's grasping claws.

The effect was exactly what he had planned and been hoping for. The mindless dead were guided solely by the urge to eat. To assuage the eternal hunger that gnawed at their rotten bellies and brains. As long as he stayed within their line of sight, the swaying undead would follow him unerringly to his preconceived destination. As one they marched forward, outstretched hands clawing at the air, rotten teeth gnashing and clacking pitifully against the ambient silence of the forest.

Glancing upward, Deadeye noted the artificial light that created a white halo effect over the trees up ahead, set against the blue-black backdrop of the Illinois autumn night sky. He knew that he had reached his destination. The boom, boom, boom of the dance music echoed outward and seemed to reverberate in the shimmering of the distant stars overhead. Unconsciously this had the effect of turning the approach of the Apache scout and the undead wave into a choreographed assault, complete with its own theme music. Reaching the edge of the tree line, Deadeye used the light refractive capability of his ZAP's armor to silently slide out of sight, instantly camouflaging himself from the approaching undead eyes. Leaping upward, the Apache grasped a low hanging branch of an ancient pine tree and pulled himself onto it. Settling into a crouch, he watched the momentary confusion of the undead as they lost sight of him only to be replaced almost instantly by the moaning rage of new prey being heard within the proximity of the swarm of undead. The deep vibration of the club music ripping through the night air now drew the undead pack forward as surely as if someone stood ringing a dinner bell. Each thundering beat of a drum and each ripped guitar chord followed by poorly rhymed lyrics called to the creatures with a primal urging, driving them forward to find their prey. Promising something to rend beneath their decaying teeth and tear the flesh from its bones.

Two men stood casual guard outside the glass doors of the skating rink. Both men had large caliber hunting rifles leaned against the side of the building's outer wall, perhaps ten feet from where they stood. They were so complacent that Deadeye wondered if they were long term squatters, random scavengers or part of the Red Baron's crew of Death worshipping bikers. He supposed alternatively that they could simply be ignorant corn farmers content at living out the remainder of their days wearing foraged John Deere baseball caps, drinking beer and smoking dope.

Even as the first of the undead shambled forward out of the forest on rotten legs, the men appeared to be oblivious, smoking their cigarettes and laughing amongst themselves. Both men held a can of beer in their hands, drinking as they talked.

Curious as to what could make two men in an apocalyptic world of the living dead so careless when on guard duty, Deadeye dropped out of the tree branches, nimbly landing on all fours without a sound. Racing to get ahead of the ever-marching Romeros, he slowed to a cautious walk when he was safely beyond the creature's imminent threat radius. Using the enhanced hearing capabilities of the ZAP armor's helmet, he quickly modulated the incoming sound to block out the music while filtering the men's conversation into the headpiece.

"So, do you really think he's gonna do it?" A young thin man in a blue flannel shirt and blue jeans asked his partner. As he spoke, the glowing tip of a lit cigarette bobbed in time with his words as it dangled between his lips.

"Do what Billy?" The second man asked. He was significantly older than his protégé and wore a black t-shirt and a St. Louis Cardinals baseball cap backwards upon his head. A bushy grey beard hung down from his chin. His jeans hung low beneath an ample beer belly. "What the fuck are you squawking about now? You turning pussy on me boy?"

"C'mon Clint. You know what I mean. I ain't no pussy. But doin' that whole Jesus thing, you know with that Army dude up on the big screen? That don' seem right ya know. Kinda sacrilegious and all…"

"What the fuck? You getting' all churchy on me boy? Tell you the truth, it don' make a fuck to me as long as it keeps my dick outta the ringer. You should try to be more like me; learn from my examples. The Baron, he don' like no shit and he don' tolerate none neither. You get in his way and he will string you up by your balls right next to G.I. Joe. Mind your own business boy. That's my motto. Nothin' but trouble if'n you don't."

From the way Billy began chain smoking his cigarettes, it was clear to Deadeye that the older man's words had delivered their desired effect. Still, Deadeye wanted to know more about who it was that these men were talking about. It was obvious that whoever it was, the man was an enemy of the Red Baron and probably military or prior military by the G.I. Joe description, but was it someone that had been dispatched from the Apocalypse Academy or a freelancer like a Paladin out here in the dead zone? Sliding slowly to his left, Deadeye kept his back to the wall of the skating rink, easing closer behind the two men as silent as a wraith. Each movement of his body was slow and deliberate, carefully maximizing every aspect of his stealth capabilities. Although he could no longer hear the music, the reverberations of the bass hummed within his suits' structure. When he was within three feet of the guardsmen, he slowly assumed a battle crouch, drawing his deadly combat tomahawk into his hand. Trusting his ZAP armor's ability to distort light and keep him hidden, even at such a close range, he listened once again to the two men talking.

"That ain't none of your business either Billy. You mind me here boy. Rumor has it that that soldier was once the Baron's own partner back afore the world went to shit. Done him dirty and ratted him out or sumthin'. Got him kicked out of the Army. He'll be lucky if all he gets is strung up. That Baron's more than a little bit nuts and vindictive to boot. Men say he's so vengeful that he would kill a thousand men just to get to the one that wronged him. No sir. You stay the fuck outta the way Billy of that one for sure. Don't cross him none and you maybe stay alive. "Besides…that soldier boy is one of those bastards that the Baron's always preachin' about. One of the ones that helped build that school for special orphans of "Z" day or some crap. Way I hear it, the Baron's getting' ready to tear that place down brick by brick. Gonna be lotsa dead soldiers when that happens, so this one is just the beginnin'. You listenin' to me boy?"

Billy nodded his head in agreement. The young man had just lit his third cigarette in the minute and a half since Deadeye had been watching them, and a tremble shook the red ember at its tip. He was clearly scared shitless.

"Anyway, him dyin' hard will send a message to any others thinkin' about crossin' the Baron. Harsh justice for anyone that crosses that man, that's the word on the street. Ain't nobody gonna fuck with us when they see this dude hangin' from the drive-in with his eyes getting' pecked out by the crows. So, you see, it's better for all of us if'n he dies ugly up…Urrkh!!!

The bearded man never finished his sentence because Deadeye's tomahawk severed the synaptic connections within his skull as the heavy tactical blade tore through skin, bone and brains. Blood splattered fully into young Billy's face, extinguishing the cigarette and completely paralyzing the teen with unnamed fear. Deadeye released the weapon from his grasp. Separated from the distortion field generated by the ZAP armor, the tomahawk seemed to materialize in Clint's forehead drawing the man's eyes upward as his body fell into a quivering heap upon the ground.

Adrenaline poured into young Billy's system, freeing him from the bloody paralysis that had gripped him subsequent to Clint's gory death. Casting his eyes frantically from side to side, he spied his rifle where it stood, leaned upon the side of the skating rink. Turning his body, he prepared to lunge for the rifle. Deadeye was faster having anticipated the move. Pivoting smoothly, the deadly Apache swung the razor bow downward in an arcing crescent. The bow's razors edge sliced smoothly through the teenager's jeans and parted the flesh across the backs of his calves. Thin flesh, firm muscle and taut tendons split around the metal of the blade and released as both legs collapsed beneath the boy. As Billy pitched to the ground on his back, both of his feet flopped loosely upward, falling back upon his own shins. Crying out in agony, the boy reached down to try and grasp his ruined legs. Deadeye flipped the blade of his bow upward and sliced all four of the teenager's fingers off of his right hand.

Looking around quickly, Deadeye saw that the assault had gone unnoticed by the patrons within the skating rink, although the walking dead continued to close the distance to where he now stood. Deactivating his armor's cloaking feature, Deadeye looked calmly down at the boy from behind his mirrored faceplate. Placing an armored boot upon Billy's chest just below the sternum, he applied enough downward pressure to keep the boy from regaining his breath. Blood poured freely from the savage wounds on the teenager's ruined hand and feet.

"I'm only going to ask this one time. If you fail to answer me correctly or sufficiently, I will make you suffer in ways that you cannot begin to imagine. If you try to scream or alert the people inside the skating rink in any manner, I will slice open your belly and let you bleed out slowly here in the dark. If you give me the information that I need, I will let you live. Do you understand what I have told you?" Deadeye said quietly through gritted teeth as he knocked an arrow onto the razor bow and drew it back to its full extension. The head of the arrow was aligned just beyond the armored boot, pointed directly at Billy's heart. Between gasping moans and pain filled tears, the teenager tried to answer the Scout.

"If...I...tell...(gag)...(wheeze)...Baron will...kill... (gag...gag...wheeze...gasp) ...please...I...can't..."

"Wrong answer." Was all Deadeye said. With a subtle shift of the bow's firing angle, the Apache loosed the arrow. Before the sound of the bow strings' release could be heard, the razor-sharp arrow had blinked through the air, penetrated Billy's bicep and pinned the arm firmly to the ground. The subsequent shriek of agony was cut short as the teenager attempted to draw in air into his lungs. Deadeye steadily ground his boot downward, collapsing the boy's chest beneath his weight, preventing the boy from drawing a breath or releasing a sound louder than a gasp.

Staring hard into the teenager's face from behind his mirrored visor, Deadeye slowly and deliberately drew another arrow from the quiver over his shoulder and knocked it on the razor bow's string. Peering up from within his helmet he saw that the Romeros were still a safe distance away, but they were closing steadily. Drawing the black arrow back once again to its full length, the Apache stared into the boy's eyes just beyond the arrowhead.

"One more time dung heap. Where did they take the soldier? Who was he?"

"Please…I don' know…I…"

Billy's eyes widened in a microsecond; realizing in that fraction of an instant that his answer would not be acceptable to the deadly assassin standing over him.

With lightning speed, the razor bow shifted aim again, targeting the teenager's other arm. No sound of release could be heard due to the steady beating of the eighty's music from within the skating rink. Ironically, the song that was currently playing across the speakers was "Hurt So Good" by John Cougar Mellencamp. It sounded as though at least twenty or thirty other people inside the skating rink knew the chorus because they were all singing along with the music. As the arrow leapt from the bow and skewered his other arm just below the shoulder socket where all of the muscles aligned and joined to provide flexibility to the limb. One hundred and ten pounds of pressure drove the broad head arrow through bone and sinew as if it were a hot knife going through butter. The boy's screams pierced the air but were well hidden beneath the beat and rhythm of the song. After a moment, the teen' screams turned to open sobs. Billy was now transfixed to the ground like an obscene parody of a butterfly exhibit.

A low, unholy moan drew Deadeye's attention upward. Even without his amplified hearing, the hungry cries of the undead could be heard over the raucous noise of the party inside. The Romeros that he had led to the skating rink had arrived, and now stood only twenty feet away, moving on unsteady feet. Nodding his armored head upward, Deadeye indicated the approaching Zs to Billy.

"Last chance. Either you tell me right now who the soldier was that you and Clint had been talking about and where they took him or I shoot an arrow into your balls and let the undead eat you while you lay here and bleed out. If you're lucky, maybe you will die before you get turned or you have to watch as they rip something vital out of your belly and eat it in front of you. Or maybe they will chew off your face and pluck out your eyes so that you cannot see what is coming, but you will feel every second of the agony as they gnaw through your skull and belly before you die."

"I'll tell…(gasp)…please. I'll tell. Don't let …
(gasp…wheeze) me die…like this!

"Who and where!" Deadeye demanded, twisting the
arrow in the boy's shoulder savagely. "Three seconds.
One…two…thr…!"

"The drive-in!" Billy screamed. They've
got…(gasp)…him…there!… The…Baron
is…(gasp)…gonna crucify…on the big…(wheeze) screen
as an…example! Leave the…body for the crows. (gasp,
gasp) Please…The Baron made …us. I
was…only…following…only following …orders!" The
boy pleaded.

"Who?!" Deadeye demanded. "Who is to be
crucified?"

"Some old Army …guy…(gasp). Named…Pig or
…Swine…or sumthin'! I … (wheeze, gasp), I don'
know…him!" Panic was clearly overriding the pain
receptors in young Billy's mind as he began to squirm
frantically around, twisting his head, trying to see the
approaching undead. The fiberglass arrows kept him
pinioned to the ground. Upon seeing the walkers only ten
feet away, the teenager began to beg frantically. Anything

was better than being eaten by the living dead. He could run. Hide from the Baron's wrath, but first he had to get away from here. Get away from this crazy ass man with a bow and arrow.

"Please...I...told you...everything that...I know. Let me go...!"

"Hogg." Deadeye said quietly. "Was it Sergeant Hogg?"

"Yeah...maybe...fuck ...I...I ...ahhh God it hurts...I...don' know...Please God!...Don' shoot my nuts!...(Gasp)...Please...let me...go!" He begged, his voice full of pain and fear.

Nodding once, Deadeye unknocked his arrow from the razor bow's string and replaced it into his quiver. Reaching down to the bearded head of Clint, he wrenched the tomahawk free from his skull with a wet sucking sound. Brains and blood flew outward from the fatal wound.

Seeing the tomahawk in the armored Apache's hand, Billy's eyes rolled up into his head with fear. He was certain that he was about to die. Deadeye leaned forward and wiped the deadly weapon off on the teenager's blue flannel

shirt, then replaced it into its belt holder at his waist.
Without another word, he turned, activated the stealth
capabilities of his ZAP armor and walked away.

"Wait!...Please!...Don't leave me!... You said you
wouldn't kill me!...Help me…!" The rest of the plea was
instantly converted to a thick gurgle as young Billy's throat
was torn out by the jaws of a Romero. Shambling undead
fell upon his body, tearing free his innards in long ropy
strands of crimson and pale white intestines. All the while,
the music thumped in a steady rhythm leaving the partiers
inside unaware of their guardian's fate. The last words Billy
cried out were, "You… promised!"

Deadeye nodded once, muttering to himself as he
walked away. "Yes Billy. I did. I guess I lied, but at least I
didn't shoot you in the balls." Then he headed for the door
to the skating rink. "By the way…" He said as he opened
the screen door. "Thanks for the information. You were a
big help."

# CHAPTER TWENTY-SIX
## FREAK'S PROMISE

Freak sat on guard duty as the first golden rays of sun
began to tint the morning sky in a wash of yellow, pink and
purple hues, much like an artist's canvas. Growing up on
the south side of Chicago, he had never really appreciated
the arts despite his Grandma religiously watching the silly
white man with the bushy hair on public television always
making happy little clouds and trees. He had always
enjoyed attempting to make little pieces of art growing up
to please his Grandma in class before the apocalypse erased
all formal schooling. In his mind, the drawings and
watercolor paintings had at best been poor imitations of
real art yet his Grandma had always created such a fuss
over them and immediately hung them by magnets on her
old, battered refrigerator, replacing any previous attempts
he had made. No matter how financially poor they had
been in reality, his Grams always made him feel like a king
no matter what he attempted to do. He really missed her.

A small, tender hand touched his armored forearm causing him to start and break the reverie that he had allowed himself to slip into. Silently he chided himself, his mind using Gram's stern voice to tell him to *"pay attention boy or sumpthin' bad might happen to ya."* Looking downward, he saw a small blond-haired girl gazing up at him with huge blue eyes that sparkled in the morning sun. The girl's pig tails had become lopsided from sleeping and stray hairs stuck out across her head like miniature antennae. Perhaps four years old, she held a battered, one-eyed pink teddy bear in her arms.

"Hey sweetie…" He said in the softest voice he could muster so that he didn't frighten the child. "What's wrong?"

"Mr. Giant Sir." She said in a sweet, timid little voice. "I'm scared. I think I heard a monster out there coming to eat us!" Tears immediately rimmed the large blue eyes as if the admission of fright had released the flood gates in her brain and small rivers of tears crested her lids and spilled down her cheeks. The effect on Freak was instantaneous. It was as if the little girl had reached through his armor and was holding his heart in her pale little hands.

"Awww Sweetness, you ain't got nothin' to be afraid of honey. As long as I'm watchin' over ya, there ain't nothin' bad gonna come your way. See, they are afraid of me…kinda like how the postman used to be afraid of them big dogs on his delivery route when he would bring the mail. Just think of me as your very own watch dog." He said with a smile.

"But what about those dead people? They want to eat me. Do they eat dogs too?"

Freak thought about his answer for a moment before he replied. He didn't want to frighten the girl any further than she obviously was. "Ya. Ya, I suppose those dead ones would try to take a bite outta an old dog at that, but that old dog; he would make them pay, you see. Make 'em pay a right big price and he would never let them get to his friends." I tell you what. I know a story about what happens to those old, rotten "Zs" if they try to mess with any of my friends. Would you like me to tell it to you?"

The twin pig tails bobbed in unison as the child nodded yes, her eyes never leaving Freak's brown face. He

341

gave her a gentle smile, sat down beside her and began to quietly beat box with his mouth, setting a rhythm and tempo for his story.

*"There once was a little girl from the city,*
*Her little pig tails looked so pretty.*
*One day she walked out to the park,*
*She had so much fun it got dark.*
*Scared of the night, she held her pink teddy tight*
*And cried out for someone to keep her safe and make it all alright."*

*"Out of the trees shambled a nasty ol' Z,*
*Wandering all around for a bite.*
*To eat up a girl like a roast and some toast,*
*But her toes was what he wanted to eat the most,*
*To savor and chew in delight."*

*"A huge giant was near,*
*There was no Zs that he feared.*
*When he heard the girl's scream,*
*He knew just what it meant,*
*And ran to her side by the slide."*

*"The giant picked up the girl, with the cute bouncing curls,*
*And placed her on his broad shoulders.*
*Then he snatched up his bat,*
*He gave the undead a huge swat,*
*And its head rolled down the slide like a boulder."*

The girl giggled and clapped as Freak held up one of the Blues Brothers to show her that he was indeed her protector.

"What happened then Mr. Giant?"

"Well, then they went back home. When they got there they had a humongous tea party with little mister Pinky bear and all of her other stuffed animals and they all lived happily ever after in a big castle that reached all the way up to the clouds and served chocolate with every meal."

As the story ended, the girl threw her arms around Freak's neck with such speed and vigor that he immediately wondered if she had changed into the living dead and was attacking him. He relaxed immediately as he heard her tiny voice coming from his shoulder.

"I love you Mr. Giant!" She quietly exclaimed.

He patted her gently on the back and stroked her hair. "What's your name sweetheart?"

"It's Danielle." She answered without lifting her head or unclenching his neck.

"Can I call you Dani? Well Dani; don't you worry about a thing. You know why?"

She shook her head slowly against the crook of his neck.

"Because" The armored man said. I am YOUR giant and there ain't no "Z" in this world that's big enough or bad enough to stop me from always keeping you safe."

The girl's arms tightened even more around his neck as she acknowledged the words of her protector with a simple "Thank you."

Freak thought back to the inherent racism of south Chicago and of all the gang and police violence that he had seen in his young life. It had all been such a stupid waste. The innocence of the world, like this little girl needed to be protected. Sheltered from all of the violence so that they could grow up to appreciate how the world was supposed to be rather than how it was. It's funny that it took an apocalypse of walking dead corpses to help him realize what his Gram had always been preaching to him…racism was for fools.

"You're welcome sweetheart." He said softly and began to hum a soft tune as he slowly rocked her back and forth. Soon the girl's breathing slowed and deepened to a relaxed rhythm that softly echoed off of his armor's plating. Comforted, she had fallen asleep.

Looking up at the bright morning sky, he had the feeling that his Grandma was looking down on him from her place in heaven and smiling her approval. He smiled back knowingly. He would die before he let any of these children ever come to harm.

# Chapter Twenty-seven
## Weary and exhausted

The intermittent sounds of various caliber weapons being discharged echoed through the tall pine trees surrounding Spartan's position. Considering the way, the sound had rolled through the trees along the river, Spartan could tell that the gunfire had been relatively close. Judging by the amount of ammunition that was being expended, there were only a few likely causes. Perhaps the walking dead had found a pocket of survivors that were currently fighting for their lives or perhaps those same survivors were battling the invading legion of Lords of Death, trying to prevent their own merciless slaughter at the hands of the undead worshipping biker gang. It could have even been the remaining members of the Phalanx or even Apocalypse Academy personnel although both of those options seemed unlikely as the expenditure of ammunition seemed chaotic and undisciplined rather than controlled and orderly as they had been taught by the Special Forces cadre at the Academy.

Occasionally a scream of terror registered on Spartan's enhanced helmet audio sensors, causing the night birds to leap into the air and take flight. He had picked up at least three or four of these throughout the course of his march carrying Dancer along draped on his shoulders. As badly as his blood called to him to rush into battle and attempt to affect a rescue, Spartan knew that Dancer was not in any shape to be participating in a skirmish of any type and leaving her behind alone and unprotected to render aid that may or may not have been useful, was simply not an option. As much as it went against all that he believed in, those people, if they were truly innocents, would have to survive on their own.

Focused on the gunshots, Spartan did not see the root jutting from the ground as it entangled his armored foot in the darkness. The thick, knotty pine root grabbed at his plodding feet as firmly as an undead corpse. Stumbling, he began to fall towards the dirty path beneath him. Desperate to prevent further harm from coming to Dancer, he torqued his torso so that he absorbed the impact with his shoulder and back while grasping the girl's semi-conscious form tightly against his chest. Although the fall did not cause him any real harm, he laid there for several seconds

347

exhausted. Silently he thanked God for the muscle enhancing properties of the ZAP armor. Without them, he would have surely fallen much sooner than now. He could feel the fatigue making him sluggish. His mind was definitely not as crisp as it should be as evidenced by his little trip into the dirt courtesy of a simple pine tree root. What if it had been a "Z" arm grasping at his boot? He could have placed himself or worse, placed Dancer in a very serious tactical disadvantage by becoming helpless upon the ground.

*"C'mon Spartan! Get your shit together!"* He quietly chided himself.

Looking down at Dancer he was relieved to see that the girl was no worse for wear due to the fall that they had taken. They had entered the White Pines Forest State Park. The second is the northernmost road. It winds its way past several stone pavilion picnic shelters and exits further up the river. Quickly assessing the threat level to be minimal, Spartan had opted to stick to the established walking trails, choosing speed and freedom of movement over stealth. If they heard someone approaching he could always duck off the path with Dancer and hope they wouldn't be detected.

He had once heard hope described as a fickle lover. He sincerely hoped that he would not have to find out just how fickle this evening. As wounded and tired as they were, he did not believe that a fight of any type would have ended well for one or both of them.

Rolling up to a seated position, Spartan quietly spoke to his Phalanx partner.

"Dance? You awake in there?"

The girl answered him in a slurred voice that sounded as if she had been drinking alcoholic beverages all night. "I'm 'wake…short…of."

At least she had been able to respond. He had spoken to her several times over the helmet communication system of her ZAP armor during their march and she had not been able to reply. Spartan remembered the first aid training with Nurse Ortega. The Hispanic nurse had stressed that it was important to keep a person that had suffered a concussion awake.

"We have to get back up and get moving. Can you stand? My foot is tangled in a root and I can't clear it off with you on my chest."

Dancer's head lolled forward onto her chest, her shoulder's slumping. Unconsciousness was only a short step away. He could see through the hole in the side of her helmet. Activating his own external light on his helmet, he peered into the hole. Bright red blood had fully soaked through the bandage that he had applied and it glistened under his light. Clicking off the light again, he grasped the girl's thigh and shook it firmly. Using a command voice that he amplified through Dancer's ZAP helmet, he issued her orders. He hoped that the change of communication tact would be enough to jolt the girl into action, by reflex if nothing else.

"On your feet soldier! We move or we die!"

Surprisingly, Dancer stood immediately. Although she weaved a bit from side to side, she was standing of her own accord. Pulling his foot quickly out of the roots, Spartan got up to his feet and quickly looked around to see if they had dropped any of their gear. Not seeing anything he used

Dancer's naginata in one hand like a walking stick and lifted the girl's good arm over his neck. Placing his free hand around her waist, they started moving forward. If Spartan remembered correctly there was a small farmhouse just outside of the park's main entrance. He estimated that he was less than half a mile away from there. If he could get Dancer inside undiscovered, then he could redress her wounds and perhaps allow themselves ten minutes or so to get their bearings.

"Stay with me Dance. We are gonna make it. Just a little bit further. Hang tough!"

To his complete and utter surprise, Dancer spoke up. It was a short, slurred and contrite statement but hearing it let Spartan know they were going to be ok.

"Blimey mate. You've got a right nice bum you 'ave."

Spartan laughed and though the girl said nothing else, her feet did not stop moving. Quickly they crossed the distance to the edge of the park. Spartan could hear that the gunfire had been silenced and he no longer heard screaming of any sort. Although he felt bad at not being

351

able to render aid, he had to think about the safety of Dancer first. That meant those people, whoever they were, had to be left on their own. Looking across the asphalt road from the tree line, he saw what appeared to be a small, brown cabin style house on the outer edge of a modest corn field. Using the thermal imaging of the ZAP armor's helmet, he saw no living creatures inside, however he noted what appeared to be two to three dozen livestock milling about inside of a corral. Switching his vision over to the green night vision spectrum, he saw that they were all small white-tailed deer. A painted sign above the corral read **"Deer Park Petting Zoo"**. The house must have been the caretaker's home. Either he was gone or dead as the animals all seemed emaciated and sluggish in their movements as though they hadn't been fed in days. At least they didn't appear to be undead. That was a perk.

Approaching the cabin, he noted that the front door was slightly ajar, creating a slim black vertical stripe in his green night vision. Knowing that he needed to get Dancer inside and try to properly redress her wounds without worrying about constantly being under attack, he leaned the naginata against the wall and just booted the door open, leveling his M-4 at the open space, content in the knowledge that he would just blow away any undead thing that tried to claw its way into the open air to Hell. Fortunately, he was able to keep the noise in the night quiet as no undead creatures popped out to try and eat his face off.

Seeing the room furnished in the mid nineteen seventies style floral and wood rustic patterns, he quickly moved Dancer over to the full-sized sofa and removed her helmet and gently laid her down. A small moan escaped her lips as did a mumbled "Thanks." Walking over to an old wooden coffee table, he swept the ancient plastic floral arrangement onto the floor and tipped the table upside down. Snapping two of the foot long legs off from where they attached to the table, he set them down on the floor next to Dancer's prone form. Leaving the girl resting on the sofa, Spartan quickly rifled through the drawers in the kitchen and laundry room looking for something to bind the wood to the soldier's broken arm. Finding nothing useful, he moved to the cabin's basement where he hoped any tools may have been kept. The basement smelled of years of mold and mildew vaguely mixed with the fresh scent of either urine or Pine Sol. Spartan couldn't be sure of which. Seeing an old sleeping bag and a discarded pile of dirty clothing lying in one corner, Spartan thought that someone had been using this area as a survival shelter until recently.

Moving quickly, not wanting to leave Dance alone in case the owner of the clothing returned, Spartan rifled through the tools and implements on the shelf under the stairs. Pushing aside hammers and screwdrivers, he finally saw what he had been looking for. Digging his armored hand into the pile, he wrapped his fingers around the two-inch-wide roll of silver tape. Seeing the roll in with the tools brought another random memory from his father to mind. He could hear the man saying, "If you can't fix it, duct it!" and laughing at the joke. Unfortunately, he still could not remember the man's face. He hoped it would come back in time and that his amnesia would not be permanent. Almost as an afterthought, he snagged a blue pillowcase from where it hung on a clothesline. It appeared clean, as if someone had chosen "Z" night to wash their sheets.

Pulling the silver roll of tape free of the surrounding tools, Spartan moved quickly back through the house. Glancing out of the open door and seeing no imminent threats in the area, he closed it and returned next to Dancer and prepared to set her arm into a more proper splint. Gently he removed the girl's good hand from where it cradled her injured wrist. The whole hand was tinted bluish-purple and had swollen to the point that none of the girl's delicate bones were visible. Removing Dancer's ZAP armor had been extremely difficult. The girl's lack of continual consciousness made unclasping her safety protocols extraordinarily difficult without hurting her.

Removing the armored gloves of his ZAP armor, he softly felt her fingertips and noted that they felt cold and waxy. Spartan knew that if she did not receive proper treatment soon then his teammate ran a risk of losing the hand due to the loss of blood circulation and infection as well. Carefully he turned the arm over and insured that there was not a compound fracture. Satisfied that the break had not penetrated the skin, he moved the inspection higher up her forearm. The break appeared to be in the lower forearm and wrist areas only. The swelling seemed to lessen significantly about mid-forearm where the ulna and radial bones extended beyond the mid forearm. The bones were clearly broken in both areas.

Knowing what he had to do; Spartan laid the two table legs on either side of his teammates' forearm. The thought of intentionally having to cause Dancer pain made him slightly queasy, but he also knew that if he didn't do something then the end result would end up much worse for the girl. Gently, he brushed a strand of hair out of her face as he spoke softly to her.

"Dance...Dancer, can you hear me?"

The girl moaned a semi-coherent response that sounded confused or maybe it was a British slang term that Spartan was unfamiliar with. He wasn't sure. Either way it didn't really matter, he had to set the arm whether she heard him or not. The conversation was more of a courtesy.

"Dancer, this is really going to hurt. I've got to set your arm and apply a splint until we get back to the academy and get you treatment from Ortega. Do you understand? Try not to move or scream."

There was a grunting exhalation that Spartan took as a confirmation. Re-donning his armored gloves he grasped Dancer's arm just below her elbow and placed his opposite hand gently but firmly at the base of her hand, just above the wrist. Taking a deep breath to steel his nerves, he used the ZAP armor's strength enhancement to pull her arm in two separate directions. As he maintained a constantly increasing pressure, he monitored the girl's pulse on his HUD display inside of his visor. He knew that the overwhelming shock of pain to her nervous system could be devastating, especially since she had already suffered a head injury as well. He could only hope that the shock of setting her arm didn't kill her.

Dancer's eyes flew open as the pressure drove red hot needles of pain spiking through her nervous system, flooding the synapses of her brain with adrenaline. To her credit, the girl did not scream. Even semi-conscious she must have been able to comprehend the potential danger that they were still in. There was a sharp hissing intake of air through her clenched teeth as Dancer fought the pain in her arm, and her armored feet unconsciously tap danced upon the floral print of the sofa, trying to mask the pain through alternative movement. Her father had trained her well.

For what felt like an eternity to Spartan nothing happened. Slowly he continued to ratchet up the amount of torque on the forearm until a sudden pop-pop vibrated through his hands indicating that the broken bone had realigned itself and was now back in its proper position. Looking at Dancer's face he grimaced inwardly. Tears silently dripped down her cheeks, creating runnels in the dried blood that had been left behind by her head injury. Her teeth were clenched against the pain. Carefully, Spartan positioned the table legs and taped the makeshift splint into place, cautious not to wrap it too tight and slow the circulation to the girl's hand. Then using the old blue pillowcase that he had found; he fashioned an impromptu sling.

"How does that feel? Too tight?"

"I'll live, but I won't be doing the Queen's royal wave any time soon I'm thinking mate." Was all she said as she wiped her good forearm across her face, creating a ghastly smear of blood and tears that was frightening to behold. "Where's my rifle?"

"Gone." Spartan said simply. "I couldn't find it after the water tower fell."

"Damn. My naginata?"

Spartan nodded his head towards the closed door. The Japanese polearm leaned against the frame, its folded steel blade glistening in the ambient lights of the ZAP armor, making it appear almost alive. Dancer breathed a small sigh of relief. The rifle was a significant loss but it was still only gear. The naginata felt different to her. Almost as if she had imbued a small portion of her soul into training with the weapon. Maybe it was because she had associated the polearm with one of the only normal periods of her life. She had loved being a flag girl for the sports teams and band at her school. Sure, the cheerleaders were more liked but in her opinion they were the dumb ones; able to only sling their assets side to side to display their limited talents. Those same bimbos had been incapable of memorizing and performing the complex choreographed sequences of the flag routines, while simultaneously twirling the flags in synch with twenty-two other flag corps members. She was pleased that Spartan had recovered the weapon.

"Your pistol is still in your holster. When you are ready we need to move to catch up with the rest of the Phalanx.

Techno is hurt bad and the other two are babysitting a nun and twelve children including an infant. How is your pain?"

She was surprised at his purely business-like questions. "I'll be ok. My arm is throbbing like hell and my head is aching like a three-day hangover, but I will survive."

"Good. There are some painkillers in the medkit. Pop a couple and drink some water to rehydrate yourself. We will move out as soon as you get your ZAP armor back on and you are ready.

"No, not while we are on the road." She answered. "I can't afford to be stoned out of my mind in case we run into any "Z's" or more biker's. Incidentally, I don't suppose you shot the bloody bastard that winged my noggin?"

"I don't know." He answered honestly. "I emptied an entire magazine into the rooftop on full auto. When the dust cleared he was gone, but I can't say for certain if I hit him or if he just fled."

"Just as well." Dancer replied through gritted teeth as she took a deep breath and struggled to stand, sliding her helmet back into place and securing the locking mechanisms but leaving the visor open. "I'd rather put a bullet or a blade in the wanker myself."

Spartan stood silently, offering his servo powered arm for support and stability to his teammate. He watched carefully as her heart rate climbed on his HUD screen and noted her very slow rate of ascent. She was really in no shape to travel but they had to get moving. They had to catch the Phalanx and get back to the Academy before the undead could travel out of Freeport en masse and spill over into Mount Morris or even invade Dixon and the Apocalypse Academy. Together they moved for the door, their faces set with determination

As Dancer grabbed the shaft of her naginata with her good hand she turned back to Spartan. Staring hard into his closed visor, she spoke briefly in clipped tones.

"Coming back for me was stupid. You put yourself in harm's way to try and protect me. As team leader, it was a stupid thing to do. You cannot risk yourself for one of us…" She paused, biting her lip as if deciding what to say. "As my boyfriend I love you for saving me. Thank you." Then as a last second afterthought she kissed his visor leaving a steamy lip print on the glass. Then she turned and walked out the door of the farmhouse using the naginata as a walking stick.

Movement across the fields was slow but steady. In the six hours since their departure from the farmhouse they had been fortunate to avoid any additional contacts; human or otherwise. The pop, pop, pop of distant gunfire led Spartan to believe that their luck was about to take a turn for the worst. Screams of pain and terror resounded through the amplified hearing systems of the ZAP armor.

Moving quickly across a small, water filled ditch and into the edge of the tree line, Spartan helped Dancer to the ground and gently leaned her against the base of a large purple leafed maple tree. The tree's broad, dark leaves and shade would help to conceal their position. Receiving a thumbs up signal from the girl, Spartan turned and crawled back to the edge of the foliage. Parting several strands of high grass and brown tipped cat tails, he used the night vision feature of his helmet to scan the field and trees around him. Magnifying his vision, he could see a small building ahead near the bend in the road.

Spartan remembered it as the skating rink that he and the Phalanx had passed on the way to Freeport on their mission. Then, they had skirted the building leaving the locals to their fun. Now it appeared to be in complete chaos as drunken locals and several bikers blazed away with guns at a large pack of Romeros that had wandered into their midst. The living people seemed to be having trouble targeting the undead with an assortment of shotguns and handguns without hitting each other in a crossfire. The "Z's" were so intertwined with the living that the situation was breaking down from any type of organized, armed defense and into an "every man for himself" situation. This was especially evident from the numerous deceased individuals that lay sprawled across the lawn, stairs and parking lot. Bloody arterial spray patterns painted the walls and dappled the grass in shiny, crimson rivulets. Even as Spartan watched, several of the corpses were beginning to twitch and he knew that they would soon be joining the battle on the side of the living dead when they rose again as Reapers. More and more people were screaming in panic and pain as the merciless undead tore hunks of bloodied flesh from their bodies. It was pure carnage.

An echoing howl of pain followed by an extremely explicit barrage of curse words drew Spartan's attention to the front of the building. An enormous biker wearing the leather vest bearing the colors of the Lords of Death with a chainmail shirt beneath was leaping about wildly, grabbing at the right rear of his buttocks. Scanning the area immediately around the biker, Spartan did not see any "Zs" near the man that were close enough to deliver a bite so he assumed that the man had been the recipient of friendly fire. Just then the burly man spun to face a Romero that was shambling up from behind his position, moaning as it came. As the man turned around to meet the threat with a heavy length of chain dangling from his hand, Spartan immediately recognized the black cloth yard shaft of an arrow that had pierced the man's armored posterior. There was no mistaking the military grade of the arrow, nor its owner. Spartan keyed the person-to-person communications frequency into his helmet's communication system and spoke into the microphone.

*"Deadeye this is Spartan. Over?"*

*"Go ahead Spartan. You're loud and clear. Over."*

*"Deadeye, I am in a tree line north of the skating rink and I am looking at a Lords of Death member holding a chain and screaming because he has a black arrow sticking out of ass. Is this your handiwork?"* Spartan asked, trying to suppress the chuckle that was tickling his ribs at the sight of the man.

*"That is affirmative Spartan. I thought that you might need fire support and a distraction so I let our undead friends chase me all the way here from the camp. How's the little lady? I heard that she was in a rough spot."*

*"Pretty battered but in truth she's lucky to be alive. She has a minor head wound, a probable concussion and a broken wrist and forearm but no bites. Thank God for small favors."*

*"Copy that. Let me ensure that these yokels and that idiot biker stay busy for a while then I will assist you in evacuating out of this place. Over."*

*"Negative, I say again negative Deadeye. Current intelligence shows an army of at least ten thousand or more "Z's" being herded*

*our way by the Lords of Death. If I had to guess, they set the fire that is burning Freeport and driving the undead our way. We have to warn the Apocalypse Academy ASAP or it will be wiped out. Even with warning I am not sure that their defenses will be strong enough to repel the horde. Besides the fire, the Lords of Death are using living human prisoners as live bait behind their motorcycles to lure the walking dead and move them forward en masse."*

*"Copy that. Primary mission parameters are changing to warning the Academy. Secondary parameter updated to evacuate you and Dancer. Just so you know, we have a third problem."*

*"Go ahead. I'm listening."* Spartan said as a group of three "Z's" finally overwhelmed the chain wielding biker and drug him to the ground beneath a flurry of clawed hands and gnashing teeth. Deadeye could hear the man's final screams over Spartan's helmet communication.

*"The Lords of Death have captured Sergeant Hogg. I am not certain of all of the details such as why he was out here but if you look on the ground outside of the side entrance to the skating rink you will see where I discussed the matter with one of his captors."*

Spartan craned his neck to see where Deadeye was talking about. A headless, eviscerated corpse lay pinned to the ground by several arrows. The Apache had shown no mercy during the interrogation it appeared.

*"I see it."* Was all he said in return.

*"After a brief yet pleasant conversation, the young would-be-psychopath divulged that the Lords of Death intended to crucify Sergeant Hogg upon the drive-in movie theatre screen for the Bloody Baron's amusement and so that everyone that passed could see his ruthless handiwork."*

*"Damn."* Spartan thought aloud. He didn't have time for another distraction but he couldn't just leave their sergeant to be slaughtered by a group of motorcycle riding death maniacs. Each option was just as crucial and time sensitive as the next. Hogg would be pissed at him if they abandoned the mission to save his gruff old ass, but they had also been taught to never leave a man behind. Fuck he hated command decisions.

*"Have you confirmed Hogg's status as a P.O.W?"*

*"Negative Spartan but the local had no reason to lie and every reason to tell the truth. "Zs" were closing in. Pinned to the ground, my third arrow was pointed directly at his balls so I am pretty certain that he was honest, at least with as much as he actually knew about the situation."*

Glancing back at the arrow-pinned corpse, Spartan spoke. *"Looks like he must have said something that you didn't like. Did he talk about your momma or something?"*

*"No. I kept my word. He still had his testicles when I left him. That was all that I promised. I never said that I would help him. If he had summoned the strength or courage to tear the arrows either out of the ground or through his arm and shoulder then he might have survived. Instead, the cowardly bastard just laid there and screamed."*

*"Copy that. War is hell and this is most definitely a war."* Spartan replied. *"Rally with me in five mikes on the north side of the road across from the go-kart track. Let's see if we can recon from there to recover Sergeant Hogg."*

*Copy. Five mikes, tree line north side of the road. Deadeye out."*

Crawling back to where Dancer was propped against the maple tree, Spartan swiftly explained the situation to the girl and helped her to her feet, guiding her by the arm as she wobbled woozily, leaning against the ancient Japanese weapon for support. Small branches and dry leaves crunched beneath the girl's feet, each crunch or crack sounding like a gunshot to Spartans amplified hearing. Quickly he turned down the gain, returning his hearing to more normal levels.

"Were you able to copy the radio traffic between Deadeye and me Dance?" He asked.

"Mostly." She replied. Spartan noted that the slur had returned to her speech. She needed rest badly. "Heard 'bout Hogg. You… planning on going after just one bloke? You sure that's the right …? I mean…, to delay the delivery of …umm… I mean…intelligence to the Academy for a chance to save just one man…especially …like him?. That …I mean…why would… could it…mean the difference in more than a hundred people dying? not just one Hogg…. should have known better." Her voice held broke and wavered; tears fell as she tried to reason past her injury.

Even though he had expected this line of questioning from Dancer, the near hysterics in her voice surprised him. She seemed almost so unstable. Spartan had never seen this side of the girl. He expected Deadeye, maybe even Freak to have a ruthless side. This was something new for Dancer. She seems like she would just abandon their Drill Sergeant. Perhaps it was a by-product of years of training with her father to be a tough as nails intelligence operative like he was. Whatever the case may be, he didn't like it. Not one little bit. There was no place for questioning orders in the field. They had all been taught that.

"Let's get this straight. This is my operation. I am in command. You have valuable input that aids the team, great...share it. You want to question my decisions and judgment then shut the hell up! Are we clear soldier?!" He barked so forcefully that the girl took an involuntary step backward. "You don't like my decisions then complain to the Colonel when we return to the Academy! Until then, soldier on and do your job and I will do mine!"

"Yes, sir!" Was the girl's sneered response, although it dripped with so much venom that Spartan was certain that her gaze left scorch marks on his armor.

"Good. For the record, he wouldn't just wander around blindly out here in the dead lands. He had to be out here looking for us. If he's out here there has to be a really damned good reason for it."

The silence in the air seemed to crackle with arcing mental electricity but Dancer either chose or was incapable of adding anything further. Her head seemed to lose its defiant positioning and droop a little towards her chest.

"C'mon Dance. Let's get to the rally point. I could really use a hand carrying you out of here."

"Are you calling me bloody fat?" The girl said with a pained chuckle, all traces of the tension and hostility from moments ago gone from her voice.

*"Maybe it was the head wound?"* Spartan thought. *"Maybe it's making her act irrationally."* He really hoped not. He would

have to render her unconscious with sedatives which would slow their movement even more.

"No, no, not at all! Maybe Husky or stout. I know…big boned. But definitely not fat!"

"You're such a bloody wanker mate!" She slurred. Spartan tried to keep her talking.

Using a mock hurt tone, he said. "How about fluffy, eh? It has a definite feminine undertone to it. The fluffy British samurai?" He laughed.

"Fluffy. Hmm, yes. Fluffy is rather feminine. In fact…it is probably the antithesis of the word that will apply to you if you keep this senseless prattle rambling on in my ear." The girl's tone of voice had shifted again. It was no longer playful. It was angry.

"Oh? And what word would that be my portly little partner?" He chuckled nervously.

Dancer planted both heels firmly into the ground, stopping their forward movement. The butt of the naginata that she had been using as a walking stick was stuck into the earth. Slowly she turned her armored head to look at him. Spartan could not help but to look at the bullet hole and dried blood in the girl's helmet. Her mirrored visor gave no hint of emotion, but the icy tone to her voice was enough to chill a polar bear on a midwinter's night in the arctic.

"Pulped or maybe castrated." She said coldly and pulled her arm loose from Spartan's hand as she again began walking to the rally point without another word.

Spartan was seriously beginning to wonder if Dancer had suffered more than a concussion with the shot that she had received in the head. Maybe there was some deeper damage there that the naked eye could not see. In the interest of maintaining his manhood, on the off chance that his British companion was even remotely serious with her chosen word of reply, he tactfully retreated, leaving her to walk several steps ahead of him.

Inside of her helmet, Dancer smiled for the first time since she'd been shot and fallen off of a water tower. *'It serves him right for being such a tool and yelling at me when I was only trying to help."* She thought to herself as her head wound pounded in time with her footsteps.

# Chapter Twenty-eight

## Jane's dissension

Cutter and his cronies on Echo team opted to delay their return to the Apocalypse Academy despite their successful supply run into the town. Armed with the firsthand knowledge of the advancing undead army that the Bloody Baron had *so generously* provided, Cutter felt it would be safer to watch the impending battle from a long way away rather than being hip deep in the undead.

Battle was perhaps an inaccurate term for what was about to happen. It would most likely be more of a siege and slaughter than outright combat. Sure, the Academy staff and underage students would put up an initial fight but with the majority of the combat trained former cadets out on missions, the staff would not be able to hold out that long. The undead horde would attempt to penetrate the medieval looking Academy's defensive structure while the Commandant and the Drill Instructors futilely attempted to repulse the coordinated attacks of the bikers and prevent perimeter breaches from occurring. The staff would be outnumbered by at least ten thousand undead with the teams deployed out on assignments. That was precisely why Cutter had informed the Bloody Baron of the timing of the missions; to allow the man access into the Academy with limited resistance. The information was sure to bring him reward and stature in the new regime under the Baron. He was sure of it. And if by some miracle the Academy staff actually survived or even won the battle he could claim total ignorance of the battle because he had been ordered out on a foraging mission for supplies.

Had the full complement of students, graduates and staff been present then perhaps an effective defense could have been mounted. Maybe even a spearhead attack in an attempt to eliminate the Lords of Death leadership and make the bikers break ranks and retreat could have occurred although it would have been a long shot. Cutter was fairly certain that rhetoric like that was precisely the kind of glorious, heroic drivel that people like Spartan and his Alpha team rejects lived for. Unfortunately for them, the Commandant had chosen to deploy all five strike teams simultaneously on different missions, leaving only a skeleton crew onsite to defend the place against intruders.

Cutter suddenly wondered what Colonel Slade would do when the end became imminently clear and he had to choose between capture or consumption by the living dead? When he knew without a shadow of a doubt that escape was impossible and that he was facing either a torturous death at the hands of the Lords of Death or watching his own intestines being pulled out like yard long sausages and being eaten before his eyes, what would he do? Would he choose to face death head on, eye to eye, like the hard charging warrior that he claimed to be? Would he surrender and give up the Academy without a fight? Would he allow himself to be turned into a snarling, carnivorous monster that no longer knew its friends from its dinner or would he eat a bullet and prevent the change from ever taking place? Cutter knew what he would do in the man's place. C-4 shaped body armor with a dead man's switch in his hand. He'd have one final knife fight with the nearest person of interest for old time's sake and then ka-boom. Game over. No coming back from that.

Their five-ton military truck sat two blocks away from the river, carefully camouflaged in an alley between an old Ace Hardware building and an attorney's office that had both been long since abandoned. His team sat nonchalantly on the stone embossed riverbank of the Rock River beside the Peoria Avenue Bridge, watching the swirling eddies of current spinning in clockwise whirls and the water being pushed swiftly away from the dam only two blocks away. Although the Apocalypse Academy was almost directly across the river, Cutter doubted that his team would be spotted as they watched for signs of the impending invasion that was destined to come from the north. His pulse raced as he imagined the forthcoming destruction about to take place.

In a way, Cutter had wanted to try and send word to Sergeant Havok about the impending invasion and report his conversation with the Bloody Baron. After all, the man had accepted the rag tag group of misfits and malcontents as Echo team and done his best to train them. In fact, they had learned a lot from the man, skills that would potentially keep them alive after the Academy's fall. They did kind of owe him a measure of loyalty. Of course, to warn him would mean either driving a five-ton truck straight into the gates without offloading any gear or supplies or sneaking someone in with a message. Either way if they were caught by one of the other Drill Sergeant's the result would be the same. Suspicion would be raised at Echo team and their loyalties. He could not allow that. Instead, if the resourceful Drill Sergeant made it out of the Academy and managed to break away from both "Zs" and the bikers, then Echo team could rendezvous with him, play the part of innocent mission completion and luckily pick him up. If not...well every war had its collateral damage. In fact, the only person that he was actually disappointed about leaving behind was Nurse Ortega. It was a shame that she was about to become a "Z" appetizer on the undead horde's buffet list because she really did look pretty damn hot in those military fatigue pants. Even after the apocalypse certain needs needed to be fulfilled and Cutter was willing to bet that the woman was a wildcat in bed. Latino heat to be sure.

Leaning his armored back against an old water oak tree that hung its branches sullenly over the river, Cutter scanned the distant horizon for any sign of the approaching undead horde. In his mind he imagined that their approach would be much like a swarm of bees. First one or two of the creatures, probably the Reapers would run into the area, buzzing about and looking for the first sign of a living person to attack. Then the Romeros would burst out of every available avenue in an overwhelming charge of stinging teeth and claws. Perhaps the walking dead were not that different from other creatures in nature. It was really just survival of the fittest to the Nth degree, although the undead really didn't "survive" because they were technically, already dead.

A soft footfall in the stone and leaves under the tree let him know that someone was approaching. Looking down at the shadow, he could tell by the dark profile and swishing ponytail that it was Lotus Jane. She held her helmet under one arm. Without turning around to look at her, he spoke. The tone of his voice bore condemnation and sarcasm fused into a single utterance.

"Are you here to tell me how wrong I am to let those self-righteous bastards at the Academy die without giving them any warning about the Baron's plan? If so, save your breath. They deserve what's coming to 'em. I wouldn't piss on 'em if they were on fire, much less save 'em." Cutter paused, letting his words ride the moment on a wave of angry emotions.

"Or maybe you're here to beg me just to save that little slant eyed boy that you've come to be so sweet on? Protect your new boyfriend if he comes back from his mission? Is that it?"

Jane's initial response choked off in her throat with a gasp. How had Cutter found out about her feelings for Techno? She hadn't told anyone and it was not like they were actually a couple. He was just a really nice boy that had been kind to her. In truth, he probably didn't even feel the same way about her. Instead, her mind whirled like a top, spinning in a vortex of unknown feelings. Trying to comprehend the magnitude of her team leader's observations was making her head swim. She reached a handout to the oak tree for support and sucked in several deep breaths.

"What? You didn't think that I would find out? I'm a lot more observant than other people give me credit for. That's why the sergeant Havoc picked me as his go to guy in the Academy and not Spartan or one of the other team leads. I see things. I know when something's wrong. I pay attention to the little details. For instance, did you know that the Havoc gave me the communications codes for every team's ZAP armor? I've been listening in to everyone inside my helmet. Hearing what they are seeing almost like I am there. Do you want to know a secret?" He lowered his voice and whispered conspiratorially. "Alpha team ain't faring so hot. Wanna know something else? You boy is hurt, maybe dying. Then he will turn. Maybe I should help them after all just so you can watch him be pacified. Would you like that?" He said and began to chuckle. The sound radiated malice and evil.

Lotus Jane's answer was written in her body language. Her head drooped forward as the tears poured from her eyes. Her shoulders drooped and shook as she cried. Her arms wrapped around herself, as if to hold back the pain of Cutter's words. She could not have appeared more guilty of Cutter's accusations if she had tried.

"Please…" She sobbed as the tears spilled freely down her high cheekbones, driving a stripe of black mascara before them. She looked at her team leader through the salty water that stung her eyes. "Please don't do this. Don't let this happen. There has already been so much death. It's wrong to not save whoever we can. I know that you hate Spartan. I know that you hate the Alphas. But Techno is an innocent kid. You've had it out for him before we were even assigned to teams. As far as we know, we may be the last living humans in any semblance of a society except for the biker's that worship the undead. Siding with them is akin to bigotry. They want everyone not like them dead. Everyone that does not bow down to the rule of the Bloody Baron is the enemy. Please...you are better than that Cutter. You are a leader. Don't let yourself become a puppet and help the Lords of Death raze the Apocalypse Academy."

She paused long enough to compose herself while Cutter looked at her thoughtfully. She could see the gears turning in his brain and believed that she knew what he wanted.

"I'll do anything you say. Anything that you want me to do... I will be loyal to only you. I will take care of your every need. I will be your toy. Whatever you want...Just please...please warn the Academy of what you know. No one will ever know. We can keep it a secret. Just us. Not even the rest of Echo team will know.... please..." Her voice trailed off as her sobs came heavier, driving rivers of charcoal-colored streaks down her face and making her appear almost clownish. Dropping to her knees, she struggled against the spasms in her chest as she fought the tears for air.

"Do you know what I think Jane?" Cutter said gently as he placed a hand on the top of her hair and began to stroke her hair and ponytail. Jane didn't look up at the physical contact, but just shoot her head no.

Cutter wrapped his fingers into the girl's black hair and jerked her head backwards so that his face was only inches from hers. Jane let out a timorous squeal of pain.

"I think that you are a backstabbing, gook-loving, traitorous little gutter slut whose brain was rotted out by way too many drugs in the alleys of the big city before "Z" day ever began."

The click-click-click of a revolver's hammer being drawn back drew her eyes upward from the ground. She had expected repercussions for her request. Perhaps even physical violence, but she was not mentally prepared to be staring down the black barrel of Cutter's .357magnum. From her vantage point at the weapon's business end, the weapon looked like a cannon. The black hole of the bore seemed to suck in all surrounding light from her vision, obscuring everything else. Her eyes crossed slightly as she peered down the weapon's abyssal-like barrel. Deep inside the darkness she caught the briefest flicker of silver and knew without a doubt that the light was the bullet that would disintegrate her brain.

"I think that I should shoot you right in your slutty face, right here, right now, and let the crows take what's left of your eyes. See, there ain't no place for a traitor in my world. Me, I gotta trust the people I'm workin' with and they gotta trust me. That's how we're gonna survive. The boys, they all trust me. They know that I am doing what's best for the Echoes. Doin' what it takes to keep livin'. Ya see, bein' part of that group of do-gooders? That ain't about livin' in today's world. It's about helpin' people and being all warm and fuzzy. Do you know what they sent their precious Alpha team to do? What they sent little Mr. Prince Charming to save?"

"No…" Was all she whispered.

"They didn't send them for supplies, or ammunition, or even to scout out the enemy! They sent them to a fucking orphanage! They sent them to bring back kids so we can have more mouths to feed when the supplies run out and to replace us when we die running their errands! Babies and children Jane! That's why your boyfriend is dying right now, lying out there somewhere? Someone else's kids! Fucking stupid! And who do you think they will send out next? When will it be our turn to go on a death-defying mission of ignorance? When will they send us out to die for what they believe in but we don't? That's why we side with the Baron. He takes what he needs. He doesn't squander resources on lost causes. He knows that we are the future."

Cutter paused, composing himself. "I'm gonna leave this up to our team. Whether you live or die will be completely up to them. Make no mistake, if the team says that you die, then I will shoot you right here, right now. No appeal, no mercy. Do you understand me?

Jane slowly moved her head up and down feeling the cold gun metal of the revolver's front sight scrape her forehead. She silently wished that she had kept her ZAP helmet on.

Raising his voice, Cutter addressed the rest of Echo team which had been watching the display of intra-team discipline from a distance.

"What do you think boys? You heard what she wants and what I've had to say about it. Do I shoot this bitch in her two-timing face for wanting to warn the other teams and the Academy? Or do I give her one last chance, let her get up and watch the Apocalypse Academy be destroyed brick by brick?"

Skull was the first one to speak up. The boy had found face paint during their supply run at one of the stores and had taken the time to paint a grim, black and white skull-like visage over his own face. Emaciated as the boy was, his eyes bugged out prominently against the black circles of makeup that surrounded them. Surrounded by the blue-black ZAP helmet, he looked eerie. When he spoke, it was with a nasally whine; a byproduct of the beating that Spartan and the giant black teenager, Freak had administered to the future members of Echo team on the first day of Academy training in the men's room.

387

"Shoot her!" The boy said with a rictus grin, the sparkle of insanity gleaming in his protruding eyes. "Shoot her good boss! Right in the face. She won't be so pretty then will she? No, she won't! Shoot the bitch!"

Cutter looked at Skull. The boy definitely had a screw or two loose. He would have to remember to keep an eye on him. Crazy people could be unpredictable and violent. Flecks of spittle and glistened on the teenager's chin and gooey foam cornered the boy's mouth as he anticipated the murder of Jane. Nodding once, he spoke aloud. "That's one vote for execution...Savage?"

The dark boy spoke in a low, cautious voice as his eyes flicked from teammate to teammate.

"Death is too quick for her. The pain of the heart will eat at her for a much, much longer time. To me that makes a more fitting punishment. Suffer knowing that you're alive while someone else you could have saved is dead. I say let her watch. If we are lucky then maybe she will even hear her precious Techno's death scream over the river. If she gets out of hand between now and then, shoot her."

"Hmmm, interesting point of view. I hadn't considered the mental torture aspect." Cutter said. "Ok, that's one vote for letting her watch." Cutter actually hated logic. Action based on impulse was usually so much more efficient in his world, although it had occasionally added problems later on, such as getting arrested for instance. But that was then and this was now. He turned to Orc, the last member of Echo team.

"Don't fuck this up Orc. I know you aren't the sharpest knife in the drawer so let's keep this simple shall we? Does she live or does she die?"

Orc's hideous face contorted as he struggled for the right answer. His pink tongue pressed between his lips and licked across his cracked and crooked teeth and his bushy eyebrows furrowed like dive bombing caterpillars upon his thick brow. He knew what decision he thought was right. The problem was that he didn't think that Cutter would agree with his decision and then would be angry with him. Instead, he asked Cutter a question.

"Uhh boss? Ain't we 'cross the river from the 'cademy?"

Cutter rolled his eyes. Looking over his shoulder he used his non gun hand to point out the castle-like structure on the opposite side of the water.

"What?" He said exasperated. "Really?  You are such an idiot? You can see the fucking building sitting there plain as day and you take the time in this serious moment to ask me something stupid like that?"

Cutter was clearly annoyed. The Echo team leader's face was turning redder by the moment. "What's your point?" He said to Orc through gritted teeth.

"Well...dat ain't but a coupla hunnerd yards the way I figure it, you know across the water. Ain't they gonna hear it if'n you put a bullet in her head and splatter her brains and be warned just the same? Ain't that what we don' want to happen?"

Cutter thought about the behemoth's question for a moment. He had been so caught up in his righteous fury at Jane that he hadn't considered the report of the heavy barreled revolver across the water. He remembered a science class in his past that sound travelled even better over water than on land. Maybe if he had had a little .22 or .25 caliber pistol it would have been overlooked but the heavy boom of the .357 would not be. Shrugging his shoulders dramatically, he lifted the gun away from his female teammate's forehead and held it at shoulder height while he de-cocked it with a smile.

"I guess this is your lucky day sweet cheeks." He said while he reached down with his free hand and grasped her cheeks from under the chin, raising her to her feet.

"But let's get this straight. This ain't a free pass. You got a long way to go to get back in good graces with the Echoes again. If you scream out or try to run across that bridge and warn anybody, in any way, shape or form, then I will use my favorite knife to cut out your tongue and feed it to the fish over there below the dam, do you understand me?" He squeezed her face harder for emphasis.

"Oh, and by the way, if you even think about stickin' me or one of the boys with your blade and I will personally hold you down while the "Zs" take turns gnawing off that pretty face. Visualize what you'd look like with no nose, no eyes, no lips and no cheeks before you think about being stupid. Are we clear?" He released her face with a small sideways shove that caused her to stumble as he waited for a response.

"I understand Cutter. It won't happen again." She said in a timid voice, her spirit broken.

"Good. Don't ever forget that you belong to Echo team. Your heart; your body...even your very soul. We own you now and always."

As she nodded her head automatically in subservience she glanced forlornly at the Apocalypse Academy and her heart felt squeezed in a vice of despair. Slowly, she tried to rise back to her feet but never saw Cutter's fist coming. The world exploded in a myriad of sparkling colorful bursts, and then mercifully faded to black.

# CHAPTER TWENTY-NINE
# CRUCIFIXION AT THE DRIVE-IN
# THEATRE

The allotted five minutes had elapsed and Deadeye still had not appeared at the rendezvous point as they had discussed. Rather than risk his scout's position by calling out to him on the communications system, Spartan chose to trust in his teammates' skills and instead evaluated the approach to the drive-in theatre. The road serpentined for approximately one hundred yards along a gravel road before coming up to a gate house where, in the days before the apocalypse, tickets had been sold to persons wanting to view a movie from their vehicle. Now the booth stood vacant and empty, a monument to days of the forgotten pleasures of the past. Spartan felt the twitch of a memory and vaguely remembered a movie about giant rats or chickens or some such. As quickly as the memory came, it faded leaving a void and a question mark in his mind. He really wished that his memory word return. It was annoying to have blank spots in his psyche.

Looking deeper into the shadows of the gate house, Spartan could not see any sign of a posted guard at the entrance. Switching over automatically to the infrared and thermal imaging systems of his helmet, he subconsciously confirmed the findings of his naked eye. There could still be someone posted on guard duty out of sight and shielded against his scanning capabilities but he highly doubted it. Still, they could be around a hidden corner or below the ground level so he would need to be cautious.

Beyond the eight-foot-high privacy fence and gate house, Spartan could make out what appeared to be the flickering half-light of a small campfire surrounded by the husks of old vehicles and at least a half a dozen Lords of Death carousing merrily as they passed a bottle between them. The men obviously felt that they were in no danger as they did not even hold a semblance of a guard on duty and instead swayed and slurred in merriment that indicated that they were all drunk.

Moving silently to his right several yards, Spartan craned his neck outward, gaining a better view of the theatre's one-hundred-foot-tall movie screen. There, spotlighted with an old police car's Q beam hung the battered form of Sergeant Hogg. The military man hung stretched out by his arms, his torso and legs dangling downward. Blood streaked the man's bare torso and face, showing that he had been savagely beaten. Spartan could not tell if the man was even alive from this distance. Tamping down the rage that was welling deep in his core, he struggled to tell if the man had been crucified in the traditional manner by the Lords of Death or if they had merely suspended him from the movie screen by ropes or cables. Enhancing the magnification of his optics, he did not see any noticeable injuries to the man's palms or wrists except where the rope had bitten in. That was good as it made the act of getting the man down from the screen easier. Not easy by any means, but easier.

A rustle behind him drew Spartan's attention. Spinning on his heel, he assumed a low crouching attack position; the Sword of Leonidas pulled back and at the ready to attack. The air shimmered and Deadeye blurred into view. Spartan relaxed his weapon and eased back down to one knee. Deadeye did the same. The Alpha team leader noted that the boy's armored fist held his tactical tomahawk tightly. Gore dripped from the heavy blade. It had seen recent use.

"What happened?" Spartan asked, nodding at the tomahawk.

"I saw a straggler from the skating rink run across the road right after we spoke. I didn't want him circling around and accidentally stumbling upon us or shouting out an alarm. For the record, he had been bitten at least twice. I did him a favor."

Spartan nodded and then turned towards the drive-in theatre. "I counted at least six separate bikers around the fire near the center of the parking lot not including Sgt. Hogg. The fire should work to our advantage and screw up their night vision. I didn't see any posted guards at this end. We will need to do this as quickly and quietly as possible so that we don't attract any unwanted attention. From the decrease in shots being fired and the lack of screams, I think that your little party at the roller-skating rink is coming to an end. On the upside, I think that these guys are so drunk that either they didn't even hear all of the commotion or just didn't care about the locals that they had teamed up with and left them to the "Zs" considering themselves safe inside the fencing."

Deadeye nodded. "The man in the woods also told me that there are two men posted at the rear exit of the parking lot at a separate gate house. That is apparently how the biker's come and go. The front gate is booby trapped with some sort of explosive device. He didn't know what kind...even under duress."

Spartan thought about their situation for a moment, considering his options for attack.

"If we jump the side walls of the drive-in and hit them hard and fast in a pincer movement like they taught us at the Academy, we should be able to pull this off. I will create the diversion. I don't know exactly what it will be yet, but you will know it when you see it. You take down as many as you can from behind. This has to be quick. We don't know if they have Comms or not. Look for anyone grabbing a radio rather than a weapon. We'll get to Hogg next, and then deal with the gate guards last. If this goes south or if I am captured, you are to get to Dancer and get back to the Academy. We still have a mission to accomplish. Pick up Freak and Techno on your way."

"Understood."

"What about me?" Dancer asked, speaking up for the first time and letting Spartan know that she had returned to consciousness. "I'm still a part of this bloody team ya know mate."

"You have no distance weapon and are physically in no shape to engage in hand-to-hand combat Dance. Your naginata requires two hands to wield it properly and with your busted arm there is no way that you can do that. I've seen you practice with that thing enough times to be confident that I know what is required. You still have your pistol. Act as a spotter for us and make sure that we do not get any surprises from the roadway. Stay outside the fencing and advise over our helmet Comms if anyone comes. That includes on foot or in a vehicle. Let me be clear. You have a severe head injury. You are not to engage in combat unless your position is compromised and you are in active fear for your life. If you can run, then run. We will catch up to you. Do you understand?"

"But…"

"No time for arguments on this one Dancer. We've got to get to Hogg. Every minute that he hangs up there is another minute that he could die from asphyxiation if he's not already dead. I'm not willing to waste that time arguing. Just do as you're told."

Being left out of a fight did not sit well with the Brit. She had been trained to fight by her father. Trained to survive almost since she was old enough to walk. One of her earliest memories was of hiking mountains while carrying a full backpack at his side. But he had also taught her how to follow orders immediately and without complaint.

"Copy." Was all that she said.

Spartan nodded his head in appreciation at the fact that the normally strong-willed girl let the decision go without debate or argument. Turning back to Deadeye he selected his avenue of approach into the parking lot of the drive-in.

"I'll come in from the east side. The wall around the drive-in is only eight feet high so I should be able to clear it using the enhancements of my ZAP armor. You take the west side. Come in from a dark spot. Once their eyes are on me, acquire and fire on your choice of targets. Eliminate as many as possible from a distance with your bow. Do me one small favor. Try not to shoot me will ya?"

"Nothing's guaranteed in the chaos of combat my friend." The Apache stated deadpan. "But I will do my best."

Spartan chuckled. He had never seen the teen miss, neither in practice nor in actual battle. "How's the battery on your ZAP?"

"Sixty-two percent." Deadeye responded after checking the digital readout provided in the helmet.

"Mine's a lot lower. I'm at forty-four percent. Dancer and I burned up a lot of juice getting out of Freeport. All the more reason to get this done quickly. I would really hate to look like the Tin Woodsman and have my armor frozen in place because I ran out of power. It would be a stupid way to die."

Deadeye nodded, wiping his tomahawk off on the grass, and then slid it back into the sheath at his belt. Unslinging his razor bow, he reached over his shoulder for one of the black Plexiglas arrows in his quiver. Drawing the arrow, he quickly knocked it onto the bowstring. Uttering a simple "Good hunting" he vanished from view into the night as his ZAP armor diffused and refracted all light around him. Without another word he moved into the forest, silent as a nature spirit.

Spartan stood in a crouch, muscles tensed, clutching the hilt of the sword of Greece's greatest warrior king tightly in his fist. Eyes focused hard on his destination at the east side fence, he started at the touch of Dancer's hand as it gently closed over his wrist. Looking over he saw the girl leaning in close to his helmet so that she could whisper softly enough for his auditory sensors to pick up.

"You watch your arse mate." She said point blankly. "These bastards may be legless on the booze but they are still Lords of Death. Don't go getting sloppy just because you think the drink has them knackered. You end them hard and quick. No mercy and no sympathy."

Spartan nodded once and turned his head back towards the drive-in theatre. Gently pulling his hand out of her grasp, he reached up, clasped her shoulder once, and then sprinted out of the woods as fast as his ZAP armor could propel him. His legs churned in a blur that swept up the fallen leaves in his wake until he entered the opposite tree line next to the wooden fence. Slowing down to a crouched walk, he quickly moved up to the fence and peered through the gap between two boards.

He could clearly see the six bikers from this position. All of the men wore the vests and colors of the Lords of Death. Each was seated in various states of reclining around the middle-sized campfire, passing a bottle of liquid frequently between them. The echoing sounds of laughter and slurred speech carried on the silent Midwestern air and the scent of various types of tobacco and narcotic smoke registered across his armor's external sensors.

Maneuvering his body to look further past the men into the parking lot, Spartan could see a large SUV that had apparently been abandoned during the apocalypse. Although it stood upright, the body was rusted, pock marked with innumerable bullet holes and all of the windows had been shattered. The vehicle sat like a rotting red metallic corpse only two rows from the wooden fence about twenty yards from his current position. While the old hulk of a vehicle would not provide him any type of cover during a firefight it would hopefully conceal his movement as he entered into the parking lot over the fence.

Moving quickly, he gauged the time elapsed and decided that Deadeye had been given sufficient time to get into position. The tall, dry autumn grasses whispered and swished with a thick rustling sound as he moved. Pausing once again he peered again through the boards. Although he knew that the noise was enhanced by his helmet sensors, he still worried that the men across the fence would become alerted to his presence, costing him the element of surprise. It was a needless worry. The men had not moved except to pass the bottle between themselves. Taking one last glance at the men, he quickly side stepped to where he approximated the SUV to be. Sliding the Sword of Leonidas into its sheath, he grasped the top of the fence with both hands and propelled himself overusing the servos of the ZAP armor to enhance his strength exponentially. Silently he landed in a crouch and redrew his weapon.

Cautiously he peered around the truck's rusted bumper. All six men still sat drunkenly bullshitting amongst themselves and passing the distinctly emptier bottle between them. Several emptier bottles littered the ground near the fire. His entrance into the parking lot had been clean and unobserved. Pulling his head back behind the engine block, he keyed his communications on Deadeye's frequency.

"Deadeye this is Spartan." He whispered. "I am over and clear. I have direct line of sight one targets. I am waiting on your confirmation before I approach."

"Confirmation given." The Apache scout advised. "I am on target as well. Engage at will."

Spartan took a deep breath and steeled his nerves. Normally the thought of combat did not jangle his senses but if he failed this time someone would surely die. Sparing a quick glance up at Sergeant Hogg where he dangled high upon the theatres screen, he felt the red rage rising in his gullet; an internal volcano beginning to erupt. He bit down hard on his lip letting the immediate pain refocus his thoughts and allowing him to force the emotional magma back down temporarily. This operation needed methodical execution, not unbridled emotion. Feeling once more in control, he stood up from behind the rusted body of the SUV and strode purposefully towards the drunken men.

# Chapter Thirty
# The Freak and the Nun

Sister Margaret walked over to where Freak sat against the rock overhang deftly dodging the sleeping forms of her charges. The children, as children will, were all sprawled out in various positions that would have made a senior yoga instructor proud. Quietly the nun addressed the giant black member of the Phalanx.

"Do you mind if I sit down young man?" She asked quietly, indicating a piece of fallen log across from where Freak sat.

"Last time I checked this was still a free country." He shrugged. Although his Granny had insisted that he be brought up with a proper church upbringing, Freak had never been especially comfortable at church, much less with direct interaction towards members of the faith. It made him feel fake inside. Like kissing an ugly Aunt. He did it because he had to, not because he wanted to. Besides, where he had grown up in Chicago, God didn't seem to be minding the store. The "golden rule" of *"Do unto others..."* had been unequivocally changed by the street gangs and thugs to say *"...before they can do unto you.* "It was a real statement about how members of the faith felt about their gods' protection when they hired armed guards during services and replaced all of the church vehicles windows with bullet proof glass. Thieves and drug abusers of every ilk were constantly trying to steal silver candle sticks and gold inlaid crosses. Once a man had even come into the service and attempted to rob the church's collection plate at gun point, during the services. It was hard to focus on a sermon about the value of life after the security guards had shot the man dead on the altar steps. Freak remembered the blood spraying across the huge bible and wondered how many other people had died for that book.

Holding the baby close to her body to keep it warm against the autumn chill, the nun used her thick pinky finger as a pacifier allowing the infant to alternately suck and gnaw on the tip. Smiling down at the cooing child, the portly woman spoke in a quiet, yet firm tone. It was a voice that was used to kindness rather than the harsh street tone that Freak had grown up with.

"I saw what you did this morning. It was very kind of you. I wanted to take a moment and thank you and your friends for risking your lives to save us and also to thank you specifically for what you did for little Danielle."

Completely caught off guard, Freak muttered "You're welcome, it was no big deal". He hoped that the praise would be the end of the conversation. He wasn't sure what he had been expecting when the woman came and asked him if she could sit down. Fire and brimstone about death and the apocalypse maybe but a kind tone and thanks most certainly were not it. It just wasn't. The nun continued.

"I wanted to tell you a little bit about Danielle's past, especially what she experienced when her parents died, so that you can understand why what you did and said to her was so significant and special. Her parents, Billy and Ashley Sizemore were average people, living average lives. Billy worked as the night shift manager at a local restaurant and Ashley was a stay-at-home mother. Together they managed a decent middle-class existence and were active participants at the church every Sunday. Well, maybe not every Sunday but enough of the time that we got to see them and recognize them as part of the extended church family. The last time that we saw them was the church picnic two weeks before "Z" night."

"The unholy eruption of the viral dead from the earth and the decimation of mankind surged through the media. Small towns in the Midwest being what they are, the news held little interest for the Sizemore's and the virus was considered to be far away; confined to the urban Mecca's such as New York, London, Cairo, Los Angeles, Mexico City and Moscow. Far away from the rural life and city limits of a northern Illinois corn town. If anyone at the local eatery even noticed the plague of the dead it was probably mentioned with the phrase "publicity stunt" or "terrorist attack" attached to it and passed like so much waste into the trash cans of everyday lives. No one thought that the virus would ever reach America's heartland. Even the church announced that we all had nothing to fear because the plague seemed to affect only those areas of the world were debauchery and decadence had set in. Sort of a modern-day Sodom and Gomorra story. We were all wrong."

"By the time the town realized that there was more than a harsh strain of the flu incubating in their midst, power grids across the country had begun to fail and hundreds of people were dying at the hands of the walking dead every minute of every day. The wave that initially struck Freeport started at the gas station near the interstate. In minutes it had magnified exponentially. In hours, they were everywhere and in a single day the city was lost."

"Billy, being of above average intelligence, had left work early and raced home to protect his family. Surrounded by undead neighbors, he fought his way into his home and slammed the door. Quickly Billy and Ashley piled everything that they could move against the door in an attempt to barricade their home and keep the family safe. Knowing that they would be unable to flee with such a small child, they chose to try and ride out the viral wave inside their home through stealth rather than force of arms. You see, Billy owned no guns and was armed only with a tennis racquet and a golf club. I know this because I found his camcorder in which he gave a statement for posterity's sake. I think he knew that he and possibly Ashley were about to die but he was hoping to protect little Danielle."

"As the front door splintered and gave way, Billy handed a pink backpack and a roll of duct tape to Ashley. The video showed Billy shove Ashley and Danielle towards the bedroom and turn to fight the approaching creatures. There were literally dozens of the hell spawn and the video bounces frantically as Ashley runs up the stairs before stopping on the second-floor landing to look back at her husband. The video records both the blood curdling screams and the gruesome death as Billy is literally torn into so many pieces by the walking dead that he can never be resurrected by the virus. Ashley's screams can also be heard as well as Danielle's hysterical crying. May God rest his soul. He was a good and brave man."

"Ashley can then be seen and heard slamming the bedroom door. At some point she sets the camcorder on the child's desk and is seen in the video wedging the desk chair under the doorknob. Frantically she runs across the room and begins flinging toys and stuffed animals out of the little girl's wooden toy box. The toy box itself was about four feet long and two feet high with a hinged wooden lid depicting a Disney elephant and her baby Dumbo."

"Ashley then took the pink backpack and a blanket and hurriedly threw them into the toy box. Tears stream down the woman's face as she kisses her baby girl, hugs her

411

tightly and hands her a flashlight. Against the girl's panicked and pleading screams and the shattering door behind her, Ashley forces the poor girl down beneath the wooden lid and begins to quickly loop the duct tape around the toy box, sealing it shut. Two, three four loops are wound around the makeshift protective box before the door finally gives way and the chair skitters across the floor from the weight of the undead assault. As the living dead begin to tear into her flesh, Ashley can be seen dropping to her knees and draping her body over the top of the child's hiding place. With every last beat of her heart, she fights to hold the toy box shut. She never stopped protecting her child, even in death."

The nun paused; her breath hitching as she quietly cried tears for the lost mother and father. Freak could see the moisture running freely down the older woman's chubby cheeks, glistening in the limited light of their camp. Composing herself, the nun apologized for her emotions and finished the story.

"I found them like that, three days later as myself and two of the other nuns went door to door searching for surviving parishioners. She has the most unimaginable night terrors to this day and probably will for the rest of her life. I cannot imagine the emotional trauma of listening to my mother and father die, much less being locked into a wooden box while they did so. That is why what you said and did for us is so significant. Even if your tale only brings the girl one night of respite, it is far more peace than she had before. For that I am eternally grateful."

Freak wasn't sure what to say. Sure, he had known that the little girl had lost someone. They all had since "Z" night. But he had never suspected anything so gruesome and heartbreaking. He wanted to rush over and pick the girl up; to hug her and tell her that everything would be alright. But he knew that was a lie. Likely as not they would all face death again and soon, at that. The Lords of Death were still out there and the horde was marching south. Emotions boiled within him and his throat felt constricted as if by a giant snake, as he licked his dry lips.

"As long as I am alive, no one living or undead will hurt that little girl ever again. Me and the Blues Brothers will make damn sure of that. You have my word."

The nun smiled faintly in the night. "I know…and so does God. Thank you."

Then she stood up and walked back into the makeshift tent without another word to check on the children, leaving the Phalanx giant all alone with his thoughts.

# Chapter Thirty-One
# Battle at the Drive-in
# Theatre

So drunk were the guards, that the first one did not even register Spartan's armored presence until he was marching directly towards them less than twenty feet away. Blackened armor glinting in the firelight like the carapace of a desert scorpion, red and yellow colors flickered and flowed in vivid, contrasting styles across Spartan's face plate, arms, legs and body. The effect was like seeing a walking mirage of ebony, crimson, and amber approaching the Lords of Death around the campfire.

Three full seconds of drunken shock further passed before the biker's alcohol saturated brains registered the imminent danger of the vicious sword dangling from the mirages' hand. This hesitation allowed Spartan to close the gap another ten feet between him and the men that were trying to prevent him from rescuing Sergeant Hogg. That delay would ultimately spell their demise.

The first of the Lords of Death to lurch to his feet attempted to reach for his rifle that was leaning against the log on which he had been sitting. He managed a brief exclamation of "What the fu…!" before a deadly black arrow streaked through the night sky and sank fully into the back of his skull, pitching him over the log and headlong into the campfire. The man was dead before he felt the white-hot flames ever touch his flesh.

The second biker decided to forego his weapon and attempted to bull rush Spartan headlong, intent on using his ample girth to bear his armored foe to the ground and hopefully gain an advantage. In his intoxicated state, it took Spartan very little effort to sidestep the man's wild charge and deliver a bone snapping round house kick to the attacker's ribs and solar plexus. The audible snap of bone and whoosh of exploding air from the man's lips burst out into the night. The sounds were immediately silenced as Spartan drove and armored elbow downward into the base of the bikers' skull. As the man face planted into the gravel and dirt of the parking lot, Spartan spun the sword of Leonidas point down and thrust it savagely between the man's shoulder blades. The razor-sharp blade vibrated as the biker's spinal cord severed with a pop. The entire attack and counterattack had lasted less than three seconds.

One of the Lords of Death, a thin man with a long goatee, rolled behind a parked car and slowly drew a two-and-a-half-foot long machete. The weapon had a razor sharp, squared off front edge and jagged teeth across its top. The weapon glinted in the firelight and Spartan momentarily wondered if the oversized knife could penetrate his ZAP armor. Twirling the big knife in circle, the thin man spoke to Spartan in a voice that indicated that he smoked a lot of cigarettes.

"I don' know who the hell you are but I'm gonna gut you. Cut you real deep with this here blade. Gonna cut you deep and watch you weep. Watch you bleed."

Spartan nodded his armored head, encouraging the fight. He could feel the returning volcanic rise of the battle rage burning for release in his chest. His heart was pounding and a red veil tinged his vision. Grinding his teeth, he fought for emotional control. Opening his mouth to speak would only increase the risk of the words becoming an outright roar of guttural fury. That loss of control would only make matters worse right now.

The biker's intoxication was countered by the rush of adrenaline. His body responded to its training and muscle memory as a skilled fighter even though his mind was cloaked in an alcoholic fog. He was obviously used to wielding the machete in battle. Two, three, four slashing cuts rang off Spartan's armor, scoring the black finish but not penetrating the polymer of the armor itself. Spartan slashed the heavier blade of Leonidas and the man deftly side stepped the swipe and rang a heavy hit across the side of Spartan's helmeted head. The blow was solid enough that Spartan was certain that he would have been incapacitated at the least and probably killed if not for the armor's resilience.

Seeing that he could not out finesse the man's superior blade work, Spartan changed tactic. Observing the man's attack vectors and technique, Spartan noticed that the biker continually chopped with the heavy, squared off blade before slashing horizontally. *Chop, chop, chop, swing. Chop, chop, chop, swing. Chop, chop, chop, and swing.* Spartan repeatedly parried these attacks with his longer blade, using the rhythm of the pattern to steadily draw him closer to his assailant. On the fourth consecutive cycle, as he brought his steel blade up to parry the horizontal slash, he allowed the attack to spin him three hundred and sixty degrees. Driven by centrifugal force, the Sword of Leonidas bit deep through the faded blue jeans and into the back of the man's hamstrings. Slashing and pulling the weapon free as he completed the spin, he immediately reversed the ancient weapon's momentum to power a backhanded swing into the base of the bikers' neck, where the head met the shoulders. The folded steel slashed through skin, muscle and bone before spinning the bandana clad head off into the dark. Blood fountained from the top and bottom of the biker's body as the corpse fell lifeless to the ground, the machete falling from nerveless fingers and landing point down into the dirt and gravel.

Ten yards away the biker's mouth moved open and closed without uttering a sound. In its severed brain it distantly remembered that a severed head could live up to two minutes without its blood supply. Fortunately for him, he only lasted another ten seconds before his eyes glazed over dead.

A shouted war cry from behind Spartan warned him that another attacker had circled around behind him during the battle and was now charging at him. Spinning on his heel, sword extended low to the rear, he saw a blond ponytailed biker wearing a long-braided beard running towards him wielding the upraised black labeled whiskey bottle over his head like a bludgeon. The bottle itself was not a truly imminent threat thanks to the superiority of the ZAP armor, but the biker still needed to be dealt with before they could rescue Sergeant Hogg.

Then as abruptly as the charge had started, the man slowed to a walk before finally coming to a stop altogether. The expression on the biker's face changed from anger to confusion as he opened his hand and allowed the bottle to drop to the ground where it shattered. Due to the shadowed firelight flickering across the biker's dark clothing and vest, Spartan did not immediately notice the black feathered arrow protruding from the front of the man's t-shirt. The biker slowly sagged to his knees, his mouth forming an "O" as he looked down at the arrow, then back at Spartan and back a final time at the arrow before toppling over onto his side. Blood gurgled from the man's mouth and leaked in twin rivulets down his chin as he slowly suffocated in his own blood.

The last two Lords of Death turned back-to-back, understanding that the attack was two sided and intent on protecting each other's flank. The first man, a bald giant easily as large as Freak bearing a tattoo of a flaming skull upon his chest faced the forest line where Deadeye was hidden. Muscles rippled across the man's bare chest and massive arms causing the skull to appear as though it was laughing when he moved. In his hands he held a sledgehammer of impressive size.

The second biker held a glistening pair of hand scythes. The wicked looking curved blades looked sharp and dangerous in the firelight. Leaner than, but just as muscular as his mammoth partner, the man worked the blades in a complex series of cutting patterns in an obvious display of skill. Spartan had no doubt that many men, women and maybe even children had felt the bite of those blades. Observing their movements, he could tell that these two men were used to fighting as a team. Slowly the two men revolved clockwise, turning to present a more difficult target for the hidden archer while they surveyed their options. Any ill effect of the alcohol that they had consumed during their fireside revelry was gone, leaving only two very deadly looking bikers in its place.

As they completed the circuit, Deadeye stepped from behind the pickup truck from where he had stood firing at the bikers and deactivated the cloaking function of his ZAP armor. Blurring into full view of the hammer wielding biker, he knocked an arrow and raised the deadly razor bow.

Without a spoken word uttered between them, the two bikers acted in unison to charge their two armored foes. Weaving in an exaggerated zig-zag pattern as he ran forward, Hammer man displayed his strength by pulling the heavy sledgehammer through a series of feints and simulated attacks. Each movement brought the heavy implement almost a yard closer to the scout who calmly tracked his movements with the knocked arrow. In the other direction, sickle man feinted, withdrew and tumbled towards Spartan with the deadly looking hooked blades constantly weaving figure eights around his torso and head. The blades moved so quickly that Spartan was having difficulty tracking the movement of the weapons even with his enhanced vision and targeting systems of the ZAP armor. It was readily apparent that the man was a martial artist of some sort and appeared, at least on the surface, that he also had extensive training with his chosen weapons. Spartan slowly shifted his footing to allow him to bring the Sword of Leonidas up over his shoulder before settling it into a downward pointed defensive stance with his longer blade diagonally held before his body.

As the brawny biker closed the gap between them to less than twenty feet, Deadeye released his first arrow. The bow string hummed as the plexiglass shaft rocketed forward, straight towards the man's' exposed flaming skull tattoo. To the Apache's surprise, the biker yanked the heavy steel head of the hammer upward at the last instant causing the arrow to ricochet away harmlessly into the night. Perhaps sensing the stunned disbelief that held Deadeye still for a moment, the biker roared and changed his rushing pattern into a straight on bull rush, hoping to crush the smaller warrior beneath the mallet's steel head before he could recover his surprised composure.

Diving hard to his left to avoid the crushing blow, Deadeye rolled on his shoulder and fired the second arrow as his body completed its revolution and returned him to his feet a yard and a half away. The Lord of Death was just trying to pull the sledgehammer's heavy head out of the gravel where he had sunken it with his violent, missed attack when the yard long black arrow ripped through the flesh of his thigh, quivering as the deadly sharp arrowhead imbedded into the man's femur. With a scream that sounded far more like anger than pain, the biker swung the hammer downward, snapping the arrow off just above his skin. Deadeye quick fired a third arrow directly into the man's face from point blank range, but again the man's reflexes were amazingly…almost supernaturally… fast.

Rather than impaling the biker through the skull, the man jerked his head sideways and the arrow sunk into and through the trapezius muscle that stood like a miniature mountain attached to the side of the goliath's neck and shoulder. The arrow punched clean through the leather and muscle, half in and half out of the front and back of the biker's body. As if the deadly arrow was nothing more than an annoyance, the Lord of Death reached up with his free hand and ripped the arrow free with a scream of rage. Whatever drug this man was on, Deadeye knew that he would only take him down with a successful kill shot.

Anything else was just as likely to piss the bull of a man off further. The Apache didn't want to waste time hoping that the giant would bleed out. Already the man's violent screams could be attracting attention from persons both living and undead outside the fence.

The massive sledgehammer swung in a wide arc towards Deadeye, looking to smash the Scout to death in a single, devastating blow. At the last instant, the Apache managed to raise the razor bow, parrying the strike with the steel body of his own weapon. The effect was immediate and painful. Powered by the mass and momentum of the crazed biker, the impact was like getting hit broadside by a runaway truck. The sheer force of the impact drove the bow back into Deadeye's own torso, forcing the teen to tumble with blow and allow it to drive him backward or risk having both arms broken. As it was, both of his arms vibrated painfully, barely allowing him to hold onto his weapon. He had never been hit so hard. Rolling hard to the side, he kept moving as the crazed biker beat a barrage of blows upon the gravel and earth causing the rock to disintegrate beneath the hammer's steel head and cause shrapnel to repeatedly chatter across his face plate and helmet. Clearly the biker was trying to crush his skull in single smashing blow to end the fight. On the fifth missed strike, the sledgehammer struck a softer section of ground and sunk its head and four inches of the haft into the dirt and crushed rock.

Deadeye used the microsecond that it took for the behemoth to rip the hammer free to his full advantage. Driving his feet upward into the air, the Apache kicked up to a battle ready, standing position and ripped the razor bow's keen edges into a deep, crosscut slash across the biker's abdomen, followed immediately by a shallower "X" cut across the man's chest. Sinewy muscle and bluish gray intestine showed through the separate slashes as blackish-crimson blood poured freely from both the arrow and blade wounds. As with the pain from the arrows, the biker merely snorted in derision at the damage and kept fighting. Deadeye felt that he now knew exactly how the matadors felt trying to wear down the mighty bulls in the old-world arenas.

Perhaps sensing defeat, the giant lifted the huge sledgehammer above his head with both hands and hurled it with all his might at the Scout. Again, the Apache rolled to the side to avoid the blow only to realize too late that the flying weapon had only been a distraction.

The Lord of Death crossed the space between them and wrapped a massive hand firmly on the juncture of the ZAP armor's shoulder and neck guard. Swinging the teen as if he were nothing more than a small child, the biker ripped the Apache backward, slamming him into a parked pickup truck. Despite wearing the battle armor, pain burst through Deadeye's lower back and kidneys and the razor bow spun off into the night. Two, three, four times the move was repeated as if the heavily armored teenager were nothing more than a rag doll, crushing the boy painfully against the grill, bumper and hood of the truck contorting the vehicle's metal out of shape with each blow.

Reaching out with his free hand, the Lord of Death grabbed Deadeye by the protective thigh guard and with a single, effortless motion hoisted him high into the air. Then taking a two-step hop, the biker launched the teenager over the cab of the truck through the air, crashing violently against the vehicles open bed and sliding him off the downed tailgate and onto to the ground. Deadeye lay stunned and unmoving, his vision bursting with colorful strobes of pain.

The initial impacts with the truck's bumper-to-bed tour had driven all of the air from the boy's lungs and left him dazed as he slid downward onto the ground, landing in a black armored heap. Even as his mind fought to draw air into his lungs, he knew that he would regret the action. He had heard at least two ribs break during the battering. Sure enough, as the first draw of air sought to expand his lungs, wildfire race across his nervous system, exploding his vision into blue-white stars. The pain was so intense that he almost blacked out. Instead, he lay deathly still, fighting for self-control of the agony while his mind searched for a solution to his enemy's preternatural strength and ferocity.

Smiling through blood coated teeth, the biker swiped his massive forearm across his bald head, wiping away the sweat and gore that had accumulated there. Almost casually the man walked over to where he had thrown his sledgehammer and hoisted it up onto one cyclopean sized shoulder. Poking a finger into his own distended intestines as he walked, the Lord of Death drew the digit out and licked the blood from it.

"Pathetic…" Was the first tangible word that the biker said aloud to Deadeye. "Mortal bodies are so weak." He did not know if the teenager was actually still alive or already dead but he fully intended to ensure that it was the latter, probably by hitting him fifteen or twenty more times with the hammer. "Say good-bye runt."

Deadeye lay motionless, sprawled below the tailgate and trailer hitch. The world was spinning and tilting crazily. He could see the insanely strong biker walking slowly towards him and he knew that he would only have one chance to escape. If he screwed it up, the giant would kill him, no doubt. He had to wait for just the right moment.

The massive biker stood by the teenagers' crumpled body and spit a bloody mass of phlegm down onto the boy's prone form. "To bad you ain't gonna survive this beatin' kid. You might've done good as one of us."

Then the gore covered biker slowly, almost dramatically raised the hammer to its full height well over ten feet in the air. Clenching all of his powerful muscles into a single deadly downward blow, the biker reversed the weapons' momentum at its apex and drove the heavy hammer down towards the Apache's armored head with all of his might.

When he was fully certain that the biker's momentum was committed to the swing; Deadeye burst into action. Kicking both feet outward as hard as he could, he was rewarded with both armored heels connecting with the front of the Lord of Death's knee cap. A sharp snapping sound and the knee reversed direction, bringing the first cry of agony from the man. The hammer slammed harmlessly into the dirt as Deadeye rolled hard to his left, again to the front and a third time to the left again, placing the truck's bed between himself and the biker that had collapsed to one knee, clasping his injured leg and roaring in fury. Quickly Deadeye activated his ZAP Armor's camouflage function and faded into visual nothingness.

The Lord of Death could not believe it. It was bad enough to have been injured by that Academy brat, but to receive the exact same debilitating injury that had cost him his life centuries before was ironic and insulting. The other Immortals of Xerxes' retinue would cause him no end of torment if they found out about it. It was bad enough posing as a human, but a crippled one? Never!

Grabbing the sledgehammer from where it lay on the ground, he used the weapon as a makeshift cane to help himself stand up. He could see his brother Immortal fighting the cursed one across the parking lot, but there was no sign of the boy he had been about to kill. Had the brat run away? Surely not. Unless he knew that he could not win. Unless he knew that the biker was something more than he appeared to be. That could not be allowed. The Baron had forbidden the revealing of their true forms to the humans. He had to find the teenager and kill him before anyone could be told of their secret.

Perhaps he could taunt the little bastard into revealing himself. He had to be hiding close by. Reaching down, he grabbed the trailer hitch with his free hand and lifted the back end of the truck three feet off the ground effortlessly as he peered beneath.

"Come out; come out little pig, little pig!" He called gruffly. Despite the pain in his knee, a chuckle escaped his lips. He did so enjoy tormenting the humans.
The demon had been so long down in the darkness, beneath the lash that he was savoring this chase. "You can't hide and you know now that you can't win. You are

431

unarmed." He said, slinging the fallen razor bow over his shoulder. "Come. Surrender yourself to the Baron. I will tell him of your bravery. Perhaps he will show mercy and grant you a place as an Immortal. You would not be the first…Believe me boy!"

The massive giant lumbered around almost blindly, seeking Deadeye fervently but allowing his frustration to grow moment by moment at the teenagers' vanishing trick. With a great roar, he screamed out his commands at the boy hidden in the night, the force of the yell causing a long, loopy length of intestine to come slithering out of his belly and causing it to dangle before him like a macabre rope swing. His patience was wearing thin. He wanted to kill this insolent human.

"When I find you I will eat your heart you fucking human! I will tear your body to pieces and feed your very soul to Ahriman, the destructive spirit! Come out and face your death! I will find you sooner or later! You cannot hide from me for long whelp!"

But the massive bull-like giant was wrong on several counts. First, if he chose to, Deadeye could hide from the

biker for as long as his batteries held out on the ZAP
armor. Second, he had no intention of running away.
Lastly, he was not unarmed. Carefully he slid the fourteen
inches of tactical black steel tomahawk from its sheath on
his belt.

*"I will win because the time to fight fair is over."* He thought to
himself as he clenched the heavy hand ax in his hand,
armored fingers wrapped around the weapon's paracord
hilt and crept as silently as a panther towards the biker. *"It's
time for you to die; whatever you are..."*

Spartan worked his keen edged sword side to side
furiously, blocking the incoming, lightning-fast attacks of
the dual hand scythes. He had blocked a dozen attacks and
dodged several more in the small amount of time since the
duel with the lanky Lord of Death had begun barely two
minutes prior. Each strike of the hand scythes had scored
his armor deeply making Spartan wonder what type of

metal the weapons had been forged from. Although none of the attacks had yet penetrated his ZAP armor, he believed that the suit would not hold out forever and sooner rather than later the armor would be breeched by a focused strike.

Time and again Spartan had used his natural athleticism and superior strength to maneuver himself into a position to parry his opponent's attacking blade outward, exposing the biker to a debilitating or possibly killing blow only to have the secondhand scythe slash inward attempting to decapitate or eviscerate him in unbelievably fast counterstrikes. Frustration was beginning to set in as he found himself continually giving up the tactical initiative in order to prevent being disemboweled.

Although the man appeared thin, his size was not indicative of his strength. Spartan's augmented strength provided by the ZAP armor placed him at levels significantly higher than normal humans, but he had absorbed several blows that had impact similar to the thunderous shots he had taken from Freak during training at the Apocalypse Academy. Perhaps the biker was hopped up on narcotics or some kind of mind-altering drugs that prevented his body from measuring its own levels of pain, but Spartan didn't think so. For one, the man leered cheerfully at him while they danced through feints, attacks and ripostes. He seemed to be fully enjoying himself. For two, the man appeared to be in complete control of his faculties. Every attack was deliberate and calculated. Lastly, the biker was exceedingly agile, leaping from car to car, pirouetting off of truck beds and even using the speaker poles from the drive in to absorb his momentum and launch him into numerous whirlwind attacks. Spartan subconsciously felt like he was watching a hokey karate movie observing some of the biker's acrobatic moves rather than fighting for his life. Perhaps the biker was a former student of Parkour and free running before "Z" night had occurred.

A missed parry and a three-inch-long gouge across his faceplate brought him out of the perfunctory considerations and refocused Spartan on the battle at hand. Even though the biker wore no armor, Spartan had yet to be able to land a blow and was constantly on the defensive against the man's whirling blades. In addition, the man was constantly able to gain the tactical positioning on the high ground by leaping and twisting from place to place above, below and around the Phalanx leader's sword while Spartan remained primarily grounded. In fact, other than his superior strength, the only advantage that Spartan had was that his longer weapon could be used for stabbing and slashing whereas the hand scythes required room to slash side to side only.

Of course, trying to take advantage of that small perk was extremely difficult in the wide-open space of the parking lot. Spinning the scythes like a bladed tornado, the Lord of Death raced in, his blades alternating in slashing and chopping cuts at Spartan as if he were a mere sheaf of grain to be hacked down. One of the hooked blades slid down Spartan's sword during one parry and parted the lighter armored wrist joint of the ZAP armor; cutting a three-inch slash across his forearm. Although not extremely deep, the cut stung and bled profusely causing Spartan's grip on his weapon to become slick and tenuous.

Spartan reciprocated stepping inside of one of the biker's wide swings, wrapping the bladed hand in an overhand joint lock at the elbow and delivering an offhand, armored elbow to the bridge of the biker's nose. Spartan's audio receptors registered the satisfying crunch of nasal bone being smashed flat as the man was propelled backward into the side of a dilapidated old Chevy. Blood burst from the man's dual nasal ports and he swung the blades blindly for a moment while he attempted to clear the involuntary tears that sprang from his eyes.

Seeing an opening in the man's defenses, Spartan pressed the attack. Continually he parried the bikers' strikes, steadily applying more and more force to his defensive blows which caused the Lord of Death to swing his deadly hooked blades wider and wider to maintain his aggressive pattern of attack. Placing a powerful blow almost directly above the man's fingers on the hilt of his right-handed scythe, Spartan drove the weapon outward to the full extent of the man's reach. Quickly, the Academy warrior stepped inside of the returning left-handed strike, catching the man's forearm against the top of his heavily armored shoulder. Spartan could feel the curved blade digging for purchase over the top of his armor, but with no leverage or momentum the blade merely scratched the surface of the complex weave. Twisting his body violently to the side, Spartan felt the tip of the hand scythe penetrate briefly into his shoulder blade through another section of connecting rubber and silicone. The pain was annoying but not enough to distract Spartan from his true purpose in absorbing the blow as he did.

Ripping his ancient blade horizontally across the lanky biker's abdomen, Spartan was rewarded with a sound not unlike the tearing of fabric. Black and crimson ichor splattered the ground as the Lord of Death's intestines and stomach ruptured and spilled out into the night. Spartan allowed the momentum of his slashing attack to guide the blade downward, drawing the disbelieving biker's eyes with it. Spinning the blade one hundred and eighty degrees in his hands, the Phalanx leader drove the deadly point of his sword upward as hard as he could. Spartan knew that if he missed with this attack then his entire chest and throat areas would be exposed with little hope for recovery or defense. Still, he was fully committed to this action, so he gave it every ounce of strength that he possessed both within and without the armor's enhancements.

A red, raging battle cry burst from his lips as he drove the razor-sharp point of the Sword of Leonidas through the tender flesh just beyond the point of the man's chin, through the soft palette and deep into the biker's brain. The sword did not meet any type of physical resistance at all until the blade burst through the top of the man's impaled skull. The effect on the Lord of Death was instantaneous. Appearing as though he were being electrocuted, the biker's arms shot outward, flinging the curves hand scythes far into the parking lot and causing the man's legs to perform a spasmodic dance of death. Blood ran freely around the biker's eyes and from his ears as his bisected brain tried to understand that he was now a dead man.

Tipping the ancient sword to the side, Spartan exposed the dead man's chin and jaw line. Placing his armored boot firmly against the side of the biker's bloody face, he shoved with his foot while simultaneously pulling with his hands on the sword hilt. The sword ground loose, like a ship being towed off of a sand bar before finally sliding out of the man's skull. The biker dropped to the ground, dead on impact.

Battle weary, Spartan looked around for his teammate. Seeing the titanic bald biker swinging his maul blindly told him that the Apache had opted to resort to stealth rather than continue with a straight up fight. He felt the first iota of concern when he recognized his scout's razor bow clenched tightly in one ham-like fist. Regardless of the fatigue that he felt, he knew that he had to help his teammate. Quickly he wiped the Sword of Leonidas on the leather riding chaps and blue jeans of the lanky biker he had slain. Unfortunately, he was so focused on the battle before him that he failed to notice the crimson and black ooze-like substance that dripped in thick gobbets out of the throat and torn abdomen of the Lord of Death before soaking into the ground and returning to the hell which had spawned it. Drawing himself up to his full height, Spartan began to march resolutely towards the hammer swinging goliath before him, intent on helping his friend and teammate eliminate this last foe. Suddenly his communications channel crackled in his ear.

"Stand down Spartan. This hairless beast is mine." Deadeye said across the intra-helmet link that they all shared.

"That's a negative on that Deadeye." Spartan replied calmly. "Or did you forget that we have an entire army of undead on our asses. We need to end this quickly then get to Sergeant Hogg."

There was a long, silent pause over the communications channel while Deadeye considered his course of action. Every instinct was screaming at him to handle the conflict against the larger man alone. There would be honor in that battle. However, his teammates and the nun and children were depending on him to get back to the Apocalypse academy. Finally, he replied to Spartan with a cold, steely resolve filling his normally emotionless voice.

"Spartan, this fucker hurt me. Hurt me bad and that really pisses me off. I'm about to rain Native American pain all over this big bastard just like my ancestors did to the white man in the old west. Don't worry, I will make it quick. Please. Win or lose, this is my fight. Go after Hogg."

"Copy. Just make sure that you *don't* lose!" Was all that he said, then spun on his armored heel and sprinted off through the parking lot towards the giant movie screen.

A wide smile split the enormous biker's face as he slowly swung the sledgehammer in lazy, arcing figure eights before him. "Looks like the only advantage that you might have had just ran away runt. Two against one you might have had a chance. One on one I'm gonna pound you into paste and use that armor as a trash can! Sooner or later, I will hit ya, then it will be all over but the cryin' little man!" The Lord of Death goaded.

Deadeye took a wide legged stance, crouching low to the ground and slowly circled to the man's left. It was obvious to him that he was not going to win a test of strength with the behemoth. Thanks to the ZAP armor he had stealth on his side but he knew that the man was right. Sooner or later a lucky blow would land and with the biker's raw, physical power he didn't know if even the advanced armor could withstand a full-strength blow from the sledgehammer. Methodically he searched for any sign of weakness. He had damaged the biker's knee, but adrenaline or drugs and alcohol seemed to have muted that pain enough for the biker to lumber around quasi-normally. Then a slight drooping movement caught his eye. He had noticed that the man could not wield the weapon as cleanly when the hammer reached its apex during the figure eights over the biker's left shoulder. This was probably due to an old injury, possibly a rotator cuff tear that had scarred over if he had to guess. It wasn't much. Still, an opening was an opening and the Apache intended to exploit it. Circling slowly to the left, he patiently waited for an opportunity to present itself.

Silently, Deadeye moved foot over foot the way that his father had taught him, making certain of each toe placement before bringing the rest of the foot down. Eyes scanning the biker, he noted that the swings had changed from a figure eight pattern into a more energy conserving frontal slash. Sweat had beaded upon the biker's bald brow and the mallet did not swish through the air with nearly as much dynamic force as it had when the contest had begun a few minutes earlier. It was clear to the scout that the man was getting tired. He intended to utilize the same hit and run tactics that the famed warriors of his ancestors had used in the history of the Apache people. *Step, move, step, move…*

Sometimes the waiting to attack is harder than implementing the actual attack itself. Deadeye's right arm began to tremble slightly as he clenched the handle of the tomahawk and held his arm cocked back, prepared to lash forward like a striking serpent at the first opportunity. Even the armor's servo enhanced power could not adjust for the odd angle of moving in one direction while holding his body canted and prepared to strike. The man seemed to realize his weakness as well as he kept either his weapon's head or haft up near the weakened shoulder at all times. Deadeye began to strategize. The fastest way to tire a man, even a giant, was through exertion and blood loss. He fully intended to use both techniques to make the enormous man frustrated and reckless until he could ultimately bring about his demise.

Seeing the man's chest heaving after a particularly wide attack, Deadeye knew that the time for his strike had come. Squatting as low as he could to avoid any potential counter swing or reflexive attack, Deadeye crept forward until he stood parallel to the bikers' left side. Ripping the tomahawk through the air as hard as he could, he slashed deep into the giant's upper calf muscle, just below the back of the knee. The effect was instantaneous. Muscles severed, the massive leg could not support the biker's bulk and he toppled over into the dirt with a surprised scream of pain. Releasing the sledgehammer with one hand, the man attempted to hold the bisected muscles back together with the other. Blood poured between the meaty fingers and Deadeye resisted the urge to stay in one place and hack at the hand. Instead, he performed a front shoulder roll behind the man and sprang back to his feet, instantly circling again.

Confusion and anger were evident on the biker's red contorted face as he frantically searched for any sign of the attacker. Unfortunately for him, he was searching for the Native American where the attack had come from, rather than attempting to prognosticate where the next attack would be. Blindly the biker slashed back and forth now one handed with the heavy sledgehammer, hoping for a lucky killing blow against the upstart that was attacking and hurting him. Gasping for breath, the giant man used the handle of the hammer as a crutch to support him as he rose up upon his remaining damaged but functional leg. Pain was evident on the man's face and sweat rolled freely across his brow, cheeks and neck. Leaning his lower back against a rusted-out Dodge, the biker bellowed blindly into the night.

"I'm gonna kill you ya little fucker! I'm gonna kill you and suck the juice out of your eyes before I take your head to the Master! I'm gonna eat your goddamn spleen you little fuck!" the giant raged.

Still, Deadeye circled, silent as death, not bothering to respond to the frenetic taunts and give away his position. Moving steadily at a low ready position, he circled behind the car upon which the biker was leaning for support. Rearing back with the tomahawk, he extended himself over the vehicles' rusted white hood and tore the weapon through the biker's right triceps tendon, just above the elbow. The hand holding the head of the heavy sledgehammer spasmed; jerking wildly as the severed muscles and tendons rolled back up into the man's shoulder girdle. The head of the mallet crashed to the ground as did Deadeye's bow which had been slung over the biker's shoulder. "Fucking human coward!" The bullish Lord of Death screamed. "Fight like a fucking man!"

Blood was draining rapidly down the biker's arm and dripping into a crimson pool that was seconded by the wound in his opposite calf. Still the man did not quit the fight or surrender. Deadeye could not believe that the man could continue battling with all of the injuries that he had inflicted upon the man's body. Perhaps he was under the influence of PCP. He had read once of it taking more than thirty bullets to put a user down before the apocalypse by police.

Choking up on the sledgehammer so that he grasped it at mid haft, the Lord of Death held his injured arm across the gaping abdominal wound that Deadeye had rent earlier in the contest. The open belly looked like a maw attempting to devour the biker's bleeding arm. The majority of the internal organs and intestines had fallen outward and drug beneath the man through the pooled blood, dirt and gravel. Slowly the biker waved the heavy hammer head back and forth before him, although the arcs were clearly meant only to ward off any further strikes against him as the man's wide eyes frantically searched the fire lit night for Deadeye.

Stopping directly in front of the Lord of Death, Deadeye silently timed the waving of the hammer to and fro. Back and forth… back and forth. On the third pass he gripped the tomahawk with both hands and pulled it back for a powerful swing. As the head of the hammer passed his position, Deadeye slashed the tomahawk as hard as he could downward. The tempered black steel bit through the flesh and bone of the man's hand before neatly bisecting the hammer's haft. The behemoth screamed as he watched the first three fingers of his hand tumble downward toward the ground and land with a red splash in the pooled blood beside the grey metal sledgehammer head. Clutching his newly wounded hand beneath the armpit of the arm with the severed triceps, the biker staggered in shock before his tortured legs dumped him unceremoniously onto his ass, shivering from blood loss in the filth. Sitting stunned, blood poured from the savage plethora of wounds that the Native American had so deftly inflicted upon him.

Deadeye deactivated the ZAP armor's cloaking feature and materialized into view directly before the dying biker.

"What are you?" The Apache asked.

The biker began to gurgle a bloody laugh despite his many injuries. "I am Immortal human. My kind shall be your death…"

"Well, I am an Apache by birth..." He said as he raised the tomahawk high above his head. "…a member of the Phalanx by choice and a sworn protector of the Apocalypse Academy. I am also your death!" Then he buried the razor-sharp weapon in the biker's skull, cleaving bone and brain down to the cerebral cortex. Yanking the weapon free with both hands, he reached into a pouch on his belt and removed a small glass vial. Taking a sample of the biker's blood, he re-stoppered the vial and carefully placed it back into the pouch. Perhaps Ortega could analyze the blood and they could learn something from it.

Walking over, he picked up his razor bow and wiped the bloody blades clean on the biker's leather vest. Turning he could see Spartan climbing the theatre screen attempting to reach Sergeant Hogg. He would talk to Spartan about the odd things that the biker had said just prior to his death when they had time. Right now, they needed to perform a rescue of Hogg if he was still living or a retrieval of his body for burial and get the hell out of Dodge. Quietly he limped over to a broken-down truck, holding his damaged ribs. Slowly he knocked another arrow into his bow and searched for anymore threats.

# Chapter Thirty-Two
## Recovering the Hogg

Lowering Sergeant Hogg from where he hung, crucified upon the drive-in theatre movie screen had been something of a magic trick in and of itself. Spartan had first attempted to secure a line under the sergeant's arms by rappelling down to him. He quickly found that maneuvering the burly, unconscious sergeant to get the rope around him was far more difficult than he had at first surmised. The sergeant had been suspended from his wrists, neck and chest by bailing wire that had dug deeply into his flesh due to the Sergeant's own weight and gravity. It was a minor miracle that the man was alive at all. After several attempts, Spartan finally managed to wrap the line tightly around Hogg's midsection, crotch and arm pits. He then carefully cut the wire that held the man in place. The parachute line groaned at the increase strain as the support wires were cut. Spartan was initially afraid that the cord would snap, sending the Drill Sergeant plummeting to his death seventy-five feet below.

Quickly, Spartan radioed for Deadeye's assistance. The Native American relinquished his covering duty to Dancer who had also arrived and began to help Spartan slowly lower the dead weight of Sergeant Hogg's unconscious form to the ground. Dancer maintained her overwatch at the top of the screen even after the battered sergeant was resting on the ground, carefully propping Spartan's M-4 on the maintenance stair railing with her one good arm. The selector switch had been moved to the fully automatic position since she couldn't properly hold the weapon to aim.

Pausing for a moment to catch his breath, Spartan spoke over the open communications channel to his team.

"How's everyone's power supply holding out?" He inquired as he silently gauged their movement capabilities back towards the Academy.

"Down to twenty-six percent." Deadeye responded through pain gritted teeth. "Fighting that big bastard while cloaked the whole time really ate up my batteries."

Spartan could hear the wheeze in the boy's words and knew that he was in serious pain. Each sentence was punctuated with pain. Still, the teen was tough. Never once did he utter a complaint, even though Spartan was pretty sure that the boy had at least one broken rib and possibly a concussion from the beating that he had taken.

"Forty percent." Dancer said. "But then again I missed the dance with these blokes."

"Mine's down to eighteen percent as well. We are going to have to find a way to recharge these batteries soon or we are going to have to ditch the ZAP armor. That will make this little journey a whole lot more interesting. Either way, we need to get moving soon."

A blood-streaked hand reached up from where the battered and abused Sergeant lay on the ground. Weakly it motioned for Spartan to come near. Turning his audio receptors up as high as he could stand it, Spartan gently grasped the man's outreached hand and listened to the whispered words that escaped the Sergeant's swollen and misshapen face. He felt like he was holding the hand of a child.

"Hid...ZAP. Under...ilk...duds. Extra...ower." The bloody hand released Spartan's and fell to the ground as the soldier fell into unconsciousness.

"Milk Duds? What the hell was he talking about…? Spartan broke off in mid-sentence as the truth came to him. Hogg must've worn his own ZAP armor out into the field when he came looking for Alpha team. When he knew that he was about to be captured he must have hidden the armor somewhere to keep it from falling into enemy hands. But where?

Looking around in the firelight, beyond the slain bodies, the rusted and battered vehicles and the sound speaker poles, Dancer spotted the snack bar.

"Seems bloody likely to me mate that the big lug might've stopped for a pint of fizzy drink or crisps or a scrummy candy bar. Buy all that lot over at the snack bar I'm for thinkin'."

Looking around, Spartan spotted what Dancer was referring to beyond the campfire. The sergeant had said "under the milk duds". That had to be it. The problem was that the building was dangerously close to the rear exit of the drive-in theatre. It was a miracle that the guards at the gate hadn't already heard all of the commotion from the fight at the fire. Looking up at Deadeye, he quickly explained Hogg's whispered comment and where he believed the spare ZAP batteries and Hogg's armor to be hidden.

"I'll take care of the guards." Spartan said. "You all guard Hogg and find the extra batteries.

Deadeye shook his head side to side. "You're down to eighteen percent with your ZAP's power Spartan. You said so yourself. If you run out of juice and your armor freezes up in the middle of melee, they'll slaughter you sure as shit. I'll take the guards. I've got a little more power. Besides, if I can get them from a distance before they ever have a chance to see it coming, we can keep everything quiet. Less chance for more bikers to happen into us."

Spartan had to admit that the plan made sense. It just rankled him to let another teammate take on the dirty work alone. Risking himself was one thing. Risking others made his head hurt. Dancer was already injured because of the decisions that he had made.

Turning to Dancer, he asked her a question. "Are you gonna argue with me too if I order you to guard Sergeant Hogg?" His tone was light to indicate that he wasn't really serious with the question.

"Of course, love. But that is what we Brits do best Gov'nur. Argue and make tea." She laughed with the first hint of her pre-injury dominant personality. "Of course, if I was so inclined, there wouldn't be a bloody thing in the world that you could say to dissuade me, but since I *am* so inclined, I'll be fine right here sitting on me bum by the good sergeant." She paused for a moment, and then added as an afterthought "You had better make sure that you bring me back some crisps and chocolate. I'm starving."

With a simple nod and a smirk that the girl could not see but knew without a shadow of a doubt was concealed behind the faceplate of the ZAP helmet, Spartan turned back to his Scout. "Ok, let's do this. You've got the guards and I'll take the snack bar. Be safe."

Deadeye acknowledged the instructions by turning away and immediately vanishing from sight as the ZAP armor's cloaking field seamlessly blended him with the night and the gigantic green-black pine boughs that overhung the movie theatre's privacy fence line. With the suit activated, the young scout was as silent as a spirit moving through the parking lot. Despite the augmented hearing sensors of his ZAP armor, Spartan could not detect any signs of movement from Deadeye. It was downright eerie just how deadly silent the teen could move when he really wanted to, and he was ghosting with severely damaged ribs. Spartan was glad that they were on the same team. He took off at a jog to the left and he knew that the Apache would play off of his movement by going right. It was amazing to Spartan how comfortable he was becoming at trusting his teammate's actions going into combat. A few short months ago he had not known any of them, now he was entrusting these people with his life and theirs with him.

Low on armored power, Spartan opted for a more direct route to his target. Steadily, he wove back and forth between the parked and abandoned vehicles, trying to make as little noise as possible. This seemed especially difficult since his every footfall sounded as if he was crushing the gravel beneath his feet to powder and making enough noise to literally wake the dead.

Reaching the little wooden building without incident, Spartan withdrew the Sword of Leonidas from its scabbard with a low, metal on metal rasp. Pressing himself tightly against the wall to minimize his silhouette in the moonlight, he listened and heard no signs of movement from within the snack bar or the adjacent film room. Pivoting quickly through the doorway, he stepped immediately out of the fatal funnel as he had been taught. Flowing down the walls interior, he used the ZAP's HUD to visually scan the room with infrared, confirming that the room was empty. Clearing the area behind the counter with a glance, Spartan stepped up to the glass snack counter. Peering through the glass countertop, he could see that the display case was empty with the exception of a single sample box and a small placard indicating the treats cost.

Bending, he steadily slid open the attached cabinets warped and decaying doors, searching everywhere that was large enough to hide the sergeant's armor. The fruits of his labor revealed numerous candies and a half dozen rats that feasted on the former sweet treats but no armor. Sweeping aside the vermin and the candy, Spartan looked at the shelf beneath. It was solid wood. Clearly, Sergeant Hogg had not put his armor in the cabinets. A likewise search of the cabinets behind him, beneath the decrepit popcorn machine, located only paper cups, empty popcorn boxes and Styrofoam plates.

Frustrated at his lack of success, Spartan let out a sigh and stood up. Using his tactical light, he scanned the room, searching for any place that the Drill Sergeant could have hidden the valuable ZAP armor. Had the Lords of Death already found it? Spartan was confident the Hogg would have gone to great lengths to keep the armor out of their hands if at all possible. No, for some unknown reason he was confident that the dead worshipping biker gang had not taken possession of the battle suit.

A pair of tables stood empty on one side of the room surrounded by both standing and knocked over chairs. Turning to his left, Spartan saw a small janitorial closet marked supplies by the plastic name plate attached to the door. Opening the closet, he pushed aside mops and brooms, plastic containers of floor cleaner and boxes of toilet tissue. Nothing to indicate that Hogg had been in there. Seeing the toilet tissue sparked an idea. Perhaps the sergeant had hidden the armor in the bathroom, out of plain sight from the bikers. A quick scan of the simple tiled room's walls and floors revealed that guess was also wrong. Looking at the energy display on his HUD, he began to worry. He was down below ten percent. He had to resolve this fast or he was going to stuck in place, immobile until somebody could come and rescue *him*.

Finally, he walked back into the snack bar, dejected but determined to try one last time to find the armor and the backup battery supplies. Methodically he scanned the common area of the room, being cautious to take note of any anomaly. His eyes passed the tables and chairs, the candy display case and the storage cabinets. No, Hogg would have never put the armor somewhere so obvious. He knew its value in the post-apocalyptic world. He would have made it difficult to find knowing that he was going to be captured.

Then he noticed something that he had missed on his first time through the snack bar. Over against the wall, near the front former of the room, stood a small, tan box; it's top standing open. Walking quickly to confirm his suspicions, Spartan used the Sword of Leonidas to tip the box onto its back. Large brown lettering on a yellow-tan box glared upward at him. Milk Duds! Kneeling quickly, Spartan inspected the old-fashioned wooden floorboards. Looking critically, he noticed several small gouge marks and scratches in the wooden surface that had been partially concealed by chocolate having been smeared into the grain. He was certain that he had found Hogg's hiding place.

Leaning the sword against the wall along with his M-4 that he had taken back from Dancer, Spartan dug his armored fingers into the wood and pried the four-foot-long floorboards loose. Peering down into the natural crawlspace beneath the floor with his tactical light, he was rewarded with the welcome sight of Sergeant Hogg's web gear and ZAP armor. Quickly searching the pouches of the web gear, he found two backup power supplies for the combat armor, four full thirty round magazines of 5.56 ammunition for the M-4 rifles and a separate thigh holster containing Hogg's personal .44 magnum revolver. Elation of an almost spiritual level filled him. Some people may pray to God for blessings to keep them safe, but in battle he was far more willing to pray for supplies and bullets to protect himself.

Quickly gathering up all of the items from beneath the floorboard, Spartan replaced his sword in its sheath, picked up his M-4 and started toward the door, his mission a success. He had almost walked outside when he realized that he was forgetting something. Rushing back over to the display counter, he reached down and brushed away several rat damaged boxes before withdrawing an entire box of unopened Hershey candy bars still wrapped sterilely within the clear cellophane sealant from the factory. Dancer was going to be ecstatic. For the first time in several days

Spartan allowed himself to believe that things were going right.

# Chapter Thirty-Three
## Status check

*"Coming in. Hold your fire."* Deadeye said into his helmet communicator, letting Spartan and Dancer know that he was returning to their area of operations rather than maintaining his stealth and risking a friendly fire incident. Better safe than sorry and with everyone as on edge as they were, it was a definite risk to just pop in somewhere unannounced.

*"Copy that Deadeye."* Spartan replied. *"Any issues?"*

*"Negative Spartan. The gate guards were laid back to say the least. Almost closer to lax. As far as I could tell they were totally unaware of our presence. The overall opinion from them while I was listening outside the gate house was that the fireside revelry must have been getting a bit rambunctious due to too much booze. Both were neutralized silently and without too much of a fight. In truth they were very unprofessional. If I had to hazard a guess they were lackeys at best. Perhaps they were new initiates to the Lords of Death from one of the nearby communities that had been overrun, but they were*

*definitely not seasoned veterans. They didn't even have their weapons within reach when I took them down."*

*"Acknowledged."* Then almost as an afterthought he added another question. *"Deadeye, did the biker you fought say or do anything strange or peculiar?"*

*"Yes. He said he was "Immortal" and that "his kind would be my death." Obviously he wasn't telling the truth on the first part. The rest remains to be seen. Oh…he also referred to me as "mortal." He also shrugged off wounds that would have incapacitated or killed most other people as if they were a minor annoyance."*

*"Ya, mine too and he moved like lightning. I had the damnedest time even hitting him initially. We need to get Hogg back to the Academy and tell the Colonel about this. I would have had difficulty believing in the supernatural if this were still the days before the dead rose up and started walking the earth. Now…well…?"*

*"Now it would not be too far of a stretch to believe that the bloody blighters could be run by demons or devils or maybe something' else lookin' to bugger all of humanity! Shit!"* Dancer added vehemently as she helped the battered and slowly moving Sergeant Hogg to Spartan's location. Reaching their destination, she let the sergeant lean away from her and handed him a canteen full of water.

"They're just cannon fodder. Low level turds meant to slow you down but not really to stop you. That's the Baron's way. Wear you down first, then come at ya full force. I taught him that trick in Somalia a lifetime ago. He left them behind to guard me sure, but you seen how alert they were. He knew that if you ever made it this far then these freaks would probably die as the horde moved forward. If not, you'd most likely waste them. Maybe he even got some of the dumb asses to volunteer by playin' to their loyalty. Idiots... Governments do it all the time unless you're a major player in whatever fucked up game they happen to be playin'. Never thought he'd be using' my own fuckin' tactics against me. Prick, cocksucker." The sergeant said through bruised and split lips, leaning against the metal leg of the swing set at the base of the theatre screen. Bloody spittle flecked his chin as he spoke, then he shrugged. "I'd have probably done the same thing if I were in his shoes. Weed out the chaff and any problem children. It also sets the example to the rest of his followers not to fuck with him."

He slowly sipped the water from the canteen that Dancer had given him. Each swallow seemed to rejuvenate him just a little. Although the water was refreshing, he would have given his left nut for a cold beer or ten. The lack of alcohol was punching his ornery button. He was feeling meaner and meaner with each swallow of plain water. *Oh well, fuck it. At least he didn't have the DT's.*

A shadow moved in the tree line and Deadeye seemed to materialize out of the darkness at a trot. Spartan stood facing him, his M-4 held at the low ready position with his trigger finger lightly balanced on the weapon's lower receiver.

"Any Intel on the horde? "Spartan asked as he handed Deadeye one of the fresh batteries from Hogg's pouches.

"Yeah… I had a chance to talk to one of the boys before he took a permanent nap. Does the name Custer mean anything to you?"

"Oh shit. That bad huh?"

"Uh huh. According to the biker there are somewhere in the neighborhood of twelve to fifteen thousand "Zs", counting Romero's only, headed towards the Academy. Perhaps a third again as many Reapers. That's not including any more towns, villages or farming communities that the horde absorbs as it marches forward. Anyone not ripped to shreds will add to the wave of undead battle numbers. It's pretty doubtful that the walls of the Academy will hold up against that type of force. Maybe the armory with its reinforced walls if everyone can get there but if they don't move soon they will be cut off with no food supplies."

"Even getting in there is at best a holding action. Eventually the fucking supplies will run out and the survivors will either have to fight or die of starvation. Almost better to end up an hors d'erve than die slow like that." Hogg said solemnly. "Not me. If I'm gonna go down, then I'm takin' as many of those fucking commie, cocksucking, puss dripping fuckers with me as I can. I might just kill a few "Zs" too while I'm at it." The big sergeant laughed morbidly.

"Damn, and Freak, the nun and the children are walking right into it. Dancer, try to raise them on Comms. We have to warn them off."

"I already tried Spartan." Deadeye said. "We are too far away. There's more. The Baron supposedly still has connections inside the Academy. Not sure who it is but the person or persons are in a position to make some command type decisions. If they succeed in bringing the horde here, then the Galena and Peoria avenue bridges as well as the railroad bridge will be blocked off by bikers. Any survivors would be forced to flee from containment north which is uphill and directly into the flow of the horde. It will be a massacre."

"Shit!" Spartan said again, lacking any other expletive that seemed to fit the situation.

"Yes, that is a fair statement..." Deadeye stated calmly. "But you could have prefaced it by adding several partial sentences to more accurately convey your overall feelings. For instance, "We are in deep shit." Or "Can you believe this shit?" or since there is a nun involved perhaps "Holy shit!" would be apropos. Unless of course you intended to use the term more as an adjective such as "shitty" or an adverb like "shitily", then you would have to restructure the entire sentence." Deadeye said, his voice devoid of any sense of humor. He was dead serious.

Spartan, Dancer and Hogg all gawked at the young Apache warrior. The boy generally spoke less than full sentences in his most liberal of conversations, yet here he was lecturing his team leader on grammar and basic communication skills? Perhaps it was a sign that the

467

normally reserved scout was in fear for their immediate future.

Spartan fought for a reply but it was the Drill Sergeant that spoke up first. "Just when in the holy hell did you become Charles fuckin' Dickens, Tonto?" The heavy sarcasm dripped almost palpably from Hogg's thick southern drawl.

"I will have you know that I was a member of the National Honor Society before "Z" night Drill Sergeant and I attended all accelerated classes including advanced English, Literature, Biology and Psychology. Would you prefer that I spoke in the more stereotypical Native American manner like you've seen on television to communicate with you as a white man? How's this sound?..." The Apache scout paused to clear his voice, lowering it by several octaves. "Me go. Scout 'em out trees. Gone many moons. You sit'em on fat white ass and wait for red man to save racist asshole. How's that? Better?"

The biting sarcasm must have gone straight over the Drill Sergeant's head as did the racist comment because he only replied "Well, yeah."

An enormous amount of irritation was readily apparent in both Deadeye's posture and tone of voice as he formulated his stinging reply to the redneck sergeant.

"Sergeant Hogg, the problems that led to "Z" night were very similar to your own ethnic insecurities. The basic and overwhelming need from most people is to communicate. To talk about their individual wants, needs and desires. To make other people bend to their will using metaphorical houses most often built of smoke and mirrors. To look back at the late twentieth and early twenty first centuries, the politicians were more lawyers than men of action. War hero Presidents who helped lay the concrete foundations of our country were inexplicably replaced by paper mouthpieces for corporations and bureaucracies. Regimes came and went, created and toppled by the individual agendas of people that preached basic democracy, but that were fueled by self-serving, individual financial gain. Greed."

"Then the firestorm that was "Z" night came and many, many, of those same politicians abandoned their constituents and their causes to fight for self-preservation. Among those who cared not at all were the paper lawyers that figuratively burned away beneath the fire of undead teeth as they found out that individualism does not preserve life, it makes it vulnerable to destruction. Even the religious leaders of numerous faiths got into the act, blaming this religion and that prophet or messiah for the destruction wrought by the HUNGER prions. Man destroyed man almost as fast as the undead did all in the holy, genocidal name of their individual gods while actually foregoing the basic tenants of their actual religions to preserve life."

"But when the dust settled and mankind paused to think about what had been lost to the walking dead, it was not the use of cars or computers. It was not military superiority nor the mega-powered title associated with any country or world leader. Yes, those happened but they were not the most significant loss. It was the loss of the ability to hear and understand the natural world. It is people like you Sergeant Hogg that destroyed our planet. You know how to command; how to give instructions but you have lost the ability to *listen*. To hear without the need to utter a response in return."

"In my tribe, the elders insured that we were never allowed to forget our connection to the living world. To be educated was not gaining the ability to read or do mathematics. It was recognizing the natural bond that unified mankind with the rushing fury of the mighty rivers, the rustling leaves of the trees and perhaps most importantly, the silence of the night sky."

"But you should not feel bad sergeant. There are very few people within the white man's world that understand this connection. Instead, they, like you, cover their ignorance and inability to comprehend by trying to increase the personal volume of their voices, insult that which they don't understand and cower in terror from their own insecurities. Just as you hide your own insecurities behind the acrid smoke of cigars, the burning intoxication of whiskey and your own self-loathing at your failures to save the people around you, even as you yet live. In the white man's world, it is called having a "Survivor Complex." You've lost the ability to enjoy the world. Do you even remember the last time that you read a book for enjoyment? Not a military regulation or a training manual. A novel. Fiction? Nonfiction? Hell, even the Bible? No, of course not because you are so self-absorbed in surviving that you've forgotten how to enjoy living."

"Yer probably right, but I ain't got much time for readin' some stupid book or listenin' to the trees during the

apocalypse sweetheart. All about assholes and elbows doin'
the work that's needed to keep people alive. Life's about
survivin' until the next day now, not understandin' why you
got lucky enough not to have a pack of undead zipperheads
snackin' on your balls." The Drill Sergeant countered.

The Apache youth considered Hogg's reaction for half
a minute before replying. He had expected the Drill
Sergeant to be angry, maybe even try to take a swing at
him. He had not expected the man to agree with him even
partially.

"Then Sergeant Hogg we will agree to disagree for I read
each and every day. I believe that by maintaining a touch
with the whimsical keeps the soul or in my case, my spirit
pliable. I will try to recall the words of a great author of the
nineteenth or twentieth century. It went something like
*"We must be cautious not to stare into the Hells of our own world lest
we become one with the monsters that we so fear."* In our case, if all
we think about is destroying the undead then we are the
exact inverse of them as all that they think about is
destroying us."

"Wow, that's pretty deep. Wish I could've been on a
beach somewhere with a gallon of tequila, a bikini wearin'

hottie on each arm and a new cee-gar to chomp on while I thought about it. Wait, I got an idea…The next time I'm sightin' in one of those puss fucks at forty yards with my M-4, I will pause long enough to consider "to be or not to be?" and then I will go ahead and vaporize the fuckers' skull. Hmmm….I guess that makes it "not to be." Got it! Thanks for clearin' up the philosophy of the world professor tree hugger! I couldn't have figured it out without some numb nuts like you that has just gotten out of diapers and ain't seen shit of the real-world tellin' me what I should do. Until you've seen half of the shit that I have, do me a favor…fuck off!" The Drill Sergeant said with a grin.

Deadeye shook his head. He had met many, many people like Hogg, even before "Z" night. Cynical, biased and prejudiced by their own life experiences too much to let go of the hatred and enjoy whatever was left of their lives. He knew that no matter what he said, he would never get through to the man nor change his point of view. Fortunately, he wouldn't need to; at least not right now. Instead, he just shook his head in silent disgust and turned back to Spartan.

"We need to move. Deadeye, you're on point, Dancer on our six. Sergeant Hogg, you're in the middle. We need to catch up to Freak and the nun to warn them. Let's go. Double time it all the way. Stealth is now secondary. If we don't get to them before they leave the park where we fought the bikers, we may not get to them at all. Let's move people."

Move they did. Powered by fresh battery packs that had come from Hogg's gear, they all but flew across the open landscape. The only sound was from Hogg gritting his teeth against the tortured muscles of his battered body as they began running. As they began to accelerate the pace, Spartan could have sworn that he heard the man say *"Great…, pivot man again."*

# Chapter Thirty-Four

## Immortal Decisions

The demon inhabiting the mortal remains of the human once known as the Bloody Baron leaned back in the leather covered executive chair with its elbows propped onto the armrests; fingers steepled before its face. It was deep in thought as it considered all of the elements of its assault on the Apocalypse Academy. Patience had never been its strongest suit, always preferring a straight-out assassination to tactical warfare. Lazing the target was the job of a grunt, not a General. Besides, it rankled him that someone else might get the glory of a kill that was rightfully his. His time in the elite forces both within the confines of Hell and upon the mortal plane had led to both types of missions and he had always found himself unsatisfied if he didn't get to perform the kill himself. It was an almost physically palpable emotion that bordered on the cusps of anger and a sense of deprivation. It always left a bad taste in the demon's mouth. Sour and bitter like alum filled lemons of disappointment that burned even through the natural bile and slime filled maw and throat.

475

Drawing a black, skull pommeled carbon steel knife from his boot holster, he watched as the razor-sharp blade mirrored the room's ambient light down the entirety of its twelve long inches. The dancing reflections were almost mesmerizing to him as he slowly twisted the blade to and fro, causing the light to shift and twist along the carbon steel, flowing its way to the weapon's point and back down to the demon's grasping hand in a macabre manner. It was as if the weapon was aware that it had been drawn and was suddenly eager to absorb the honey sweet life essence of a living creature.

The knife was by far his favored method of killing and by extension also his most favored possession. It had been a gift from Dahaka himself after the lesser demon had successfully infiltrated and influenced Adolph Hitler into indulging into supernatural research that had allowed many of its kind to escape the bonds of Hell and penetrate into the human world. The dagger even bore the lightning bolts and swastika upon its cross guard that had become the fashion in Nazi Germany during the war years. The demon chuckled to itself for just a moment, considering how easily the "Aryan master race" had been manipulated by his kind. Hate, destruction and death on a massive scale had been so easy to foment when a few subversive comments were made that played upon a nihilistic human's ego, patriotism and greed.

The blade of the knife itself was like no other upon the earth. Razor sharp, black carbon steel had been infused with the organic essence of blood spawn, what humans called vampires or nosferatu, allowing the weapon to not only slay its victim but also to drain its life force and provide the wielder of the blade an equitable amount of rejuvenation. The stronger the victim; the greater the effect. In addition, demon magic further enhanced the blade, providing it the tensile strength and diamond sharpness to cut through almost any armor as if it were butter.

Sure, he could utilize most modern and ancient weaponry as well as his own claws and teeth if the situation were dire enough. The greater weapons such as grenades, rockets and even missiles were capable of killing in larger numbers than his knife. That was indisputable. But there was something intimate about a well-crafted blade severing a soul's life chord and drinking in its essence. It was intoxicating to the point of drunkenness and over the millennia he had found that he cared less and less for destruction on the large scale and took much greater pleasures in the personal elimination of his foes with his dark god gifted knife. It was as if every soul taken by the blade gave the weapon a bit more character...more panache. A bloody tempering of the carbon folded steel that stole essence as well as its victim's health.

Besides, a bullet or a bomb could not perform the type of exquisitely prolonged pain that he could with the knife. Sure, it could maim or kill, but it could not be surgically controlled to maximize the agony of its victims. If he wanted to interrogate an individual and extract information without causing immediate death, (Humans all died eventually. They were such a weak species.) then he could administer hundreds of razor fine, shallow cuts across the body. He could insert just the fine tip of his blade into the belly of a muscle and twisting it ever so slightly, slicing through tissue and wreaking havoc on the creature's nervous system without causing it any noticeable damage. Severed tendons and ligaments increased the levels of pain, to say nothing of the wretched agony that came to the victim when he pierced an organ such as an eye or an ear drum. More often than not, just the mental visualization of the impending pain was enough to encourage the subject to spew information. It had been that way for time immemorial. Pain brought loose lips and physical compliance.

Of course, occasionally there were those strong-willed mortals that attempted to resist both mentally and physically. The torturous arts had been refined for centuries and all of the most successful demons had served in at least one human war as an inquisitor, an interrogator or a "Special Operative". Techniques such as water boarding (which was especially entertaining when actually using a water elemental to suffocate the victim repeatedly) were effective if not overly imaginative. The demon Baron preferred to use his Hell blessed knife to incapacitate his victim first by severing either an Achilles tendon or perhaps a hamstring. In his experience, of which the Nazis had provided him a plethora of opportunities to experiment upon, a person whose hope of escape were eliminated immediately was much more likely to acquiesce to requests for information, even if they knew that death was the only freedom that they would ever receive.

Lastly, there was the art of death. Subconsciously the Baron ran his tongue lengthwise down the black blade causing a thin line of blood to well up as it passed over. So focused on reminiscing about the pleasures of the blade was he that he did not even notice the paper-thin cut. Death by his blade could come in so many different ways. A single thrust could be quick and painless if inserted into the heart or brain or it could be slow and lingering such as piercing the lower intestine and allowing a human's own toxicity to poison their bodies. Which method he used depended solely upon his mood at the moment and the needs of his mission. Either way; slow or fast, his victims always responded the same way. There is a flash of searing pain as the knife enters the flesh, and their mouths form an "O" of shocked surprise. Then, the search for mercy within his cold eyes as he watched the candle bright light of their souls dimming until it was finally snuffed out completely and their souls moved into Hell's inferno. A gift to the dark master Dahaka.

It was that final moment that he savored most of all. There was nothing like the vibrant feel of a soul entering his blade and charging him with additional power. He remembered the time when the mortal shell that he currently inhabited had been fully human. The dark promises that he had made to coerce the man into accepting his presence in an effort to save his daughter. The fool. It was truly disheartening to know that the

Demon God had decreed that the man's partner, the idealistic Sergeant Hogg and all of the brats of the Apocalypse Academy would not get to sample his blade's finery. But the dark God had decreed that the undead were to rule this world. There was an agenda to maintain. He would just have to be satisfied with watching the Academy warriors die beneath the tearing claws and teeth of the risen corpses…unless of course he could slip his knife in somewhere unnoticeable. A demon had to maintain its ambition after all.

Chuckling to himself, he admired the glimmering black blade one last time and prepared to replace it into its sheath. Seeing the traces of blood on the blade, he wiped it casually across his pant leg and put the weapon away. It was time to get down to business. Reminiscing was fun, but less than productive. With a bellow, he called for his Aide de Camp.

"Magic! I require a report! Now woman!"

The Baron's voice echoed within the single-story building's open office. He had chosen this particular building intentionally due to its location north of the Academy but also because it stood in the direct route of the

horde when it flowed southward into town. As an added
bonus, the city park that was located across the street was
donated by the Lions club. He had so enjoyed donating
Christians to the lions during the Roman times. Such
bloody fun.

The raven-haired witch appeared into the room, her
boot heels clicking on the marble flooring as she walked.
She must have been nearby because only seconds passed
between his call and her arrival. The girl was a course in
opposites. Her overall appearance was a bizarre cross
between a gothic wannabe biker, a voodoo priestess and a
catholic schoolgirl. The brown eyed girl did not so much
walk into the room as flow. Knee high leather stiletto boots
accentuated the red plaid mini skirt that barely extended
down below the girl's crotch. A thin chain hung about her
waist serving as a grizzly belt holding her Gris Gris bags
and a bleached human skull. Her torso and ample bosom
were covered in a faux leather tank top that had been
altered to expose her taunt, muscular belly. Her navel was
pierced and a silver skull charm with glimmering red ruby-
like eyes peered out at him in an almost mesmerizing
manner, swaying side to side with the girl's hips like a cobra
prepared to strike. The charm looked like an unholy artifact

when she undulated her hips, tanned muscles flexing beneath it. The Baron wondered not for the first time if he could speak directly to the dark masters through the natural feminine portal that the girl's body surely contained below it. The entire ensemble was covered by an open, full length black leather duster that blew backward behind her when she walked, traversing to and fro about the girl's heels.

She could have been a model before "Z" night. The way that she looked and preyed upon the sexual urges of men meant that she had had experience manipulating the opposite sex and bending them to her will. The woman wore beauty the way other women wore emotions. She could be sultry and appealing in one moment and brutally deadly the next. In fact, she would have been an extremely compatible concubine were it not for the fact that the last two attempts to bed the woman, one by man and one by a demon, had met with the dismemberment of the most important of man's nether regions. She had allowed the poor bastards to suffer for days, pleading for mercy while staked to the ground in a bed of fire ants before she had finally beheaded them beneath the blade of the red katana that she wore strapped across her back.

Only after the punishments had been doled out had the Baron learned that the woman and her sister had been brutally raped by a group of scavengers during the earliest days of the apocalypse. Her sister had been so traumatized that she eventually had killed herself; a tortured soul that now languished in Dahaka's dark domain. In an unholy ceremony, the girl who had been raised in the backwoods of Louisiana, had summoned a voodoo curse upon the defilers and had foresworn any physical pleasure until she found the ones that had been ultimately responsible for her sister's demise. The demon did not know the specifics of the curse but he was willing to bet that it was evil personified, if he knew Magic. It was possible that her particular blood debt would go unpaid as many early survivors had since perished beneath the undead's rampage across the world. Still, he hoped that she found at least one of the offending mortals. It would be entertaining to see what types of misery she could foster on their behalf. Besides, if she eventually found out that all of the perpetrators had died, then she could renounce her vow to abstain from physical pleasure. The "Baron" was really looking forward to that day because he considered the woman to be of a kind of hot that paralleled the very fires of the abyss. He could spend an entire day just thinking of the laundry list of sexual exploits that he wanted to indulge in with her. Without the katana, of course.

"Has the tracking device that I put on Hogg's armor begun to move yet? The Academy brats should have reached him by now if they were coming."

"Yes M'lord." He liked when she called him that. It sounded faintly medieval and spoke of servitude. "They should arrive at the Apocalypse Academy no later than noon tomorrow if they maintain their current pace. We have no reason to believe that they will not meet that schedule. Our spies have reported in and stated that the group is no longer moving stealthily, with much less attention to their surroundings. They have passed two stalker teams already without seeing them."

"And the undead?"

"They will arrive by midnight of the same day. The motorcycle teams have reported that there was a small delay in obtaining the live bait necessary to lure the Romeros and Reapers forward; however, I instructed them to use any survivors from the skating rink in the place of civilians despite their earlier pledges of fealty to you M'lord. I felt that the continued success of the mission was worth the loss in the eyes of Dahaka. The survivors have been chained and even now serve our dark lord by bringing the horde forward. We are currently back on schedule as planned."

"Excellent and a fine use of available resources! I am pleased." The Red Baron murmured. "And the other Apocalypse Academy teams?"

"All have been engaged by the Lords of Death and the walking dead. Many of the teams have reported casualties and deaths. A number of the former cadets were pacified by their own people as they turned which will add to the demoralization of their forces. Currently, all teams except the Alpha and Echo teams are isolated and pinned down. They will not be able to render aid to the Academy when the horde arrives. We are one step closer to the children of Dahaka inheriting the earth. Perhaps they are the meek that the Christian bible referred too?

The Baron shook his head slowly in agreement, causing the light to reflect off of both his clean-shaven pate and his monocle. His demonic essence found the presence of hair to feel unnatural and he had chosen to keep his head bald. It felt much more in tune with his natural hairless state. In addition, although he did not need the small piece of circular glass to actually see, he found that the item made his appearance as the resurrected German warplane pilot much more believable. The fact that he *had actually inhabited the consciousness of the Red Baron* of Germanic lore did not actually matter. He had been many personas over the eons as had his brethren. Humans, by large, were not capable of sowing death and destruction on an equitable scale as the Hell born. But when the dark god Dahaka had needed one hundred demonic essences to form the resurrected Immortals of Xerxes' legions, many saw a fresh opportunity to cause chaos again upon the mortal plane. He himself, a young demon Princeling had been the very first to reenlist. How he loathed humans. Well except for the females; they had their uses.

Privately he wondered about his Voodoo Priestess's zealousness towards the historical Rapture and its resurrection of the dead. Was she the crazy Catholic school girl? She didn't seem to be the overly religious type being so versed in pagan voodoo magics but one could never tell. Certainly, he had fostered the belief amongst the humans that the rising dead were an event of biblical proportions. It was a means to an end. A way to form his own army of blood thirsty bikers who felt that the fact that they were still living and not part of the rapturous return meant that their God had judged them and found them wanting. That their souls were stained by evil and that the only way to purge the taint was by slaying those more wicked than themselves. Of course, that meant that he and the other Immortals painted people such as the Apocalypse Academy personnel as sinners in the eyes of the Lords of Death. Those that did the "work of God" would find redemption when they were finally released to the afterlife, only to be raised into the embrace of undeath for all time. Their sins cleansed beneath tooth and claw. Murder the innocent in the name of the Savior. He still found the deception wickedly delightful.

Humanity had become so decadent prior to the apocalypse that the need for belief in a long dead carpenter as their Savior was all that many people held onto. Of course, this was a ridiculous notion. He had been present when his brethren had crucified and slain the mortal. He had even taken a personal moment to stab a spear into the flesh of the man's side ensuring that he was dead. Was he God's son? Who knew, but he died just the same.

During his various stints as a human, he had learned that almost most everything that mankind wrought against itself was not due to supernatural interference but more often than not it was directly due to the crazed mind of a dictator, the piqued curiosity of a group of scientists, the power grabbing quest of the military or just some mentally unbalanced nutjob that felt that the total annihilation of humanity was a better option than history recording them as losers. He had even guided the occasional Hollywood stalker just for fun.

Of course, at each and every turn the crackpots and dictators needed advisors. They needed trusted people to whisper the truth directly into their crazed ears and to originate the evil thoughts for them. What they didn't realize was that the blackness that consumed them and allowed them to create these scenarios within their tiny mortal brains always originated within the madness of demonic possession. It was one of the demon's greatest pleasures to taint the pure and turn them to evil. It had been done thousands of times throughout the centuries and the rise of Dahaka's apocalypse was no exception. A demonic tweak of a scientific mind coupled with the application of technology had opened the rift to the Abyss and spilled the prions that formed the H1N1GR virus into the world. The rest, as they say, was history.

People like Magic, if she was in fact a true religious zealot, were perhaps the most dangerous people to taint because their beliefs prevented them from fearing the normal mortal consequences of their actions. They did not fear death or the loss of her soul. History had been filled with religious martyrs of every race, creed and denomination. Still, for now she served his dark purposes as the priestess of the Lords of Death. When and if the time came that she ceased to be an asset, he would feed her piece by piece to the undead horde.

That was not saying that he wouldn't have some fun first. He would definitely tie her down and tap that special stuff a few times and listen to her scream. He might even share her around the proverbial campfire with his brother demons. After that she should be ready to walk willingly into the oncoming flood of undead to ease her own pain and suffering. Or he could just use her and then shoot her in the eye. Demonic possession contained so many complex decisions.

"Ah, decisions, decisions." He said aloud to no one in particular.

"Beg pardon M'lord?" The raven-haired priestess asked inquiringly.

"Oh, nothing. I was just musing about the future." He said, returning his mind to the task at hand. "Advise me when the horde enters town so that I can savor watching the Academy fall. And be certain that I have an entire cooler full of cold beer to go with it. Their destruction has been long in coming and I intend on savoring the moment with a few beverages to celebrate our imminent victory. When the Apocalypse Academy has fallen, we shall celebrate as they did in the old days over the heads of our enemies!"

Magic did not understand the historical reference but understood the remainder of the orders perfectly. "As you wish M'lord." She said, bowing low and giving the Bloody Baron a full view of her cleavage. Then in a swirl of rasping leather and plaid, she turned on her spiked heel and exited out of the front door of the bank.

# CHAPTER THIRTY-FIVE

## REUNITED

Galvanized by the knowledge of the potentially impending deaths of their teammates and a dozen children, Spartan and the rest of his half team pushed their personal fatigue levels into the distant recesses of their minds. While they still felt the exhaustion and pain of the extended sprint, they refused to let it slow their pace. Spartan was personally worried about the three warriors beside him. Dancer had suffered her head injury and a definitely broken arm. Hogg had been beaten to a pulp and had God knows what for injuries and Deadeye was wheezing through his busted ribs. To a man they did not utter a single complaint but he knew that they were miserable. In addition, he was worried that if he pushed them too hard then they would be unable to fight once they arrived back at the academy.

Even with the fresh power cells in their ZAP armor, the toll on the warriors' bodies was enormous. They had been pushing the need for speed for greater than the proscribed thirty-minute sprinting maximum that they were supposed to be able to safely maintain. The windbreak of pine and hardwood trees that lined the roadway blurred by in a fiery show of green, brown, yellow and red colors. To the running warrior's enhanced vision, it almost appeared as if the flames of Freeport were chasing them all the way to the Apocalypse Academy. Drooping power lines seemed to repeatedly rise and genuflect before the inhuman velocity that the ZAP armor was allowing them to maintain.

After two hours of breakneck speed and brutal endurance running, they saw the first visible sign of the children in Freak's care. It was the Apache Scout's keen skill of observation, even while running that allowed Spartan's group to see the tiny, brown smudged fingerprints along the trunk of an old Chevrolet Malibu that sat broken down upon the road. The freshly eaten wrapper of a Hershey bar stirred idly in the emergency lanes' gravel. The car's pale-yellow finish appeared to have been playfully finger painted, as evidenced by the melted chocolate smiley face on the trunk and several gooey stick figures coupled with several brown racing stripes running down the vehicles' street side doors. Once they knew where to look, it wasn't hard to follow the trampled path of the chocolate bearing toddler-a-saurus's into the forest ahead.

Pointing off the roadway into the tree line, Spartan held up flashed hand signals which ended with his fist up indicating that he wanted his team to stop running. For one of the few times there was no debate and no commentary. Everyone was too busy gulping down breaths of air to attempt sarcasm. After several seconds of getting his own labored breathing under control, Spartan keyed his communications frequency and called out to Freak. It was better to slow down enough to ensure that they wouldn't catch up to the group, only to get shot by their own man. He could only imagine the stress levels that his resident giant had to be experiencing. Running with three full grown adults that were injured was difficult enough. Trying to run, while carrying a fully incapacitated teammate, while towing a middle-aged, battle-hardened woman of God and twelve crying, pooping, snotting or whining children had to be its own level of Hell. Personally, he thought he would rather face an entire army of the living dead that to try and maintain his sanity with that group. He'd have to remember to thank the Colonel for this mission later, even though he and his team had actually selected it after winning the Dante and the honor of Cadet of the Cycle.

"Freak, this is Spartan. Can you read me? Over..."

"Welcome back Dawg." The big man said. "It's good to hear your voice. I read you loud and clear."

"We are coming up on your six. Hold your fire. Deadeye will provide the visual confirmation hand signal."

Freak was confused. There was no "visual confirmation signal" that he knew of. Was the team being cautious or was something wrong? He paused for a long second before replying, unaware that he had subconsciously already keyed the microphone.

"Copy that Dawg." He would just wait and see what was up before he let the kids out of his sight. If there were any of those Bikers tailin' his bro's then they were some dead mothers. "I'll be watchin' fo' da injun."

Again, the big man left the microphone keyed open for just a couple of extra seconds. It was just long enough for Spartan to hear the snippet of a song in the background.

"...*love you, you love me...*"

Maybe the nun was bolstering the children's spirits with some music, but he hoped that they were careful. Any noise could bring a wandering pack of undead racing their way. It would be a stupid way to die.

Looking over at the scout, Spartan nodded his head once and the boy took off like one of his own arrows. Deadeye moved at his best possible speed for several minutes, weaving through the trees and around the foot catching underbrush before he finally caught sight of his team's giant, resplendent in his black carapace of shining armor. Immediately he threw up the team's hand signal, extending his middle, armored finger and flipping Freak the bird.

Seven long minutes later, the exhausted Hogg, Dancer and Spartan walked into view. Spartan had been forced to slow their pace as the rest break had actually worked against them, allowing muscles to tighten and old wounds to renew throbbing. Rather than being met by a group of sad faced, snotty-nosed kids, Spartan was surprised to see a gaggle of happy, soft singing children that were actually giggling. It was a confusing, out of place sight in a war zone.

Freak walked up and reported to his team leader.

"All's well here Dawg. We are some tired asses but between me and Sister Margaret we are doin' ok keepin' the kids happy. We don't have that far to go. Through the park, down the road and into our beds at the Academy. I can't wait to get some shut eye."

Spartan frowned. "I guess Deadeye didn't give you the bad news."

He said Dancer got clipped and had a broken arm. Also mention that your homeboy Hogg got beat up pretty bad by the Lords of Death. Is there something else man?"

The Phalanx team leader blew out a huge sigh. "Ya bro. There is." Pausing to remove his helmet, he took a deep breath of the fresh forest air then told Freak about how the Lords of Death had been leading the walking dead towards the Apocalypse Academy and their intent to overrun it.

"She-ee-it! We ain't got the manpower to fight that many "Zs" Dawg, even if we had every last person back. Some might be there but we all went out on missions at the same time and I ain't heard shit for radio traffic to indicate that anybody has made it home yet. What are we gonna do?"

"We've gotta get there and warn them. Maybe if we can get there fast enough, we can evac everybody out before they get trapped inside by the Reapers, Romeros and Lords of Death. When can you be ready to move from here?"

"Dawg, I can get these kids up and movin' in no time. Give me twenty minutes."

"Ok, twenty minutes and we move out." Then as an afterthought he asked a question. "I gotta ask. How are you keeping the children in such good spirits? I was expecting a bunch of crying kids and you and Sister Margaret to be stressed out. Instead, I hear singing and find smiling, happy faces everywhere."

The enormous teen looked genuinely embarrassed which surprised Spartan. Sheepishly he muttered "Well, it was Sister Margaret's idea mostly. I just kinda made it into a reality Dawg."

"What was Freak? Spit it out already."

Freak tried to answer but found himself sputtering to formulate the right words that would not humiliate or embarrass him to his team leader. Instead, his response was limited to a repeating series of "buts" and "wells" with the occasional "you see" thrown in to further confuse the comment.

Sister Margaret spoke up. "He was very, very brave." Spartan had not heard the rotund nun approach but looked at her quizzically as she continued. "Only a real hero could have done what he has done for these children by removing their fears so completely."

Spartan turned back to Freak. "Well *hero*, are you gonna spit it out or what?"

The titanic warrior threw up his hands towards the sky in a manner of submission to the Phalanx team leader and blew up a frustrated breath.

"Dawg, I swear if you laugh then the "Zs" or them biker chumps will be the least of your worries." He warned. "I did this fo' them kids. I wanted them to feel safe and not be screamin' ya know?"

Staring to turn his back to the team leader, he put his ZAP helmet onto his head. The image of a huge purple dinosaur bearing an ear-to-ear smile grinned back at the leader of the Phalanx, drawn in sidewalk chalk upon the armor. It was an image that evoked instant pre-"Z" night memories of toddler music, childhood adventure and clean spirited fun while learning. Spartan immediately erased the broad smile that had spread across his face before his enormous friend could see it. Deadeye however had walked up at the same moment when Freak had turned around and was now almost falling over with hysterical laughter. The laughter was instantly infectious to everyone nearby. After so many close calls between the walking dead and the bikers, it was a relief to share a happy moment together. Even Freak accepted the laughter from the children by wiggling the tail that had been drawn in purple chalk on his buttocks. Deadeye couldn't even comment because his laughter had him doubled over in great guffaws that were leaving him breathless and in pain from his damaged ribs. Freak restrained himself from belting his partner, even when he mentioned that Freak and the dinosaur's butts were actually the same size between gasps and giggles.

"You are a bloody, brilliant genius my friend!" Dancer said, nodding her head in approval.

When the initial mirth died down, Spartan clapped his gigantic friend on the shoulder. Speaking softly where none of the other people could hear him, he addressed Freak. "Your Granny would have been proud of you bro. Swallowing your pride is not an easy thing to do and you hit a home run doing it this time. Well done."

"Thanks Dawg. To be honest, their laughter and those songs that I remembered from my own childhood kinda took away some of the dark shit that has been weighing on me. Gran always talked about the healing power of music. I guess now maybe I understand it. I wish it could've worked for Techno. Spartan, I…I'm not sure he's gonna make it. He seems like he's busted up really bad and we can't get him to talk at all. He's been unconscious this whole time. I think he's gonna die." He finished sadly.

"Dancer…" Was all that Spartan said, but when he turned to finish the statement the Phalanx team medic was already moving past him to check on their injured teammate. Sergeant Hogg was close on her heels, going to lend whatever aid that he could. As the team's medic,

Dancer had learned more advanced techniques from Nurse Ortega with regards to stabilizing severe injuries. Spartan assumed that Hogg was versed in these as well. With Dancer only having one arm to work with, it was good that the Drill Sergeant was there to help her.

He hoped that they were up to the task or the Alpha Team Phalanx would suffer its first casualty.

Look for book 3 in the

Apocalypse Academy soon!